It was as ~~unwelcome~~ sight of her in that absurd candy-cane sweater, her belly swollen, her pale face without makeup, her hair tumbled around her shoulders in a tangled mess, should've done the trick. He should've been cured, his clear thinking restored.

But instead...instead...

Irresistible You
by Barbara Boswell

She had to make the man fall in love with her. Her life depended on it. Her life and the lives of her two babies. She was going to have to make herself irresistible. And she would have him in wedding clothes by the end of the week....

Wife by Contract
by Raye Morgan

BARBARA BOSWELL

loves writing about families. "I guess family has been a big influence on my writing," she says. "I particularly enjoy writing about how my characters' family relationships affect them." When Barbara isn't writing and reading, she's spending time with her *own* family—her husband, three daughters and three cats, whom she concedes are the true bosses of their home! She has lived in Europe, but now makes her home in Pennsylvania. She collects miniatures and holiday ornaments, tries to avoid exercise and has somehow found the time to write twenty category romances.

RAYE MORGAN

has spent almost two decades, while writing over fifty novels, searching for the answer to that elusive question: Just what is that special magic that happens when a man and a woman fall in love? Every time she thinks she has the answer, a new wrinkle pops up, necessitating another book! Meanwhile, after living in Holland, Guam, Japan and Washington, D.C., she currently makes her home in Southern California with her husband and two of her four boys.

The Wedding ARRANGEMENT

BARBARA BOSWELL
RAYE MORGAN

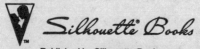

Published by Silhouette Books
America's Publisher of Contemporary Romance

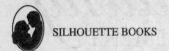 SILHOUETTE BOOKS

ISBN 0-373-23008-7

by Request

THE WEDDING ARRANGEMENT

Copyright © 2003 by Harlequin Books S.A.

The publisher acknowledges the copyright holders
of the individual works as follows:

IRRESISTIBLE YOU
Copyright © 2000 by Barbara Boswell

WIFE BY CONTRACT
Copyright © 1997 by Helen Conrad

Printed in U.S.A.

CONTENTS

Dear Reader,

I decided to write a book about a couple being thrown together for jury duty while I spent an entire day waiting to be chosen, or not, to serve on a jury myself. Though I wasn't picked—the sweetest rejection I've ever had!—I did come up with a story for the hero Luke Minteer, whom I'd been asked to write about. Luke had been a not-so-nice secondary character in several of my other books and I wasn't sure if he was hero material. Making him do penance on jury duty seemed like a start to redeem him. I knew, to intrigue him, his heroine would have to seem totally unavailable and that those two would never have crossed paths or willingly spent time together unless forced to. Serving on a jury trapped them both.

Marriage and children, extremely important to Luke's big family, was the only way for him to win his way back to them. Brenna, the heroine, always so alone, needed him as much as he needed her. I love reading and writing about the influence (and even the interferences!) that families have on characters, and Luke's family certainly had both. I hope you enjoy it.

Happy reading!

Barbara Boswell

IRRESISTIBLE YOU
Barbara Boswell

One

Jury Duty!

Luke Minteer was still in shock. As of tomorrow morning he was supposed to be a juror in a civil case. And from the few facts the opposing lawyers had revealed about the case during the juror interview, Luke already deemed it a major time waster. Of *his* valuable time!

This, after he'd been such a good sport about the situation. Despite the major inconvenience of being summoned to join his fellow citizens in the potential jury pool, he had dutifully—albeit grudgingly—shown up at the courthouse for the selection. That should have been the end of it, as far as he was concerned.

He expected to be rejected; he was counting on it. For the first time ever, rejection was infinitely appealing, and his past days as a tarnished hotshot political operative seemed to guarantee it. Who would want the likes of *him* on a jury?

Apparently the judge and the attorneys on both sides would—because he'd been selected.

Desperately he looked around at the other chosen jurors sitting with him in the box, while a bailiff instructed them on their upcoming obligations. They were now expected to put their lives on hold, to be held captive in a courtroom—and all because two idiots, aided and abetted by their mercenary lawyers, had decided to sue each other.

He was Luke Minteer! He didn't do jury duty!

Eight of the chosen were years older than he was. *Decades* older! Two young men who appeared to be in their early twenties sported multiple tattoos and piercings on various parts of their bodies—their eyebrows, their noses, their lips and of course their ears, with at least ten earrings per lobe.

Luke glanced at the final juror, the young woman sitting next to him, who was very visibly pregnant. She looked like a teenager, though he knew she couldn't be. In the state of Pennsylvania, jury duty fell only to those who'd reached the legal age of twenty-one.

Luke couldn't gauge how advanced her pregnancy was. Unmarried and not a parent, he steered clear of the mysteries of pregnant women.

What mattered in this situation was that she was unmistakably pregnant, the young men looked like circus freaks, and the elderly people were very, very old. One of them coughed continually.

Luke groaned. "I don't have a prayer of getting out of this."

"You just said exactly what I was thinking," said the pregnant woman, looking surprised.

Luke was surprised, too. He hadn't intended to speak his own thoughts aloud like that. Another sign of how rattled he was by his unexpected inclusion.

"They must be desperate for jurors to pick this crew," she murmured, now voicing his observation. "I'm due to deliver my baby in six weeks. The lawyers for both sides said the trial would be all wrapped up long before then, though," she added hopefully.

"Don't believe everything you hear," Luke grumbled. "Especially when a lawyer says it. I worked in politics. I know."

"Didn't you tell them you worked in politics?" Her gray eyes widened. "It seems that would instantly disqualify you."

"Why would I be disqualified on those grounds?" Never mind he'd believed the same thing—wrongly. "This case has nothing to do with politics, it's a battle-of-the-sexes case."

"And a really stupid one," she added glumly.

"You took the words right out of my mouth." Luke heaved a groan. "The facts of this case read like the rejected proposal for a really bad book. Guy gives girl engagement ring, then dumps her. She refuses to give back the ring, which he claims is a family heirloom—and which he wants for his new fiancée. Let's call her fiancée two. So he sues fiancée one to get the ring back."

"But fiancée one claims the ring was a gift, hers to keep," his pregnant fellow juror interjected.

"Or to sell. In order to finance the breast implants she claims are essential to her career as a nude dancer," Luke added dryly.

"And she also countersues him for harassment or interfering with her civil right to work or whatever." The young woman rolled her eyes heavenward. "I tuned out at that point."

"Did you hear that both parties are demanding punitive damages for their emotional pain and suffering? As if either one feels any emotion except pure greed—and possibly revenge."

"Why can't they settle it themselves like civilized human beings? Why do they have to go to court and drag all of us into it?" she railed. "Who can side with either one, anyway? He's a fickle cheapskate and she's a manipulative—"

She paused for a moment.

"Perhaps litigious, silicone-endowed nude dancer is the term you were looking for?"

"I had something a bit less flattering in mind. Already, I can't stand either one of them, and I've never even met them."

"Did you say that to the lawyers?" quizzed Luke.

She nodded. "Oh, yes."

"So did I. Must be why we were picked. Better to dislike them both than to side with one. The lawyers would consider that fair and impartial."

"It's a lot like politics after all," she said thoughtfully. "Where you don't like either candidate but are supposed to vote for one. It boils down to the lesser of two evils at worst, or at best, two jerks."

"Evil or jerk." Luke held back a sigh. "I'm going to take a wild guess that you think all politicians are unlikable, morally corrupt, sleazy.... Feel free to jump in and stop me at any time."

She didn't. Which apparently meant she agreed with his assessment?

"I was attempting to be ironic," he said to enlighten

her. "There are exceptions to the corrupt politician ste-
reotype, you know."

"I'll take your word on that." She looked bored with
the subject.

From his past work in the field, Luke was aware that
politics tended either to bore or inflame, and unless one
was canvassing for votes, a change of topic was advis-
able. Still, he was unable to let it go.

"One exception is my brother, Matt Minteer. He's a
congressman." Luke's voice held a note of fraternal
pride. "Matt is the representative for the Johnstown district, which includes this county, so that would make
him your congressman."

"Matt Minteer," she repeated. "Is he the one who
fired his own brother for dirty tricks or nasty campaign
tactics or something like that? I heard about it when I
moved here last year."

This time Luke didn't suppress his sigh. He let it out
heavily. "Yeah, that would be Matt. The nasty, dirty-
tricks-playing brother is me. I was fired two years and
eight months ago, but the story is still being told, I see."

"And those lawyers picked you for the jury anyway?" The young woman was incredulous. "Wow!
They are really, *really* desperate."

"No charges were ever filed against me. It's not as
if I'm a convicted felon." Luke was defensive. "Although as far as my brother's staff is concerned, I might
as well be. They're a very traditional group, set like
cement in the old ways. When I tried to be innovative
and competitive, to take some risks and implement
some new ideas and methods for—"

"Translation," she cut in. "When you used dirty
tricks and nasty tactics, they didn't approve, and you
got the ax."

Luke scowled. "Are you always so...blunt?"

Though she'd pretty much summed up the situation, it didn't mean he liked hearing it.

"Yes," she said...bluntly.

"Well, why should you be different from everybody else?" Luke was aware that his voice held just the faintest trace of self-pity. He didn't care. "No one else in the district bothers to hold back their opinion of me, including my own family. Everybody reminds me that, though to the world at large I may be a bestselling crime fiction writer these days, in this district, I'm still Congressman Minteer's brother, the weasel."

She arched her dark brows. "Crime fiction?"

Luke brightened. Even the locals who disapproved of him as an innovative, risk-taking political mastermind bought his book. Everybody, everywhere, had, bringing him national success as an author.

"I wrote a bestselling crime novel about a serial killer that was published in hardcover and did well and then hit number one on the *New York Times* list when it came out in paperback. It's still on the bestseller lists, although farther down by now, of course, and—"

"I don't read crime fiction, and I'd *never* read about serial killers," she said disapprovingly. "Why would anyone want to read about such evil and ugliness? Why would anyone want to write it?"

"You aren't the first to ask that question." Instead of taking offense, Luke grinned. "In fact, most of my family does. But I do have one favorite aunt who tells me to make the crimes in my next book even more grisly."

"Well, I don't agree with your favorite aunt. Glorifying crime is...is toxic."

"I don't glorify—" He began to argue, but inevitably, his sense of humor kicked in. "You are *brutally* frank. Opinionated, too. Those lawyers in this trial might think you're a malleable little mommy, but it looks like the joke is on them. You'll probably hang the jury and they'll have to try the case all over again."

The bailiff appeared again, instructing the chosen twelve to report back to the courtroom tomorrow morning at nine-thirty for the beginning of the trial. Then he excused them for the day.

Everybody stood up. None of the selected jurors looked happy with their fate.

"It's four o'clock," muttered one of the older men. "The day is already completely wasted. Why did they take so darn long to pick us? All those foolish questions they asked us..."

"I had to take two buses to get here," complained an elderly woman. "Now I have to take two to get home—*and* do it for heaven only knows how many more days, until this is all over."

"I'm bringing my knitting with me every day," said another woman defiantly. "I have to finish an afghan for my great-niece's new baby in time for Christmas. That's little more than a month away."

The two pierced, tattooed young men slunk off. Luke stared after them, bemused. He noticed that the pregnant woman was looking at them, too.

"What are the odds of two jurors sporting identical dragon tattoos that stretch the length of their arms?" he murmured. "I'd never put that in a book. My editor would say, 'Come on, Luke, that's too over the top.'"

"Sometimes truth is stranger than fiction. Which is a creepy thought, considering some of the fiction being written these days."

"I assume that's another potshot at my writing ca-

reer?'' drawled Luke. ''Nobody can accuse you of being subtle.''

She and Luke faced each other.

''Since we're fellow jurors, we might as well introduce ourselves. I'm Luke Minteer.'' He offered his hand
to her.

''Brenna Morgan.'' She shook his hand but withdrew
her own quickly.

''You look like you want to wipe your palm on something. Don't worry, I'm not infectious,'' Luke said
drolly. ''I'm merely the bad-guy brother of your good
and honorable congressman, and that is not contagious.''

She looked ready to debate the point. ''You switched
to a career writing crime novels about serial killers.''

''And you don't know which is worse. My political
chicanery was disgusting, but my writing is morbid and
sick.'' He smiled slightly at her startled look. ''No, I'm
not a mind reader, Mrs. Morgan. I'm just quoting my
mom and my sisters, my grandmother and my aunts,
except for Helen. You'd get along famously with them.
They never miss a chance to lecture me on the perils
of writing about evil.''

''But you enjoy writing about evil?''

She was looking at him as if he were Satan incarnate
on a book tour. Luke felt compelled to offer some sort
of defense.

''Look, I'll try to explain to you the way I've tried
to explain it to the family. Inventing a crime and a case
and solving it is fascinating. You can enter the mind of
your characters and set up the cat-and-mouse game between the criminal and the police. Plus, on the practical
side, it's been a very good career move.''

Okay, he wanted to brag a little about his writing

success, Luke acknowledged to himself. Was that so bad, in light of the fact he'd been viewed as a disgrace to the Minteer clan, as the district pariah? His writing had elevated him to something akin to celebrity status.

Celebrity or pariah? That choice was a no-brainer.

"A person's got to make a living, you know," he added, with a practiced touch of boyish charm.

Brenna Morgan stared impassively at him, uncharmed. "And since you'd already been kicked out of dirty-tricks politics, creating serial killers was the logical next step? There's nothing in between? Not anything in the retail industry or in the business world or the—"

"Aha! Now you're joking. I see the glint of humor in your eyes, despite your best efforts to hide it behind that deadpan facade."

This time Luke flashed his most winning smile, the one on the back cover of his book's dust jacket. He'd gotten fan mail based on that picture, from women who hadn't bothered to read the book.

Brenna slowly, almost reluctantly smiled back.

Luke knew she would. No woman was immune to his special smile, not even pregnant ones who thoroughly disapproved of him and his profession. That is, unless she happened to be related to him. To his female relatives, his smile and his charm were distinctly underwhelming.

"I really wasn't joking," Brenna insisted.

"Sure you were. Those big gray eyes of yours are still shining with amusement."

"No, they aren't."

"Are you one of those types who always has to have the last word? Your poor husband—and those hapless lawyers who have no idea that they've chosen an intractable force of nature to be on their jury.'' Luke laughed. ''Yeah, it'll be a hung jury, all right.''

The two of them started walking toward the door, toward freedom. They fell into step, side-by-side. Luke cast a swift glance over at her.

He always noted a woman's height, and he made no exception this time. She was wearing flat shoes, which allowed him to correctly estimate that Brenna Morgan was not quite five-four. At five feet ten inches, he seemed to be towering over her. Luke enjoyed the sensation in spite of himself.

After all, he'd made peace with his less-than-six-foot height *years* ago. He didn't mind being the shortest of the four Minteer brothers, he didn't care that his three sisters were nearly his height. That two of his teen nephews already were as tall as he was and were still growing.

It wouldn't be long until he was surpassed in height by another generation of Minteer brothers. Not that Luke minded, of course.

And to prove it to himself and everybody else in the world, he deliberately dated tall women, women close to his own height or even taller, especially in very high heels. He liked the elegance, the challenge of height. He was *completely* comfortable being one of the less-tall Minteers and didn't need short women to make him feel—well, six-feet tall.

In fact, he assiduously avoided pairing up with a petite woman. To prove his point to himself and everybody else.

He cast another surreptitious glance at Brenna Morgan.

She was pretty. That renegade thought fleetingly crossed Luke's mind, surprising him. He did not, as a rule, take note of a pregnant woman's looks. A pregnant woman obviously belonged to another guy, and he wasn't the type who poached on his brother man's territory.

He might be viewed as a snake by some—okay, by many—but he did have a certain code of ethics that he followed. Cheating with another man's woman was strictly taboo.

Besides, a pregnant woman was a mother-to-be, and mothers deserved the utmost respect. The Minteer brothers had that canon drilled into them by their own mother and grandmothers, by their aunts and great-aunts and older cousins, too.

He certainly respected mothers too much to think of them as pretty, Luke reminded himself. Because thoughts of prettiness too easily led to thoughts of desirability, which logically progressed to thoughts of sex.

Mothers, those paragons of maternal virtue, were not sexy! At least, they weren't to Luke Minteer.

But Brenna Morgan, with her long black hair curving just over her shoulders, her thick bangs accentuating high cheekbones and big, clear gray eyes fringed with dark lashes, with her firm little chin and full, sensual lips... No, not sensual, he quickly amended. Sensual and pregnant just didn't go together.

Still, Brenna Morgan was definitely a pretty woman.

To cleanse himself of the disturbing thought, Luke allowed his gaze to drift over her totally nonexistent figure. She looked like a balloon overinflated with helium, the skirt of her blue maternity dress swirling around her swollen feet and ankles.

Luke expelled what might have been a sigh of relief. He admired long, shapely legs on a woman. Though he

couldn't see Brenna's legs under the long blue skirt, her
puffy ankles certainly failed his desirability test.

As well they should. She was pregnant, some kid's
mother-to-be.

She was some guy's wife. She was of no interest to
him whatsoever.

"Is your husband going to be ticked off that you're
stuck with jury duty and that your poor unborn child is
going to be exposed to lawyers and their sleazy clients
for days on end?" Luke asked jovially, purposefully, as
they reached the main entrance of the building.

Brenna, in the midst of pulling on her oversize light-
brown parka, looked up at him, in that serious, earnest
way of hers. "I don't have a husband. This baby is mine
and mine alone."

She pushed the double doors open and walked off,
leaving him staring after her, his jaw agape.

"You were picked for jury duty in your condition?
Are they nuts? Did you tell them the baby is due in six
weeks?" Cassie Walsh, Brenna's next-door neighbor,
was outraged on her behalf.

Cassie's three-year-old daughter, Abigail, sat on the
floor, transfixed by a video of *Winnie the Pooh,* and
didn't look up as Cassie rolled an ottoman toward
Brenna, who was resting in the armchair.

"I told them." Brenna wearily propped her swollen
feet up on the ottoman. "It didn't matter. The judge
told us at the beginning of the day that they were cracking down on people getting out of jury duty."

"How can you be expected to sit for hours when
you're so far along in your pregnancy?" Cassie demanded. "Can't you get an excuse from your doctor?"

"But then my name would go back in the jury pool

and I might be chosen after I have the baby. I'd rather get it over with now. Anyway, sitting in the courtroom isn't any different from sitting in an office all day—or me sitting in my studio drawing for hours, right?''

"I suppose so.''

"Uh, one of the jurors is the brother of our congressman, Matt Minteer,'' Brenna added, keeping her voice carefully casual.

It bothered her that she had to make an *effort* to sound uninterested. She should be naturally uninterested! Even worse was the realization of how much she wanted to talk about Luke Minteer to Cassie, because she knew that Cassie's brother, Steve, was a lobbyist in Harrisburg and a reliable source of information about Pennsylvania politicians. And maybe about the brothers of politicians, too?

Brenna blushed. She was attempting to pump her friend for information about a guy—like some infatuated thirteen-year-old! A wave of hot embarrassment swamped her.

"Which brother?'' asked Cassie. "Matthew Minteer has three brothers, Mark, Luke and John.''

"Luke,'' mumbled Brenna. She still couldn't believe she was playing this game. It was so very unlike her!

"Ah, Cambria County's most notorious bachelor.'' Cassie chuckled. "He'll sure bring a wealth of experience to any jury!''

Brenna stared silently into space. She was too preoccupied with Luke Minteer, and that was not a good thing, she warned herself. She could visualize him so clearly in her mind's eye, it was as if he were standing right in the room with her....

Brenna gulped. Luke Minteer was one of those too-handsome, too-charismatic, too-masculine-for-his-own-good men. Certainly, for *her* own good.

She saw his thick, dark hair, cut slightly long, which gave him a certain rakish air. And then there were those blue eyes, such a brilliant and distinct shade of blue. The strong line of his jaw, his well-shaped mouth. Oh, that mouth!

Brenna laid her palms against her flushed cheeks to cool them. But those visuals of Luke Minteer in the courtroom kept coming.

His long-sleeved blue chambray shirt seemed to accentuate, not conceal, the breadth of his shoulders and chest and the rippling muscles in his arms. And he'd boldly worn jeans, in spite of the dress code printed on the jury summons that said "no jeans or shorts allowed."

Never mind that half the people who'd shown up were wearing jeans, too, Luke Minteer wore his jeans too well, like a sexy cowboy in a magazine ad. Brenna gave her head a quick shake to dislodge *that* uncensored thought.

By wearing jeans Luke Minteer had deliberately flaunted the rules, that's what she intended to think. And what else could you expect from a political dirty trickster who'd been fired by his own brother? Brenna tried hard to summon up some hearty disdain for the man.

Instead, she found herself picturing his hands.

They were large and strong, with long, well-shaped fingers and short, clean nails. That she had been aware of such minute details, had seemingly committed them to memory, appalled her. And then additional mental pictures flashed before her, scenes that dropped below his chest to his flat stomach and—

Brenna sat bolt upright in the chair.

"Brenna, are you all right?" Cassie was immediately concerned.

Brenna nodded weakly. "A...little twinge. A cramp, I think."

"That'll keep happening the farther along you get," Cassie, a mother of three, said sympathetically. "Braxton-Hicks contractions. Try not to let it worry you."

Brenna gulped. She wasn't worried about twinges and cramps; she'd read all about them, she even expected them. But this alarming awareness of Luke Minteer...

That was totally unexpected. What was the matter with her? Was she losing her mind? She was heading into her ninth month of pregnancy, and the last thing she should be thinking about was—

And suddenly a blanket of calm descended over her. Of course. She was heading into her ninth month of pregnancy.... That explained it all.

Hormones!

Every pregnancy book she'd read—and there were plenty—had claimed that her hormones would go into overdrive and could cause wildly irrational thinking, emotions and even behavior. So far she had remained remarkably immune from all that, but now it appeared she had succumbed at last.

"You had a long, tiring day, Brenna," Cassie continued, her tone soothing. "Why don't you stay for dinner tonight? Ray has a meeting at the high school and will be home late, and Brandon and Tim are eating at their friend Josh's house. I made macaroni and cheese for Abigail and me, and there's plenty of it. *And* we have chocolate cake for dessert, my grandma's recipe."

"Thanks, Cassie, but I...I really should go home," Brenna said weakly. "I ought to work on my—"

"Stay!" Cassie insisted. "I'll fill you in on your fellow juror, Luke Minteer. According to my brother, Steve, Luke was kind of a legend around Harrisburg when Matt was in state government there, but he managed to contain himself back then."

"What kind of legend?" murmured Brenna, in spite of herself.

Her unborn baby kicked so hard, the movements caused the material of her blue dress to bob and weave.

"Oh, the kind who played mind games to psych out opponents—and who played lots of games with lots of different women, if you know what I mean." Cassie cast a quick glance toward little Abigail, but the child was engrossed in the video and paying no attention to the adult conversation.

"Luke was a player, and I'm sorry to say that in those bad old days, my brother used to be one, too," Cassie said, lowering her voice a bit. "Steve and Luke moved in the same circles. But at least Steve matured and reformed and is a good family man now," she added, clearly relieved by the transformation.

"Not Luke Minteer, though," guessed Brenna.

Not that she cared, she assured herself. She was simply passing the time, chatting with Cassie until dinnertime. She'd decided to stay; the macaroni and cheese and chocolate cake were too tempting to pass up. She could work later this evening.

"No, not Luke," Cassie agreed. "Matt Minteer was elected to Congress and Luke went along to D.C. as his administrative aide, the same position he'd had in Harrisburg. But in D.C., Luke was unleashed. He ran wild down there."

"How?" Brenna prompted. "Uh, not that I want a

detailed account," she added hastily, her face flushing again.

"I'll give you the abridged version. Luke got in with a very fast social crowd plus a very nasty political crowd. Maybe he could've stayed unnoticed in one, but not both. Steve said rumors about him were constantly flying from D.C. to Harrisburg and, of course, back here to the district. Matt ended up firing Luke. Boy, were the Minteers mad!"

"At Luke or at Matt for firing his brother—or both?"

"At Luke, only at Luke. They let it be known how much they disapproved of him and encouraged everybody else to tell Luke their own unfavorable opinions of him, too."

"I wonder why he came back here?" Brenna mused. "It seems like a strange choice for someone like him, to come back to a small town and be ostracized and criticized by his own family."

"Maybe he was trying to get back on their good side. But if he was, it didn't work. And then he wrote this really successful novel. I heard it's going to be made into a movie, which would mean even more money, but his family still disapproves of him." Cassie shrugged. "They're a tough crowd, the Minteers."

"He has a favorite aunt who likes his book. He, um, mentioned her."

"I don't know which one she is. There are so many Minteers in the area, especially when you count the aunts, uncles and cousins. Abigail goes to preschool with Luke's brother John's little boy, David. Sounds like some sort of six-degrees-of-separation chain, doesn't it?" Cassie smiled. "Or maybe fate?"

Brenna swallowed hard. "What do you mean?"

"Well, who knows what could happen between you and Luke when—"

"Nothing," Brenna said firmly. "Cassie, I'm having a baby, for heaven's sakes."

"Who needs a father. Because there isn't one in the picture."

"And from what you've told me, Luke Minteer sounds just like the kind of man who would love to step in and play daddy to someone else's child." Brenna's voice dripped sarcasm. "As if he would ever find a pregnant woman attractive in the first place!"

"Okay, I concede your point." Cassie gave up. "The only thing that will happen involving you and Luke Minteer and jury duty is a verdict."

Brenna ran her hand through her hair. "And maybe not even that. What if it's a hung jury?"

She thought of Luke's amused prediction that she would be the one to hang the jury, but didn't share the remark with Cassie. She didn't want her friend to know how long she and Luke had talked, especially after Cassie's outlandish speculations.

Besides, she'd already spent too much time thinking about Luke Minteer—and way too much time talking about him to Cassie. It was puzzling, and disturbing, too.

And then there was the most puzzling, disturbing thing of all—that remark she'd made to him upon leaving the courthouse.

Why hadn't she simply played along with Luke Minteer's belief that she was married? Why hadn't she pretended that a "Mr. Morgan" actually existed?

Luke had assumed one did, that she was a married woman—until she'd quashed that notion flat.

Why had she done it? Brenna mused throughout the evening. By morning she still didn't have the answer.

TWO

All twelve jurors arrived on time the next morning for the beginning of the trial. They introduced themselves to each other, and one of the older men, Roger Hollister, was elected foreman. The lawyers for both sides seemed pleased with the jurors' first group decision; Hollister, whose nickname was Sarge, had served in World War II and knew a thing or two about leadership.

In the jury box before the opening argument, Luke once again sat next to Brenna Morgan. A natural gravitation process had already occurred among the twelve. Sarge Hollister and the other two men in his age group sat together, as did the five elderly women. The two pierced and tattooed young men, both named Jason with different surnames, stuck together, which left Brenna and Luke with nobody but each other.

Or so Luke told himself. Never mind that in his political incarnation, he had prided himself in fitting in with any group, regardless of age or sex. That was then, this was now, and he and Brenna were their own group strictly by default.

He glanced over at her. She'd gone for comfort over formality today, trading in yesterday's blue maternity dress for black slacks and a long bottle-green top. He had opted for jeans again—after reading the prissy advisory not to wear them to court, of course he would never wear anything else—and an equally casual plaid flannel shirt.

But Brenna had followed the dress code, such as it was. She'd pulled her dark hair high in a ponytail, and the ends of it brushed against the nape of her neck. Luke's eyes lingered on the soft, creamy-white skin exposed there, and he quickly lowered his gaze.

She looked as if she had a beachball stuffed under her shirt. Her breasts and belly seemed to merge into one big shapeless bulge, but her black tapered pants revealed that despite her advanced pregnancy, her legs were nicely shaped. Her ankles weren't swollen today. He noticed that, too.

Luke frowned.

"Why aren't you married?" he blurted out in a low whisper.

Brenna turned to look at him, visibly startled by the question. Luke himself was startled. He was doing it again—blabbing his thoughts aloud. The influence of the courthouse, perhaps? It was an old gothic-style place, vaguely creepy, where strange things might be expected to happen—like him imagining that he was being influenced by the atmosphere!

"Because I'm not," she replied coolly.

She might as well have come right out and flatly said,

It's none of your business, because her answer, her voice and entire demeanor conveyed just that sentiment.

Still Luke didn't back off. "Did your boyfriend dump you when he found out you were pregnant?"

"Are you speaking from personal experience? Is that what *you* would do in a similar situation?" Brenna went on the offense, her chin rising defiantly. "Or maybe you've already done it, for all I know." She didn't meet his eyes.

"No! I didn't—I wouldn't—I've never—" Luke paused when the attorney for Brad, the plaintiff, stood and began to present his opening argument.

Brad sat at the table, listening to his side being presented, nodding his head at every point. His former fiancée, Amber, visibly bristled, grimaced and vehemently shook her head in disagreement.

Everybody in the jury box stared at the feuding former lovers—everybody except Luke Minteer, whose eyes remained riveted on Brenna.

He leaned a little closer to her, his voice low in her ear. "Don't try to turn this around and sling mud at me, lady. This isn't about *me*."

"True. It has nothing to do with you," she murmured between clenched teeth. "And please stop talking. The judge is giving us a dirty look."

"And God forbid we get on the wrong side of His Honor," taunted Luke. "We might get thrown off the jury. Wow, *that* would be a heavy price to pay."

"Excuse me." The judge pounded his gavel, interrupting the attorney. "Jurors nine and ten, conversation will be conducted outside the courtroom, not during the trial. I don't want to have to mention this again." He glowered at Brenna and Luke.

Brenna blushed and she stared at the floor. Luke

shrugged, scowling, but unintimidated by the reprimand.

"Don't look so guilty," he whispered to Brenna a moment later. "It's not like we're criminals on trial here. *We're* the ones giving up our time to do our civic duty so that *Brad and Amber* can stick it to each—"

"Will you please shut up!" Brenna said desperately. "We're going to get jailed for contempt of court or something if you keep—"

"Juror nine!" thundered the judge, glaring at Brenna.

She slumped lower in her chair. "I'm sorry, Your Honor."

"She isn't feeling well, Your Honor," Luke spoke up. "She is very advanced in her pregnancy and needs to take a break right now. If you would be kind enough to excuse her for a few minutes..." He stared at the judge expectantly.

The judge looked nonplussed. "I...see. All right, we'll all take a ten-minute break. Court resumes in ten minutes." He strode from the courtroom.

"If we take ten-minute breaks every ten minutes, this trial will never end," one attorney complained to the other, loud enough to be heard in the jury box.

"You guys are the ones who picked a very pregnant woman to be on your jury," Luke called back to them. "So live with it, boys."

"I'm going to the rest room," Brenna murmured, and quickly left the courtroom.

Luke was in the corridor standing against the wall when she emerged from the bathroom. She would have walked past him, but he approached her.

"I came to your rescue," he said proudly. "Pretty fast thinking on my part, hmm?"

"Is that how you see yourself? A kind of gallant

knight in shining armor?'' Brenna headed directly to the courtroom, Luke at her side. ''What you seem to forget is that you're the reason I got in trouble in the first place.''

''Honey, you got in trouble long before I came on the scene.''

''If that's an attempt at wit,'' Brenna ground out, ''it failed.''

''Mmm-hmm. So you were dumped by the daddy when you told him you were pregnant?'' Luke surmised with a knowing nod. ''You wouldn't be so defensive and angry unless I'd really hit a nerve.''

''I'm not defensive but, yes, I'm angry. Because you're a...a—''

''Jerk,'' Luke supplied amiably. ''Weasel. Snake. Rat. I've been called all those things and much worse. Deservedly, too, no doubt. But I never knocked up a woman and walked away, leaving her, uh, holding the baby. Literally. I don't blame you for being furious, and if it helps to direct your rage at me, go ahead. Your boyfriend is lower than fungus slime and—''

''I don't have any rage to direct at you or anyone else!'' Brenna exclaimed, exasperated. ''I don't have a boyfriend who dumped me when he found out about the baby, either. There is no boyfriend and never was. Period.''

Luke said nothing. They walked to their seats and sat down. They were the first two jurors to return to the box.

''Go on, ask me,'' Brenna growled, after a few more moments of Luke's silence. Oddly enough, it disturbed her more than his questions and speculations. ''I can almost hear what you're thinking. So just say it.''

''I'm not one to criticize anyone else for being impulsive.'' His lips quirked into a wry smile. ''I used to call it being spontaneous back when I was your age.''

''Back when you were my age?'' Brenna scoffed. ''That wasn't so long ago, was it? It's not like you were in World War II with Sarge and company.''

''I'm thirty-five and it's been a long time since I was—'' Luke gazed down at her. ''Twenty-one?'' he guessed. ''And crossing the line from spontaneous to indiscriminate can result in—''

''I'm twenty-six. And having my baby wasn't an impulsive act, it—'' She broke off and stared at him, aghast. ''You think that I had multiple *spontaneous* one-night stands and wasn't careful?''

''You said you could hear what I was thinking,'' he reminded her.

''I didn't think it was *that!*'' Her voice rose in indignation. ''Ick! Sleeping around indiscriminately? *You* might have, but I would never do that.''

''Don't get too self-righteous, honey. You're pregnant, and that means at least one sexual encounter with at least one man. Since you were so adamant about not having a boyfriend, naturally, I assumed you'd, er, scored with more than one guy and didn't know which one was the father of your baby. Not that I'm condemning you for that,'' he added. ''I'm very open-minded.''

''How generous of you!''

''I guess I might've sounded a bit self-righteous myself there.'' Chagrined, Luke took a deep breath. ''I apologize.''

''Don't bother, because it doesn't apply. Just because you *scored* with a string of one-night stands doesn't mean that I did. And I *do* know who the father of my baby is. I personally selected him. He's a medical student, tall, blue-eyed and blond, of Swedish-English ancestry, with no inherited diseases in his family. He has a strong bent toward the sciences but also enjoys music and sports, particularly—''

"You sound like you're reading a description out of a catalog." Luke's dark-blue eyes widened suddenly. "Good Lord, that's what you did, isn't it? That's how you picked this guy, from a…a sperm bank catalog?"

She didn't deny it. She nodded her head, confirming it.

Luke gaped at her, stunned.

"I was anything but impulsive about this." Her gray eyes were as calm and serious as her tone. "I methodically researched everything very carefully and—''

"That's…that's so premeditated, so calculating," Luke cut in. He almost had to gasp for breath. "No, *demented* is what it is."

"You're the one who's demented! You wouldn't condemn me for a series of one-night stands or for not knowing who the father of my child is, but you're scandalized that I went to a sperm bank to—''

"Shhh!" he hushed her. "Unless you want to broadcast this to our fellow jurors, I suggest you keep quiet."

Brenna looked up to see the eight older jurors filing into the box. "You're right. I wouldn't want to shock anybody else," she murmured caustically.

"I'm not shocked, I'm just…" Luke's voice trailed off.

What exactly was he, then? He didn't know, couldn't identify the weird feelings roiling within him.

"Shocked," Brenna insisted. "And you don't like the sensation because shocking people is *your* specialty, right? You want to be the one to shock people, not the other way around."

"All right, guilty as charged. Now, can I ask you a personal question?"

She sighed. "You're going to ask it anyway, aren't you?"

"Are you gay? Is that the reason you've gone the, er, test-tube route? Because your, uh, significant other is a...a woman?"

"You should hear yourself, stammering like a shocked and disapproving candidate who is trying extra hard not to be politically incorrect." Brenna grinned. "Were you this tactful when you worked in politics?"

"Of course not—which is why I no longer work in politics. Well, are you?"

"No, I'm not gay. I don't have a significant other of either sex, and I don't want one. There's just me and my baby, and that's all either of us will ever need."

The two Jasons came shuffling in and had to climb over everybody to get to their seats at the end of the box. Both wore short-sleeved T-shirts, providing a clear view of the long and colorful identical dragon tattoos on their respective arms.

The sight was enough to break anyone's train of thought. Brenna and Luke stared in silence at the two dragons, then at each other. Seconds later the lawyers trooped into the courtroom with their clients. A moment after that, the judge reentered.

"Proceed, Counsel," the judge ordered.

Brad's attorney continued to explain how his client had been wronged by the duplicitous, avaricious Amber.

Luke gripped the arms of his chair.

Just me and my baby, that's all either of us will ever need. Brenna's statement swirled in his head. She sounded so sure, yet he knew she was wrong.

He had three brothers and three sisters, along with a

myriad of cousins; all were married with children. He'd seen firsthand that a new mother and a newborn baby needed a lot more than each other. They needed a support system.

At the very least they needed *one* other committed person involved—first, with the pregnancy, and then with the infant itself. The baby's father ought to own that role. Every child deserved a good father.

Brad's attorney sat down, and Amber's counsel, a young woman who looked to be right out of law school, rose to her feet with an impassioned declaration about women's rights and jealous-male greed.

Luke wasn't listening. He was too astounded by his own unexpected thoughts on parenthood. It sounded as if they'd been lifted directly from one of his brother's family-values speeches.

He knew Matt believed all that stuff, but Luke didn't. At least, he thought he didn't. He'd always considered himself to be an anything-goes kind of guy.

But the thought of Brenna Morgan and her baby, alone except for each other, struck something deep within him, summoning beliefs and feelings he hadn't been aware of harboring.

Luke looked up at the high ceiling, at the old-fashioned windows that looked as though they hadn't been opened in the past century. This courthouse really was a strange place, where his brother's speeches played inside his head. Where he couldn't stop thinking about a pretty, young pregnant woman whom he didn't even know.

Except it felt as if he knew her well. From the moment they'd started talking yesterday, something had clicked, as if they'd known each other for a long, long time. As if there had never been a time when they

hadn't known each other. They were open and frank
and honest with each other; conversation between them
came too easily for them to be total strangers.

But they'd never met...not in this lifetime.

Luke was unnerved. Now he seemed to be channeling
his youngest sister, who believed in all that past-life
nonsense. Luke didn't. He was a live-for-today kind of
guy who tried not to think of next year, let alone a next
lifetime. Or a past one...with Brenna Morgan?

A diversion was definitely in order before he lost his
mind completely. Luke tried to redirect his thoughts to
his new book, which was coming along fantastically
well.

His newest serial killer, a charming land developer,
was on the trail for fresh victims, and a small town
hosting a national pageant for teenage beauty queens
had invited him there, in hopes of becoming the site of
his next lucrative mall....

Luke shifted in his chair, picturing the calculating
killer and the teen beauties, especially the one about to
meet her doom....

And his mind abruptly went blank.

If he leaned to the right, he nearly choked on the
heavy scent of musk oil emanating from one of the
dragon twins. But if he leaned to the left, his shoulders
brushed Brenna's and he inhaled the light, fresh scent
of soap and shampoo and powder, a wholesome yet
somehow alluring scent.

Luke sat straight up, suddenly, wildly alarmed. It
couldn't be happening. His body was acting as if he
was aroused.

He was aroused!

His pulses thundered in his head, drowning out the
lawyers' voices, the whir from the heating vent in the

wall, the dried fallen leaves being blown against the glass windowpanes by the wind. Brenna Morgan, sitting next to him and oblivious of the effect she was having on him, completely commanded his senses.

He could see her and smell her, but that wasn't enough. He needed more. He was filled with a faint sense of anger at his involuntary response. *This would not do!*

But he could barely stop himself from reaching over to touch her, right here in the middle of the courtroom. He desperately wanted to feel if her hair was as silky as it looked, to run his fingers along the lines of her beautifully shaped mouth. To insert his thumb inside.

Luke pictured her lips parting, then allowed his imagination free rein, erotically expanding the scene in every way....

He bent forward, straining and aching and pulsing with need.

Jason M. in the chair beside him suddenly elbowed him.

"She's hot, huh?" the younger man whispered.

Startled, Luke followed his gaze and realized that not only had Jason noticed his predicament, he had attributed it to the defendant, Amber, seated at the nearby table, her enormous chest thrust forward, her cherry-red lips pouting. Amber repeatedly flashed provocative glances at the jury, zeroing in on the three younger males in particular.

"I think she likes us," the other Jason chimed in with a snort and a chortle.

Which drew the attention of the judge. "No talking in the jury box!" he snapped.

The Jasons lapsed into sullen silence, but Luke was grateful for the reprieve.

With a sidelong gaze, Luke resumed his covert study of Brenna. Her skin, glowing and natural, her delicate features, put Amber's heavily made-up mask in the shade. As for figures...

The two Jasons might be slavering over Amber's ample assets, but Luke found himself thoroughly fascinated by the sudden visible movements of Brenna's pregnant belly. Beneath her knit shirt, the outline of the baby's head—or its rump?—was discernible as it rolled over within her.

Brenna laid her hand over her belly, as if to soothe the restless baby. And Luke, unable to stop himself, did the same thing. He felt the warmth of her belly and the movements of the unborn child beneath his fingers.

And then his hand touched Brenna's.

It was as if an electric current had passed between them.

Brenna's head jerked up, and she drew in a sharp, shocked breath. Her eyes met Luke's, and he instantly lifted his hand, unable to come up with an excuse—or at least one he considered acceptable. Not to mention believable.

"Uh, sorry," he muttered. "Irresistible impulse."

He'd tossed around that phrase in his books, not really believing such a thing existed. It was merely an easy motive to attribute to a character's behavior, almost a cliché.

Now he knew that irresistible impulses were real indeed, because he had been seized by one himself when he'd put his hand on Brenna. But how could he ever expect her to understand that, when he didn't understand it himself?

Luke watched Brenna draw back, trying to move as far from him as possible within the confines of her chair. He couldn't blame her. After all, he had invaded her personal space and touched her like some sort of out-of-control psycho.

He wrote about those—he wasn't supposed to act like one!

Luke closed his eyes and massaged his temples with his fingertips. What was happening to him? And *why?*

The morning session was adjourned for a one-hour lunch break. The two Jasons were the first to go, barreling past the other jurors and the attorneys and casting smirks at Amber as they passed her.

The eight senior members of the jury decided to go together to Peglady's, a restaurant near the courthouse. They were halfway to the door when Sarge, the foreman, turned around to look at Brenna and Luke, still standing side-by- side in the box.

"Hey, you two want to come with us?" called Sarge.

"No, thanks," Luke answered for both himself and Brenna. "Uh, you didn't want to go with them, did you?" he tacked on as the eight jurors departed with surprising speed.

"Too bad for me if I did," said Brenna. "I'd have to run to catch up with them, and I'm not in running condition these days."

"Yeah, they are hotfooting it out of here," observed Luke, unrepentant. "I guess they're hungry. Well, Peglady's serves big portions so there's plenty to eat, plus extra to take home. Too bad the food is inedible."

"How can that be? I heard one of the women, Wanda, I think, tell the others that Peglady's is an institution here in Ebensburg."

"Yeah, it's an institution, all right. Like prisons,

schools, state hospitals. Name one of those renowned for its great cuisine.''

"Point taken." Brenna made her way out of the box.

Luke followed. He wasn't following her per se, he assured himself. To get out of the courtroom, he had no choice but to trail her, unless he wanted to be rude and push past her. And he did not want to be rude.

"So where are you going for lunch?" Luke didn't like trailing behind, so he caught up to her, easily matching his long strides to her waddling ones.

It was true, she did waddle like a duck, an observation noted by his writer's eye for detail. Being so very pregnant, he knew she couldn't help it. How did she walk when she wasn't pregnant? Sexily, with her hips swaying seductively from side to side? Gracefully, like a dancer? Or—

"Maybe I'll brave Peglady's, despite the inedible food." Her voice intruded on his ruminations. "At least it's close. I don't want to walk too far in the cold. What about you?"

"I think I'll go home. I live about twenty minutes outside of town, up the mountain."

"Twenty minutes up and twenty minutes back. That won't give you much time to eat," Brenna pointed out.

"Approximately twenty minutes. It's sweet of you to care."

Brenna looked up at him. His grin and the glint in his eyes matched his teasing tone.

"Don't waste your boyish-delight act on me," she said tartly. "It'll probably go over well with Amber, though. She couldn't take her eyes off you and the Jasons, but I think she'd choose you, given any encouragement at all."

"Boyish delight?" Luke arched his brows. "Ouch.

As for Amber... Since we jurors are forbidden to discuss anything about this case among ourselves, I suppose I can't accuse you of having a jealous fit of pique because Amber was looking me over. It could be grounds for a mistrial."

They walked into the jurors' lounge where the coatroom was located and found their coats. She had her big pale-brown parka, he had a navy-blue winter jacket that deepened the color of his eyes. Both carried their coats instead of putting them on.

Luke held the elevator doors open with his arm until she was safely inside the car. And then a group of people appeared, seemingly from nowhere, and pushed inside, shoving Brenna hard against Luke.

"Hey, people, quit rushing like a herd of stampeding buffalo," Luke ordered sharply. "This woman is practically nine-months pregnant, and she was almost knocked down. Every one of you owes her an apology, and if she doesn't get one, *I'm* getting your names. And this is a courthouse, so just use your imagination as to what I'll do next."

"Luke!" whispered Brenna, dismayed.

Everybody in the crowded elevator began offering her abject apologies, making sure that Luke saw and heard them. She stood pressed against him, her back molded to his chest and the cradle of his thighs. His hands rested on her shoulders. They felt heavy and warm, just like his body felt against hers. She had to fight to keep from relaxing against him and melting into him. It seemed like the most natural thing in the world to do.

Heat permeated through her, and it felt good, keeping her warm even when the doors opened to a blast of the chilly November air that filled the first floor of the courthouse. The drafty entrance foyer, the source of the unwelcome cold, was just ahead of them.

"Every single one of those people told you they were sorry," Luke said, sounding awestruck. "And I think they genuinely were sorry, too. Sometimes people surprise me."

"The unanimous apologies aren't surprising at all. Everybody in that elevator knew you were watching them. They probably considered you dangerously prone to filing lawsuits. If you had told them to sing Christmas carols to me, they would've launched into a chorus of 'Joy to the World.'"

"You have a tendency to overanalyze. I suggest that you simply accept things at face value, Brenna."

"I suggest you stop making suggestions, Luke."

"That's the first time you've said my name," he murmured, staring down at her.

"So what?" Brenna didn't look at him; she kept her gaze focused well over his shoulder. "It was the first time you'd said my name, too," she added defensively.

"So you called me Luke in retaliation for me calling you Brenna?" The glint was back in his eye, the drollery in his tone. "You really go for the jugular, don't you, babe?"

She made no reply.

"I do have another suggestion to make," Luke instantly filled the silence between them. "I suggest you thank me for defending you against those boors in the elevator. I stood up for you, remember?"

"I didn't ask you to. I didn't want you to. I don't like to make a scene, and you certainly turned that elevator ride into one."

"Well, for one who doesn't like to stand out, you sure picked a helluva way to get pregnant, honey. Taking the sperm-bank route inspires curiosity, which means lots more attention than simple, old-fashioned procreation ever would've.''

They stood a few feet away from the doors while they donned their coats. Luke easily shrugged into his, then helped Brenna, who was struggling with hers while also shifting her purse from side to side.

He let his hands linger on her shoulders while she fumbled with the zipper.

''I've never told anybody about—about how I got pregnant,'' she said, so quietly he had to strain to hear her. ''And I'd appreciate it if you would keep it to yourself.''

Brenna gave up on the zipper and hurried to the double doors. Luke was right behind her, and this time he pushed them open, holding them for her.

''You haven't told anybody else?'' He was incredulous. ''Nobody knows the truth but me?''

''No. It's a fact, I really don't like making a scene or being the center of attention. And as you pointed out, something kind of…unconventional, like the donor catalog and bank, pretty much guarantees…speculation and gossip.''

A blast of wind hit them as they stepped outside. Shuddering from the cold, Brenna clutched the sides of her coat together.

''Come on, my car's right down there.'' Luke pointed to his enormous black Dodge Durango truck parked along the curb, almost directly in front of the courthouse.

He took Brenna's arm and walked her through the wind to his truck. She ducked her head, letting him guide her, the cold air stinging her eyes, making them tear. Moments later she was seated in the front passenger seat while Luke revved up the engine.

"Isn't this spot reserved for a VIP or something? How did you park here without getting ticketed?" Brenna flexed her icy fingers, pulling on her knit gloves. "Yesterday they told us to park two blocks down—if we could find a place in the free lot there. Otherwise, we were on our own and good luck."

She zipped up her coat just as the heater began to work, quickly warming the interior.

"One of my cousins is a cop," explained Luke. "He suggested this spot and said he'd pass the word that my truck was right where it should be."

"I thought your relatives didn't like you—except for your favorite aunt who enjoys grisly murders."

"Well, some of the younger cousins, especially the guys, think I'm cool." Luke swung the truck into the sparse flow of traffic. "And I shamelessly buy their friendship by taking them out to lunch or dinner or whatever."

"Are you trying to get back in your family's good graces?" Brenna asked curiously. "Is that why you came back here after..." Her voice trailed off.

"After my brother fired me and my family told me I was insufferable and full of myself, a sleazy showboat, and a vain big shot who was in danger of losing my immortal soul?" Luke chuckled wryly. "Mixed metaphors don't bother the Minteers, and they freely fling them."

"But why—" Brenna stared out the window. "Where are we going?"

"To lunch, remember? We have a little less than an hour."

"I'm not going to your place in...in the mountains!" Her voice rose in panic. "Let me out right now!"

"I'm not going home. You were right, there's not enough time." Luke cast her an inquisitive glance. "You're scared," he observed thoughtfully. "Of me?"

"I admit that I do have issues with being taken somewhere against my will by a man I hardly know," Brenna replied tersely.

"Issues," he scoffed, his dark brows narrowing. "The current buzzword. An annoying one, too. Nobody has problems anymore, everybody has issues. Although it seems to me what you really have going on is an overload of hormones. You were operating in high maternal-protection mode."

"Maybe so." Brenna folded her arms and rested them on the shelf of her belly. She tried to will her pounding heart into beating a little slower.

"Were you freaked when I touched your belly in the courtroom earlier?" Luke blurted out. A flush of heat spread up his neck to his face. "I didn't intend to scare you, but when I saw the baby moving, it—I—"

"It's happened to me before," she said briskly. "People wanting to touch my belly to feel the baby move, except it's always been elderly women, and they always ask."

Once again she tamped down the swell of feelings the touch of his big hand on her belly had elicited within her. They meant nothing; they were a physiological reaction, she reminded herself. Insisted to herself. Hormonal overload and nothing else.

"It really was an irresistible impulse," explained Luke. "You see, I have a scene in my new book where a pregnant woman—"

"You're not going to have a pregnant woman murdered by a serial killer?" Brenna was aghast.

"No, but the killer does touch the pregnant woman's belly. It's very, very suspenseful. I want the reader literally shaking and screaming at the killer, 'Don't you dare hurt that mother and child.' And when he doesn't, the reader's relief will be—"

"You never did say where we're going," Brenna cut in sharply. He'd been exploring the mind-set of his serial killer character when he'd touched her? She shuddered.

"I'm kidnapping you to the China Palace, a few blocks from here. Ever been there?"

"Yes. And jokes about kidnapping aren't funny."

"That's what the homicide detective said to the serial killer in my first book," joked Luke. She didn't smile, and he sighed. "Well, the humor worked in the scene in the book."

"I'll take your word for it."

"I guess you'll have to, since you never intend to read a word I write. Okay, we'll move on to a neutral topic. The China Palace. It's owned by the Lo family, who ran a successful place in Philadelphia but moved here because they wanted to try a small town for a change. They're very strong supporters of my brother. Held a fund-raising dinner for Matt right here in the restaurant."

Luke pulled into the parking lot of the China Palace. Inside, the hostess and a waitress, both young Chinese women, greeted Luke enthusiastically and escorted them to a choice table by the window.

It appeared that Matt wasn't the only Minteer to enjoy support here, Brenna noted. And the admiration appeared to be mutual. Luke chatted and joked with the two young women as Brenna seated herself and opened the menu.

"Okay, which one are you?" asked one of the young women, finally acknowledging Brenna's presence.

It took Brenna a moment to realize that she was the one being addressed. And she had no idea what the answer to that question might be. She stared at Luke, baffled.

"Jennifer wants to know which one of the many Minteers you are," he explained, toying with a salt shaker.

"One of the sisters or one of the cousins?" prompted Jennifer, smiling invitingly at Luke.

Brenna met Luke's eyes. He shrugged. "I'll let you decide since you're the fiction writer," she said dryly.

Luke cleared his throat. "Actually, she isn't a Minteer. This is Brenna Morgan. Brenna, meet the Lo sisters, Jennifer and Isabelle."

"Hello," Brenna offered politely.

The Lo sisters gaped at her, barely managing to mutter a response before abruptly departing.

"What was that all about?" Luke frowned. "I've never known them to be rude before. I've been snubbed by plenty of people in this town but the Lo sisters have always been exceptionally friendly."

"Yes, I noticed. And they weren't being rude, they were stunned." Brenna was amused. The astonishment on the Lo sisters' faces had been comical. "No doubt it was the shock of seeing you with a pregnant woman who wasn't related to you."

"What are you implying?" Luke demanded.

"Me? Nothing." Brenna turned her attention back to the menu.

Luke looked over at the Lo sisters who were blatantly staring at him and Brenna. "I've been the object of enough gossip to know *that* particular look they're giving us,'' he muttered.

"I'm sure you have. I've heard some of the stories." Brenna never glanced up from the menu.

"For crying out loud, we're serving on a jury together. It's our lunch break!" exclaimed an aggrieved Luke. "And who told you stories about me? And, er, what were they?"

"When I told my neighbor that Congressman Minteer's brother was on the jury with me, she told me her brother knew you back in Harrisburg, in your pre-D.C. days." Brenna closed the menu. "I think I'll have a bowl of wonton soup, an egg roll and chicken with cashews."

"Who's your neighbor's brother?" pressed Luke.

"Steve Saraceni, the lobbyist."

"Uh-oh." Luke actually gulped. "Did she, um, go into specifics?"

"No." Brenna smiled sweetly.

"Well, it doesn't matter, anyway, because it's all ancient history, water over the dam. A place in the past we've passed out of." Luke paused to catch his breath. "Those days are over. Saraceni would say the same thing himself."

Brenna sipped her water. "I'm so thirsty. The air in that courtroom is too dry."

"Okay, the stories out of D.C. were even worse, I can't deny that." Luke fiddled with his napkin. "But that's—"

"Ancient history? Water over the dam? A place in the past you've—"

"Isabelle!" Luke stood up and waved the waitress over. "We're ready to order now."

Three

The afternoon session moved at a glacial pace, and several of the jurors had trouble staying awake. Brenna was one of them. Her eyelids felt heavy, keeping them open was an effort and a numbing lethargy spread through her.

It was too warm in here, the lawyers droned on and on, citing one dull legal reference after another. Plus, she'd eaten too much for lunch. The combination was narcotizing. She allowed herself to close her eyes. It would be all right to close them for just a moment.

Brenna drifted in the netherworld between sleep and wakefulness....

Images glided through her mind. She saw herself and Luke sitting at their table in the China Palace eating lunch. He used chopsticks—adeptly, too—while she and everybody else in the restaurant ate with plain old forks. Brenna smiled now, as she had then. She didn't know why, but his prowess with the Asian utensils amused her.

And then he'd put down his chopsticks and asked her quietly, "Why did you tell the truth about your pregnancy to me and nobody else?"

Brenna was faced with the very question she had asked herself when blurting out the truth she'd kept carefully guarded all these months. Why had she told Luke?

"I think it was because you were goading me," she'd replied slowly.

Luke nodded, seeming to accept the answer. Brenna was glad he did, but she didn't buy her own explanation. She should've dismissed Luke's speculations with a shrug, not caring what he thought. Instead, she'd told him her deepest secret. It made no sense at all, or else it made very revealing sense.

"What is the story you've told everybody else in town?" Luke demanded.

"Unlike you, I'm not too well known in this town, so everybody doesn't want to know about me. I did tell my neighbors and my doctor that I, uh, was in a relationship that didn't work out, and when I found out I was pregnant, the baby's father left."

"Which is exactly what I thought at first—until you emphatically informed me that there was no boyfriend," Luke reminded her. "Hasn't anybody else pushed for more details?"

"No. Nobody else has been that rude. Or pushy. Or intrusive. They've respected my privacy."

"Maybe they figured talking about it—about him, the supposed father—would upset you," surmised Luke.

"Or maybe they just weren't interested enough to ask you anything more."

"Maybe," she'd agreed.

After that Luke had grown very quiet. He hadn't spoken much at all as they finished their meal and drove back to the courthouse, where he reclaimed the VIP parking spot for his truck again.

"We will now take a brief recess!"

The judge's stentorian tones plus the bang of his gavel startled Brenna back into full consciousness. Her eyes flew open, and she jerked forward. She felt a hand close over her upper arm, steadying her.

It was then she noticed how very close she was sitting to Luke. Their shoulders were touching, and she was leaning heavily against him. His hand was on her arm. Was she imagining it or was his thumb lightly stroking?

Brenna stood up as quickly as she could. Unsteady on her feet, she gripped the front rail for support.

"I...think I fell asleep," she murmured, running a hand through her hair.

"You and everybody else on the jury except Wanda and me." Luke rose to stand beside her. "Wanda has her knitting to keep her alert, and I'm used to sitting for long stretches while my mind wanders."

"Into serial killer land?" Brenna yawned, still drowsy.

"It's an interesting place to go. Although I was somewhere else this time." Frowning, Luke gripped her elbow. "Come on, let's go get a cold drink from one of those machines in the lounge."

She let him lead her into the jurors' lounge, where a TV set was tuned into the Weather Channel. The meteorologist was in a frenzy of excitement about a blizzard that was "crippling the plains." Scenes of blinding snow and abandoned cars along an interstate highway played on the screen.

"I wonder if they drag out the same old blizzard footage every time a new storm hits?" mused Luke, gazing at the television. "Who would know? All snowstorms look alike."

"As a devoted weather fan, that's blasphemy to my ears." Brenna sipped the cold soda from the can Luke had given her. "Thanks for this," she added.

"Consider it my contribution to the judicial system." Luke was flippant. "Keeping the jury alert and functioning is necessary to end this stupid trial as fast as possible."

"Then you can get back to creating murder and mayhem full-time."

"Yeah." He watched her sip the soda. "What do you do, full-time?"

"I draw."

He waited for her to elaborate. She didn't. She silently sipped the soda from the can, her eyes affixed to the blizzard on the television screen.

"Okay, I'll bite," Luke said at last. "What do you draw?"

"Mostly children and cute animals. I'm a freelance artist. I've illustrated children's books and magazines and drawn paper dolls and sketched children for sewing patterns and books."

"Has your work been published?" He looked startled.

She nodded.

"And you earn enough to support yourself…and the baby?" Now he looked even more amazed.

His incredulity irked Brenna. Did she appear stupid?

Incapable of possessing artistic talent? What was so un-believable about her being paid for her work?

"Well, that's cool." Luke shrugged laconically, his surprise fading into indifference.

Which bugged her even more. "Oh, I'm glad you think so. I was worried you might find me *un*cool."

"Yeah, right." He laughed. "You couldn't care less what I think. And I like that too. You're...not boring."

"People who care about your opinion bore you? That sounds terribly jaded." Brenna tossed her empty soda can into the nearby trash bin, then walked over to the window and stared outside.

Moments later Luke again was by her side. "I am jaded," he said, resuming the conversation exactly where they'd left off. "Remember all those stories about me?"

"'Enough about me, let's talk about what you've heard about me'?" Brenna mocked.

Luke looked nonplussed. "I didn't say that."

"I understand subtext."

"Huh? What subtext? What are you talking about?"

"Never mind." Brenna turned and walked away from him.

Luke followed. It was as if he were on a leash and she held the end, dragging him along after her, wherever she went. The insight was appalling, yet he kept going, not stopping until he realized she was heading purpose-fully to the women's rest room.

She stayed there, not emerging until it was time to return to the courtroom.

Luke was already seated when she took in her chair in the box. She didn't look his way; she struck up a conversation with Wanda instead, admiring the colors in the afghan the older woman was knitting.

Luke found the discussion about yarn dull. He tried to enliven it. " All ready to hear more about those zany star-crossed lovers Amber and Brad?'' he joked, interrupting.

''We're not supposed to discuss the case until deliberations.'' Brenna's tone was frosty, as if she didn't know he was kidding.

Luke knew she did. He heaved a deep, martyred sigh. ''Brenna, I know you're mad, but—''

The judge entered the courtroom, and everybody rose in deferential silence. There were no more breaks until court was adjourned at four-thirty.

Later that evening Brenna was in her studio, an upstairs bedroom she planned to completely remodel someday. Right now it was empty except for her draft table and state-of-the-art desk chair, worth every cent she'd paid, considering how much time she spent in it. A ledge she had installed ran the length of one wall and held the tools of her trade, pens and pencils, both lead and colored, rulers and erasers, sable brushes, watercolors in every hue imaginable.

The lighting equipment had been another major expenditure, necessary to enable her to work at night, even though she preferred the natural sunlight of daytime. When the baby came, she might not be able to adhere to her normal routine of working all morning and afternoon. The baby would dictate her schedule, and that might mean working nights, when it was dark.

Brenna was prepared. Her new lighting made the room as bright as day.

Piles of books and magazines were stacked haphazardly around the room; getting shelves to put them on was another future project. An illustrated book of costumes lay open in front of her.

Brenna reached for a sharp yellow pencil to color in the loop-tied pigtails of the little girl with a turned-up nose and mischievous sparkle in her pale-blue eyes.

The little girl was six-year-old Kristin, who was wearing clothes in the style and colors that a child of that age in the year 1908 would have worn. Brenna had drawn Kristin's dress and bloomers, big ribbons and button shoes after researching her invaluable aid: *A Hundred Years of Children's Wear: 1850-1950.*

One of her favorite CDs, *Broadway Sings Happy,* a collection of peppy anthems from various shows, accompanied Brenna as she drew. Since that momentous day when she'd learned she was pregnant, Brenna had played nothing but upbeat music, songs about hope and love and laughter, songs that lifted her spirits. She firmly believed that maternal moods affected an unborn baby, and it was her duty to protect her child from any of her own less-than-positive emotions.

A boisterous rendition of ''76 Trombones'' filled the small house, and Brenna hummed along. When the telephone on the wall beside her began to ring, she picked up the portable receiver and tucked it under her chin while deftly coloring Kristin's hairbow a pale-pink.

''Oh, so you have a parade going on in there,'' said Cassie Walsh on the other end of the line. ''That's why you haven't heard your doorbell ringing or the knocking—I mean, the *pounding*—on your door.''

''Somebody's at my door?'' Brenna quickly lowered the volume of her CD player.

The doorbell was ringing insistently, with some knocking—no, pounding was more descriptively correct—occurring at intermittent intervals. All the houses on the street had been built close together on small lots, enabling her neighbors to hear what she had blocked out with her music.

"Can you see who it is?" asked Brenna. She knew Cassie had a clear view of her front porch from the Walsh kitchen.

"It's a man," Cassie said. "That much I can tell, because it can't be a woman with that build. And if it is... Well, she has my deepest sympathy. You know, if you'd put your porch light on when it gets dark, I'd have a better view, Brenna."

There was a slight note of reprimand in her voice. Cassie had a younger sister and often fell into that role automatically with Brenna when it came to things like safety tips.

"Did I forget to put the porch light on again? Sorry, Cass. I guess I'm still not used to living in a house after a lifetime in apartments. Can you tell if it's a policeman? Because I'm not opening my door to anyone else, and I'm not even sure I'll—"

"I'm sending Ray over there right now," Cassie said decisively and hung up.

Amid the ringing and pounding, Brenna crept quietly down the stairs. There were no windows in her small entrance foyer, and her door was solid oak, with no glass panes to reveal her presence to the person outside.

"I'm Ray Walsh and these are my boys, Brandon and Timmy." Through the door, Brenna heard Ray Walsh, Cassie's husband, the principal of the town high school. "We live next door. Can we help you?"

"I'm a friend of Brenna's, and I'm starting to get concerned. She isn't answering her door, and I know she must be in there. All the lights are on, and I could hear music playing a couple minutes earlier. I know she's inside—but maybe she can't get to the door?"

Brenna uttered a small astonished gasp. She also recognized that particular male voice. It was none other than her fellow juror, Luke Minteer.

And he was at her door? Why?

Automatically she opened the front door. A hard-blowing wind rushed into the house, and Brenna shuddered, rubbing her hands over her arms. Her long red maternity sweater, decorated with candy canes, wasn't enough protection against the cold night air.

"You are here!" Luke sounded triumphant.

His eyes met Brenna's, and their gazes locked.

"Hi, Mrs. Morgan," Brandon and Tim, both pre-teens, chorused.

Luke arched his brows sardonically, and Brenna quickly looked away from him, to greet the boys warmly.

"Thought we'd drop over and see what you're up to tonight, Brenna," said Ray. He tilted his head toward Luke. "Friend of yours?" He left the option open for Brenna to confirm or deny.

"Yes, I know him." The breathlessness in her voice surprised her. She supposed it must be from the shock of cold air.

"Luke Minteer." Luke extended his hand to Ray and then to each boy. "Nice to meet you. It's good to know Brenna has such reliable neighbors," he added with a smooth sincerity that made Brenna's lips curve into a wry smile.

It wasn't hard to picture Luke out campaigning for his brother. He sounded as if he were chatting up potential voters right now.

"You're the writer, aren't you?" Ray eyed Luke thoughtfully. "And…the brother?"

Luke grinned. "Things are really starting to look up when I'm 'the writer' before 'the brother.' It used to be the other way around—I thought it always would be."

"Your book was amazing," Ray said eagerly, dropping his initial reserve. "Had me laughing one minute and on the edge of my seat the next. And the ending! *That* sure was unexpected! What a great read!"

"Thanks." Luke beamed. "I had to go to the mat to keep that ending. The editors wanted me to—"

"If you'll excuse me, I have to get back to work," Brenna injected. She started to close the door.

"Wait!" Luke stepped into the doorway, preventing her from shutting him out.

Brenna paused, her hand on the knob.

"Can I come in?" asked Luke.

She was certain he'd only asked because Ray and the kids were standing there. Otherwise, she had no doubt that he would've pushed his way inside without bothering to seek her permission. But since he had…

Brenna remained still, with the door partially closed and Luke half in and half out, while she debated whether or not to let him inside.

Luke cleared his throat. "It's urgent, Brenna."

Another gust of wind delivered yet another icy wallop. It was too cold to stand there indefinitely. Brenna stepped aside, allowing Luke to enter.

"Brenna, if you need anything, give a call." Ray was already herding the boys from the porch. "I'm looking forward for your next book, Luke," he added with enthusiasm. "Don't make us wait too long for it."

Luke gave a friendly wave, then turned and closed the door behind him. "Nice guy," he remarked.

"And an admiring fan of yours." Brenna folded her arms, resting them on her belly. Inside her body, the baby had ceased its earlier gymnastics and was probably asleep. "If you want to continue your discussion with Ray, go on over. I'm sure he'll be delighted."

"I didn't come here to discuss my writing with your neighbor."

"Why *are* you here?" She eyed him warily.

Luke opened his jacket and slipped it off, tossing it toward the post of the wooden railing along the staircase. The hood snagged the top of the post and hung there.

"Sort of a slam dunk," he said with satisfaction. "Not bad, huh?"

"Let me guess—you played basketball in school?"

"High school," he confirmed. "Never made the team in college. Not, er, enough height, according to the coach."

She looked up at him. Flatfooted in her slipper-socks, it seemed she had to look way up. "I guess they only want those seven-foot-tall giants playing college ball."

"Yeah. If you're six feet tall—like me—you're out of luck." Luke squared his shoulders and looked even taller to her.

She noticed that he still had on the same clothes he'd worn in court today, faded well-fitting jeans and the plaid flannel shirt, its colors muted, as if it had undergone repeated washings. She knew that the fabric was soft and warm because she had felt it against her cheek as she'd slept against him in the courtroom this afternoon.

The sensory memory hit her like a blast of frigid air, jolting her, making her feel a little dizzy. The breathlessness she'd originally attributed to the cold wind was back, which meant there had to be another cause for it.

This time Brenna didn't kid herself into believing it was anything other than his stunning sensual impact on her.

She gazed up at him, so male and tall and strong. So virile.

What was the line in that old, country song, something about "looking better than he had a right to"? Oh, that was Luke Minteer! And he was here in her house, staring down at her with his piercing Irish-blue eyes. She felt an unfamiliar melting warmth ooze through her, pooling deep in her belly.

Brenna gulped. "I know you're not here to discuss your ex-basketball career. You said it was urgent."

"I meant it was urgent that you make up your mind to let me in. I was freezing my, er, I was really getting cold standing out there." He rubbed his palms together. "Any coffee?"

"I don't drink it. I've never liked it. I have tea and hot chocolate," she added reluctantly. Was she obliged to offer hospitality to a drop-in visitor?

"No, thanks." Luke made a face as if she'd offered him rat poison. "Anyway, why I'm here...I know why you blew up at me in the courtroom today."

"I didn't blow up at you!"

"Figuratively speaking. Hey, you were mad, Brenna. Come on, admit it."

"I wasn't mad," she insisted. "I—" She broke off, then began again. "I'm working this evening, Luke. I don't have time for guests."

"I'm not a guest. I just stopped by to tell you that I figured out what got you so riled this afternoon. It was because I didn't give you a chance to talk about your job.'' He wore the satisfied smile of one who has discovered an elusive truth. "I didn't mean to cut you off, but somehow—''

"The conversation got turned around to focus on you? Funny how that always seems to happen, isn't it? You do love talking about your favorite subject—you!'' She was fighting hard to hold back a smile of her own. He was tangibly turning on the charm; she could feel it.

"And that made you mad, isn't that right, Brenna?''

"No, I was simply tired of talking to you, of talking about you, of listening to you.''

She was particularly tired of the roller-coaster thrills being in his company provided her, but Brenna was not about to add that. Better to offend him by letting him believe she found him a tiresome bore. Because if he were to suspect these *feelings* he'd stirred up in her...

A pregnant woman, at the mercy of an overload of hormones, developing a schoolgirl crush on the town's bachelor rogue? Oh, it was too embarrassing to contemplate.

"Serving on a jury means enduring all the lawyers' blather, not the other jurors,'' she added baldly.

Luke gave a huff, his expression one of disbelief mingled with indignation. "Well, you don't have to worry, I won't continue to *bore* you. In fact, I'll spare you from having to endure any more of my...blather. From now on, I won't talk to you at all.''

"That works for me,'' Brenna said glibly. "Good night.''

"Good night!'' He retrieved his jacket from the post.

Brenna felt her baby awaken with a sudden thrust and begin to kick forcefully. She drew a sharp breath after a particularly enthusiastic strike.

Luke, his hand on the doorknob, had turned around in time to see her reaction.

"You flinched." He scowled. "Are you okay, or do you intend to go into labor right now?"

"I'm okay. Susannah or Simon's foot connected with one of my internal organs. A kidney, I think."

"Simon," Luke repeated, dropping his hand. "*Simon?* Don't tell you you're thinking of naming the kid Simon?"

"Only if it's a boy. If she's a girl, she'll be Susannah."

"Susannah is all right, I guess, but Simon as in 'Simple Simon Met a Pieman'? As in Simon Says? And that arch villain Simon Legree? You can't be serious."

"Simon is a wonderful name!" Brenna was defensive. "It's a classic, biblical and timeless. It's strong but stylish and not overused—"

"You sound as if you're quoting from one of those baby-name books. You can't take them seriously. Case in point, one of those books claims that Hortense is ripe for a comeback."

"Not one of the name books I've read says that," protested Brenna, "and, anyway, there is a world of difference between Simon and Hortense."

"The sperm donor was half-Swedish, so why not choose a Viking name? Might as well play up the kid's heritage, since it's the only thing he'll ever get from his father."

The implied criticism stung Brenna. "You were just on your way out the door, after promising you wouldn't talk to me anymore, remember?" she needled him.

Luke's mouth thinned into a straight line. "You can be really bitchy at times, Brenna."

"True. I can be. And a charming smooth operator

like you doesn't have to put up with it. I'm sure this town is filled with nonbitchy types who would love it if you dropped in on them. So why don't you?'' She opened the front door and held it for him.

"That's a blatant invitation for me to leave,'' accused Luke.

"As blatant as I could make it,'' she agreed.

Cold air was beginning to fill the foyer again, thanks to the opened door. Brenna shivered.

"Why am I still here?'' Luke tossed out the question, glaring at her, as if challenging her to supply the answer. "Why did I come over here in the first place?''

His eyes swept over her, taking in her defiant stance, her feet planted wide apart, one hand on her hip while her other hand kept pushing the door open wider, letting the wind blow inside. She was probably hoping a gust would blast him right out of the house.

To his extreme consternation, Luke couldn't decide if her aggressive posture infuriated him or turned him on. Or both.

Worse, he already knew the answers to the two questions he had posed, though he could only hope *she* didn't.

He was here because he couldn't stay away from her. Because the need to be with her had somehow overpowered his common sense and his willpower to stay away from her.

His mind had short-circuited this afternoon when he'd learned she was a successful artist, one who actually made a living from her work. He'd been impressed, and the odd vicarious pride that had streaked through him unnerved him. If he hadn't stopped himself, he would've deluged her with questions and given himself away. So he'd played it cool and *she'd* turned cold.

But instead of being relieved, all he could think about was how to make things right with her again. After staring blankly at his computer screen tonight for over two whole hours without typing a single word—his first-time-ever case of writer's block—he'd conceded that writing was a lost cause. His imagination had been taken over by Brenna Morgan!

It was as if he were possessed, so he'd hightailed it over here seeking exorcism. Her unwelcoming bitchiness, coupled with the sight of her in that absurd candy cane sweater, her belly swollen, her face pale without makeup, her hair tumbled around her shoulders in a tangled mess, should've done the trick.

He *should* have been cured, his clear thinking restored. He *should* have been able to go right home and write that scene where the serial killer touched the pregnant woman's belly, the one that he'd improvised on the spot today, after touching Brenna.

Instead, instead…

"Damn," Luke swore softly. "What have you done to me?"

He reached out and cupped her cheek with his hand. Her skin was soft and warm, and he lightly stroked it with his fingertips.

A moment later she backed away from him, her gray eyes flashing. "What are you doing?"

"Good question," murmured Luke. He moved swiftly to close the door, then leaned against it, his back chilled by the cool wood. "But the only answer I can come up with is that I'm not doing enough."

His arm snaked out and he seized her wrist with his hand.

Brenna stared down at his fingers manacling her wrist. "Don't, please!"

He heard the fear in her voice, and it called to mind her momentary panic in his car this afternoon, when she'd thought he was taking her to his house.

"Are you afraid of men in general or me in particular?" he asked quietly. He didn't loosen his hold on her wrist.

"Let me go." Brenna licked her lips, and he followed the movement of the tip of her tongue with avid eyes.

"I won't hurt you, Brenna." He slowly, gently, but inexorably pulled her toward him. "Don't be afraid of me."

"I'm not afraid!" she exclaimed fiercely. "I might have…issues…about being manhandled, but I'm not afraid!"

"Manhandle you? Never, honey. I'm known to have a slow hand." Luke chuckled softly. "A light touch."

She was only an inch or two away from him now. "Sounds like song lyrics to me," she said huskily.

He touched her cheek. "If you're not afraid of me, prove it, Brenna."

"By doing what?" Brenna's breathing was hard and fast, her pupils dilated wide.

With arousal, Luke was certain of that. Not fear, never that. She couldn't be afraid of him. He gave a tug, pulling her against him, as close as her pregnant belly would allow.

"I'll think of something," he said lazily, sliding both his hands to her hips.

"Have you lost your mind?" Brenna gaped at him. "I'm almost nine months pregnant, for godsakes!"

Four

"There can be no doubt about that," Luke agreed. "I actually can feel Susannah or Sam kicking." His blue eyes grew round as saucers. "What a weird sensation!"

"Try experiencing it from the inside, if you want weird," murmured Brenna, noting his renaming of her son.

"Thankfully, I'll never have to," Luke's relief sounded heartfelt. "Women are a helluva lot braver than men when it comes to certain things, and having a kid tops that list."

Brenna felt the grip of Luke's hands on her hips loosen as the baby's strongest kicks became noticeable to him. While he was distracted, she should take the opportunity to shove him away. She could make a dash into the downstairs bathroom, only a few feet away, lock herself in, open the window and scream for Cassie and Ray.

They would hear her, she knew. They would be over here within moments to rescue her.

So why didn't she do it? Brenna asked herself as Luke's fingers tightened once more, keeping her right where she was.

"And it's Susannah or *Simon,* not Sam." Instead of escaping from him, she corrected him.

"We'll discuss that later." He widened his stance and settled her more intimately into the cradle of his thighs, then began to nuzzle the side of her neck.

His arousal pressed thick and hard against her. Brenna's heart began to pound against her ribs so wildly, she wondered if Luke could feel that, too. Yet her arms remained at her sides, and she made no attempt to push him away from her. Her uncharacteristic passivity shocked her.

"See." Luke's mouth blazed a trail of nibbling kisses to her ear. "Nothing to be scared of, Brenna." His lips traced the shape of her ear, and he carefully enunciated each word.

Brenna's hands slowly glided to his chest—to finally push him away, she thought. But they seemed to be operating of their own volition, because instead of giving Luke a hearty shove, her fingers curled around his jacket.

"I already said I'm not afraid of you," she whispered.

And she truly wasn't. Which would completely explain the mystery of why she felt no need to involve her neighbors in what was a very private matter. She neither needed nor wanted to be rescued. She hardly had time to process that insight when Luke's lips brushed lightly, sensuously over hers.

"Good." His warm breath, scented with an enticing mix of coffee and peppermint, flowed over her.

Brenna's head spun. What he was doing felt so good…everything did—the feel of his big hands anchoring her against him, her breasts crushed comfortably against the solid wall of his chest, his mouth so warm and seductive on hers.

Brenna quivered, clinging to him as an unfamiliar melting pleasure began to pervade her body. Her nipples, so sensitive during her pregnancy, tightened into taut points and began to tingle in the most disconcerting way.

She'd been aware of the changes in her breasts as her body prepared her to nurse her child, but the sensations evoked by the close contact with Luke's chest were brand-new. She wondered what it would feel like if he touched her there, with his fingers, with his mouth.

Brenna froze. These images and feelings, the wildness and the sensuality… They were overwhelming her; she couldn't handle it. What if she were to simply give in to them…?

I was overwhelmed and overpowered by my feelings, Brenna! I just couldn't help myself! Her mother's voice, girlish and plaintive yet subversively pleased, echoed in Brenna's head like a ghost from the past.

And Brenna's own silent response was the same as it had been when she'd been a child, listening to her mother's dramatic confessions. *But try to, Mom! If only you would at least try to fight the overwhelming, overpowering feelings.*

A futile wish, because Marly Morgan adored being at the mercy of her overpowering, overwhelming feelings; she thrived on being *helpless with passion,* her favorite dramatic description of her favorite state.

The very concept made Brenna cringe, then and now.

Her mother's perennial can't-help-myself excuse had inspired Brenna early on to control her impulses, her emotions, her wants. Even her needs. Brenna Morgan would not be overpowered or overwhelmed, she would not be made helpless by anything or anyone.

But here she was, on the verge of all those things— with Luke Minteer.

It seemed that it was time she took her own advice and at least *tried* to fight these overwhelming, overpowering feelings.

"What is it, honey?" Luke was attuned to her sudden emotional withdrawal, but he continued to hold her.

"This is just plain crazy. I'm not thinking straight." Brenna nearly wailed. "My common sense has…has been usurped by a hormonal blitz."

"Usurped, huh?" Luke gazed down at her, studying her delicate features, his eyes lingering on the alluring fullness of her lips. "There's a word that doesn't come up in everyday conversation. At least, not in mine."

"It's an effective word. And applicable." She lowered her eyes to avoid his intense scrutiny.

"Hmm, wonder if I can work it into the dialogue in the current chapter of my book?"

"Would that be between the killer and his victim of choice? Ugh!"

"Ah, my little muse. How did I ever manage to write without your invaluable guidance?"

Luke was on the right track, keeping it light and glib, Brenna thought, relieved. She would wisely follow his lead and defuse the emotional intensity building between them. Hopefully her common sense, which had gone missing when he touched her, would quickly return.

It occurred to her that moving out of his arms and away from him would be a considerable aid to that process. Instead, Brenna remained where she was. In his arms.

Despite her intentions, the syrupy warmth diffusing throughout her body made her feel too languid and lazy to do anything else. She decided she could be glib just as easily here as from across the room.

"A muse," she repeated. "You'll understand that I'm less than thrilled to be considered a muse who inspires horrific scenes like a serial killer terrifying a pregnant woman. Not to mention whatever awful scene you might dream up using the word *usurped*."

Luke laughed softly. "In other words, don't try to blame my nauseating sensationalist writing on you, Brenna?"

His words, his tone, were smooth and flip, but the way he was holding her—Brenna stole a quick look at his face and quickly averted her eyes again—and the way he was looking at her, was not.

The mixed signals confounded Brenna, but she played gamely along. "You took the words right out of my mouth, Luke."

"I'd like to put something *in* your mouth, honey. Are you going to let me?"

Brenna nearly choked.

They were definitely having two separate conversations on two different levels, the jokey spoken one, and the intense nonverbal one being conducted by their eyes, their hands, their bodies.

"You see, *you* have a hormonal blitz as your excuse." His tone was no longer quite so light and breezy. "So what's *mine*, Brenna? You might not believe this, but I've never put the moves on a pregnant woman before.''

"No?" *Keep it light, Brenna*, she silently repeated her mantra. "And here I was thinking you did this sort of thing all the time."

"You think I get some kind of kick out of, uh, being kicked by the baby within?"

"Not that I'm condemning you for that," she said, parroting his own words back to him. "I'm very open-minded."

"Don't, Brenna." Luke made a strangled sound that was something between a laugh and a groan. "Don't make me laugh. Don't make me…like you more than I do already. It's bad enough that I want you as much as I do."

"You want me," she repeated, the words affecting her viscerally.

Hearing him proclaim it was as potent as feeling the physical evidence hard and insistent against her. That surprised her. She wouldn't have thought herself susceptible to sexual sweet talk—if that's what it was.

"You know I want you, Brenna. And we both know it's ridiculous." He sucked in a gulp of air, peering down into her wide gray eyes. "Don't we?"

"Yes," she agreed, nodding fervently. "Absolutely ridiculous."

"You should tell me to get lost. Pronto."

"Yes, I should. And I will."

"But not yet," he added quickly.

Too quickly, Luke acknowledged ruefully. She had to know how very much he didn't want to leave her. That would give her power over him, and he felt a pang of foreboding. During his political operative days he'd learned that ceding power to anyone for anything could

be costly indeed. It was a lesson he'd mastered all too
well, one that had stayed with him despite his career
change. Or perhaps because of it.

What would be the cost of giving in to this urge to
kiss her? Luke was shaken by how very badly he
wanted to.

He could almost *feel* his normally dependable sharp
and calculating mind getting derailed by the touch of
her hands, the feel of her soft breasts pressed against
him. Desire was a potent force, but one he was familiar
with, one he could control. This was different.

Luke gazed at Brenna. He enjoyed talking to her,
looking at her, simply holding her. Combined with this
desire he felt for her...

How did a man resist that staggering, potent combination? To make matters more complicated, Brenna had
fully agreed with him that their predicament was ridiculous, so he couldn't even argue with her—which he
would've done, gladly, had she challenged him.

But she hadn't, thus giving him no grounds for a
quarrel, which would've created some head-clearing
distance between them. Instead they remained close, on
every level. Though she was nine months pregnant and
they hadn't even kissed, the simple act of embracing
her was fast transporting him to a higher high than any
he'd previously experienced.

Could he ever remember feeling such desperate urgency, such aching need?

Heat surged through him like molten lava. What
Brenna Morgan stirred in him was new, a most intoxicating thrill. He wanted to explore it further, to see
where this subtle but powerful sensuality would lead.
He held her even closer.

Brenna locked her arms around his neck, squirming

against him, tormented by the unfamiliar, aching frustration of wanting but not having. Of being close but not nearly close enough. Of longing to let go but not daring to.

Was this what happened on the road to becoming helpless from passion? To being overpowered and overwhelmed to the point of not being responsible for her actions? For the first time, Brenna saw the seductive appeal in that excuse. And tried to fight it.

"Luke." She gasped his name. "Please! It's...it's too much."

"You've got it backward, sweetheart." His voice was as thick and husky as hers. "What you mean is, it's not enough. But we can remedy that. Right now."

His mouth took hers in a hungry, possessive kiss.

Brenna felt his tongue prod her lips and, reflexively, she opened them to him, allowing him entry to the moist warmth within. The intimacy was startling yet not alarming. Tempting and certainly not disgusting. All her previously held beliefs and fears of intimate contact seemed to be dissolving in the exciting fire of his kiss.

She felt his mouth moving over hers, evoking a fierce pleasure deep within her. His tongue touched hers, then rubbed seductively, invitingly, and she followed his lead, imitating his actions, returning the pressure of his lips, the thrust and parry of his tongue, with her own.

Pleasure and excitement and desire exploded inside her, obliterating a lifetime of caution and control, transforming it into aching, urgent need. She felt his big hand glide slowly upward to cup her breast and gently caress it, his thumb teasing the tip. The dual barriers of her sweater and sturdy cotton bra were no impediment to the electrifying effects of his touch.

Brenna moaned softly and arched into him.

"This is what you want, isn't it, honey?" he murmured hoarsely.

His hand moved again, under her sweater, over her bra, his fingers seeking and not finding a front clasp, and then nimbly undoing the double hooks in the back.

"I know it's what I want." He groaned the words as her swollen, unrestrained bare breasts filled his hands.

He fondled her, nuzzling her neck, rubbing against her as she whimpered, mindless with pleasure, clinging to him.

"I don't want to rush you or hurt you, Brenna." Luke slid his hand between her legs. "There has to be a way we can do this. We'll just have to be, uh, creative."

His words swirled in Brenna's head, but she hardly comprehended them. Her eyes were closed and she clung to Luke while her entire body reacted to the warm pressure of his hand. His fingers stroked her lightly, deftly through her leggings. Brenna knew he must feel the telltale moisture there, but she was too dazed to feel self-conscious or embarrassed.

Pleasure, extreme and intense, rocketed through her. She'd never known it could be this way, that she could feel like this.

And then, abruptly, the excitement turned frightening. She was no longer standing! Luke had swept her up in his arms. It was nothing less than terrifying not to touch the ground, to be held high against his chest, as if she were light as a doll instead of an almost-nine-months-pregnant woman, weighing the most she ever had in her life.

Reflexively, Brenna hung on to Luke, her arms tightly around his neck as he started toward the staircase.

"Where's your bedroom, honey? I'm guessing upstairs." His voice was deep and low, almost guttural.

The sound alarmed Brenna as much as her helplessness. The baby didn't like what was happening, either; she was sure of that. She felt the increased activity in her womb, as if Baby X were trying to kickbox the big intruder away from its mama.

The perception, whimsical though it might be, made Brenna tense. She knew all about children attempting to take care of helpless, foolish parents, having been such a child herself. No way was she going to be the mother of one. It was another promise she'd made to herself and to her unborn child—and one she intended to keep.

Starting right now.

"Put me down!" Her voice shook, sounding neither as forceful nor clear as it could have. As it *should* have!

No wonder Luke didn't take her command seriously. "It's okay, sweetie. You're not all that heavy."

He thought she was being polite, looking out for his well-being, saving him from lower back pain and strain! Brenna felt giddy laughter bubble up in her.

No one was more shocked than she when she burst into tears instead. And began to strike at him with her fists.

Her blows caught Luke off guard, though he ducked his head in time to miss getting smacked in the face.

"Brenna, what are you doing?" Luke stopped in his tracks halfway up the staircase.

His voice, stunned but not angry, jolted Brenna back to the present. Aghast at her own violence, she stopped hitting, her fingers quickly uncurling.

"Brenna? Honey?" Luke stared down at her, concern

replacing the desire and subsequent astonishment that
had clouded his eyes. "What is it?"

"I asked you to put me down." To her mortification,
a fresh flood of tears overtook her. Each word she spoke
was punctuated with a sob. "And you...you didn't."
She couldn't seem to stop crying.

"Oh, God, it's the baby, isn't it?" Instead of putting
her down, Luke raced back down the stairs, carrying
her into the small living room off the entrance foyer.
He looked stricken as he gently laid her down onto the
sofa.

"Are you in pain? Should I call the doctor? Yes, of
course, I should. I will, right now!" He careened from
the room, only to return a second later. "Who is your
doctor? And where's the phone?"

Brenna sat up. He looked wild-eyed and panicked and
was zooming around like a cartoon character. Clearly,
he'd misunderstood her protest, and the entire situation
suddenly struck her as hilarious. Not to mention absurd.

This time her laughter came as quickly as her tears
had moments before.

Luke did not join in the merriment. "You're hyster-
ical." He bent down and took both her hands in his.
"Brenna, it's going to be all right, honey, I promise
you."

Using his hands as leverage, Brenna pulled herself to
her feet. She was calming down now, her emotions beginning to level. The baby must have known it, because
the frantic kickboxing slowed to mellow pokes.

"Sit down, Brenna," ordered Luke, trying to push
her back down onto the sofa. "Better yet, lie down. I'll
call the doctor and we—"

"I don't need a doctor, Luke." This time her voice
held all the clarity and strength it had lacked during the

debacle on the stairs. "I just want you to leave. Immediately." Her tone also possessed the steely, icy edge she had honed to perfection over the years.

It was one that Luke had never heard from her, and it visibly affected him. He stared at her, uncertain and uneasy.

"Brenna, what happened tonight—"

"Won't happen again, Luke. Not ever." She hoped she sounded threatening enough to be taken seriously. "Get out of my house and leave me alone. I'll…I'll make you very sorry if you don't."

It worked! She must've sounded as menacing as a henchman working for the Sopranos, because Luke strode from the room and out the front door without a backward glance.

Brenna sank slowly back onto the sofa and rested her elbows on her knees, her head in her hands.

She sat there, consumed by memories of the inexplicable, terrifying and wondrous passion that Luke Minteer had evoked in her. And that she had evoked in him?

Brenna wasn't sure. After all, he had a reputation with women, and for all she knew any available, willing female might turn him on—despite his claim that he didn't, as a rule, fancy pregnant women.

Well, she'd been willing—at least for a short while there—but she would never, ever be available to him or to any other man. Brenna thought of her mother's terrible relationships with all the wrong men and, finally, with the man who had committed the one act not even Marly Morgan could excuse.

"Brenna!"

Cassie Walsh's voice startled Brenna from her increasingly disturbing reverie.

Brenna jerked her head up and stared in astonishment at her neighbor, standing in front of her.

Cassie sat down beside her. "I heard Luke Minteer peeling rubber, racing out of here like a speed demon at about a hundred miles an hour." Cassie was thoroughly disapproving.

"So you came over here to see if the reason he writes so successfully about serial killers is because he happens to be one?" Brenna managed a wavering smile. "I'm fine, Cassie."

"Your front door was unlocked." Cassie put a sisterly arm around Brenna's shoulders. "And you've been crying, Brenna."

Brenna touched her fingers to her cheeks, which were still wet with tears. She'd almost forgotten she had cried. And in front of Luke Minteer! Since she never cried in front of anybody, the act seemed as intimate as…Luke's touch. As her responses to him.

Brenna heaved a soft groan. What an embarrassing, unnerving mess this was! How could she ever face Luke in the courtroom tomorrow?

Maybe she could call in sick. Surely her doctor would vouch for her if she were to tell him she was feeling ill and needed to stay at home in bed. Weren't there alternate jurors available to fill in for such emergencies?

"Brenna, I want you to know that you can trust me." Cassie was looking at her with concern and speculation. "I mean, we've only known each other since you moved in last year, but I think we've become really good friends and—"

"We *have* become really good friends, Cassie," Brenna agreed, interrupting. "And I'm so grateful to have you and Ray and the kids living next door as neighbors and friends."

Cassie leaned forward attentively, as if prompting Brenna to continue. But Brenna had nothing more to say. The two sat in silence for a few moments, and then Cassie rose to her feet.

"Well, I guess as long as you're okay, Brenna…" Her voice trailed off.

"I am, Cassie. Honest. And thanks for checking up on me," Brenna added with a smile. "It's nice to know somebody cares about us." She patted her swollen belly. The baby was quiet now. "About Susannah or Simon and me."

To Brenna's surprise, Cassie's eyes misted with tears. "Brenna, we do care. And I have more than an inkling of what you're facing. I was a single mother myself for a number of years."

"You were?" Brenna was surprised. The Walsh family seemed like such a close, tight-knit unit, the type of family who'd always been together.

Cassie nodded her head. "My first husband left me and the boys when they were just babies. That was a really rough time. I took Tim and Brandon home to live with my parents and grandmother and my sister. I don't know what we would've done without them. But you don't have a family to fall back on, Brenna."

"No, but don't worry about me, Cassie." Brenna didn't bother to add that basically she'd been on her own for years. Having someone "to fall back on" was an alien concept.

Brenna Morgan depended on herself.

"I'm fine," she reiterated.

"You always say you're fine." Cassie frowned. "Even if you weren't, you wouldn't admit it. But, Brenna, you and your baby need family, you need—"

"How about if you and Ray and the kids are my

honorary family?'' Brenna suggested brightly. "There couldn't be a better family to have than you Walshes." She paused. "I never knew Ray wasn't the boys' real dad, Cassie. He treats them the way he treats little Abby. Just like his own."

"He legally adopted the boys right after we were married. And now they are his own kids in every way, just like Abigail."

"Ray is a wonderful man," Brenna said warmly. "It's good to know guys like him actually exist in real life."

"Yes." Cassie's face darkened. "Unfortunately, good-for-nothing jerks who contribute nothing but their genes to the next generation also exist in real life. You can't imagine how much I detest men who shirk their duties as a father, the…the emotional and financial obligations that each and every father *owes* to his child. To just opt out, to blithely assume the mother will handle everything… It makes my blood boil, Brenna!"

Brenna assumed that Cassie was thinking about her sons' biological father, who must have been one of those detestable shirkers. She wasn't sure how to reply. To bash Cassie's ex or to praise Ray Walsh again?

She tried to do a little of both. "Some men are responsible and kind, and others aren't." Brenna gave a philosophical shrug. "That's just the way it is, I guess."

"There has to be a better way," Cassie muttered fiercely as Brenna walked her to the door. "*Somebody* has to do *something* to make things better for mothers and children."

"I guess garnisheeing men's wages to pay child support is a step in the right direction, at least financially," remarked Brenna.

"And we have that law in Pennsylvania. Think about

it, Brenna. At the very least, your baby deserves its father's financial support.''

Brenna thought of the medical student who didn't even know he was going to be a father, though his contribution had enabled her to be blessed with this wonderful gift of a child.

"It doesn't matter to me. I know I'm very fortunate to be able to support my baby all by myself," she assured Cassie.

Cassie did not appear reassured as she left Brenna's house for her own. She looked furious, no doubt still enraged by the heartless abandonment of her sons by their birth father. Brenna considered calling Cassie back, to urge her to put the disturbing memories of the past behind her.

It was the best way to get on with your life after something bad had happened to you, Brenna knew. It was what she had done herself.

Except every now and then those bad memories would boomerang into your new, good life. Flashbacks—a not uncommon symptom of post-traumatic stress, so she'd been told.

Brenna swallowed hard. Undoubtedly that's what had happened to her tonight, when she'd been assailed by terror as Luke attempted to carry her up the stairs.

His size and strength and her own vulnerability to it triggered her panic. And though the circumstances tonight couldn't have been more different from—*that night*—her reaction, so deeply ingrained from *that night's* trauma, had been the same.

She'd pleaded and cried and tried to physically fight back.

To no avail, back then. But tonight she hadn't been harmed. She had won.

Or had she? Was it winning when there was no fight? Luke hadn't used his strength against her, he hadn't been trying to hurt her. Or to scare her.

But she'd certainly scared him! Brenna thought of Luke's own panic in response to hers and couldn't help but smile a little. He'd feared she was going into labor and had morphed into a stereotypical, nervous expectant father, a sitcom staple.

It was rather dear of him to be so concerned, especially since he wasn't the father, she decided.

And then she remembered how cold she had been to him while he raced around wanting to help her. She hadn't been able to appreciate his motives at the time, not when she was still in the fearful grip of past threats.

So she'd driven Luke away with her words and her tone. He had left immediately, undoubtedly glad to be away from such a moody irrational shrew, and who could blame him?

Brenna certainly didn't.

After all, she wasn't looking for a good man like Ray Walsh to come along and take care of her and her baby—not that Luke Minteer had been auditioning for the role.

Why *had* he come over tonight, anyway? The longer she sat here thinking about tonight's strange events, the more Luke's actual reason for dropping in eluded her. Hadn't he mentioned something about her being angry with him at the courthouse this afternoon because he'd expressed no interest in her job?

As if he cared about either—her anger or her job!

As for him wanting to make love to her...

Now that she was firmly back in her right mind, Luke's professed desire for her was beyond comprehension. Why, how, could he want her in her current condition, her body swollen with child? A child who wasn't even his own.

She preferred not to think of her desire for him. There was only so much confusion a person's mind could deal with at any given time.

Brenna gingerly rose to her feet and slowly climbed the stairs to her studio. The partially colored-in figure of mischievous little Kristin, surrounded by her 1908 clothes and playthings, lay on the desk before her.

With considerable relief, Brenna picked up a pencil and got back to work.

When the phone rang fifteen minutes later, Brenna ignored it. Though it was a bit late for telemarketers, some ambitious ones had probably extended their calling hours. The answering machine would take care of that.

After six rings, she heard her own voice politely recite her recorded message, inviting whoever to leave a name and number. Telemarketers never accepted the invitation.

"Pick up. I know you're there, Brenna." Luke's voice boomed into the machine. "I know you're screening your calls."

Disconcerted, Brenna dropped her pencil. As always, while working, she'd been too absorbed to think about anything but the characters and their lives she was creating with her drawings. It put her into another world, which was her refuge, her escape.

And now Luke Minteer had invaded that private, peaceful place by crashing back into her consciousness.

He wasn't welcome. She had come up here expressly to work—and to avoid all thoughts of Luke Minteer. Now, here was his voice, filling her studio. Filling her head!

"If this machine cuts me off before you pick up, I'll simply call back, Brenna. I'm relentless about getting through to people who are trying to dodge my calls. I never give up. It was one of my greatest talents as a political hatchetman."

Brenna found herself smiling in spite of herself. She'd never heard anyone admit to being a hatchetman. In her experience, people tried to sugarcoat their less-than-admirable traits and deeds. Or deny them completely.

The machine clicked off, and the studio was quiet. For a moment. Then the phone rang again, and this time Brenna picked it up.

"I knew you were there," said Luke.

"Congratulations. Your record of getting through to people trying to dodge your calls still stands."

There was a split second of silence.

"I also considered the art of ironic distance to be another specialty of mine," Luke said wryly. "But you're as good at it as I am. Maybe even better."

"I'm not sure you mean that as a compliment."

"I don't. It just occurred to me how annoying ironic distance really is. Tiring, too."

"Well, since we're both annoyed and tired of each other, let's hang up and pretend that—" she gulped for breath "—that none of this ever happened."

"I can't forget, Brenna. I terrified you tonight, and I'm sorry." There was no flippancy, no ironic detachment in his tone now. He sounded genuinely concerned and contrite.

Brenna winced. "Don't, Luke."

"Don't what, Brenna? Don't apologize? Don't think about what you—"

"Yes, don't think about me," she cut in eagerly.

"Think about *you*. About how furious you were when you left here."

"You don't get it, do you?" Luke heaved a long sigh. "Do you know why I left when I did, Brenna?"

"Of course. Because I kicked you out. And off you went—at about a hundred miles an hour, according to my neighbors."

"Brenna, the reason why I left so abruptly had nothing to do with you kicking me out. In fact, it's impossible to kick me out. Just ask anybody who's ever tried. When ordered to leave, I take it as a challenge and deliberately stay put. Needless to say, it irritates the hell out of people."

"Another one of your valuable talents, no doubt?"

"Unquestionably."

"I can see that politics' loss is publishing's gain," Brenna cracked.

"Brenna, listen to me," Luke's tone grew serious once again. "I left tonight because you were extremely upset, and I knew if I stayed, it would only make things worse for you. I had to go when you ordered me to, because if I didn't get out right then and there, I would've scared you even more. I didn't want to hurt or scare you, Brenna. I realized that you had to know you were in control of the situation."

Brenna stared uneasily into space, discomfited. Luke had analyzed the situation—and *her*—a bit too accurately. Not that she would tell him so.

"*All* women want men to...to leave them alone when they say so," she pointed out. "It's why there are stalking laws."

"Brenna, I know it's more than that. I've been doing a lot of thinking about this. Something bad happened to you, didn't it, Brenna? Something involving a man, or—'' there was an audible gulp from him ''—men?''

Brenna closed her eyes. His voice was quiet and low, with understanding, with concern. It washed over her like a warm, soothing wave.

''Brenna?''

She had a sudden vital urge to pour out the story of that long-ago terrible night, but she fought against it. The very few times she'd ever talked about it had elicited what she didn't want. Pity.

She didn't need pity; she knew it could only be detrimental to her. Brenna well remembered the frequent bouts of self-pity her mother had indulged in, and look where *she'd* ended up!

As if he could see her across the telephone line, Brenna straightened her shoulders and lifted her chin to convey her resolve.

''Yes, something bad happened to me,'' she said brusquely. ''But it was years ago, in the…the distant past. It's over, so let's just leave it at that.''

She heard Luke's sharp intake of breath. ''Brenna, you…you didn't have a…a run-in with a serial killer, did you? Or…or someone you loved wasn't murdered by one?'' He sounded completely shaken, ready to hit the ground from sheer horror.

Brenna couldn't help herself. She started to laugh. ''No wonder you decided to write crime fiction! You do have the imagination for it. No, I've never crossed paths with a serial killer, and I've never met anyone who has. Thank the good Lord for that.''

It took her a moment before she noticed that Luke was not sharing her amusement. There was no laughter, only silence, on his end of the line.

Brenna felt a pang of remorse. ''Luke, I'm sorry for

laughing at your, um, kind concern but it was just so—''

"Serial killers aside, something bad happened to you and it involved a man," Luke said quietly. "You admitted as much, and I can't find that funny, Brenna."

She waited for him to press for details. When he didn't, when the silence on his end continued, she relaxed. "I know this is probably the last thing a cool rogue type like you wants to hear, but you're basically a nice guy, Luke Minteer."

"There was a time when that description of me would've been like a knife in the gut, back when I was intent on being the coolest rogue of rogues." Luke's laugh was self-mocking, without mirth. "But now, being called a nice guy...well, it doesn't sound all that bad."

"I'm glad. Because I...I appreciate your call tonight after...well, you know." Brenna couldn't bring herself to say any word to describe tonight's "incident" with Luke. She wasn't going to step into the landmine evoked by words like *kiss, touch, or passion.*

Luke must've known it, because he made no further reference to the "incident" either. "I'll see you in court tomorrow for the next riveting installment in the Who Gets the Ring Saga," he said lightly.

"Yes." Thanks to this call, she no longer had to dread seeing him tomorrow. She wouldn't have to fake an illness and pester her doctor for an alibi. That in itself was a relief.

But before hanging up, Brenna couldn't help adding, "Luke, let's not mention *it* tomorrow, okay?"

"You want to pretend *it* never happened. I hear you, Brenna."

"No hard feelings?" She was a bit surprised she even

cared about Luke Minteer possibly harboring hard feelings against her.

"No hard feelings at all. After all, we're, uh, buddies,
Brenna. Jury buddies, right?"

"Right." She smiled. "You really are a nice guy,
Luke Minteer."

"Yeah, it's a well-kept secret, but I'm a gem. A mod-
ern-day Prince Charming. The kind of man a girl is
proud to bring home to Mother. Shall I continue, or
have I run the analogies into the ground?"

Brenna thought about that last one he'd mentioned.
She wouldn't be bringing any man to meet her mother,
and despite Luke's belief that he was some kind of
rogue, Brenna knew that Marly Morgan would probably
regard him as tame as a pussycat, as straitlaced as a
Sunday school teacher.

Marly's tastes ran to what she described as "bad
boys." Law enforcement had another term for them—
felons.

Brenna shivered, remembering. And then, determinedly, she dismissed her dark thoughts.

"You'd better quit with the analogies, Luke," she
said dryly. "You've not only run them into the ground,
you've buried them six feet under."

"That's exactly what a snotty newspaper critic said
about all the snappy similes in my first book. I guess I
don't have to add that he isn't a fan of my writing."

"Oh, what does he know? The bestseller lists can't
be wrong."

"Now you sound like my agent. Good night,
Brenna."

Five

A snowstorm, complete with gray sky, icy wind and a blinding gust of flakes greeted Brenna when she opened her front door the next morning. Not for the first time, she wished for an attached garage to keep her car indoors, protected from the elements. Plus, she wouldn't have to endure winter's slap in the face first thing in the morning.

Brenna glanced longingly over at the Walsh house, where she knew the whole family was cozily ensconced for the day. According to the radio's list of closings, the entire school district was taking a snow day, citing frigid temperatures and the possibility of more snow later in the afternoon.

But court was in session. There had been no mention of the courthouse being closed in deference to the bad weather. Which meant she had to get herself there this wretched winter morning.

Mentally Brenna listed the tasks to be completed before driving to the courthouse. Snow needed to be brushed from the windshield and the rest of the car windows; she probably needed to scrape off the inevitable buildup of ice, too.

Through the whirling snow, she could barely discern the outline of her car, parked along the sidewalk in front of her house.

The necessary tools were inside her car, and hopefully her key wouldn't freeze in the lock, as it had on similarly frigid days. That would mean a return trip to her kitchen for the small de-icer that Ray Walsh had so kindly given her after she'd had to borrow his a few times.

Brenna's head was lowered to spare her face and eyes from the bracing chill of the wind, so she didn't notice anyone coming up her front walk until a pair of hands closed over her shoulders.

She jerked up her head, and her eyes met Luke's. Somehow she must have intuited who it was before she saw him…because if she hadn't, Brenna knew she would have screamed.

Being grabbed unexpectedly had that effect on her.

"Let's go. I'm parked right in front of your car." Luke wrapped his arm around her, holding her close against him, using himself to shield her from the wind.

Moments later Brenna was packed into the passenger side of his big black SUV. The car was blissfully warm, the heat on full blast, the radio tuned to a fast-talking disc jockey who was making jokes about the latest celebrity arrest in New York City.

Luke slammed her door shut to walk around to his side, and for a moment Brenna was alone and enclosed in the warm quiet confines. Well, it would've been quiet, if only that DJ would shut up. Automatically she reached over and turned off the radio.

Luke climbed into the driver's side. "Hey, what happened to—"

"I can't stand that guy yammering in the morning— well, not at any time, actually. The other local station will have weather and traffic updates," she added helpfully.

"Stating the obvious. Like we can't see for ourselves that it's snowing, and traffic is going to be hopeless."

Luke didn't turn the radio back on, and Brenna was pleased until it occurred to her that she really had no grounds to take command of the airwaves while in his vehicle. The particular "shock jock" whom she abhorred had a lot of devoted listeners; Luke might very well be one of them.

She felt guilty, disturbing his morning routine. "Do you want me to turn the radio back on to—"

"Nah, leave it off." He pulled into a deserted, snow-covered street that was lined with the residents' parked, snow-covered cars. "Looks like everybody is staying home today."

Brenna nodded. "The school district called off classes and most businesses are shut down for the day."

"But there's no such break for us worthy citizens serving in the courthouse. They must figure the wheels of justice are equipped with snow tires and chains."

"Maybe trials are supposed to be like the mail. You know, going on through rain and hail or sleet and snow," suggested Brenna. "Remember that old jingle?"

"How could I forget it? My great-uncle Marty the mailman used to quote it endlessly. Uh-oh."

As he pulled up to a stop sign at a four-way inter-

section, they watched a car skid, nearly sliding into another car, which managed to swing out of its path at
just the right moment.

Brenna expelled a nervous breath. "The roads are
bad," she murmured. Unfortunately, she identified with
the skidding driver, not the artful dodger.

"The trucks are out plowing and salting the main
highways first. By the time they get to these little neighborhood streets—no doubt in the spring—the stuff will
have melted on its own."

She had to smile at his hyperbole. "They're not quite
that slow."

"Creative enhancement, as we in the political arena
liked to call outright lying. Has a much more positive
connotation."

Brenna was back to staring anxiously at the snow and
skidding motorists. "I don't remember them predicting
snow for us yesterday. Of course, I didn't watch the
eleven o'clock news with the weather report."

"I did, so I knew it was coming. The Midwest blizzard moved faster than anybody thought it would. I
thought you were the Weather Channel junkie. How
could a snowstorm catch you unaware?"

"I was working till past midnight and didn't even
have the TV on," Brenna admitted.

"Do you have to have complete silence to work?"
he asked curiously.

"No, I play music." Brenna thought of her show
tunes, which never failed to touch her, to uplift her. "I
have lots of CDs and tapes of really lovely songs."

"I *have* to have music while I'm writing. Total silence would drive me nuts. But I don't think my tastes
would fall into your 'lovely' category." Luke cast her
a quick sly glance. "That's your cue to make some

wisecrack about Music to Create Murder and Mayhem by.''

''I've heard way too many jokes about my love for show tunes to dump on your music. Everybody is entitled to their own tastes .''

''Ah, the perfect carpool passenger. Sucking up to the driver. Next you'll say you tried to buy a copy of my book, but it was sold out at the bookstores,'' he added dryly.

''Perfect passengers don't take control of your radio,'' she reminded him. ''And you can count on me never buying your books, unless you switch to writing romance novels with a guaranteed happy ending.''

''Just the thought of that is more bone-chilling to me than this weather.''

''Your devoted readers probably feel the same way. I really do appreciate the ride this morning, Luke. I'm sure the jurors' parking lot won't be plowed yet, which would mean driving all over town trying to find somewhere else to park and—''

''Finding a place to park was the least of your troubles this morning, Brenna,'' Luke cut in bluntly. ''You could've easily slipped on the ice and fallen flat on your face. Or on the baby.''

''Actually, I hadn't thought of that.'' Brenna was surprised that she hadn't—and even more astonished that Luke *had*.

In fact, Luke had visualized that alarming possibility last night, when the weatherman on the local news had warned about the likelihood of snow this morning.

He'd made up his mind right then to pick her up and drive her to the courthouse this morning, if court was in session. Which, unfortunately for those having to brave the as-yet-untreated roads, it was.

Luke braked to a stop at a red light and stole a glance at Brenna, sitting quietly beside him. He wasn't one to enjoy silence—he equated it with boredom or awkwardness—but he felt neither bored nor awkward with Brenna.

He felt comfortable.

What was that quote his brother Matt used when describing his relationship with his wife, Kayla? Something about "speaking in silence being the most intimate connection between people"?

Luke had never quite comprehended what on earth Matt meant. Now he felt he might have an inkling.

Were he and Brenna "speaking in silence"?

Or was he going totally nuts?

She must have felt him looking at her, because she turned her head and met his eyes. Her lips curved into a half smile.

"What?" she asked.

"What do you mean, 'what'?" Luke attempted to sound blasé. He wasn't sure he succeeded.

"You look as if you want to ask me something." Brenna's smile widened. "Well, go ahead. This is your car and I'm the grateful passenger."

Now that she'd brought it up, there was something he desperately wanted to ask her, something he'd been thinking about since last night. Something he had lain in bed ruminating over, long after he should have been asleep.

Luke took a deep breath. "When that…bad thing you mentioned last night happened to you, uh, were the police involved?" he blurted out. "Was the—for lack of a better term—the perp ever caught?"

Her smile instantly disappeared, like in a comic strip panel where a smile flipped upside down into a deep frown.

"I told you I don't want to talk about that." Her voice was as cold as the wind whipping the snow around outside. "I told you it happened in the distant past and it's long over. What part of that didn't you get?"

"You said I looked as if I wanted to ask you something." Luke was defensive. "You said to go ahead and ask. So I did."

She gave an impatient huff. "I thought you wanted to listen to that idiot on the radio. I thought you were going to ask whether I minded if you turned his show back on."

"So much for speaking in silence," muttered Luke.

As far as he and Brenna were concerned, their silence was spoken in two vastly disparate languages. Which was exactly as it should be, because there was no "intimate connection" between them.

There was no connection at all. His lack of sleep was getting to him, making him imagine all sorts of foolish things that had somehow gotten stuck in the grooves of his brain.

Defiantly Luke turned on the radio.

The DJ's voice filled the air. He was raucously proclaiming, between snorts and guffaws, that men want to get laid all the time, therefore making platonic friendship between the sexes impossible.

"Idiot!" snarled Luke and switched the radio off again.

Brenna stared at the windshield wipers, which were getting a heavy workout in the storm. Her hands rested on her huge swollen belly.

"You don't agree with him?" she asked impassively.

"That all men think about is getting laid?" he snapped. "No, I don't agree. We—I think about other things. Although you probably don't believe me because of what happened last night," he added testily.

"You promised you wouldn't mention that."

"Sorry. You have so many conversational taboos, it's hard to keep track of them all. Refresh my memory…exactly what am I allowed to talk to you about besides the weather?"

"Stick to the weather and we'll get along fine," she retorted.

They drove along in silence, a smoldering silence, complete with dueling glares. Every time Luke shot her one, she gave it right back to him.

His sense of humor began to get the best of him. Brenna Morgan could be as annoying as hell, but somehow she amused him, too. Her stubborn refusal to back down reminded him of his younger sisters, Anne Marie, Mary Catherine and Tiffany.

Those little hellions had always stood their ground—and still did, though they were all happily married now with little hellions of their own.

Not that he thought of Brenna as a little sister. He stole a quick glance at her. Did he?

Brenna caught his look. It wasn't a glare, so she didn't return it. "You stopped glaring at me. Are you over your snit?"

"I don't have snits. Only girly-men have snits."

"I'll probably regret asking this, but would you please describe what you consider to be girly-men?"

"Oh, you know, those hapless twits who can't hit a ball with a bat and are mocked at their company softball games. The ones who can't tie good strong knots so

when they're moving or on vacation, their stuff flies off
their cars or pickup trucks and ends up all over the
road.''

"No wonder the poor souls have snits," Brenna said
dryly. ''They strike out at softball and are laughed at,
their stuff gets strewn all over the highway and the driv-
ers passing by are laughing and calling them girly-
man.''

"True."

"Actually, that's a useful bit of information, Luke. If
my baby is a boy, I'm going to make sure he can hit a
ball and tie a strong knot.''

"He'll thank you for it." Luke smiled. "And if you
need any assistance, give me a call. Every Minteer male
hits 'em out of the park and ties knots of steel.''

"No doubt from the age of five," Brenna added, getting into the spirit.

"Three," corrected Luke, and they both laughed.

Luke turned onto the street where the courthouse was
located. The usually crowded, bustling area was empty,
every reserved VIP parking place in the front of the
building unoccupied.

"Where is everybody?" murmured Brenna. She
looked at the dashboard clock. "It's normally packed
around here at this time. Court should be starting shortly
and—"

The sharp, wailing sound of a police siren abruptly
silenced her.

Moments later a uniformed policeman leaned in the
window Luke had opened on his side.

"Hey, Patrick, what's up?" Luke asked. "This place
is as deserted as an Arctic outpost.''

Brenna wondered if this was Luke's cousin, the policeman who'd authorized their special parking privileges.

"The courthouse is closed today, Luke," said Patrick. "Didn't you hear it on the radio or TV?"

"I sure as hell didn't!" Luke added a few choice expletives. "And I listened to the whole list, too. Took forever! I heard every school listed, every meeting, just about every store in the whole damn mall, but not a word about the courthouse being closed today!"

"Yeah, word didn't go out till late. The powers that be waited until fifteen minutes ago to officially cancel." Patrick heaved a disgusted sigh.

"Why?" demanded Luke.

"Packed schedule. There's a trial in every courtroom, including that double homicide at the gas station last summer. The judges and lawyers want to speed things along on account of the holidays coming up," explained Patrick. "But when nearly 90 percent of the jurors called the courthouse or police station saying they wouldn't be in… Well, there was no choice. Court is closed for the day. I'm here to tell the diehards who show up to go home. So far you're only the fourth diehard, Luke."

Luke groaned. "Go ahead and substitute moron for diehard, Pat. I deserve it, I should've known."

"We both should've guessed, just from looking out the window," interjected Brenna, willing to accept her share of the blame. "I mean, when you really think about it, is there any way that Wanda or Roger or the others would've ventured out in this, with or without an official cancellation?"

Patrick leaned his head farther into the car. He looked at Brenna, then an expression of undisguised astonishment crossed his face as his gaze lowered to her unmistakably pregnant shape.

"Who are you?" he fairly gasped.

Brenna stifled a grin. Obviously, the sight of Luke Minteer in the company of a pregnant woman unrelated to him was as stunning to Officer Patrick as it had been to the Lo sisters in the China Palace.

"Brenna Morgan." Feeling devilish, she leaned over and offered her gloved hand for Patrick to shake, leaving him no choice but to stick his hand across Luke to grip hers.

"Patrick Minteer, Luke's cousin. Pleased to meet you, Brenna. You, um—" he glanced furtively at his cousin, whose face was a half inch away from their handshake "—a friend of Luke's?"

"I'll have to ask him." Brenna wondered at this strange impulse she had to tease Luke Minteer. But it was too irresistible not to give in to. "Are we friends, Luke?"

Luke's reply was a fierce scowl.

Patrick immediately dropped Brenna's hand and withdrew from the window.

"Luke, be careful driving, okay? Better yet, stay off the roads today. Even a fender bender could be nasty with, er, her in her…her condition," Patrick added uneasily, heading back to the patrol car.

"We're free! I feel like a kid who just heard school's been canceled," Brenna exclaimed jubilantly.

Luke stared stonily ahead. "Why did you do that?"

"Do what?"

"'Are we friends, Luke?'" He did a mocking, high-pitched imitation of her response to Patrick's question.

Brenna flushed. Suddenly her small joke didn't seem all that funny. Certainly, Luke found no humor in it.

She felt embarrassed, defensive. "He asked me a question and I wasn't sure of the answer. I thought I'd ask you since I don't make a practice of lying—or you might prefer *creatively enhancing*—to police officers."

"Oh, so it would've been *lying* to say, 'Yes, I'm a friend of Luke's'?"

"Maybe," she snapped. "I don't know if you consider me a friend of yours or not."

"Well then, what about a simple 'We're serving on a jury together'? That is certainly the truth. No need to consult me on that."

"You're right. That's exactly what I should have said. I'm sorry I didn't, but never mind, I'll go set the record straight right now."

She unlocked the door and pushed it open. Wind and snow gusted into the interior.

"Brenna!" Luke reached over to grab her, but she had already stepped down onto the sidewalk.

She was surprisingly fast for an almost-nine-months-pregnant woman, and it certainly helped that the sidewalks had been salted. By the time Luke gathered his wits and clambered from his side of the vehicle, Brenna had reached the passenger side of the patrol car.

Patrick Minteer leaned across the seat and opened the door for her. "What can I do for you?" he asked warily.

"Officer Minteer, would you mind driving me home? Your cousin—"

"That's enough, Brenna." Luke was right behind her, his hands on her forearms, his body surrounding hers like a protective shell. "I don't know what stunt you're trying to pull but it—but I—"

"Let me go." Brenna began to struggle. "I want to go home."

"I'll take you home." Luke began to pull her away from the patrol car.

"No!" Brenna grabbed hold of the car door and hung on. "Don't bother. I wouldn't want you to inconvenience yourself for another minute on my behalf. Your cousin said he would give me a ride."

It suddenly occurred to her that the young policeman had not yet agreed to her request. "Will you please, Officer Minteer?"

"Of course," he agreed.

"Stay out of this, Patrick," growled Luke. "It has nothing to do with you."

"Yes, it does!" cried Brenna. "A police officer giving a ride to a juror falls into the category of official civic business or something like that."

She thrust herself forward with such force, she succeeded in loosening Luke's grasp on her. She would've landed face first in the front seat of the police car if Patrick hadn't reached up to catch her by her shoulders.

"Holy Mother of God, Luke, she almost fell! And in her condition!" Patrick was distressed. "What's going on with you two?"

"We're serving on a jury together," Brenna said through gritted teeth. "Nothing else is going on. We're strictly fellow jurors, right, Luke?"

She was kneeling in the front seat, firmly trapped between the Minteers. Patrick was in front of her, still clutching her shoulders; Luke was behind her, his hands on what would have been her waist. If she still had a waist.

"Will you both let go of me? I feel like a steak bone caught between two dogs!"

Patrick immediately dropped his hands, but Luke moved even closer to consolidate his hold, wrapping his arms around her abdomen, around the baby. She couldn't get away from him if she tried—which she did, wriggling ineffectually in his arms.

"I'm taking her home, Patrick," Luke announced. "I'll get her out of your hair right now, figuratively speaking." He flashed his cousin a charming smile. "Literally, I'll get her out of your car."

"No!" Brenna's voice rose. "I said no. You can't let him drag me away, Officer Minteer, or you'll be aiding and abetting a…a kidnapping. One juror has no right to abduct another juror."

Patrick Minteer looked uncertain, glancing from Brenna to Luke, then back to meet Brenna's eyes again.

"Please, Patrick," she said softly, suddenly sure he had decided to side with her.

Until Luke spoke again.

"Don't pay any attention to her, Patrick. She's too emotional to know what she's doing. Remember every time Aunt Molly got pregnant…." Luke's voice trailed off.

Patrick instantly recoiled, returning to his place behind the wheel. He adjusted his hat, which had been knocked askew during the brief scuffle, and didn't look at Brenna again.

"You've really, really, *really* done it this time, Luke." The young officer gripped the steering wheel with both hands. "Go on, take her home. But you know it won't end here. Oh, wait, just wait till…" He groaned and shook his head.

Luke half pulled, half carried Brenna back to the Dodge Durango, still idling along the sidewalk, with both doors wide open.

"Some policeman your cousin is!" she said crossly as he packed her inside. "He actually let you take me away against my will. I should file a complaint. And who is Aunt Molly? Patrick looked totally spooked at the very mention of her name.''

Luke didn't answer until he'd pulled the SUV into the street and was heading away from the courthouse. ''Aunt Molly had these, er, memorable mood swings— every time she got pregnant. Which was five times! All in all, they made an indelible impression on many of us Minteers.''

''I'm sure. But why did you let your cousin believe that *I* was a hormonal basketcase?'' argued Brenna. Never mind that she'd invoked that same argument to herself, about herself, while trying to rationalize her feelings for Luke Minteer. Brenna grimaced. Now was not the time for even more rationalizing! ''I only did what you wanted,'' she insisted. ''I told Patrick we were fellow jurors. Then you came roaring after me like some...some wild Neanderthal. What was that all about? Just who is the crazy one here?''

''You know I didn't want you to go running off in the middle of a blizzard to tell him anything,'' Luke said tightly. ''And I did not roar like a Neanderthal.''

''I beg to differ. Now take me home right now or I'll...I'll get out at the next red light and knock on somebody's door and ask them to call me a cab.''

''Oh, that would fix me, wouldn't it, Brenna? You wandering around in a subzero blizzard knocking on doors, hoping to find a cabdriver insane enough to come out in this weather to drive you? Yeah, that would hurt me a lot more than it would hurt you—or your baby.'' He gave a disdainful huff. ''You sound like a little brat threatening to hold your breath till you turn blue because you think that'll really punish the grown-ups.''

Brenna was appalled. He was right, of course. Her

juvenile threat wouldn't hurt him at all—but it would certainly do harm to herself and the baby. She leaned her head back against the headrest and wondered if she was becoming as wacky as the Minteers' fabled Aunt Molly.

Luke was silent, pretending to concentrate on driving through the storm. But he was a native of this area and had driven through far worse storms, so he had ample opportunity to think while navigating the roads, to reflect on the staggering fact that yes, Brenna Morgan had hit exactly on the best way to punish him.

The image of her running away from him to roam through the frigid snow-blinding streets was as horrifying as the most heart-stopping murder scene he'd ever written. More so, in fact. His fictional creations and their fate had no power over him; he didn't care if an imaginary killer offed an imaginary victim.

But Brenna...oh, she had power over him. There was no use denying it when the possibility of something happening to her—even as stupid and unlikely as her bratty little threat—could unsettle him this way.

He switched on the radio, as much to hear the latest storm updates as to try to distract himself from his disturbing insight.

She was bad news, he lectured himself sternly. She was every "must avoid" he had ever warned or been warned about.

"This just in!" exclaimed an eager newscaster. "A giant old pin oak tree was uprooted by the wind and ice and has fallen across a portion of Route 128, knocking down power lines. Both the tree and the live wires are blocking the road, and 128 is closed indefinitely so crews can begin the removal and repairs. Motorist are advised—"

"Ah, this day keeps getting better and better." Disgusted, Luke turned off the radio. "I can't get home if 128 is closed. It's the only road that leads to Mountainview Trail, where I live. And even if I could get there, I'll have no power till they get the lines back up."

A moment of dark humor struck him. Well, at least he had something else to think about besides Brenna Morgan. He could now dwell on the massive inconvenience of no electricity and no way home.

"What will you do?" It was the first time Brenna had spoken since issuing her threat. She had been sitting in chastened silence ever since.

"Maybe I'll run the blockade and try to jump the oak and the live wires. That always seems to work in the movies." Luke turned the corner onto her street. "Just kidding."

"I'm glad you clarified that." She arched her brows wryly. "It wasn't too hard to imagine you trying it."

"Yeah, we roaring Neanderthals often do double duty as foolhardy stuntmen."

Brenna caught her lower lip between her teeth. "You weren't being a Neanderthal. I was out of line, the whole time." She swallowed hard. " And I…I apologize, Luke."

Luke frowned. How was he supposed to demonize her when she apologized to him in that sad little voice, with confusion all over her sweet face? How could he focus on everything that was maddening about her while her pretty white teeth worried the soft pink fullness of her lips?

At this rate, how was he ever going to convince himself he couldn't stand her, that he would rather be anywhere than around her?

"I was out of line, too," he said grimly. "The Aunt

Molly comparison was uncalled for. Unfair." He heaved a sigh. "Untrue. Sorry."

Their truce silenced both of them once more, until they pulled in front of her house.

"Looks like you've got some friendly neighborhood helpers." Luke pointed his thumb at the two young boys, bundled heartily against the elements, who were shoveling her walk.

"Brandon and Timmy Walsh. Their mom makes them shovel my walk and dig my car out every time it snows, but she refuses to let me pay them. So I slip them money on the sly. I really think I ought to pay them for doing all that work." Brenna frowned thoughtfully. "Do you think I'm sabotaging Cassie by—"

"No, because I agree with you. The only snow shoveling I did for free as a kid was for my parents and grandparents, and that was out of sheer self-preservation. They would've brained me with the shovel if I'd dare to ask them for money. The neighbors all paid me for my work. And look what a model citizen I grew up to be," he added cheekily.

"Well, actually, that's true. You serve when jury duty calls, you don't cheat on your taxes. Um, do you?"

"No way. One credo I've always lived by, even at my political operative worst—or best some might argue—was Don't Mess with the IRS."

He braked the SUV to a stop, and Brenna reached for the door handle.

"Stay there. Let me get that for you," Luke ordered, jumping out to come around to her side and open the door.

Luke lifted her down, and this time there was no mutual fury to mask the effects of their proximity to each other, as in the police car just a short while ago.

This time their gazes met, their bodies touched, and the heat that rose between them was steamy enough to melt the blustery snow.

"Hi, Mrs. Morgan!" bellowed Timmy, waving his arm.

The intensity was broken, for at least a second or two. Then Luke took Brenna's arm to walk her to her door, and their closeness catapulted them back under the spell of their attraction.

"Was the 'Mrs. Morgan' bit their mother's idea?" murmured Luke, leaning down to speak softly into her ear.

So the children wouldn't hear. But mainly because he couldn't resist the temptation of touching his lips to her delicate earlobe.

"Yes. Cassie thought with the baby coming and all..." Brenna paused to breathe. It was freezing cold, but she felt as if she were on fire with a raging fever. "Cassie thought the *Mrs.* would be easier for them to understand," she added breathlessly.

"She means easier for her to explain to them. Around here a divorce is far more respectable than a deliberate foray into single parenthood."

His breath warmed the icy tips of her ears. "P-probably," she agreed, feeling weak.

They walked on the cleared pavement, approaching the two boys.

"Mrs. Morgan, you should wear a hat or at least earmuffs in this cold," Brandon admonished, undoubtedly echoing a parental warning. "Mom says it's like a chimney or something."

"Or something," said Luke." Your mom is absolutely right, too." He stopped and reached into his coat to pull out his wallet. He removed two twenty-dollar bills and gave one to each boy.

They stared at the bills, stupefied by the amount. So was Brenna. The two dollars apiece she usually slipped them seemed incredibly paltry compared to Luke's largess.

"Thanks for taking care of Brenna's place, guys," Luke boomed.

He led Brenna to the porch, shielding her from the wind as she fumbled with her key in the lock.

"Can I come in?" he asked quietly, as she pushed open the door. "For a cup of coffee?"

Brenna went still and gulped for breath.

"Wait, I just remembered, you don't have any coffee because you don't like it." Luke leaned his arm against the doorjamb, watching her. "Okay, I'll go with hot chocolate, then. I've been known to choke down tea at times, too."

Brenna reminded herself that it was midmorning, that he had driven her to and from the courthouse in this inclement weather, inconveniencing himself. Plus, the road to his house was currently inaccessible.

The least she could do was to provide him with a hot drink before sending him on his way—wherever that may be.

"How about it, Brenna?" His voice was so soft, she had to lean closer to him to hear it.

Their eyes met again, and she knew that if she were to invite him inside this morning, it would be for more than a hot drink. As for sending him on his way...

"Come in, Luke," she heard herself say.

They entered the house, and he closed the door behind him. With the snow covering the windows and blocking the sight of the outdoors, it seemed as if they were the only two people in the world.

Brenna stood, tense and expectant and aching. She had just given her okay to recreate the sensual events of last night, hadn't she?

Her heartbeat pounded in her ears, her breathing was shaky and shallow. She waited for Luke to make his move and wondered how she would react to him this time….

Six

"I'll put on water for the hot chocolate," Luke called over his shoulder as he strode toward the kitchen. "Do you have anything to eat? I skipped breakfast and I'm starving."

Brenna stood in the foyer, nonplussed. She'd expected him to make a move, but on her, not her kitchen. She heard him turn on the faucet to fill her kettle with water; she listened as the refrigerator was opened and closed, along with cabinets and drawers.

She walked to the door of the kitchen and peered in to see Luke assembling an assortment of food on the kitchen counter.

"You have everything needed to make one of my specialties." He must have heard her approach because he didn't turn around, remaining busily immersed in his project. "Peanut butter and banana with cream cheese and jelly on honey wheat toast. Care to try it?"

Brenna shuddered. "Never."

"It's nutritious for the baby. Contains all the major food groups. Protein, fruit, dairy, grains."

"Thanks, but the baby and I will pass. I have some chicken left over from dinner last night." She entered the kitchen, moving toward the counter where Luke stood. "Wouldn't you rather make a sandwich with chicken?"

"No, but I'll make one for you if you want."

She shook her head. "I'm not hungry for lunch yet."

She eyed him dubiously as he spread a third slice of bread with cream cheese. The other two were thick with peanut butter and strawberry jelly. And then he began to chop up the banana. "Are you really going to eat that?"

"Sure. It's one of my all time faves. I'm not much of a cook, but I'm a helluva sandwich maker. You could say I'm a professional one, from all the years I put in as sandwich boy in the family tavern kitchen."

Brenna moved a step closer. "Your family owns a tavern?"

"The eponymous Minteer's Tavern in Johnstown. It's been run by Minteers since before the famous flood swept it away. The family rebuilt, and it's been open and operating six days a week from noon to 2:00 a.m., staffed mainly by Minteers."

"Your roots in this area go way back." She came to stand beside him, watching him build his revolting con-coction. "No wonder you wanted to come back here, no matter what."

"I'm touched that you would attribute such noble motives to me. Which poses something of a dilemma.

Should I play along or tell you the truth about my return?'' Luke mused lightly.

"Last call. Are you sure you don't want one?'' He put the finishing touches on his sandwich and carried it over to the table.

"Believe me, I'm sure.'' The kettle began to whistle. Brenna removed it from the burner and began to prepare two cups of hot chocolate. "But I am curious why you came back here when your family was so furious with you. I've been wondering about that since I first heard it.''

"Wonder no more, Brenna. I came back because after Matt fired me, I was as furious with the family as they were with me. And I knew *nothing* would enrage them more than having me living here in the area, when they couldn't stand the sight of me.''

He took a hearty bite of his sandwich, reaching over to pull out a chair for Brenna as she carried the steaming mugs to the table.

"Coming back home was the best revenge I could think of. The success of my book was the frosting on the cake, so to speak,'' he added, grinning.

Brenna sipped her chocolate. "I don't know if I believe you.''

"Well, I didn't have to come back here, I had other choices. My services as a political operative were in big demand—outside Matt's district, that is. I had plenty of contacts, and it was well-known that I knew how to play the game of politics.''

"But you'd condoned dirty tricks and things,'' Brenna reminded him. "You had a bad reputation.''

"Honey, in some circles those were considered the outstanding features on my résumé. But moving to some other state—especially a faraway one like California where my most tempting offer came from—would've been exactly what my family wanted. Me, the black sheep, out of sight and out of mind. I was too mad at Matt, at my folks, at everybody, to be so accommodating.''

''So instead of conveniently disappearing, you came back and worked on your grisly crime book—and it turned out to be a big success.''

''Meanwhile, I showed up everywhere, at church, at the tavern, at every family member's birthday or baptism or funeral. My very presence was an affront, and I relished every moment.''

Brenna wasn't sure if she bought his perverse motive for his return or not. She suspected the true reasons were a lot more complex than Luke allowed himself to believe. ''Are you still so angry with all of them?''

''No, not anymore. After all, things worked out pretty well. If I hadn't come back, I wouldn't have written the book and found a whole new career. Turns out that I like writing more than politics—not to mention that it pays better if you happen to hit the bestseller jackpot.''

''What about your family?'' Brenna watched him finish his sandwich, down to the last crumb. ''Are they still mad at you?''

''A bunch of them still disapprove of me, but I think they're mellowing. They've finally resigned themselves to seeing me around the district. When my house was finished, I threw a big housewarming party and everybody came. Mainly to tell me I was nuts to build a place on the mountain so far from town.''

''With weather like this, they have a point,'' observed Brenna, as a heavy blob of snow dropped from the kitchen window.

''Nah, I knew exactly what I was doing when I

bought my lot dirt cheap a couple years ago. Several new houses are being built out there. It's a great place to live, and word is getting out, increasing property values. There's a fantastic view, big lots, plenty of privacy and—''

''You sound like a real estate agent trying to close a sale,'' Brenna interjected dryly. ''Naturally, that pesky, road-inaccessibility factor isn't mentioned.''

''Downed trees and power lines are freak accidents,'' protested Luke. ''And the road will be open by tonight, if I'm lucky.''

He glanced at his watch. ''Well, I'd better get going. I'm sure you have stuff to do, and my laptop is in the car, so I'll head to the library to work on my book. Thanks for the late breakfast—or early lunch. I guess we'll have to call it brunch,'' he concluded.

He rose from his chair.

Brenna gaped at him. ''You're leaving?''

Disappointment tore through her, and though she quickly lowered her head, she had a sinking feeling he had seen it in her eyes, on her face, in those first unguarded seconds.

''That surprises you?'' Luke stood over her. ''Why?''

When Brenna lifted her head to meet his penetrating blue eyes, her impassive mask was firmly in place.

''I'd better stop wasting time and get upstairs to work if I want to finish my paper-doll book before the baby is born. I've been contracted to do a series called Children of the Twentieth Century, decade by decade, and I'm only in the first one. The ohs or the aughts. Who knows what to call it? It's the same dilemma we're having in this century.''

''You're babbling,'' Luke said bluntly. ''I'd like an answer to my question.''

"I'd forgotten that talking about my work bores you." Brenna tried a diversionary tactic. "Don't worry, I won't do it again."

Her tactic didn't work; Luke was not diverted. "You expected me to try a repeat of last night, didn't you?"

Brenna winced. "I know you're busy and have work to do. So do I. I completely understand."

To her horror her voice trembled and she felt sudden, unexpected tears welling in her eyes. What a rotten time for her hormones to run amok! Brenna swallowed hard, pressing her lips together tightly, fighting for control. Not for anything would she let her hormones make her cry.

"Exactly what do you *think* you understand, Brenna?" Luke's tone was almost mocking.

"Just drop it, okay?" snapped Brenna. "Believe me, I'm well aware that I'm almost nine months pregnant and as big as a...a cow. I don't blame you at all for wanting to leave."

Immediately, she clapped her hands over her mouth in dismay. "I didn't mean to say that! It—the words just slipped out. Oh, I really am acting like a hormonal headcase—just like your aunt Molly!"

"Compared to Aunt Molly's antics, you're as repressed and restrained as a Puritan, Brenna. And you're not big as a cow, and I'm not leaving because I don't want to stay with you."

"Yes, of course, you have a deadline to meet," she murmured, striving to regain her lost poise. And to once more offer him the diplomatic out.

Which Luke immediately rejected. "My deadline isn't a problem. I have plenty of time before my book is due."

"I see," Brenna said tautly.

"No, you don't see," growled Luke. "I'm leaving because if I stay, I'll give in to the need to touch you, I'll pull you into my arms and kiss you until you're moaning and sighing and clinging to me the way you did last night. And then I'll pick you up and carry you upstairs...and scare the hell out of you, the way I did last night."

He laid his hand on the top of her head, smoothing his fingers over her silky dark hair. "I'm not a Neanderthal, remember? I'm not going to go caveman on a woman who was raped and is still traumatized by—"

Brenna jumped to her feet, nearly knocking over her mug and her chair in the process. "How did you know I was raped? Who told you? Who else knows? I didn't tell anybody in this area, I haven't told anyone in years."

"Nobody told me, Brenna. And if you haven't told anyone around here, I'm sure nobody knows. But I had enough clues to put it together." He cleared his throat. "You don't want to talk about it, I know. That much you've told me."

"It's not a place in the past I care to return to," she said bitterly. "Talking about it takes me there."

"Return to?" Luke slowly rubbed his hand along the length of her arm. "Sweetheart, I don't think you've ever left it. You're still stuck there. Your trip to the sperm bank, your determination to avoid a relationship with a man, the way you flipped out last night when it looked like we were going to have sex—it all adds up to some serious, er, issues, Brenna."

"I think I'm coping very well!"

"Yes, yes, you are," Luke agreed quickly, his tone tender and supportive. "And I'm not going to do anything to, uh, take away from how well you're coping.

Or give you more to cope with.'' He looked tense and increasingly flustered. ''I can't exactly find the right words, but do you get what I'm trying to say?''

She nodded her head. ''Yes.''

And she did; she understood what he was trying to say to her on every level.

Brenna felt her apprehensive reserve dissolving fast and wondered how Luke inspired such confidence within her. Why was she able to drop her guard—the impenetrable one she'd maintained for years—only with him?

He was a renegade and a rogue but had been honest and open about it. And early on, she had gleaned that there were good qualities within his character, at odds with his purported reputation. From his treatment of her, she knew she'd been right.

''I get it, Luke.''

''Good!'' Luke sounded relieved. ''I've never been so inarticulate before. I can usually make my point at least, though I've never been known for making it with eloquence.''

''And eloquence is a prized commodity in politics, isn't it?'' The corners of her lips slowly curved into a smile. ''Especially when it's packed into a twenty-second sound bite.''

''True. Luckily, I was never a speechwriter. I can play a good game behind the scenes, but when it comes to talking the talk... That's my brother Matt's department, and he excels in it.''

He leaned down and kissed her forehead. ''Getting back on topic—I wish I could find some eloquent way to say I'm sorry you were so badly hurt, Brenna.''

''You are eloquent. Because I know you mean it, Luke.'' To his obvious surprise, she linked her arms around his neck. "I don't want to be stuck in the past. And when I'm with you, for the first time ever, I feel different. I feel brave."

"I'm glad, Brenna."

"It's more than that." She gulped. "To be perfectly honest, you make me feel things I didn't know I could ever feel. And I was scared last night, at first, but then, later..." Her voice trailed off.

"Then, later, you decided that maybe you weren't so scared?" He rubbed his nose lightly, affectionately, against hers.

"When you came in the house with me today—" she moved closer to him, her eyes closing as he continued to gently nuzzle her "—I thought that maybe, if something happened this time, I might, I could—well, I didn't think I would flip out," she added wryly, using his own description of her reaction.

"Maybe if something happened?" challenged Luke. "Come on, Brenna, take it a step further and admit that you *expected* something to happen when you invited me in today. You *wanted* it to happen. You still do."

"And if I don't admit it, you'll probably tell me in exact detail how you've drawn that conclusion?"

"Baby, there's no *probably* about it, I'll *definitely* tell you. You looked crushed when I said I was leaving, you looked like you were ready to burst into tears."

She opened her mouth to automatically, defensively, deny it. And ended up balling her fingers into a fist and lightly punching his arm.

"Jerk," she muttered, not without a certain affection.

"Thank you, darling." His hand enclosed her fist and carried it to his mouth. He kissed her knuckles. "That's one of the nicer terms used to describe me."

They both ended up laughing. Brenna was amazed.

What could've turned into a dreadful, melodramatic scene had ended in laughter.

She looked into his warm-blue eyes and knew then and there that she loved him. It had happened impossibly, ridiculously fast, but the real miracle was that it had happened at all.

She had given up any hope of falling in love years ago, believing she was too damaged by the sexual trauma in her past to overcome it. But it seemed that she had, because she knew she was in love with Luke Minteer...and she wanted desperately to make love with him.

"Show me where you work," Luke said, cupping the nape of her neck with his hand. He headed in the direction of the staircase, taking her along with him. "In case a translation is needed, I'm encouraging you to invite me up to see your etchings."

"Consider yourself invited. But we'll walk up the stairs this time. I don't want you to break your back trying to carry me."

"I could smoothly counter that you're not heavy, you're a mere featherweight, except you'd probably punch me and call me a jerk again," said Luke, taking her hand in his.

"Hey, there's no *probably* about it, I'll *definitely* tell you."

They mounted the staircase, holding hands.

Her studio was at the top of the stairs, her bedroom two doors down the narrow hallway. Brenna hesitated for a moment.

And then Luke dropped her hand and strode swiftly into her studio, directly to her draft table.

"Hey, this is really good!" He stared at the completed full-color drawing of Kristin, which Brenna had finished the night before.

"The little girl looks like a real kid. Everything you've drawn looks real—the baby doll, the clothes, the kitten. As for the title of the book, here is a little professional advice—you should label the first decade of the century The Ohs. *Aught* sounds like a joke."

"Is that advice from your experience in politics or publishing?" Her voice wavered.

"Both. *Aught* just doesn't work." Luke looked up at Brenna, who was still standing in the hall. "Show me some more stuff you've done, Brenna. I want to see all of it."

She stared at him, confused and uncertain. Hadn't they come upstairs to…go into her bedroom?

Luke had no trouble deciphering the silent question in her eyes.

"I'm not going to pounce on you, Brenna. Show me your work, tell me about it."

He glanced outside. "From the way this snow is coming down, we aren't going anywhere anytime soon. We have all the time in the world. I'm not going to rush things. Okay?"

"I'll cede to your greater experience in this area," Brenna said, surprising herself with the small joke. She never joked about anything remotely sexual.

"Good. Now come in here…"

Brenna enjoyed showing Luke her work, the greeting cards and sewing patterns, the paper-doll books, the artwork she'd done for various children's books and magazines over the past few years.

She kept one copy of everything she'd had published

in a bookcase, and Luke picked up each item and studied it with interest.

Brenna was flattered by the attention; she couldn't
deny it.

The number of paper-doll books that she had researched and drawn visibly astounded Luke. There was
the set of Century Women's Wear, a series of ten books
covering various women's fashions over the past millennium. The Century Children Series, including ten
books featuring children and their clothing and playthings of the past millennium. The Children of the
World series, featuring ten books filled with children
from each continent and their ethnic costumes and toys.

"You've done *thirty* of these paper-doll books—plus
all these other things!" Luke exclaimed, impressed.
"And each paper-doll book has sixteen pages of drawings—I counted them! How do you do it, Brenna?
You're too young to have been working for very many
years. Unless you started when you were about four?"

Brenna smiled. "I started drawing about then, but I
published my first book when I was in art school."

"At The Rocky Mountain College of Art and Design
in Denver," interjected Luke. "I read your bio sketch
in one of your books here. Is speed-drawing a course
requirement there?"

He was now leafing through the several dozen children's magazines, each featuring a paper-doll or paper-
toy page by Brenna Morgan.

"I work fast, and I work all the time." Brenna gave
the same answer she always did when asked about her
prolific talent.

She didn't feel it necessary to mention that chronic
insomnia added many hours to her working day. She

didn't go to bed until she was so exhausted she literally fell asleep the moment her head hit the pillow.

"Hmm, that sounds like a stock answer," Luke observed. "I can spot them instantly, they're a prerequisite in politics. I also have a few of my own for writing, especially when I'm asked where I get my ideas."

"Do you say you subscribe to *The Serial Killer's Digest?*"

"How did you know? Although, I actually say *Murderers' Monthly* or *The Gruesome Gazette*. But I like your little jest better. Mind if I swipe it?"

"Be my guest."

"How many of your paper-doll books are still in print?" He studied an *Asian Children of the World* book with all the elaborate paper-doll costumes she had drawn and colored.

"All of them. The publishers said they have no plans to discontinue any of them," she added modestly.

Luke gaped at her. "I'm no authority on publishing, but I know that means all your books must be selling well. And you have a contract for a new series, too. You've got to be some kind of publishing phenom, Brenna!"

She shrugged. "I'm just grateful I'm able to earn a living doing what I enjoy. And that I'll be able to support my baby. My publishers were kind of depressed when I told them about the baby, because I also said that I intend to slow down considerably."

"The baby," Luke murmured. He gazed down at her pregnant belly, bulging beneath her dark-rose maternity tunic top. "Sometimes when we're talking, I actually forget you're pregnant."

"Hmm, have you had your eyes checked lately?" She chuckled. "There could be some problem with your sight. My pregnancy is the most noticeable thing about me these days.''

"It was the first thing I noticed about you when we met. But not too long afterward, I stopped giving your figure—or the lack of it—a thought." He smiled sheepishly. "I have to admit that's a first for me."

"I'm guessing that you've always required a shapely woman on your arm?" Brenna dared to tease.

"Oh, yeah. And other places, too." Luke's eyes gleamed. "Go on and call me a shallow jerk."

"Only if you'll call me a frigid headcase."

Moving slowly, as if not to startle her, Luke wrapped his arms around her in an embrace that was more protective than amorous. "It's not the same at all. Shallow jerks make choices, but you didn't have a choice, Brenna. You were struck by circumstances beyond your control."

"You've never even heard the details, and you're giving me the benefit of the doubt?" Brenna leaned against him, letting her head loll against the hard wall of his chest. "That means a lot to me, Luke. And I really don't think you're a shallow jerk—although maybe you used to be one," she couldn't help but add, looking up at him, her gaze unmistakably flirtatious.

Luke's response was immediate. He scooped her up in his arms, grinning as she gave a surprised squeak.

"Luke, I can walk!"

"I know. But I want you to trust me enough to let me carry you."

"This is supposed to be a love scene, isn't it? Not an…an Outward Bound experiment in building trust."

Luke laughed. "Maybe it's both. Do you trust me not to drop you *and* to make love with you?"

Brenna considered it. "I must. Because here we are."

"Yeah, here we are."

He claimed a fiery kiss before he carried her from her studio into her bedroom, holding her high against his chest. Brenna relaxed against him, her lips brushing along his jawline. Daringly she allowed the tip of her tongue to taste his salty skin.

Inside her bedroom Luke set her gently on her feet, facing him. He framed her face with his hands, kissing her forehead, the tip of her nose, the curve of each high cheekbone.

By the time he finally claimed her mouth, she was shivering with anticipation.

Her lips opened on impact, admitting his tongue inside. It seemed perfectly natural to welcome him by rubbing her tongue softly against his.

Brenna heard his moan and enjoyed the rush of sensual feminine power that filled her.

They stood together kissing, one long, deep kiss melding into another. Their kisses were both leisurely and urgent, ravenous but fulfilling, an exciting sensual paradox.

"Who'd have ever thought kissing could be this good?" Luke wondered aloud.

Both were panting and breathless when they finally had to surface for air.

"You sound downright awestruck." Brenna touched her fingers to her lips that were moist and swollen from his kisses, then traced his own mouth, equally moist and swollen from kissing her.

"I am. Once I, er, reached a certain age and a certain stage, I viewed kissing as a strictly preliminary step, to be gotten through as quickly as possible to reach the main event. But with you—" his expression was one of almost comical astonishment ''—it's like kissing *is* the main event.''

Brenna smiled. "That's very romantic, I think."

"Come here."

Luke turned her around and pulled her back against him, fitting her into the hard male frame of his body. He moved his big hands along the length of her arms, then back to her shoulders. Pushing aside her hair with his fingers, he kissed the curve of her neck, nibbling with his teeth, soothing the sensitized skin with his tongue.

And then he slid one hand down her back, following the zipper of her maternity tunic top.

"Let me take it off," he whispered huskily, his nimble fingers already unzipping.

Brenna drew a quick breath. If she didn't want this to proceed any further, now was the time to speak up.

But she didn't say a word as he peeled the unzipped tunic open and slowly moved it down her arms, over her breasts, over her bulging belly. It finally landed in a deep rose-colored pool at her feet.

Brenna stared down at her breasts, cupped firmly in her well-fitted maternity bra, designed for exactly that purpose. She laid one hand on the stretch panel of her maternity leggings that covered the hard swell of her abdomen. Within her womb, the baby was quiet, probably sleeping. There was no movement to observe beneath the material.

"Like we said earlier, this…this shape isn't what you're used to seeing when you're in a woman's bedroom," she said faintly.

"No, it isn't," Luke agreed.

For a moment she imagined the women in his past, those women whose curvaceous figures had tantalized him. But the past was just that, past. And if he was no longer a shallow jerk who demanded certain things, then she wasn't a frigid headcase to be intimidated by them.

Luke linked his hand with her own, interlacing their fingers. His other hand covered hers, which rested on her belly.

"I like the way you look, Brenna." His voice was husky.

She glowed from the warmth in his tone. It mingled with a raw sensuality that enticed, rather than unnerved her. She couldn't resist him or these wonderful feelings he was evoking within her.

An urgent need to feel his lips on hers again surged through her, and she turned in his arms, clasping his head with her hands to kiss him until she felt too dizzy to stand. But there was no cause for concern, for standing was no longer required.

Luke picked her up again and carried her over to her bed. With precision expertise, he pulled off the flowered quilt comforter while still holding her, then carefully placed her in the center of the bed, on the matching flowered sheets.

Standing beside the bed, he deftly, swiftly, pulled off his clothes.

Brenna stared at him, her eyes wide. He was muscled and well built, his body fully aroused and taut with desire. A thin sheen of sweat glistened on his skin. The sight literally took her breath away.

Luke noticed. "Breathe, Brenna," he reminded her, and reached out his hand to smooth her hair. "Are you sure you're okay with this? Because you don't have to. You know that, don't you?"

He waited for her answer.

His control, his concern for her, despite his own heightened state of desire, reassured her.

Brenna met his blue eyes, which glittered with sexual hunger. He wanted her, but he wouldn't force her if she were to call things to a halt right now.

Which she didn't want to do, Brenna realized with certainty.

She wanted this; she wanted him...because she loved him. Brenna put her hand on Luke's.

He responded at once to her invitation and sat down beside her on the bed.

"I know I don't *have* to," she murmured. "It's my choice." Just saying the words empowered her.

"And you choose me," he said huskily. "I'm glad, Brenna. And proud, too. I'm proud of you." He gazed at her. "I admire your courage and your resolve in handling whatever was thrown your way."

His eyes, his tone, his expression, invited her to confide in him, to tell him about whatever had been thrown her way.

Brenna shifted. "Luke, I don't want to tell you my life story, especially not here. And especially not now. I just want this to be between you and me, with no ghosts from the past."

"Okay. But can I say that from what I've guessed, you were dealt a crummy hand and played it well? And that having a woman like you want me, only me—well, it validates me. Do you get what I'm trying to say, Brenna?"

"I hope it's not that you see me as some kind of ticket to redemption for your, uh, disreputable past?" she asked lightly. "Because that is one melodramatic role I don't care to play."

"I see you as a woman I want very much." He smiled into her eyes. "Better?"

"Much."

Luke unhooked the back clasp of her maternity bra and slowly drew it from her body. Her breasts were swollen and full. He liked the idea that nature—not silicone implants—was responsible for the enhancement.

He continued to stare. Her nipples were large, dark and taut. The size of her nipples fascinated him; they were full and pouty, ready to nurse a child. He had never seen the breasts of a pregnant woman before and had never wanted to, but the sight of Brenna transfixed him.

Their mouths met in another slow, sultry kiss while one of his hands moved lightly over her breasts, cupping one, then the other, learning the feel and shape of each. His fingers caressed her nipples, circling the aureoles, toying with the full, tight tips.

Brenna whimpered, twisting closer, clinging to him. It was so much, so pleasurable and exciting, yet she needed, she wanted…more.

As if magically attuned to her thoughts, Luke proceeded to undress her. There was a time when she would have been mortified to be naked in front of any man—and to be naked and pregnant in a male's presence would've been awful beyond imagining.

But being here, doing this with Luke, felt neither embarrassing or unreal.

It felt good. It felt as if this was the way it was supposed to be.

They lay down on the bed together, nude, their bodies entwined, kissing and caressing for an endless time. Brenna felt his manhood, hot and swollen pressing against her, and curiosity and desire flooded her, drowning her past fears in a tidal wave of passion.

She was on the verge of reaching for him, of succumbing to the unexpected need of touching him *there*, when he lifted his lips from hers and glided his hands over her belly, over her hips.

"I can't get enough of you, Brenna," he whispered, nibbling on her neck. "The more I touch you, the more I taste you, it's not enough."

His words swirled through her head as he kissed her along the length of her collarbone, then moved his mouth lower, to her breasts. He nipped and suckled her, lightly grazing her ultrasensitive skin, teasing each rosy peak.

The sensation was excruciatingly pleasurable, like nothing she had ever known. She wanted him to stop, because she didn't think it was possible to sustain this level of physical intensity, she wanted him to go on and on and never stop....

And then his lips continued a downward path along her body, probing her belly button, which pregnancy had pushed outward, with his tongue, nuzzling her abdomen. And moved lower...

Brenna gasped for breath when it dawned on her where he was heading, what he was intent on doing with his mouth....

She grabbed a fistful of his hair, abruptly stopping him.

Luke raised his head and looked at her, his blue eyes questioning.

"Sorry. I...didn't mean to pull your hair out by the roots." She released her grip and sat up. "But I—I've never—" she blurted out, blushing. She turned her head, unable to hold his gaze. "Luke, I've never done that before. I—I've never even tried the…the, uh, missionary position.''

She cringed, blushing fiercely. ''What I'm trying to say is that I'm not experienced at sex.''

With violence, yes. She had experienced that. The addendum leaped into her head, but she didn't say it aloud and she pushed the thought away. No ghosts from the past allowed, not here and not now.

''I pretty much figured your sexual experience was limited,'' Luke said conversationally, pulling himself up to sit beside her. ''And if you wouldn't even try the venerable old missionary position—conservative enough, even for missionaries!—of course you would never attempt anything else. You especially wouldn't allow an intimacy that means giving up total control, opening yourself completely both emotionally and physically—''

''You sound like a sex therapist on cable!'' Brenna interjected hotly.

''If that's a compliment, thanks. If it's an insult, ouch.'' Luke shrugged. ''But what I mean to say is that I understand, Brenna. There is a lust-into-trust coalition that has to occur, and until it does, you're not ready.''

The affection in his tone bolstered her like a shot of brandy. ''Does the coalition ever go the other way? From trust into lust?''

''I don't see why it couldn't.''

He kissed her long and lingeringly, his hands resuming the gentle fondling of her breasts. Brenna felt herself melting—all her inhibitions, her anxiety and fear, seemed to just flow away.

When their lips briefly parted, they both opened their eyes, and their gazes met and held.

"I don't know which coalition occurred, but I'm ready," she whispered.

She knew she trusted Luke…she certainly lusted for him! She had already granted him intimacies she would never have anticipated with any other man. And she was ready for more.

Luke kissed her again, slowly, taking his time with her, not shortchanging an inch of her skin with his lips as he resumed his intimate journey of her body.

He kissed her legs from her thighs to her ankles, first one and then the other, before parting them with his hands. His mouth nipped and laved the soft skin of her inner thighs, before moving to her center, opening her to him, tasting her.

The intimate contact made her arch instinctively and cry out. She was unprepared for this, after all, and a self-conscious flush suffused her skin from head to toe.

Luke lifted his head and reached for her hand, holding it until she opened her eyes. Brenna saw him watching her, saw the desire in his hot blue gaze.

"Relax, Brenna. Let me take you there." His voice was softly compelling.

"I feel like a freak," she confessed nervously. "Most women my age aren't so…so—"

"You're not a freak, and this is just between the two of us, remember? Other women your age aren't allowed in here."

The warmth and humor, the soothing patience in his tone, convinced her. Brenna's eyelids fluttered shut, and she breathed deeply.

When Luke continued his tender seduction, she gave in to the all-consuming need. And she gave complete control to Luke Minteer.

Complete control.

It was a dizzying surrender. She felt the sensual, primal waves rising and surging within her. Brenna moaned, unable to stay silent as she was swept away in a tornado of whirling emotion, of searing passion and pleasure that built and built until she was sure she would implode from the sheer intensity of it all.

She screamed Luke's name as she shattered into rapturous spasms. A shower of tiny fireworks flashed behind her closed eyes; her whole body pulsed with currents of sensuous electricity.

Slowly, very slowly, she began to drift down from the soaring heights to which he had taken her. His strong arms surrounded her, her head was resting against his chest, his voice low and smooth.

"Luke," she managed to whisper, but her eyelids were so heavy she couldn't lift them.

"I'm here, my love."

Brenna wanted to open her eyes and gaze into Luke's, to tell him about the emotions he had released in her, to thank him for setting her free. For she felt free and light as air, floating in a bubble of pure euphoria.

She wanted to reciprocate, to send him to the same thrilling peaks of ecstasy where he had so unselfishly taken her. But her sated body's demand for sleep overruled her.

Snuggling deeper in his arms, inhaling his unique Luke-scent, Brenna slipped into a deep sleep.

Luke held her, watching her. Her breathing was deep and even, her body totally relaxed. From the pleasure and satisfaction he had given her.

A smile curved his lips. He had given her much pleasure. And though his own body was aching with unassuaged need, he found his lack of fulfillment relatively easy to ignore.

Because the unfamiliar feeling of tenderness that suffused him was something of a reward in itself. Amazingly, by putting her needs first, he had never felt more of a man.

He felt a slight jab on his wrist and looked at her naked belly. Was that a tiny foot or a hand moving under there, making contact with him?

"Are you doing push-ups in there, squirt? Or pretending to kick a soccer ball around?"

He placed his palm over her abdomen and felt the now-rolling movements of the baby within, who had obviously awakened and was exercising.

"Sam or Susie? Which one are you?" He rubbed her tummy as if he were tousling the hair of the child within. "Boy or girl, you're gonna be cute, because your mom is a real babe, if you'll pardon the unpolitically correct expression. And you've also got those tall, blond chromosomes from, uh, the Swedish guy."

For some reason, he couldn't bring himself to refer to the medical student sperm donor as a father. This baby belonged to Brenna; Dr. Test Tube was out of the picture forever.

Which left an opening in her life and in the baby's life, too. There really ought to be a man in the picture, a man who cared about Brenna and her child.

Luke reached down and grabbed the quilt comforter from the floor, pulling it over Brenna and himself.

Gradually, his body stopped throbbing from unfulfilled urgency, and his arousal faded and dissolved into exhaustion. He fell asleep in Brenna's bed, his arms protectively cradling her and the unborn baby.

Seven

Brenna awakened, feeling groggy and disoriented.

She glanced around her bedroom and noticed that the curtains weren't drawn. For her to be in bed with the curtains open was a definite anomaly; she ritually closed them before climbing into bed at night.

Focusing more clearly, she saw snowflakes falling desultorily outside the window and realized that it wasn't nighttime, after all. The skies were gray and cloudy, but it was definitely daylight out there.

And then, abruptly, Brenna came fully awake and sat upright in bed, as if struck by a bolt of lightning.

She was nude under her quilt! The sensual memories accompanying that observation struck her with avalanche force.

Brenna sprang from the bed as fast as her pregnant shape would permit, ignoring her clothes, which were still on the floor where Luke had dropped them while undressing her.

She snatched her oversize fleecy blue robe and pulled it on, shivering, though she felt hot, as if her entire body was one heated red blush.

Perhaps she woke the baby with her fast and frantic motions, because all at once she felt him/her turning a somersault, first one way, then the other.

And while the baby enjoyed its afternoon workout, Brenna thought of herself with Luke, visualizing him, feeling the touch of his lips…

What had she done?

Oh, what she had done!

"I'm sorry," she whispered aloud, her hand on her belly.

The words echoed in her head, mocking her. How many times had she heard *I'm sorry* from her mother after Marly had done something extraordinarily stupid? Enough times to discount the apology completely and to know that there would be another one, equally meaningless, forthcoming after Marly's next misadventure.

And now here she was, Brenna herself, repeating the same words to her own child after having a misadventure of her own.

That it was a misadventure, Brenna had no doubt. The fact that she was alone, that Luke Minteer was gone, spoke volumes. Marly Morgan inevitably had ended up alone, too. Brenna groaned aloud.

She should head right into her studio and get to work putting the final polishing touches on Kristin's wardrobe. She could lose herself in that world, in the decade of the "ohs."

Not *aught*.

Once again Luke filled her head.

Brenna headed purposefully into the bathroom, turned on the shower and shed her robe. The warm water sluiced over her skin, and she rubbed coconut-scented liquid soap over her body.

She willed herself not think about her mother or about Luke Minteer. Somehow, here in the shower, it was easier to occupy her mind with other things. Like her work.

Since she was almost done with the Kristin paper doll, she would concentrate on the next decade of the twentieth century, the teens. At least she knew what to dub that decade. World War I had dominated the teens, so she would draw a little boy with toy soldiers and flags and a hat made from folded newspapers. He would have a hobby horse and a puppy....

Brenna was deciding what to name her paper-doll boy—Simon, perhaps?—as she climbed out of the shower and wrapped a big beach towel around her. She'd bought several to use after showering as her pregnancy advanced.

She was lost in thought, picturing little Simon in the early months of 1918, deciding which books would best serve as references for that particular period.

The last thing she expected was to find someone in her hallway.

So when she literally walked right into Luke Minteer, Brenna was caught completely off guard.

She let out a bloodcurdling scream.

Luke was so startled by her outburst that he gasped, and they both jumped back, to stand a few paces apart and stare wide-eyed at each other.

Luke recovered first. ''I heard water running and knew you were up.''

He attempted to smile. It was more than obvious that Brenna was stunned by the sight of him. Alarmed, too?

"What are you doing here?" she asked warily.

"Brenna, why wouldn't I be here?"

She looked genuinely perplexed, and Luke frowned.

"I got up about two hours ago. You were sleeping soundly and I figured you wouldn't wake up for a while, so I went out to my car and got my laptop. I've been working downstairs in the kitchen."

"Oh."

"Did you think I'd left?" Luke's brows narrowed and he studied her intently. "Or are you on some Lady MacBeth guilt trip, taking a shower, attempting to wash away all traces of—"

"Oh, please! I'm not *that* clichéd!"

"It's not a cliché, it's an image. A powerful image. I used it in my first book. The killer's girlfriend washes her hands compulsively after finding out what her lover has been up to."

Brenna rolled her eyes. "The more I hear about that book, the worse it sounds."

"Yeah, I'm starting to hate it myself, although I'll always love those royalty checks from it. The new book I'm working on is much better."

They looked at each other.

"You'd better dry off and get some clothes on," Luke said at last. "It's chilly in here. This house is definitely not energy efficient. Your heating bills must make gas company officials smile."

As he mentioned it, Brenna felt the cool air on her damp skin. Her freshly shampooed hair was under the towel she'd wound around it, turban-style. She was also suddenly aware that while she stood here wearing only a beach towel, Luke was fully dressed.

"The road to your house is blocked. It won't be open until tonight, if then," she said carefully.

"That's not the reason why I'm still here, Brenna." Luke heaved a sigh. "Although I know convincing you of that isn't going to be easy. You practically jumped out of your skin when you saw me because you were sure I'd taken off. How am I reading you so far? Right on target?"

She nodded her head.

"Will you let me take you to bed and show you I—"

"No!" exclaimed Brenna. "I just want to get dried and dressed."

"Okay, I hear you." Luke shrugged. "I'll be downstairs writing in the kitchen."

He turned and headed down the stairs, leaving a flummoxed Brenna standing in the hall. Luke hadn't left. He wasn't acting any differently toward her despite their intimate interlude earlier.

She hadn't anticipated this turn of events and wasn't sure what they portended. It was mind-bending to have your entire world view altered in an afternoon, and being naked and wet only made it more surreal.

Brenna quickly put on a chocolate-brown maternity outfit with matching shirt and pants and dried her hair.

Next, she went into her studio. She took some notes, bookmarked several pages of her reference books and even did a quick preliminary sketch of Simon. Though immersed in her work, she didn't forget for an instant that Luke Minteer was downstairs in her kitchen, writing about a serial killer.

But she was back in control of herself and worked for almost three hours before allowing herself to venture downstairs. Since she'd heard no doors opening or closing and no car engines starting, she knew Luke hadn't left the house.

And sure enough, there at her kitchen table sat Luke Minteer, working on his laptop, just as he'd said. Even forewarned, the sight amazed her. She paused on the threshold, and Luke looked up.

Their eyes met.

"Yeah, I'm still here," he said dryly. "And you're still shocked that I am. By the way, I heard on the radio that route 128 was opened about a half hour ago, so that reason is eliminated, Brenna."

"They must've sent extra crews to get the work done so fast," she suggested weakly.

"They must've. If I were to say that the reason it was taken care of so quickly is because the mayor's daughter and her family live up there, I'd sound cynical, wouldn't I?"

"Very cynical," she agreed. "I'm sure His Honor is deeply concerned about *all* his constituents being inconvenienced by downed trees and power lines."

Luke laughed and turned in his chair, holding his arms open to her. "Get over here, Brenna."

Acting on pure impulse, without giving herself time to think or consider or analyze, Brenna rushed into his arms. Luke pulled her down on his lap and held her, as she buried her head in the hollow of his shoulder.

"This is how it should've been when you first woke up," he said quietly. "I should've—"

"There was nothing you *should* have done, Luke. Nothing you could have done. I probably would've been just as spooked if you'd been there when I first woke up. And then we probably would've had a fight and I would've kicked you out." She smiled up at him.

"At least this way we avoided a scene, and we both got some work done."

"It's been a very productive day." His tone gave the innocuous words a sensual meaning all their own. And then he kissed her gently, lingeringly.

When he lifted his lips, she gave a small, contented sigh and rested against him.

"Brenna, I want you to know that even if we'd had a big fight and you'd kicked me out, I would still be here. And not because of the snow or the road."

"Because when ordered to leave, you take it as a challenge and deliberately stay put. Irritates the hell out of people." She repeated his boast back to him, softly brushing her lips over his as she spoke.

"True. But in your case, my motives are worthier. I'm here because I want to be with you, Brenna."

They kissed, tenderly at first, then deeply, torridly, with a burning urgency. Luke resisted the almost over-whelming desire to take her back to bed, to seek the satisfaction he had so unselfishly denied himself earlier.

Brenna gave no signs of being averse to that; it would be the natural progression of such fierce, ardent passion.

And yet, instead of doing what he wanted, Luke found himself in the unique position of being unselfish yet again.

"You haven't eaten since breakfast," he heard himself say.

He was putting his sexual urges on hold and her nutritional needs first? Now that was a new one. Plus, he sounded a lot like Grandmother Minteer. She faithfully kept track of who'd eaten what and when while under the same roof.

"You and the baby need some food," he added, sounding even more Grandmotheresque.

Brenna laid her hands on his shoulders. "I don't feel hungry for food right now," she murmured, her dark eyes cloudy with desire.

"Sam or Susie begs to differ." Luke's hand rested on his abdomen and felt the wild dance going on within her womb. "He or she is going to kick its way out of there if you don't send down some chow right away."

As if to second Luke's observation, her stomach growled, an embarrassingly loud noise that could not be ignored.

"I guess you're right." Blushing, Brenna stood up. "I'll make spaghetti. I have marinara sauce and meat-balls from Volario's Market. Would you like to stay for dinner?" she added uncertainly.

Luke gazed at her kiss-swollen lips and her tousled hair and decided he'd never seen such an erotic picture. "Oh, yeah. I'd like to stay."

After they'd eaten, they sat at the table and talked. Luke told her a bit about the new direction his novel was taking; she told him about her plans for little Simon and his World War I era toys and clothes.

"Calling a paper doll Simon is a good way to get that name out of your system," Luke approved. "So now if the baby's a boy, you'll name him Sam?"

"Your campaign against Simon has been surprisingly effective," acknowledged Brenna. "I've decided against using it. But Sam is a name that comes with its own baggage. Uncle Sam, Yosemite Sam, Son of Sam. No, I'm not going with Sam, either. I think I'll switch to another letter of the alphabet."

"How about *X*? I think Xerxes has a certain ring to it."

"It has the ring of getting beat up in the schoolyard."

"Okay, let's try *L*. What about Lucas? It has all the

masculine charm, strength and popularity of Luke but
is slightly different. And you could add Minteer, too.
Around here the name Minteer is golden.''

"Don't you think the name Lucas Minteer Morgan
might cause some talk around town?''

"So what?'' Luke grinned. "Talk is cheap. And today's big news is tomorrow's nobody-gives-a-damn-
about-it story. A whole industry is based on that infal-
lible premise—it's called publicity, and a savvy PR
person can—''

"You might be right, but I've been the subject of
enough gossip to last a lifetime,'' Brenna cut in fervently. "I don't want to be big news for even one day.
Now that I'm here where nobody knows anything about
me, I intend to stay blissfully anonymous.''

Luke's mood, his expression, abruptly shifted from
lighthearted to dark.

"Don't,'' Brenna whispered.

"Don't what?''

"Don't look that way. So angry, so filled with hos-
tility.''

"But that's how I feel when I think about you being
hurt. I'd like to dismember the creep who did it, and I
don't need any of the details, Brenna. It's enough to
know that you were raped by some scumbag, and if I
could kill the guy—''

"You can't. Someone beat you to it.''

The odd expression on her face, the way her voice
trembled, told him that the "someone'' was not irrelevant to the case. Or to Brenna.

"Will you tell me who did?'' he asked quietly.

"My mother.'' She lifted her chin and met his eyes.
"He was her latest boyfriend. I told her right after he
moved in—Mom's boyfriends inevitably moved in with

us or we moved in with them, after they'd been dating a week or two—that the way he acted around me was scary. She laughed it off and told me I was being prissy, that he was just a fun-loving teaser. No big deal, she said.''

"God, Brenna." Luke laid his hand over hers and she grasped it, wrapping her fingers tightly around his.

"Turned out she was wrong. One night when Mom went out with some friends from work, he came into my room and raped me," she said flatly.

Luke muttered an expletive.

Brenna swallowed hard and then determinedly pasted a practiced smile on her face. "But that was a long time ago, thirteen years ago, another lifetime ago, for all practical purposes. I don't dwell on it, I've moved on with my life.''

Luke knew she was giving him the chance to drop the charged topic and switch to something less sordid. To something superficial and pleasant. He also knew there was a time when he would've eagerly done just that. He had never been one to willingly open himself to another's pain.

But today he didn't try to escape hearing about the pain and horror Brenna had faced. It was a part of her, and he realized that he wanted *all* of her. Not just the pleasant social side she showed everybody else, but everything that she was.

"Thirteen years ago, you were only thirteen! Brenna, you were just a little girl!''

Luke felt rage course through him. "No wonder your mother killed the bastard.''

Brenna stared at their linked hands. "You know those books and movies where the mother is an irrepressible free spirit and the daughter is the wise one of the pair, the one who assumes the responsibility and all? Well, in books and movies, it ends well for both—the mother learns a lesson and finally grows up and the daughter gets to be a kid again, after all. But in real life it doesn't work out that way.''

''No. I can see how it wouldn't.''

''Everything was so different when I lived with my father,'' Brenna continued, as if reciting an old dream that she'd repeated many times. ''Daddy married my mother because she was pregnant, and they were divorced shortly after I was born. My dad got custody of me, and I lived with him and his parents. Mom rarely visited. I have very few memories of her, until my dad and grandparents were killed in a car accident when I was six.''

Luke wanted to say something comforting, something wise and profound, but he couldn't find the words. Her history chilled him. At six he'd been mischievous and carefree, secure within a big family, while she had faced the wreck of her whole world.

''Did you go to live with your mother then?''

''Yes. There was insurance money. Taking custody of me was the only way Mom could get her hands on it.''

''Your mother sounds like a mean piece of work, Brenna.''

''Marly described herself as zany and spontaneous,'' Brenna said wryly. ''She couldn't understand why the rest of the world didn't acknowledge how special she was. I can remember her ranting about it. She was completely estranged from her own family. According to her, they were 'dull, hateful prudes.' My guess is that they were appalled by her and glad to cut the ties. I have no idea who they are or where to look for them, so I never have.''

''And from the age of six you were essentially without protection, dragged along with your mother's parade of boyfriends?''

''I didn't like any of them, and they didn't like having me around, either. The only thing that made it bearable was my drawing.''

Brenna smiled, a genuine smile of pleasure. ''I started drawing when I was really little, and Daddy and Gramma and Gramps always encouraged me. By the time I started kindergarten, I had stacks of sketch books and boxes of colored pencils and pens. I could copy almost anything, and I used to entertain the kids at school by drawing pictures of cartoon characters. When I went to live with my mother, school became my refuge. All sixteen of them.''

''You went to sixteen schools?'' Luke was incredulous.

''Marly wasn't one to stay in the same place for very long. During the seven years I lived with her, I went to sixteen different schools, but thankfully, I made friends in all of them. My artwork was the key. As I got older, I could do original pictures instead of just copying things, so I'd draw the kids in class as whatever they wanted to be—superheroes, supermodels, even animals. Whatever. I drew the teachers and the mothers of my friends, too, and always made them look gorgeous. It was a surefire way to please people.''

''But you were a just a child. A kid shouldn't have to go from school to school, learning how to ingratiate herself. Geez, it's like a candidate running for office, always having to be likable while scrounging for votes.''

Brenna actually laughed. "I guess it sort of is. Just think, if I hadn't been able to draw, I might've ended up as a politician."

Luke didn't join in the laughter. He was thinking of his own school years. The same school from kindergarten through eighth grade, then the same high school for the next four years. His sisters, brothers, cousins and friends had all led the same structured, predictable lives.

So very different from Brenna's.

"Why did your mother keep moving?" he pressed.

"She was constantly looking for a fresh start." Brenna heaved a sad, reminiscent sigh. "But it was always the same for her, plunging into new relationships. She would meet a woman who would be her new best friend—until the inevitable blowout that ended the friendship within a few months, if not weeks. It was even worse with men, because she would fall madly in love, invite the new lover to move in or else move in with him, and then the fighting began and the breakup was bitter. The few times a man wanted to stick around and try to work things out, Mom was the one to end it, claiming she felt trapped."

"She sounds nuts, Brenna!"

"She had a personality disorder, according to the court psychiatrists, but that isn't considered mental illness." Brenna grimaced. "Mom didn't think there was anything wrong with her, ever. Even at her trial, she got on the stand and insisted that it was everybody's else's fault and she was the true victim."

"I bet that went over big."

"According to Mom, the jury and the judge all hated her, and so did her own attorney." Brenna shrugged. "It could be true. I remember her attorney took me to lunch and bought me some art supplies and advised me to cut off contact with Mom when she went to prison. 'I know Marly's your mother but she's bad news,' he said."

"Is your mother still in prison?"

"Yes. She got a life sentence and won't be eligible for parole until she's served twenty years."

Luke let out a low whistle. "For killing the man who raped her daughter? I'm no lawyer, but it seems like that might qualify as grounds for temporary insanity or some kind of manslaughter. And having to serve a full twenty years before becoming eligible for parole could be considered severe."

"The police and the prosecution didn't see it that way."

"Which means I'm not seeing the whole picture, just an incomplete outline of what actually happened," Luke concluded.

"It's such an ugly story, Luke."

"We don't have to take it any further if you don't want to, Brenna. But you've risen above whatever ugliness happened. Never lose sight of that fact."

Brenna gazed at him gratefully. He seemed to instinctively know when to encourage her to talk and when not to press her. She loved him for that, for his tact and his kindness to her.

She loved Luke Minteer—and along with that insight came the realization that loving him freed her to share the whole ugly truth with him.

"That night after he—" Brenna began to speak, but she never said the monster's name, not then and not now "—was done with me, he left, and I called a friend whose parents came and took me to the hospital. The ER nurse called the police to report it. I went home with my friends that night, and the next day I told my mother what happened. She didn't believe me. First she said I'd made it up, then she said I was the one who seduced him because I was jealous of her. When he came sneaking back a few nights later, she didn't call the police, she let him in. Greeted him with a smile and a kiss.''

Luke looked sick. "Brenna, what did you do?"

"I got out of there fast. I ran to my friend's house, and they called the police. But by the time they got to our place, Mom had already—done it.''

"She'd killed him," Luke verified.

"Yes. Mom said he was drunk and told her about that night with me and said that I was—" Brenna paused and took a deep breath "—sexier than she was. Then he passed out and she loaded the gun and shot him. The D.A. said it was the insult to her ego that caused her to kill him, not any maternal concern for me. The jury agreed and convicted her of first-degree murder.''

Luke said nothing, nothing at all.

"Yes, that part always renders people speechless.'' Brenna's tone was resigned. "It's so vile and trashy, I learned not to tell anybody. Because after the listeners recover enough to speak, they always say the same thing—'You poor thing.' And then there's more silence. I see either distance or pity in their eyes, and—''

"Brenna, if you see either distance or pity in my eyes, you're misinterpreting, because all I want to do is take you in my arms and hold you and try to make the pain go away.''

Luke reached for her. Brenna drew back.

"The pain is gone, Luke. I dealt with it a long time ago.''

"Did you, Brenna? Or is it still ruling your life?''

"I was very lucky and had a lot of help coping with it, Luke. After the trial, some of the parents of my friends at school arranged for me to be sent to Denver, a few hundred miles away, to a group home for girls who couldn't live with their families because of abuse or neglect. It was nondenominational but run by nuns, and the girls placed there had to meet certain qualifications—their grades had to be decent and they had to be considered at risk for getting into trouble but not delinquent. The hope was to show the girls who held promise that there were alternatives to…to the way they'd been living."

"And you fit the bill."

"Yes, fortunately for me, I went to live there."

"And while you were there, you made friends and loved school?" Luke guessed. His dark-blue eyes shone with affection.

"I was there until I graduated from high school, and I loved the discipline and the routine and the order. There was lots of warmth and encouragement and fun, too. I won a scholarship to art school and…well, I've just kept on drawing."

"So how did you end up here in Pennsylvania? It's a long way from Denver."

"I accepted a job with a commercial ad agency in Philadelphia two years ago. It was a good salary with benefits, and I thought I ought to at least try working for a company instead of freelancing. I moved there…and hated the job from the first day."

"You preferred being your own boss, setting your own hours," surmised Luke.

"I liked drawing what I wanted, the way I wanted too much, to conform to the company way. I also decided I wanted to leave Philadelphia for somewhere smaller.''

"This area isn't particularly well known, even throughout the state, Brenna. How did you come to be here?'' Luke asked curiously.

"One of my friends in Philadelphia was Angela Volario—you know, whose family owns the Italian market here. She talked about her hometown a lot, and I came along with her to visit one weekend. It seemed like a good place to live and raise a child, and I really wanted a family. I'd gotten past my fears that I might turn out to be a mother like mine.''

"That will never happen, Brenna,'' Luke assured her. "Never.''

"I know that now. The nuns said over and over that we have free will and make our own choices. I finally realized I wasn't doomed to be like Marly, that I'd had a good father and grandparents and friends and teachers I could emulate. I could be a good, loving parent.''

"All true. But I'd bet my next contract advance that the nuns wouldn't wholeheartedly cheer your trip to the sperm bank and your plan to have this baby solo, without—''

"I haven't told them anything about it yet.'' Brenna averted her eyes. "When I take the baby back to Denver to visit—which I'm definitely going to do—I know they'll be happy for me. And they'll be proud that I'm such a good mother,'' she added, her eyes flashing, daring him to disagree.

"I have no doubt you'll be a great mother, Brenna.''

Her brief show of defiance seemed to evaporate, without an argument to fire it. Her shoulders drooped; she appeared physically spent. Luke felt a surge of compassion for her. No wonder she didn't want to revisit her past—it was a grueling ordeal, too draining for a woman in her condition.

He cupped his hand around her nape and began a gentle massage. She leaned into it, closing her eyes.

"Has there ever been a man in your life, Brenna?" Luke asked softly.

"No. I was more interested in directing my thoughts and energy into my drawing. Having a boyfriend was never a priority to me."

"For *boyfriend,* substitute *poisonous snake*—or *sex-crazed rapist?*"

"I guess I do have a few issues still pending in that area."

"Yeah, your sperm bank visit is proof of that."

She smiled slightly. "It seemed like the ideal solution. A way to have a baby without having to endure sex to get one. Until I met you, I never even had the desire to—" She broke off and shook her head, her eyes gleaming. "You can see what a clueless numbskull I am in the male-female arena. Admitting to you—a notorious smooth operator—that you're the first and only man I've ever wanted is pretty pathetic."

She stood up and smoothed the wrinkles from her maternity top. "Feel free to ignore my lack of...cool, especially since a hormonal pregnant woman is hardly a—"

"I don't want to ignore it." Luke stood up, too. There was a sexy glint in his blue eyes. "And you know I think you're *cool.*"

Brenna had to laugh at his inflection, at the word, at the strange circumstances they were in.

"I want to take you to bed and show you how much

I want you, too, Brenna. I want to show you that there is nothing to endure. Are you ready to let me?''

''Yes,'' she breathed, her tone filled with both surprise and wonder. ''I am, Luke.''

Eight

They walked hand in hand to the staircase, pausing to kiss at the foot of the stairs.

"Do you want me to pick you up and carry you?" he asked, leaning toward her as if readying himself to do just that.

"Please don't. Maybe it's because of the baby, but being carried is—unnerving, Luke." Brenna swallowed. "I'm sorry."

"No apologies necessary." Luke put his arm around her and led her up the stairs. "I'll never make you do anything you don't want to, Brenna. You don't ever have to be afraid that I will."

She reached for his hand resting on her shoulder and linked her fingers with his. "So there will be no more pressure from you to name the baby Sam or Lucas, if it's a boy?" she teased, feeling playful and younger than she could ever remember feeling.

"Let me qualify my last statement. I'll never pressure you sexually. Otherwise, I'll try my damnedest to get you to do things my way. Winning over the opposition is part of my ex-political-operative charm."

They both laughed as they reached the top of the stairs and headed toward her bedroom. This time she felt no trepidation as he undressed her, she made no apologies for her pregnant figure. No apologies necessary, she reminded herself. Luke had seen her before, and he had stayed. He'd even made the return trip to her bedroom!

So when he told her how feminine and beautiful she was, Brenna allowed herself to believe that he meant what he was saying. That he believed it himself.

They kissed and caressed each other for a long time, with no sense of rush, no need to hurry things along. Each touch was special, each kiss meaningful, as tenderness and passion built and merged together into a loving conflagration.

They lay on the bed together until Luke helped her on top of him, to sit astride him, putting her in a position that paradoxically made her both vulnerable and powerful at the same time.

Brenna wanted more, more affection, more reassurance. More of him.

Leaning forward, she twined her fingers through the springy thickness of his hair. The sensitive tips of her breasts brushed his chest as she kissed him, her mouth open and demanding, hot and wild

Luke's hands skimmed along the length of her back, tracing the fine line of her spine and the small dimple at the base of it. After a few of these sweeping caresses, he cupped her buttocks, filling his palms with them and lushly squeezing.

She moaned her arousal and wriggled sensuously atop him, bringing her into full contact with his throbbing erection.

Luke reached up to fondle her breasts, teasing the nipples until she arched her back, tipping back her head so that her hair dangled down her back.

She closed her eyes as Luke lowered his hand and his clever fingers caressed her with an erotic expertise. Perspiration glowed on her skin as a primal instinct guided her into a position which most maximized the pleasure.

Brenna felt her body sinking into the sensual rhythm provided by his hand, and the delicious tension built, growing tighter, burning hotter. Her head lolled on her neck, frenetically turning from side to side, and her lips parted as she breathed his name and moaned her pleasure.

Her eyes remained tightly closed. Opening them would require too much effort, and her whole being was focused on what he was doing to her, what he was making her feel.

He murmured love words, sexy words that excited her even more. Luke was good with words; the thought flashed through her feverish brain. He was also very good with his hands.

She nearly smiled at the thought, except at that moment, he slowly, carefully inserted his finger inside her. First one, then another while his thumb maintained just the right amount of light pressure on the small swollen bud that ached and throbbed for his touch.

''You're close now.'' His voice was low and deep and seemed to exert a hypnotic effect on her.

''Yes. Please,'' she mumbled, as if in a trance.

''Please what, sweetheart?''

"You—you know." Her words were thick and almost incoherent.

"Tell me what you want, Brenna. And say my name," he added, a possessive note creeping into his tone.

Embarrassment and fear had lost all meaning; she felt sensual, she felt free. To say and do and feel. "Let me climax, Luke. Please."

"Yes, Brenna. I'll do anything for you."

And then he did, and a searing flash of heat exploded within her, making her writhe and rock and scream his name as her entire body convulsed with the power of her surrender.

It was a wondrous, rapturous tidal wave of heat and passion and release crashing over her. Before she could come down, as her body still quivered with aftershocks of pleasure, Brenna felt his big strong hands on her hips, settling her directly over him.

Guiding himself inside her.

She felt her body opening to his penetration, accepting him within her.

"That's it, sweetheart," he rasped. "I want you so much. You feel so good, so soft, like hot velvet. You're my love, and I'll never hurt you. You know that, don't you, Brenna? Don't ever be afraid of me."

Fear was the farthest thing from her mind, Brenna thought dizzily as she felt her body stretching to sheathe him. The fullness felt wonderful, an indescribable contrast to that empty ache that she'd known only since Luke had first aroused her. He was her first everything, and their bodies seemed exquisitely attuned to each other's.

Her insides pulsed thrillingly with his every rhythmic stroke. He adjusted her position once again until she could feel his manhood rub more directly against her most sensitive place.

"Better?" he muttered huskily.

Brenna saw shards of color streak like fireworks behind her closed eyelids. She whimpered. *Better* was definitely an understatement. It was the best, the most marvelous, the wildest and hottest...

And then their bodies both plunged over the precipice into a sublime free fall.

Luke held her as feelings he'd never experienced gripped him. He'd had intercourse before, of course, but this was the first time it went beyond physical pleasure for him.

He felt as if Brenna had absorbed him as he had entered her, that the two of them had merged and become one. She was on top of him and he was inside her, he could taste her on his lips and feel her passion-slick skin against his own. A rush of protectiveness and pride swept through him. She was his.

Her body was trembling, and he could feel her delicate little shivers as he gently eased himself out of her.

He placed her down beside him, keeping her close and tucking her into the curve of his body, like nesting spoons. Smoothing a lock of her hair away from her cheek, he gently tucked it behind her ear.

He loved her. The insight struck him with the force of a two-by-four to the head, leaving him feeling slightly giddy. For the first time in his life, he was truly in love.

He guessed there might have been—there most certainly had been—a time in his life when, if someone had told him he would fall in love with an almost-nine-months-pregnant woman carrying another man's child, he would've laughed himself silly.

Of course, nobody would ever have said such a thing, because it was just too improbable for anybody to imagine. He was the Minteer with the best imagination, and not even he could have come up with a scenario more unlikely than this one.

But it had happened, and Luke decided he wouldn't have it any other way. He wanted Brenna, only Brenna, and if she happened to be almost nine months pregnant, that's how he wanted her. Just the way she was.

His hand automatically came to rest on Brenna's abdomen, where the baby lay quiescent within her womb. Never mind the med student who'd biologically fathered this child via the sperm bank—the man whom this child called "Daddy" was going to be Luke Minteer.

"Luke?" she murmured, her voice quavering.

"I'm here, honey." He kissed the corner of her jaw, her earlobe, the curve of her neck.

"Could you go home now?"

It took a while for him to fully process what she'd just said. When it finally dawned…

"You're kicking me out?" Luke was staggered. "You're not only kicking me out of your bed, you're kicking me out of your house?"

"I want to be by myself. Please, Luke." Her voice rose to a nervous plea. "I really need some time alone."

"Tough." His hands drifted over her body, caressing, soothing, apologizing for his stand. But not reconsidering. "You've already spent too much time by yourself, Brenna. Now I'm with you, and I'm staying with you. Deal with it."

"Oh, I've done it now, haven't I?" Brenna groaned. "You've taken my request as a challenge and decided to stay put."

"It wasn't a request, it was an order, and you can't say you weren't warned about what would happen." Luke nipped her shoulder, then laved it with his tongue. "A less secure man might go running off, but luckily I have a strong male ego and am not taking your attempted rejection personally."

Within his embrace, Brenna rolled onto her other side, facing him, her arm sliding reflexively across his middle. She regarded him gravely for a moment. Her lashes were spiky with tears, her eyes shimmered with them.

"There are those who might say your ego is more than merely strong, it's overinflated, which makes you overbearing. And that you should take my attempted rejection personally because—well, what could be more personal than a woman kicking you out of her bed right after...after—" She bit her lip and shook her head, unable to continue.

Luke lifted her hand to his mouth and kissed each finger, punctuating his words with the light touches of his lips.

"After we made love and you loved every minute of it?" he suggested.

Brenna flinched.

"You're absolutely right, you know," Luke continued calmly. "There are those who would say all those things you just said. But I have a thick skin. So even though you feel compelled to say stuff to send me away, I can just shrug it off. And I'll stay with you, just like you want me to, Brenna."

She glowered at him. "What do I have to say to get you to go away and leave me alone?"

"Your body language is saying all I need to know, honey."

Brenna glanced down at her arm, draped across his stomach, at her leg which had slipped between his.... She hadn't even realized what she'd done. It was as if her limbs had moved of their own volition in direct opposition to her stated demands.

"So I've come to this—saying one thing and doing another," she said grimly. "Which makes me a total nutcase who is—"

"You're not nuts and you're not hormonal," Luke cut in, his voice ringing with that confidence and assurance he projected so well. "Your mother was a wacko and surrounded herself with similar kinds, which meant that you had to endure too many of them during those rotten years with her. So you learned not to let your guard down, and it's hard to break old defensive habits. That's all it is, Brenna."

"It's hard to argue with someone who's arguing that you're not crazy." Brenna's voice was tinged with irony.

"Yeah, it is. So stop arguing and go to sleep."

"Will you be here in the morning?" Brenna's heart hammered wildly in her chest.

"I'll be here, Brenna."

He didn't say anything else, and neither did she.

Was Luke right? Brenna wondered, confused. Did she really want him to stay here with her?

Already she was beginning to reconstruct those invisible walls around her heart. She reminded herself how much she cherished her privacy and how much time alone she required.

As for sharing a bed all night with him...well, that wasn't going to happen. It couldn't. At the school in Denver, she'd had a terrible time sleeping while sharing a *room* with another girl and hadn't shared a room with anyone since. Let alone a bed.

Brenna tried not to think of what she'd done with Luke today. Her mind was already on overload. Reliving the wild, hot memories would probably short-circuit it! But try as she might to suppress them, those feelings sneaked past her guard, evoking everything.

What they'd done. What they'd said. How wonderful it all had been.

And he was still here, holding her in the dark silence of her room, warming her with his body heat. His steady breathing echoed in her ears. It was a calming, reassuring sound.

She would lie here for just a little longer and then convince him to leave.

But wrapped in Luke's arms, Brenna felt as if her tired mind and her satiated body were floating away as she slowly drifted into sleep.

''The good news is that it's stopped snowing and the roads have been cleared,'' Luke announced the next morning.

Brenna, who'd awakened moments earlier, struggled to a sitting position in bed and watched him look out the window.

He was dressed in his clothes from yesterday, but his face was smoothly shaven and his hair still damp from the shower. He looked vigorous and alert and cheerful—whereas she felt nowhere near any of those enviable states.

''The bad news is that it's stopped snowing and the roads have been cleared—and everything is open and running on time today,'' Luke continued. ''I heard it on the radio, which means we have jury duty today. Ready for another go-round of Gimme That Ring?''

Brenna closed her eyes and tried to stifle a moan. She didn't quite succeed.

''My sentiments exactly.'' Luke chuckled. ''When we jurors get together to deliberate, I'm going to suggest that the court confiscate the damn ring and donate it to charity.''

Should she try to explain that it wasn't the prospect of serving on the jury and listening to Amber's and Brad's attorneys do their best to portray each other's clients as greedy/stingy, shameless/shameful wretches who did/did not deserve the diamond ring?

No, it was the thought of having to sit next to Luke Minteer in the jury box all day, and wondering what to say and do after the courtroom session ended.

Brenna gnawed nervously on her lower lip.

Suppose he asked—no, Luke didn't ask, he just did as he pleased—and suppose it pleased him to come back to her house with her again tonight? To make love to her and spend the night with her again? Why, she'd intended to send him on his way last night—except she'd fallen asleep first.

And for it to occur two nights in a row? She couldn't handle so much intimacy. Brenna shivered. The very idea made her claustrophobic.

But suppose it didn't please him to be with her? Suppose yesterday had been both the beginning and the end of her involvement with Luke Minteer?

She couldn't handle that, either!

For the first time in her life, Brenna felt a sharp flicker of recognition. This awful uncertainty must have been what her mother's chaotic romantic life had been like.

Brenna was aghast. She had spent years avoiding men to save herself from falling into the same traps that had constantly ensnared her mother. Yet here she was, so like Marly, falling in love and into bed with a man she hadn't known long enough. Wasting her time and brain cells worrying about what would happen next. Would he call? Wouldn't he? What did every nuance of his every word and expression mean?

Brenna steeled herself against it. She would *not* subject herself or her baby to any of that futile nonsense.

"You went into the bathroom about four times last night," Luke said.

Brenna's eyes flew open, and she felt a hot blush spread over every inch of her skin. She saw Luke studying her, and she didn't meet his eyes. She couldn't. The physical intimacy they'd shared last night didn't extend to this morning—nor to pointed observations on her bathroom habits!

"Was it because you're so far along in the pregnancy or because of the sex?" Luke's brows narrowed in concern.

"The pregnancy," Brenna replied brusquely. "I've been getting up a lot at night for the past month or so." She threw off the covers and swung her legs over the side of the bed.

She was naked, a fact she'd forgotten. Looking down at herself while making an ungainly escape into the sanctuary of the bathroom made her cringe.

But she made a successful, if ungainly, escape to the sanctuary of the bathroom, closed the door and locked it.

"I'll make some breakfast," Luke called through the door. "What do you want?"

"Anything. Whatever you're going to have." She

turned on the shower, and the roaring sound of the water precluded any further conversation.

After a quick breakfast of juice and cereal, they drove to the courthouse in silence. There had been an argument about taking two cars. Brenna insisted on driving herself. Luke said it made no sense as parking was sure to be scarce since the snowplows had been utilized to clear the district's roads, not the parking lots. However, the VIP spots in front of the courthouse would surely be cleared.

Why should Brenna drive around town, searching for what might be a nonexistent parking space? Luke argued. Even if she found one, there would be a long cold walk to the courthouse, and the sidewalks might be slippery. If she fell, she could hurt herself or the baby.

Brenna accused him of being manipulative for bringing the baby into this. Luke replied it was impossible not to bring the baby into this, as it was inside her.

In the end Brenna decided it was easier simply to ride to the courthouse with Luke. His points were too valid to ignore. Besides, she could tell he wasn't going to budge on the issue. He assured her that he wouldn't, and she'd come to realize that he always meant what he said.

Luke swung the Dodge Durango into the cleared VIP spot directly in front of the courthouse, came around to her side and lifted her out of the truck.

"There's just one thing," Brenna said, as he set her on the ground.

She was breathless from being handled by him and wanted nothing more than to lean into him and tuck her hand into his. But she kept it at her side.

"And what's that?" Luke reached for her hand and

slipped it into his pocket, pulling her closer to him in the process.

Brenna felt his body brush hers and a honeyed warmth oozed through her. "I want to go right home after we're finished here for the day."

"Okay, I'll take you right home," he replied easily.

"And—I don't want you to come into my house or ask if you can. Because my answer will be no," she finished in a rush.

"Well, I guess this is one of those damned-if-you-do or damned-if-you-don't situations." He sounded more resigned than angry or sad. "If I agree to drop you off without any protest, you'll assume I want to leave you. If I refuse and insist on coming in with you, you'll accuse me of stalking you. Of not knowing how to take no for an answer."

"You *don't* know how to take no for an answer. I don't have to *prove* that," she added.

Even to her own ears she sounded cranky and ill-tempered. She really wouldn't blame Luke if he dropped her hand and stomped off inside the courthouse.

Instead, Luke laughed. They kept on walking together, up the stairs and into the building.

In the jury box, the jurors exchanged tales of yesterday's storm and how they'd weathered it. Everybody but Luke and Brenna complained about the lack of accessible parking spaces since the lots had only been partially plowed.

Brad and Amber and their attorneys sat at their respective tables, ignoring each other.

Everybody rose when the judge entered the courtroom.

"Your Honor, yesterday afternoon the Pennsylvania

Supreme Court upheld a ruling by the Superior Court that pertains to this case,'' Brad's lawyer announced, looking very pleased. "If I may cite the ruling…''

Brad, clearly aware of what was to come, grinned from ear to ear.

Amber's lawyer looked as if he knew, too. He grimaced and seemed to brace himself as he whispered something in his client's ear.

"Amber looks ready to hit something, or somebody, probably Brad or his lawyer,'' Luke whispered to Brenna. "Maybe both.''

The judge, giving nothing away by his expression, told Brad's attorney to continue.

"In a case with circumstances closely paralleling this one, the Superior Court ordered the fiancée to give back the engagement ring after the engagement was terminated,'' the lawyer continued in a majestic baritone. "The Superior Court considered this case to be a 'case of first impression.'''

He turned to the jury and added in an aside, "That means the Court's ruling would be the standard for similar cases in the future.''

"I read the ruling, Counselor,'' chimed in the judge. "The Supreme Court justices said that the state had adopted a no-fault divorce statute back in 1980 and should apply similar principles to cases spawned by broken engagements.''

"It's long overdue for these personal issues of blame and fault to be removed from the courtroom, Your Honor,'' Brad's attorney said smugly.

The judge shot him a warning look. "I hereby order the ring returned and dismiss this case.''

"No!'' shrieked Amber, jumping to her feet. "That's not fair!''

"Sit down and be quiet, young lady," ordered the judge, pounding his gavel. He turned to the jury. "The jurors are dismissed with the Commonwealth's thanks for performing your civic duty."

"They didn't do anything but sit there and stare at me!" howled Amber.

"You see why I broke up with her?" Brad addressed the jury himself. "Would any of you guys want to marry her?"

"She's pretty hot, though," one Jason chortled to the other.

After another pound of the gavel and another demand for silence, the judge departed. The attorneys attempted to shepherd their bickering clients from the courtroom as Amber cursed furiously at the preening, triumphant Brad.

The jurors filed out of the jury box.

"Let's go before we're witnesses to a homicide and have to come back to testify," joked one of the older women.

Beside her, Brenna felt Luke freeze in place. She glanced up at him to see him staring down at her, a look of concern on his face.

"Brenna, what she said..." Luke murmured. "She didn't know about your—"

"I know," Brenna said quietly. "I don't take jokes like that personally." Her lips tightened. "But when it comes to books that make crime seem exciting and criminals seem interesting, *those* I take those personally."

Roger, the jury's elected foreman, invited everybody to Peglady's to celebrate their unexpected freedom.

"Do you want to go?" Luke asked Brenna.

She shook her head. "I want to go home. Alone!"

"Anything you want, you've got it," said Luke. Then he hummed a few bars of it.

As she'd requested—demanded!—Luke drove directly to her house. He politely assisted her to the front door, and when Brenna opened it, he made no move to come inside.

Her heart sinking, she watched him stroll back down the walk. This was the way she wanted it, Brenna reminded herself sternly.

It was just that she didn't want him to want it that way, too! Brenna realized she was on the verge of tears. She fought against them, appalled by her weakness.

"Do you want me to pick you up at six or six-thirty for dinner tonight?" Luke called to her, just before he climbed behind the wheel.

The jolt of relief she felt was palpable, throwing her so off balance that she feared she would lose her already tenuous control and start to cry, if she attempted to speak.

Oh, the effect of all these hormones, causing her moods to shift crazily from low to high!

Or was it the effect of Luke Minteer?

"Okay, six it is," Luke answered for her. "See you then, Brenna."

Nine

Luke's phone was ringing as he walked into his house. It was cold inside, and he kept his coat on. All those hours without electrical power gave the place the ambience of an igloo.

He made it to the phone just before his answering machine was set to pick up. And was astonished to find Steve Saraceni, a Harrisburg lobbyist and pal from his bad old days in the state capital, on the other end of the line.

"Hey, Luke. Hope I'm not interrupting your perp in the middle of slicing and dicing his latest victim," joked Steve.

Luke tried to recall the last time he'd talked to Steve Saraceni. Probably while he was still working for Matt and living in D.C., wheeling and dealing in the world of politics. Among other things.

None of which explained why the lobbyist was calling him now.

"What can I do for you, Steve?" Luke was curious.

"For me? Nothing, actually. I'm calling because my sister called me earlier today and—" Steve paused and cleared his throat. "I guess I should explain that my sister, Cassie Walsh, lives next door to a, um, a friend of yours. A *very special* friend of yours."

"My very special friend," Luke repeated, putting together the pieces.

It seemed that Steve Saraceni's sister had done some piece fitting herself—and Luke's instincts told him that she'd come up with the wrong picture.

"Oh, damn, Luke, we've known each other too long and too well for me not to come straight to the point. Cassie is irate because she says you're the father of this girl's unborn baby, and not only do you refuse to take responsibility, but for months you've been pretending you didn't even know her. According to Cassie, this young mother-to-be has to deal with everything, including all expenses, completely on her own."

Luke sank down on a chair, clutching the phone. His instincts had been right on target.

"Luke, are you still there?"

Steve's voice seemed to reverberate in Luke's head. "Yeah, I'm here."

"Go ahead, tell me it's none of my business." Steve heaved a sigh. "Because I know it isn't. I just wanted to—well, I wanted to find out if it's true, or if my sister might have misconstrued things."

"And why would she do that, Steve?"

"This girl is pregnant and Cassie saw her with you, the only man who's ever even visited her. She found the girl crying after you left, and you've spent the night over there.''

"And that's all the evidence?'' Luke drawled. "Don't know if you could indict me with that, Steve.''

"I know. Cassie is a sweetheart, but she gets downright militant on the subject of fathers' responsibilities toward kids. She had a bad experience with her sons' deadbeat dad and can be evangelical about looking out for...for—''

"—children whose fathers abandon them?'' Luke filled in. "Who can blame her? Certainly not me.''

"You still haven't denied anything, Luke,'' Steve pointed out. "You've done some dodging and weaving but no denying.''

"And we both know that a nondenial might as well be a blatant confirmation. I might not be playing anymore, but I haven't forgotten the rules of the game, Steve,'' Luke added with a wry, reminiscent chuckle.

"So it's true, then?'' Steve audibly gulped. "You and this girl are—''

"Her name is Brenna. And your sister is right about Brenna being pregnant. She's due within a month.''

There was a long silence. When Steve spoke again, his characteristic silky-smooth tone held a distinctly disapproving note. "You're pretty cavalier about the whole thing, Minteer. Does your brother know?''

"Matt? Of course not. Until now, nobody in Harrisburg knew, either. But you're about to change that situation, right, Steve?'' Luke gave a sharp laugh. "After all, we also both know that in the political world, information is valuable currency. And you know how to spend it better than anybody.''

"Same old Luke,'' Steve said, with a touch of malice. "Don't say I didn't check for the facts first. And I promise that I'll spend this *currency* to the best of my ability.'' Then he hung up.

Which meant that there would be a discreet, immediate phone call placed to Congressman Matthew Minteer's office in D.C. from Steve Saraceni himself.

Luke could almost hear the oh-so-congenial-and-concerned lobbyist say to his brother, ''Just wanted to give you a heads-up on a certain rumor circulating in your district, Matt.''

In this district of traditional values and strong family ties, rumors of a Minteer getting a young woman pregnant and then leaving her to fend for herself would go over about as well as a nude orgy on a church lawn.

Congressman Minteer would be indebted to Steve Saraceni for tipping him off in time to do some damage control, and in the political world a personal debt was golden. Even better than information.

Same old Luke. The phrase echoed in Luke's head.

Except he *wasn't* the same old Luke. That Luke, the one Steve Saraceni had known, would have had nothing to do with a pregnant Brenna Morgan in the first place. Apart from the obligatory hello and goodbye bestowed on all his fellow jurors, the same old Luke would not have bothered talking to Brenna at all.

Thus forever missing his chance with the woman whom he knew was irrefutably the love of his life.

Of course, the same old Luke wouldn't have cared, because he had been seeking other things, like power and thrills. He hadn't been looking for love in his life.

Just as Brenna wasn't looking for love in hers. Not from a man, anyway. She was having a baby to love and to love her. Which was fine, but she needed more and so did the baby.

They both needed him—the new improved Luke Minteer—the man who had been redeemed by love.

He would do anything he had to do in order to become a part of their lives, Luke vowed. And he wouldn't settle for some vague peripheral role; he wanted nothing less than a vital, dynamic position with Brenna and Baby.

"Begin at the beginning" was his brother Matt's mantra, when faced with a seemingly insurmountable political hurdle.

Well, the first step was getting Brenna to realize that they belonged together—which might not prove as easy as he wished.

But it was not an insurmountable hurdle. No such thing existed for the Minteers. They inevitably prevailed. And fortunately, he'd retained just enough tenacity, including a bit of underhandedness, from the same old Luke to achieve his goal.

Brenna was in that trancelike state she achieved when deeply immersed in creating the world where her paper dolls came to life. Everything in her own life faded deep into the background of her mind as she concentrated on the drawing paper in front of her.

Ideas came easily, and her fingers deftly sketched and measured and colored as characters appeared, accompanied by their individual histories and characteristics, their wardrobes and possessions.

She completed the little boy Simon and moved into the next decade, the twenties, drawing Peggy, a child with bobbed hair and dresses with dropped waistlines similar to the flappers of that era.

She'd already thought ahead to the thirties. There definitely would have to be another little girl, one with

Shirley Temple curls and short, frilly dresses to define that decade.

Each little paper-doll girl, Peggy and the Shirley lookalike, would have a doll with matching dresses. There should be pets, too, but what animal? She'd drawn so many cats and dogs over the years; it would be fun to do something else.

Would her editor think a parrot or a monkey was too exotic for a child in the twenties or thirties to own?

The doorbell rang several times before the sound registered with Brenna. She frowned at the intrusion. It always took her a moment or two to totally return to her life away from her books.

The first thing she noticed was the clock on the wall. It was just after five.

And then everything came back to her in a rush. Luke, his insistence on picking her up for dinner at— hadn't he said six o'clock?

Her heartbeat accelerated to warp speed, and Brenna tried to mock herself into staying cool and calm. After all, she wasn't a dizzy teenager eagerly waiting for her first boyfriend to pick her up for their big date! Why must she feel like one?

In spite of her resolve, Brenna stopped in the bathroom and checked herself in the mirror. Her hair needed brushing, and she brushed it. Her cheeks were already flushed, which eliminated any need for more color. Her eyes were bright, too bright. Brenna wondered how she could make them stop glowing.

And before she could stop herself, she applied a light coat of pink lipstick.

Reminding herself that it wasn't safe for the baby if she dashed down the stairs, that falling was a possible risk, Brenna forced herself to walk down the staircase slowly and carefully, holding on to the handrail.

The doorbell rang again, and she opened the door, expecting to see Luke.

She planned to tell him that she hadn't consented to this dinner date, plus he was almost an hour early for it. Drop-in visitors were unacceptable, a detriment to her work schedule. She hated being unexpectedly interrupted. Furthermore...

Brenna stared at the three women standing on her small porch. There was an older woman, probably sixty-something, and two younger ones, perhaps in their late twenties or very early thirties, all bundled in heavy coats.

They stared back at her.

"Sweet saints in heaven, it's true," the older woman murmured, her eyes sweeping over Brenna's very pregnant figure.

Brenna, suddenly self-conscious, straightened her long, pale-pink maternity sweater, tugging it farther over her maternity jeans.

"Of course it's true, Mom!" exclaimed one of the younger women, the tall, dark-haired, blue-eyed one who looked a lot like Luke. "As soon as Lisa told me, I knew it had to be true. Why would Cassie make up something like that?"

Brenna's eyes darted to the older woman with the same blue eyes and fair skin as her daughter. Her dark hair was heavily streaked with gray.

"I don't think we've met." Brenna managed to get the words out and was once again inordinately grateful to the nuns, who had stressed good manners so long and so often they'd become truly ingrained.

She extended her hand, which, to her consternation, was shaking. "I'm Brenna Morgan."

"Anne Marie Minteer," said the dark-haired young woman, clasping her hand. "Taylor," she added, almost as an afterthought. "This is my mother, Rosemary Minteer, and my sister-in-law Lisa. She's married to my brother John."

"Annie and I went to high school together," Lisa, a petite blonde, put in helpfully. "And my son, David, goes to preschool with your little neighbor Abigail Walsh. Her mom, Cassie, and I have become good friends this year. David and Abby like to play together."

Lisa seemed to run out of steam at that point and lapsed into silence.

"I've heard Cassie mention David," Brenna said politely, still mystified as to why the three were here. "Abby's mentioned him, too, I believe. The Walshes live right next door," she added, and pointed to their house, right next door.

Just in case the trio had come to the wrong place by mistake.

But the three women made no attempt to leave. Instead, Rosemary Minteer moved toward Brenna and attempted to put her arms around her.

"Brenna, you poor dear sweet girl."

Reflexively Brenna backed away in alarm. "What…what do you want?"

"You don't have to pretend with us, honey." Rosemary's blue eyes were filled with sadness and sympathy. "There is no need for you to stay silent any longer."

"Cassie told me today when we picked up the kids

at preschool. I called John and Anne Marie and a few others right away," Lisa said earnestly.

"Please don't think that we blame you, Brenna," exclaimed Anne Marie. "None of us do, honest! We want you to know we're all firmly on your side in this."

"Everybody knows, my dear, so there is no reason for any more secrecy," chimed in Rosemary. "Why, I'd just hung up the phone from talking to Anne Marie when my sister-in-law Eileen called me. Her Patrick said he simply couldn't stay silent any longer, he said he didn't feel right keeping such a secret from the family. So he told his parents, and of course they called us right away."

"And Matt called Mom from D.C. a little while ago," Anne Marie said, glancing from Brenna to her mother. "He got the word straight from Harrisburg. The gossip isn't all over the district yet, though it soon will be, of course. But when you and Luke get—"

"Luke," Brenna repeated.

It was the only name among all those mentioned—aside from Cassie and Abigail Walsh—that held any relevance for her. She was still baffled about what her uninvited guests were talking about.

What did "everybody" know?

For one grim moment Brenna thought of her past, of her mother and the trial and that terrifying night with the monster who had set it all in motion. If everybody knew all about that, she couldn't remain in town.

Been there, done that! Starring as the object in a sordid round of gossip was something she did not care to repeat, and she would not subject her child to it, not even as an infant.

But logic quickly prevailed, and Brenna discarded that premise.

They'd cited Cassie Walsh as a source, and Cassie knew nothing about her past. And was the Patrick who'd been mentioned Luke's cousin, the young police officer? Patrick Minteer knew nothing about her, either, except that she had been in Luke's SUV and they'd had an argument....

Brenna tilted her head, assessing the two taller women with their piercing blue-eyed stares.

"Are you Luke's mother and sister?" Brenna surmised. Lisa's identity as an in-law, married to John Minteer, had already been confirmed.

"Goodness, didn't we explain who we are?" Rosemary shook her head. "I'm sorry, honey. It's just that this news was so unexpected, so out of the blue, that I guess we're not quite back to ourselves yet. Yes, I am Luke's mother, and Anne Marie is his younger sister. We're delighted to meet you, Brenna, but I can't help but wish we had met under more, well, conventional circumstances."

"As if Luke has ever been conventional!" Anne Marie rolled her eyes.

A sharp blast of icy wind whirled around them, and Lisa shivered. "Could we come inside?" she asked.

Since Lisa's teeth were practically chattering, and her lips were purple from the cold, Brenna reluctantly ushered the three women into her house.

She didn't know what they wanted with her, and she really, *really* didn't want to have to entertain them. Still, she refrained from suggesting that they go back to where they'd come from.

Etiquette drills aside, they were Luke's relatives.

Plus, they didn't look as if they would be any easier to evict than Luke himself, if determined to stay. Brenna suppressed a sigh.

"Would you like some tea?" she asked, silently mocking herself.

She had slipped effortlessly back into her people-pleasing ways. What next? Asking if they would like her to draw paper dolls of their children? How had Luke described her how-to-win-friends behavior during her schoolgirl years?

Ingratiating. And that description fit her right now, too—the ingratiating Brenna Morgan.

"We'd love some tea," Rosemary said, and they followed Brenna, single file, into the kitchen.

All three Minteer women exclaimed over everything they passed along the way—the carpeting, the pictures on the walls, the color of the walls. Even the overhead light fixture!

They marveled over her exquisite taste in everything.

Brenna had to smile. It appeared that she wasn't the only one who was being ingratiating this evening.

She prepared the tea while the three Minteers continued to enthuse over everything in her kitchen, as if Brenna were the most inventive, tasteful decorator since Martha Stewart. Which, of course, she was not.

It would've been comical, if she hadn't sensed the undercurrent of tension in the trio—which actually seemed more like a riptide than a current, Brenna concluded. What was really going on here?

She arranged the mugs of tea and the cream and sugar on a tray to carry to the table for them.

"How handy that you have a tray!" squealed Lisa with abject delight. "And the sugar bowl matches the little cream pitcher. You have such flair, Brenna!"

She had flair because she owned a tray and a matching sugar bowl and creamer? It was just too much. Brenna began to grow exceedingly alarmed. Something was *very* wrong, and she couldn't wait another second to find out.

She turned to Luke's mother with wide, questioning eyes. "Please tell me why you're here," she said bluntly, throwing ingratiation to the wind.

"Brenna, it's time to end the pretense." Rosemary met her gaze squarely. "We *all* know…your neighbors the Walshes, the entire Minteer family. We know you're carrying Luke's baby."

"Carrying Luke's baby?" Brenna echoed incredulously. "How did you come up with that?"

"Cassie *told* me that she probably wouldn't admit it," Lisa said knowingly. "Cassie said Brenna has kept her relationship with Luke so secret that she wasn't even aware the two of them knew each other, until they were both summoned for jury duty."

"But we didn't know each other till then," Brenna interjected.

Lisa and Anne Marie exchanged glances laden with disbelief.

"Brenna, there's no further need for this…charade," Anne Marie said with Luke-ish firmness. "Cassie told Lisa how you asked her questions about Luke your first day of jury duty—to carefully establish that you didn't know him. She said that looking back on that day now, she realized that you were nervous and clearly trying to hide something."

Brenna thought back to that day when she'd quizzed Cassie for information about Luke Minteer. She actually had been trying to hide something—her unexpected attraction to Luke. And that really had made her nervous!

But Cassie and the Minteers had drawn the wrong conclusions all the way down the line.

"You're putting one and one together and getting three!" Brenna protested.

"Exactly." Rosemary nodded vigorously. "There are three of you. The baby and you and that…that son of mine. Oh, Luke has disgraced the family before, but never, ever to this degree! This time, he's taken *everything* we believe in and hold sacred and he has—"

"Blown it off," supplied Anne Marie.

"Yes," agreed her mother. "I'm heartsick. For a son of mine to bully a defenseless young woman into silence after making her pregnant—because he doesn't want to get married—just sickens me."

"Luke has made his opinions on marriage very clear at every wedding." Lisa frowned. "He tried to talk John out of marrying me because he said John was too young to lock on the old ball and chain!"

Brenna could almost hear Luke saying it, his dark brows arched, his tone droll. "It does sound like one of his jokes," she murmured.

"No, he wasn't joking," insisted Anne Marie. "Luke tried to talk all of us into waiting to get married. He suggested waiting decades!"

Which only proved to Brenna that he really had been kidding—a suggestion to wait *decades* to wed was clearly a joke—but this time she declined to say so. The verdict was in, and the Minteer family jury had already pronounced Luke guilty of being anti-marriage.

"Though we don't like it, we've learned to live with Luke's smart-aleck attitude toward marriage and family," Rosemary continued darkly, "but for him to blithely disregard the welfare of his own child and its mother is completely unacceptable. Now that we know the truth, we won't passively stand by and let that happen."

Rosemary's voice rose with every word, and her face turned crimson. Brenna knew it wasn't physically possible for a person's head to explode, but if it were, at that particular moment, Rosemary Minteer's head would have detonated right there in her kitchen.

Yet all the furious disapproval was based on a false premise! Brenna hastened to set things straight.

"This isn't Luke's fault. Please don't be mad at him!" Brenna implored.

She thought of how he'd come back to his hometown in disgrace after his D.C. antics, determined to win back his family's favor, of how hard he'd worked to regain their acceptance, showing up at every family occasion, happy and sad, boring or fun.

Oh, he made jokes about it, but Brenna knew how much his family meant to Luke. To have him branded an outcast again, this time over something that was not even his fault, was too much to bear.

She couldn't let that happen to him!

"You have no reason to be mad at Luke," she added more forcefully.

"No reason?" Anne Marie gaped at her. "Brenna, as much as it pains me to say it, because he is my own brother, Luke is a snake! The way he's treated you is terrible! Carrying on a secret affair and carelessly getting you pregnant! Then not even acknowledging his own baby, telling you to pretend you don't even know him and letting you handle the—"

"You don't understand!" Brenna interrupted, feeling frantic. As much as she valued her privacy, she couldn't let this falsehood go unchecked.

"You have it all wrong! Luke isn't the father of my baby! I...I went to a sperm bank. In Philadelphia.

That's where I got pregnant. Luke had nothing to do with it.''

Though she hadn't wanted to broadcast her child's origins—and telling the Minteers something seemed akin to announcing it over the airwaves—Brenna felt relief when she admitted the truth. She couldn't let Luke's family ostracize him when he was completely innocent of their accusations.

Brenna leaned back in her chair and closed her eyes, feeling drained, yet filled with a sense of conviction. She knew she'd done the right thing by sparing Luke another bout of Minteer condemnation.

Total silence followed her announcement. When Brenna raised her head and looked around the table, she saw that the three women watching her didn't seem at all placated and relieved by the truth.

They looked more enraged than before!

"A sperm bank?" snapped Rosemary. "In Philadelphia? Oh, that sounds exactly like Luke Minteer, all right. Mr. Big Shot Storyteller himself!"

"I can almost hear him saying it," said Anne Marie, blue eyes flashing. "He'd go, 'Hey, Brenna, if anybody should find out, say you went to a sperm bank—in Philadelphia because it's too big and far away for anybody to try to check out facts.' He thinks we're dummies!"

"Luke believes he is so clever, but I can see right through him," added Rosemary, her voice, her face, taut with fury.

"How could Luke be so cruel?" Lisa was distressed.

"Luke isn't cruel!" cried Brenna. Impulsively she reached over and grasped Rosemary's wrist. "And you don't see him at all if you can't see that he is a kind and loving person who has been patient and understanding and—''

"Are you sure you're talking about *our* Luke?" Anne Marie looked nonplussed. "Luke Minteer? Because nobody has ever described him in those terms. And as his family, we know him best."

"As his family, you don't know him at all," Brenna countered fiercely. "Luke is incapable of making up a big lie to shirk responsibility for a child, especially if it were his own."

"Poor thing, Luke really has you snowed," Anne Marie said, not unkindly. "But if you—"

"This conversation is pointless." Brenna stood up. "I don't want to be ungracious, but I would appreciate it if you would all leave now."

She stalked out of the kitchen, an unmistakable cue for them to follow her to the door. It didn't matter how well-meaning they thought they were or how rude they thought she was, Brenna just wanted them gone.

It was quite a shock to find herself face-to-face with Luke in the hall. His winter jacket hung open, revealing a light-gray sweater and a pair of dark-gray cords.

Brenna came to an abrupt standstill. Her heart seemed to stand still, too.

"What are you—how did you—" she stammered.

"The door was unlocked so I let myself in." Luke reached out to touch her, but Brenna quickly stepped back, out of range. "After I'd talked to my brother Matt, I thought I ought to head over here, although it's a little early for our dinner date."

By now his mother, sister and sister-in-law had crowded into the small hallway with them.

"Looks like this particular triumvirate beat me here though," Luke added. His smile, his tone, were undeniably baiting.

Brenna gazed at the wicked gleam in his blue eyes,

at the way his teeth flashed white against his shadowed jaw, which had been clean shaven in the morning.

He'd once mentioned that if he were going to some special function in the evening, he had to shave twice a day. Brenna found the notion exotic—sexy and virile, too.

And when she realized the path her thoughts were taking—while three outraged Minteer women stood there looking at Luke as if he were a vampire they'd like to stake—she wondered if she was beginning a slow descent into madness.

One thing was certain. Though Brenna felt herself beginning to succumb, his relatives were plainly not charmed by his teasing or by that devilish grin. Cold-eyed and scowling, they did not stop glaring at him.

"How long have you been here, Luke?" Anne Marie demanded crossly.

"Long enough to hear the sperm bank story," admitted Luke. He closed the gap between him and Brenna, and this time when he reached over and laid his hand on her shoulder, she didn't move away.

"I told you they'd never buy it, honey. The sperm bank part alone stretched credibility—but placing it in *Philadelphia?*" He made the city sound as remote as an outpost in Siberia. "That boosted it into the realm of the preposterous, Minteerwise. Nah, I knew that tale wouldn't play in this town—and especially not in this family."

For the first time since she'd met them, Brenna saw doubt and bewilderment on the Minteer women's faces.

"Luke Minteer, if you knew about—" his mother said, then gave her head a shake and started over. "Why in the name of God would you—" She broke off again, this time focusing those intense blue eyes of hers on Brenna rather than Luke.

"Is he saying *he* didn't make up that…that sperm-bank-in-Philadelphia nonsense?" Rosemary directed her question to Brenna, as if she didn't trust Luke to answer honestly.

Brenna felt a flare of resentment on Luke's behalf, and momentarily forgot she was annoyed with him herself for his faux I-told-you-so. "Mr. Big Shot Storyteller himself," his mother had called him. And she was 100 percent wrong!

"Of course he didn't make it up. Luke wouldn't do that." A reluctant smile quirked the corners of Brenna's lips. "He'd rather rub the unpleasant truth in someone's face than make up some face-saving lie."

"One of the many reasons it was best that I exit the political world," Luke said dryly. "How well she knows me," he added, using his hand on her shoulder to draw Brenna even closer to him.

"But if Luke didn't make up that sperm bank story, then…then *you* were the one who did, Brenna?" Lisa gasped at the implication. "But why?"

"I didn't—" Brenna began.

"She didn't want to marry me," Luke cut in smoothly. "She still doesn't. Nor does she want my name on the baby's birth certificate. But I'm not giving up. Brenna is going to be Mrs. Luke Minteer, if not before the baby is born, then afterward. Count on it."

"No," cried Brenna, feeling tears burn in her eyes and chiding herself for them.

This sudden urge to cry at the drop of the clichéd hat had to stop. But just hearing Luke talk about marriage, something she'd never aspired to—because she felt it was out of reach for someone with her past?—made her want to weep.

"I won't take no for an answer, honey. You know us Minteers, Ma." Luke flashed a grin at his mother. "You didn't raise us to be quitters."

"Oh, Luke, we thought—we were sure—" Lisa was chagrined. "I'm so sorry. I'll call Cassie right away and set the record straight."

"Why don't you want to marry my brother?" Anne Marie demanded of Brenna at the same time Rosemary was asking her, "Why don't you want to marry my son?"

Brenna felt the way she had on that long-ago night in the hospital, when the nurse had given her a shot of something "to calm her nerves."

Everything seemed unreal. Voices floated around her, but nothing being said made much sense. Faces seemed to morph wildly from one expression into the next, and it was hard to interpret them quickly enough to keep up.

The strength of Luke's arm holding her tightly against his solid, warm body was real, though. He was her anchor in this sea of confusion; his smile and his warm blue eyes were like a touchstone.

She'd had no one to cling to on that drugged night in the hospital so long ago, but today she had someone. She had Luke Minteer—who claimed he was going to marry her?

"Mom, Anne Marie, don't badger Brenna, that's my job," Luke said dryly. "Anyway, it shouldn't be any mystery why she doesn't want to marry me. Why would any woman want to marry a snake like me? I'm a cruel, big shot storyteller, I'm the family disgrace. Hardly the man of your dreams, right, Brenna?"

An uncomfortable silence descended. There was regret written all over the faces of the three Minteer women.

Brenna glanced up at Luke, who was grinning broadly, clearly on the verge of laughing out loud. Obviously, he'd heard everything his relatives had said about him and was thoroughly enjoying using their own arguments against himself.

She contemplated this glimpse into Luke's relationship with his family. They took many things very seriously, and he was a natural-born teaser who couldn't pass up a chance to needle them. They loved each other, but the chemistry was wrong.

Sometimes that happened within families, the nuns had said in an attempt to explain messed-up familial relationships to the girls back at the Denver school. Though the girls couldn't choose their relatives, they could wisely choose partners who fit with them in all the right ways. A simple message, but the words had apparently struck a chord with Brenna, because they were playing in her head right now.

She thought of her own responses to Luke. When he teased or baited her, she needled him right back. Sometimes she mocked him first. Their senses of humor were in tune. The chemistry was right.

Luke met her eyes, and their gazes locked. Brenna felt herself being drawn into his sensual blue depths and was instantly flooded with memories of making love with him. How he'd felt inside her, smooth and hot and hard, filling her up...

Oh, yes, the chemistry between them was right in ways the good sisters had *never* mentioned. And now Luke was talking about marrying her—to spare her

from becoming Today's Big News on the gossip grape-
vine? He knew how she felt about that.

And though she loved him even more for his quixotic
gesture, she couldn't take him up on it.

Brenna pulled away from him and moved quickly
into the entrance foyer.

"Time to go." She opened the front door and held
it open, impervious to the cold air rushing in. "'Bye,
everybody. Thanks for dropping by."

Ten

"**S**he's kicking us out," Luke explained to his mother, Anne Marie and Lisa. All of them had followed Brenna into the foyer. "You three had better go, since you don't enjoy making unwelcome pests of yourselves. Since that's never bothered me, I'm staying."

"I have to ask Brenna one question before I leave." Anne Marie planted herself directly in front of Brenna. "You're obviously in love with my brother. You flew to his defense, you said he's kind and loving and patient and understanding. Believe me, you'd have to be *madly* in love with Luke to see him that way. And you're having his baby, so why won't you marry him?"

"Maybe it's the likes of us that are keeping her from marrying Luke," Rosemary said sorrowfully. "After all, there are so many Minteers and we're too nosy, too opinionated, too close—maybe too much of everything for this quiet little girl. Our reputation has scared her

off, and she doesn't want her or her baby to be Minteers. We've only ourselves to blame.''

"Oh, no, that's not true at all!'' exclaimed Brenna,
aghast that she'd hurt the older woman's feelings. ''It's
just the opposite, in fact. You wouldn't want *me* to be
a Minteer!''

"And why not?'' pressed Rosemary.

"You didn't approve of Luke's dirty tricks, and you
hated his book,'' Brenna said nervously. ''And if...if
you think he's a disgrace, well—''

"We don't condone bad behavior, and we don't like
reading about immoral criminals, that's true,'' his
mother agreed. ''But that has nothing to do with you,
dear.''

"Disgrace and bad behavior and criminals have everything to do with me. My mother is in prison for
murder,'' Brenna blurted out.

"Brenna, Brenna, Brenna.'' Luke pulled her away
from the door with one hand and pushed it shut with
the other.

She was shivering from the cold, and he wrapped his
arms around her swollen belly, and held her back
against him. ''I can't believe you fell for Ma's sad-eyed,
guilt-inducing routine. That hasn't worked on me since
I was about three years old.''

"Two,'' his mother corrected. ''And it's not a routine. I am sad that Brenna feels we would judge her,
based on her mother's actions. There's certainly been a
murderer or two among the Minteers.''

"There has?'' Anne Marie's ears perked. ''Who?
When?''

"Over in Ireland, before the grandparents came to
this country, and it's not up for discussion, miss,'' Rosemary replied so quickly that Brenna knew she was mak-

ing the whole thing up to put Brenna at ease. *There's a murderer in your family? No problem, we've got them, too. Doesn't everyone?*

Brenna gave Luke's mother a tremulous smile. Unconsciously she relaxed against Luke. His body surrounded her, warming her with his male heat.

He spread his fingers wide, and they spanned nearly the entire circumference of her belly. The baby began to turn and roll and kick, as if acknowledging Luke's presence.

He kneaded gently, and Brenna almost sighed with contentment. If there hadn't been witnesses, she knew she would have sighed. But the presence of the Minteer women was effectively inhibiting.

"Brenna would like to keep the whole matter about her mother private, Anne Marie," Luke told his sister sternly. "She doesn't want it blabbed all over town. That goes for you too, Lisa. Both of you, keep your mouths shut. I know you'll convince them to keep this confidential, Ma," he urged his mother.

"Of course. We respect Brenna's privacy and won't say a word," Rosemary promised.

"He makes us sound like horrid gossips and we're not!" complained Anne Marie, shooting her brother a baleful glance. "You can trust us, Brenna. We wouldn't dream of telling anybody anything."

"Except I am going to tell Cassie Walsh that Luke wants to marry Brenna," Lisa put in. "And that he's just waiting for her to set the date. It's not fair to brand Luke as a rat who won't accept responsibility when it's not true."

"My family's staunch support of me is touching," Luke smiled sardonically. "Now, the sooner the three of you are on your way, the sooner Brenna and I can

GET 2

HOW TO GET YOUR
2 FREE BOOKS AND FREE GIFT!

1. Peel off the MIRA® sticker on the front cover. Place it in the space provided at right. This automatically entitles you to receive two free books and an exciting surprise gift.

2. Send back this card and you'll get 2 "The Best of the Best™" books. These books have a combined cover price of $11.98 or more in the U.S. and $13.98 or more in Canada, but they are yours to keep absolutely FREE!

3. There's <u>no</u> catch. You're under <u>no</u> obligation to buy anything. We charge nothing – ZERO – for your first shipment. And you don't have to make any minimum number of purchases – not even one!

4. We call this line "The Best of the Best" because each month you'll receive the best books by some of today's most popular authors. These authors show up time and time again on all the major bestseller lists and their books sell out as soon as they hit the stores. You'll like the convenience of getting them delivered to your home at our special discount prices . . . and you'll love your *Heart to Heart* subscriber newsletter featuring author news, horoscopes, recipes, book reviews and much more!

SPECIAL FREE GIFT!
We'll send you a fabulous surprise gift, absolutely FREE, simply for accepting our no-risk offer!

5. We hope that after receiving your free books you'll want to remain a subscriber. But the choice is yours – to continue or cancel, anytime at all! So why not take us up on our invitation, with no risk of any kind. You'll be glad you did!

6. And remember...we'll send you a surprise gift ABSOLUTELY FREE just for giving THE BEST OF THE BEST a try.

Visit us online at
www.mirabooks.com

® and TM are registered trademark of Harlequin Enterprises Limited.

BOOKS FREE!

THE BEST OF THE BEST™ — Here's How it Works:

Accepting your 2 free books and gift places you under no obligation to buy anything. You may keep the books and gift and return the shipping statement marked "cancel." If you do not cancel, about a month later we will send you 4 additional books and bill you just $4.74 each in the U.S., or $5.24 each in Canada, plus 25¢ shipping & handling per book and applicable taxes if any.* That's the complete price and — compared to cover prices starting from $5.99 each in the U.S. and $6.99 each in Canada — it's quite a bargain! You may cancel at any time, but if you choose to continue, every month we'll send you 4 more books, which you may either purchase at the discount price or return to us and cancel your subscription.

*Terms and prices subject to change without notice. Sales tax applicable in N.Y. Canadian residents will be charged applicable provincial taxes and GST. Credit or Debit balances in a customer's account(s) may be offset by any other outstanding balance owed by or to the customer.

If offer card is missing write to: The Best of the Best, 3010 Walden Ave., P.O. Box 1867, Buffalo, NY 14240-1867

BUSINESS REPLY MAIL
FIRST-CLASS MAIL   PERMIT NO. 717-003   BUFFALO, NY

POSTAGE WILL BE PAID BY ADDRESSEE

THE BEST OF THE BEST
3010 WALDEN AVE
PO BOX 1867
BUFFALO NY 14240-9952

NO POSTAGE
NECESSARY
IF MAILED
IN THE
UNITED STATES

go out to eat. Baby X is starving in here.'' He rubbed her belly.

The trio trooped out to their car, and Brenna and Luke stood in the foyer, the door open, watching until the vehicle was out of sight.

Luke released Brenna from his hold. "I thought they'd never leave! Get your coat and we'll—"

"We can't just casually go out for dinner and act as if nothing's happened!" she exclaimed. "Your family thinks my baby is yours! They expect you to marry me!"

"And your point is?"

"Luke, we're not getting married."

"Sure we are, sweetheart. And my name is going to be on the baby's birth certificate on the line that says 'father.'"

"Luke, your family might've thought the sperm bank in Philadelphia story was far-fetched, but it's the truth," Brenna reminded him.

"It's also irrelevant, because I'm the only father the baby is going to know. I'll be a very good father, Brenna," he added seriously.

"I know you will, Luke. Someday, to your own child. But this is my child, and I can't stay here and have your family try to pressure you into marrying me and then condemn you when it doesn't happen. I—I'm moving back to Denver. I have to."

"Listen to yourself, Brenna," Luke said sharply. "Planning to run away. Dragging your child off to somewhere else because suddenly things aren't going exactly the way you wanted. Doesn't that strike you as a familiar pattern? One you promised yourself never to follow?"

"Luke, that's not fair. This situation is nothing like—"

"Here's something else to think about, Brenna. If a man wanted to stick around and try to work things out, your mother took off because she felt trapped. Is that how you feel now, Brenna? Trapped?"

Brenna swallowed hard. She felt weak and weepy and tried to work up some indignant wrath to bolster herself. "You're badgering me," she said huskily, failing to stir up either indignation and wrath.

"Of course I am." Luke laughed softly. "Didn't you hear me tell Ma and Annie that was my job?"

"You really are incorrigible." Brenna grimaced. "And you've been this way since the age of two? Your poor mother!"

"I was a hellion, all right. The family is convinced that I still am. But that's not how you see me, is it, Brenna?" Luke's voice lowered. "I was standing in the hall when I heard you defend me. I heard everything you said about me, calling me kind and loving and patient and understanding. Saying that I would never shirk responsibility for a child. You told my family they didn't know me but you did, and the person you described—"

"I described you, Luke," Brenna assured him.

"Anne Marie is right. You must be madly in love with me if you see me like that. Are you going to admit it or play it cool, Brenna?"

Brenna heaved a resigned sigh. "Oh, what's the point in trying to play it cool? I've never been cool. Yes, Luke, I love you. You know perfectly well that I do."

A wide smile crossed Luke's face, and he swiftly yanked her into his arms. "So why are you giving me such a hard time? Spouting this nonsense about going back to Denver, about not marrying me.''

"Until a very short while ago, you'd never even mentioned marrying me,'' Brenna pointed out. "You didn't ask me to marry you, and I certainly didn't expect you to. After all, you don't love me and—''

"Oh, what's the point in trying to play it cool? Though I've always been cool, there are times when I don't need to be. I love you, Brenna,'' Luke paraphrased her own declaration, his blue eyes warm with humor. "And after I got that call from Saraceni, I decided to speed things along even more, so I called my cousin Patrick and told him to tell his mother that I had a pregnant girlfriend. Aunt Eileen and my mom were best friends before they were sisters-in-law, so I knew how fast that news would fly.''

"Speed things along when everything has been moving at the sound of light, anyway?' Brenna smiled as tears slowly trickled down her cheeks.

"And if you didn't know it before, I want you to be sure of it now, my love,'' he murmured, his lips brushing her forehead. "I want to be the man I am in your eyes. I want to be the father to our baby. This one,'' he patted her stomach, "and whoever comes next. Say yes, Brenna. Say you'll marry me.''

She was laughing and crying at the same time. "I'm an emotional basket case right now,'' she warned him.

"All the better to take full advantage of you, my sweet.'' Luke swept her up in his arms.

She clung to him, holding on tight. "You sound like the Big Bad Wolf in a fractured fairy tale.''

"And didn't Big Bad and Little Red end up in somebody's bedroom?'' Luke fractured the fairy tale even more.

They made it the whole way to Brenna's bedroom before Brenna told him, Yes, she would marry him.

"I wasn't going to go back to Denver," she admitted. "Not really."

"I know. You were panicking but I had to let you know how serious I am about you. I knew it wasn't the time to toss off a glib, 'Denver? Cool! I'll help you pack.'"

"You know me so well," she borrowed his words, and they both laughed.

Very quickly the laughter turned into kissing. Deep, lingering kisses accompanied by caresses that grew more intimate as they took turns removing every item of clothing from each other.

Their passion was burning hot, their actions tender and desultory, and before long they were both naked.

Together they lay back on the bed.

"I love you, Brenna," Luke murmured huskily, kissing her swollen belly. He smoothed his cheek over it, feeling the movements of the baby within. His baby. "I love both of you."

"I love you, Luke," she heard herself say, and the words evoked an emotional power that emboldened her.

His tongue explored her navel, and she combed her fingers through his hair, feeling the springy thick texture, tracing his scalp.

His lips closed over her right nipple, and he suckled gently, erotically.

Brenna gasped.

"Did I hurt you?" he asked, raising his head, instantly solicitous.

"No." She somehow remembered to breathe. "I just saw fireworks in my head again." Her body was humming, her mind floating.

"Now let's try for a Zambelli International Finale,"
kidded Luke, pulling her over him.

He cupped her, positioning her to receive him, and
her moan of anticipation urged him to slide in farther.

He moved and she rocked back and forth, tentatively
at first, then with more confidence and power, matching
her rhythm to his.

His pace became hot and feral, and she kept right up
with him, her head tilted back, her eyes closed in ecstasy. His hands were everywhere, on her belly and her
breasts, her thighs, between them.

Brenna was overwhelmed with sensation. He was so
deep. Deeper and deeper. She lost the rhythm she'd
been carefully keeping and abandoned herself to the ex-
hilaration of Luke moving within her. White-hot pleasure rocketed through her, sending her soaring.

She could feel the climax building, her body tensing.

"Let go," Luke rasped. "Let it happen. I've got you,
sweetheart, you're safe with me."

And she knew she was and always would be. She let
go and went tumbling into a glittering, perfect, oblivion.
Luke was with her all the way.

They sent out for pizza around ten o'clock, a late
dinner but the happiest, most romantic one either had
ever had.

Later Luke called his parents.

"Good news, Ma," he said exuberantly. "We're engaged. Sure, I'll tell her. But, here, why don't you tell
her yourself?" He handed the receiver to Brenna.

She clutched it, a little nervously. After all, she'd
pretty much kicked her future mother-in-law out of her
house only hours before. "Hi, Mrs. Minteer."

"Call me Rosemary and welcome to the family,

Brenna, darling. You're perfect for our Luke. It's as if you were special-ordered for him.''

''Now that you mention it, I was, kind of. And he was for me, too.'' Brenna's eyes sparkled. ''By the Cambria County Jury Commissioners.''

Epilogue

It snowed on Christmas Eve, just a light coating of white on the ground to make it the traditional, nostalgic white Christmas of movie and song. Brenna and Luke saw the snowfall because they were up twice that night. Little Jack Morgan Minteer demanded milk every four to five hours around the clock.

After his 4:00 a.m. feeding, baby Jack decided not to go back to sleep and remained wakeful in his parents' bed, gazing at their faces with his big, serious dark eyes. The infant clutched his father's big finger tightly.

"Hey, little guy, Santa Claus doesn't come until the kids are sleeping, you know," Luke said softly.

Jack seemed unconcerned. There was a pile of wrapped presents under the Christmas tree, many with his name on them. Who needed Santa Claus?

"He's growing so fast." Brenna sighed with wistful, maternal pride as she stared down at her son. "Look how well he fits into this little red suit that was too big for him only two weeks ago.''

"Good thing he's got a closetful of sharp new clothes to grow into." Luke leaned down to smooth a lock of hair from Brenna's cheek. "He's so beautiful, Brenna. Everybody says he's the most beautiful baby they've ever seen, and they aren't just saying it to be polite—they really mean it!"

Brenna smiled. "All babies are beautiful to their family, Luke."

"Yeah, yeah, but Jack is extra special. He looks just like you, Brenna. The dark eyes, the hair, even the shape of his little ears. They're yours. Are you sure you didn't have yourself cloned in Philadelphia?"

She chuckled and snuggled back against him. "Your mom and grandma told me Jack is the spitting image of you when you were a baby. Except your eyes were blue, of course. They plan to dig up the old photos to prove it."

Brenna and Luke exchanged amused glances.

He kissed her gently, his arms encircling her and the baby. "Jack's mine, Bren. I couldn't love him more if I'd been there the day he was conceived."

"I know. And you were the one to give him his name. Jack Morgan. You said I should call him after my father. I hadn't considered it till then. After I lost him, it hurt so much to think of my dad, I wouldn't let myself."

But building her new life and a family with Luke had allowed her to access those good memories from so long ago. To honor the late Jack Morgan with a namesake.

Luke himself had filled in the baby's birth certificate.

Child's Name: Jack Morgan Minteer. Father: Luke Minteer. Mother: Brenna Morgan Minteer.

They were a family, now and forever.

*   *   *   *   *

Dear Reader,

There was a time, not so long ago, when it was said that weddings were going the way of the dodo. Who needed them? Equality of the sexes made marriage a matter of choice few women would make.

Wrong again! Marriage is back, and so are the weddings that sign, seal and deliver on those promises made in the moonlight.

I'm always fascinated by the many different ways couples come to the realization that getting married is their destiny. *Wife by Contract* involves a mail-order bride in Alaska who winds up with a man who never ordered her or her two little children. But destiny calls, and though Joe Camden resists, Chynna Sinclair is a determined woman. One way or another, her babies are going to have a safe home. No one is more shocked than Joe to realize that he's started to care about that just as much as she does.

Another wedding in the offing, another marriage in the wings. Ah, romance! What could be better?

Hope you enjoy this one!

Raye Morgan

WIFE BY CONTRACT
Raye Morgan

One

Joe Camden hadn't expected to get a lump in his throat. Sentimental emotions weren't usually his style. But something happened when he got out of his car and looked down at the old ramshackle house.

Home. That was what it was, even though he'd been gone for fifteen years, even though he'd run as fast and as far away as he could when he'd had the chance.

"Ah, you'll miss it," Annie Andrews had said, shaking her gray head and laughing at him the day he took off. He'd stopped by to get supplies for his hitchhiking odyssey in her tiny combination post office and general store. "Alaska will call you back."

"Not me," he'd said, sure enough of that to grin at her. "It's bright lights and big cities for me from now on."

"And girls," she added for him, laughing again.

"It's true, we don't have enough girls here for you young men. It's no wonder you all run off."

His wide mouth twisted in a half smile as he remembered that day and thought of all the things that he'd been through since. Now he was back, and Annie was half-right. The Alaska grandeur, the white peaks, the forest green meadows, the water tumbling through the gorges still had the power to stir him. But it really wasn't home any longer. He belonged in L.A.

Still, everything was the same as ever. It hardly looked as though anything had changed since he'd left. The old house where his brother, Greg, still lived looked as beat-up as ever. Evidence suggested Greg was as allergic to responsibility as their father had been—but then, Joe hadn't expected anything else. In fact, that was why he'd come back.

A rustling caught his ear, and he glanced toward the nearby trees. He caught a glimpse of what looked like brown fur in the underbrush, and the past came tumbling back to him even more strongly.

"Champ," he murmured, remembering his childhood pet, the energetic brown dog who would hide in the bushes and then jump out at him, licking his face and wriggling in his arms. Without thinking, without wanting to remember that Champ had died when he was eighteen, he went toward the brush and stuck his hand into the leaves where he'd seen the movement, as though he could find that puppy just as he had so often so many years ago, as though he thought he might be able to reach back into yesterday and pull the dog up by the scruff of the neck.

"Champ?"

Champ didn't answer, but something with teeth bit

down on his hand, and he yanked it back, swearing. "Ouch. What the hell...?"

A small boy emerged from the underbrush, running as fast as his chubby little legs could take him, his brown hair bouncing on his head as he ran straight for the house.

"Hey," Joe called after him, but the little boy didn't turn. He ran on, stumbling but not giving up, as though the devil himself were after him, aiming to snatch him up and carry him off. Joe realized, with a twinge of regret, that to this kid, he probably was the devil.

"Hey, I won't hurt you," he called after him half-heartedly, frowning as he looked down at the unmistakable imprint of teeth on his hand. He'd seen them often enough before, when he and his brother, Greg, were young and he would pin Greg down and Greg would fight back any way he could.

He shook his head as though to clear it. Too many things were echoing the past, and he was beginning to feel a little weird about it. There was no Champ, and this kid wasn't Greg. But what was he doing at Greg's house?

He started down the hill after him. Before he'd gone more than a few feet, a woman appeared, coming out through the front door to stand on the porch. The sight of her surprised Joe, pulling him up short.

She raised her hand to shade her eyes against the slice of noonday sun that hit her face. "Rusty?" she called out to the boy as he raced toward her. Then she looked up and saw Joe, and she seemed to freeze, just as he had done.

He stared. He'd never seen anything like her in Alaska before. Out here, conditions were rough and the women dressed appropriately. This woman wore a

white wool suit with heels and stockings. Her silvery
blond hair shimmered around her face in a chic, professional style, catching the sunbeams, setting off a
glow, so that she seemed to be standing in a shaft of
golden light.

He shook his head slowly, drawn even more out of
sync with this situation. It just didn't fit his experience
of Alaska, didn't fit with his past, didn't fit with what
he knew of his brother's present. He felt unbalanced.
Who in the world was this woman, and what was she
doing in his brother's house?

Chynna Sinclair saw the man coming down from the
rise, saw the car in the background, and her mouth went
dry.

"Oh, darn it," she whispered softly to herself. He'd
already seen Rusty. There was going to be no way to
hide the boy now, even for the first few minutes while
they got acquainted.

Rusty reached her and threw himself against her,
wrapping his little arms around her knees and burying
his face against her skirt. She looked down at him and
tousled his hair lovingly.

Oh, well. Maybe it was best that they get the worst
over with right from the beginning. She looked out at
the man again. Why was he just standing there, staring
at her?

"Come on into the house," she told her son, gently
untangling his arms from her legs. "Come stay with
Kim while I talk to the man."

Maybe if she got the kids quieted down and playing
with something, she would have time to talk to him and
prepare him....

But whom was she kidding? There was no more time

to hide, to make up stories. She'd been putting if off all during the plane ride from Chicago, all during the flight from Anchorage in the little six-seater plane; even in the ride from the landing strip, when the pilot had kindly borrowed a car to get them here, she'd told herself it was time to make a decision on what she was going to say when she saw him. But now it was too late. He'd already seen Rusty. He already knew that the mail-order bride he'd ordered, the pretty young woman he expected, had brought along some baggage she hadn't warned him about.

Hurrying her son inside, she settled him and his little sister with coloring books in the living room and went back out on the porch. He was still standing there, staring at the house. She hesitated, thinking she should walk out to greet this large male she hoped would be her husband soon, but knowing her heels would sink in the mud if she tried it. She knew she wasn't dressed for the area, but she'd done it on purpose. This was a selling job she was going to have to do here, and image, as her boss used to tell her in Chicago, was everything. She waited instead, fingers curling around the post at the top of the stairs, her heart beating like a wild thing in her chest.

What if he didn't want her? What if he didn't want her kids? She had to convince him. There was no choice in the matter.

She still didn't know what she was going to say. This was so hard to explain on the spur of the moment. It was the sort of thing it would be better for him to learn about gradually, as he got to know her, as he got to know the kids. As he got to know them, he would understand. But how could he possibly understand when it was dropped in his lap in one large lump like this?

Taking a deep breath, she forced a smile. "Hi, there," she called to him. "I guess you missed us at the landing strip. The pilot drove us over."

As though she'd flicked a switch and brought him back to life, he started walking slowly toward her.

She wet her lips and smiled a welcome. "I hope you don't mind. Your house wasn't locked and I...I went on in."

He was closer now and she could see his face, and something inside her relaxed. She hadn't allowed herself to believe in the picture he'd sent her. It showed a man so handsome, she'd told herself to assume it was taken ten years ago, or was a phony in some other way.

But no. The picture hadn't lied. This was the same man, all right. In fact, with his broad shoulders and dark hair and glittering blue eyes, he looked even better than he had in the photograph. He wore crisp jeans and a leather bomber jacket, and neither was old or dirty. They looked, in fact, startlingly fashionable for this neighborhood.

She'd had a picture in her mind of what she would find here, and this wasn't really it. She'd imagined a farmer-hunter type, rough-hewn and bashful. This man was none of those things. This man looked a little too good to be real.

He'd reached the porch and was coming up the stairs, his face drawn into a frown as he looked her over, as though she puzzled him, or annoyed him, or something. She stepped forward quickly.

"Hi," she said, holding out her hand and bringing back her quick smile. "I'm Chynna Sinclair, and I'm very glad to be here."

He took her hand and seemed to marvel at it. Then he looked into her face and shook his head. "What's going on here?'' he asked her, searching her eyes for answers. "Where's Greg?"

But his last question was drowned out by a shriek from inside the house and then by the sound of something breaking. Chynna whirled, glanced at him quickly and muttered, "Uh...I'd better see what happened" before running in to tend to her children.

Joe followed her, then stopped just inside the entryway, turning slowly to take it all in. The house was just the same as it had been before he'd left. Greg hadn't changed a thing.

He could hear Chynna settling some sort of argument that was going on in the next room, but he didn't pay any attention. He was looking at the picture of his grandfather that still hung on the wall, his flinty pioneer eyes still staring at his grandson with the same old sense of disapproval; at the snow shovel propped in the corner, the one that always gave him splinters that lasted longer in his skin than the snow lasted on the ground; at the tall, elegant breakfront where his mother had kept her precious dishes and porcelain figurines. Only a few were left, the ones she didn't care about. He supposed she'd taken all the rest when she moved to Anchorage, five years before. Nothing had changed.

Nothing—except Joe himself.

The woman who called herself Chynna Sinclair came back into the entryway, and he looked up, blinking, wondering how she managed to seem to carry the sunlight with her. She was certainly a pretty thing, but she looked so out of place here in the Alaskan wilderness. He supposed she must be Greg's girlfriend, though he could hardly imagine where Greg could have met her. Greg wouldn't go near the city, and this was city bred, all the way. But then, what did he really know about his brother these days? If only Greg were here, these things could be cleared up right away.

"I...I have to introduce you to my children," she said, stuttering slightly, and he looked into her eyes with surprise. Why was she so nervous? "This is Rusty. He's five. And Kim is three."

He looked down at the two sets of eyes, both open very wide, looking as though awe had struck them silly, and he smiled and nodded. "Hi, kids," he said casually, his mind still on the woman.

"Children," she told them, "this is Mr. Greg Camden. I...I think you should call him Mr. Camden for now."

Joe's gaze shot up to meet hers. She thought he was Greg? This was crazy. "No, wait a minute...."

She grabbed hold of his arm, stopping him from speaking, and said to her children, "You go on back and color for a few minutes. I have to talk to Mr. Camden."

She was trembling. He could feel it but he had no idea why she would be so emotional about this. Still, her fingers dug into his arm as the children filed out, and he waited, since that was what she seemed to want.

He gazed down into her soft hair, catching a hint of the scent of roses. She seemed small, slender, and for a moment he was reminded of the time he'd found a young silver fox caught in a rusty trap in the pine forest. It had trembled, too, as he'd used one hand to quiet it while working it free with the other. That had been a fool thing to do. He'd known the whole time that the fox could turn at any moment and lash out at him, hurt him badly. But it had been something he'd had to do. The fox had struggled at first, but then it had lain still, and once free, it had streaked off into the woods. Joe had never seen it again.

Her children had finally straggled out of the room, and her head turned. Her dark eyes met his, but there was nothing wary in them, nothing fearful. They were huge and soft and warm, but there was a challenging look to them that caught him by surprise and made him wonder if he'd only imagined that she was nervous. Maybe she'd been shivering from the cool air.

"Okay," she said crisply. "We can talk."

"Listen," he began, anxious to get this identity thing cleared up.

But she shook her head, still clinging to his arm, looking up into his face and talking very fast. "No, you listen. I know this isn't fair. I know I should have told you. But…but this is the way it is and the way it has to be. If you don't want us, I'll understand. But you have to give us a chance. You can't just turn us away without giving us a chance."

He stared at her, completely at sea. He had no idea what she was talking about.

"I didn't tell you about Rusty and Kim," she went on earnestly, "and that was wrong. But I wanted you to see them before you made up your mind. I wanted you to get to know them. They're good kids—they really are. They'll grow on you—you'll see."

A shriek from the other room made her wince, but she forced a smile, despite the fact that Joe was shaking his head.

"Listen, kids are not my thing—" he began.

"I know," she broke in, throwing out one arm as though that were the most natural reaction in the world. "Of course not. Living out here in Alaska, you probably hardly see kids. So you don't really know, do you?"

He made a face and shrugged. This conversation was crazy, but she looked so cute trying to convince him, he wasn't sure he wanted it to end. "I was a kid once," he reminded her.

Her eyes brightened. "Kids have improved since then," she told him artfully. "You'll see."

He grinned, appreciating her spirit though he knew better than to believe her. "You know what?" he said. "There's no use trying to convince me. Because I'm not Greg."

Her eyes widened, and she stared at him for a long, long moment. Then a look of skepticism crept over her face.

"Oh, I see," she said, her eyes turning as chilly as her tone. "You're going to try to get out of this that way, are you?"

"No," he said, half laughing. He ran a hand through his dark hair and gazed down at her, perplexed. "Look, it's true. I'm not Greg. And I'm not even sure why you're here."

"I'm here to marry you. Remember?"

"Marry…?" Words failed him, and he lost his breath. All he could do was stand there, staring down at her. The word had hit him like a flash of lightning, shutting off all thought processes as the shock skittered through his body.

"Yes, marry." She tried to smile, but his reaction had thrown her off her game. "That was the plan."

He shook his head, struggling to put his feelings into words. "Oh, no, I can't believe that. Marriage…" He thought of his brother and his isolated ways and shook his head again. "No, that can't be."

Her eyes narrowed, and her pretty mouth set. Turning, she whipped an envelope out of her purse and handed it to him. "Then what is this?" she demanded.

The envelope was slit open at the top. A letter was tucked inside, along with a photograph. The letter was from his brother. The photograph was of Joe.

"A deal is a deal, mister," she told him firmly as he unfolded the letter and glanced at it. "You contracted for a bride. You looked through an extensive catalog and you chose me. And here I am."

Words still stuck in his throat. He looked at her. He looked at the picture. He looked back at her. And nothing came out of his mouth. If he took her at her word, if he took what she was saying literally—well, then she had to be a mail-order bride. He swore softly, shaking his head. What had he done, stepped back in time? People didn't do things like this anymore. Did they?

Grasping at straws, he waved the envelope at her. "This is a joke, right?"

She stared at him for a moment, then tossed her head and turned into the kitchen, taking off her suit jacket as she went. "Is there an apron in here somewhere?" she asked, then grabbed a large tea towel and tied it around her waist without waiting for an answer.

"What are you doing?" he asked, following her, still clutching the envelope, still feeling very much at sea.

She looked up at him with cool defiance. "I'm going to make you something to eat. I'm going to cook."

He frowned. "You don't need to cook for me."

"Why not? Aren't you hungry?"

He hesitated. It had been a long time since he'd eaten breakfast. "Well, yes, but…"

"Then I will cook for you," she said, opening the refrigerator and staring inside. "Consider it a form of audition for the job."

He couldn't hold back a grin. "This is crazy," he said, shaking his head.

She nodded, pulling eggs and bacon out and placing them on the counter. "I think so, too," she said coolly. "But you seem to need to be convinced."

He slumped back against the counter, watching her, pushing back the erotic fantasies that threatened to break into his thoughts. He had an urge to pinch himself. Could he be dreaming? Talk about dreams come true—here was this woman, offering herself up to...

No, he wouldn't think about it. That would only end up getting him into big trouble—trouble he didn't need.

"I don't mean to ridicule you, you know," he told her softly. "But I just can't believe that a woman like you has to resort to something like...like mail order...to get a man." He grimaced. "It just doesn't compute."

She spun and confronted him. "Look. You picked me out of the catalog. You must have liked something about me. You wrote me that nice letter and sent me your picture. You signed a contract with the agency." She searched his blue eyes, looking for answers. "You sent money for my plane fare. What did you think? That this was all a game? That I would never actually show up?"

He started shaking his head before she was finished and kept shaking it. "That was my brother Greg who did all that," he tried to explain once again. "My name is Joe. It wasn't me."

She grabbed his hand and looked up into his face, her eyes huge with determined entreaty. "Give me a chance," she said softly. "Please. I'll be a good wife. And my kids..." She shook her head, and for a moment he was afraid her eyes would fill with tears. "They're good kids. You just wait. They won't be any trouble at all. You're going to love them."

Loving kids had never been one of his goals, but he had to admit he was beginning to feel a definite temptation in other directions. He liked her big brown eyes and the way her breasts filled out the pale pink silk shell she wore and the way her lower lip seemed to pout when she was annoyed with him. His mind began to wander for just a moment, mulling over what it would be like to order up a woman like this from a catalog and have her appear on the doorstep, ready to be a wife. It was a caveman dream, but he kind of liked it.

But before he had time to indulge in it for more than a few seconds, a cry came from the living room, and suddenly a huge crash shook the house.

"Yeah, those adorable kids," he muttered to himself as she jerked away, spun and started for the living room. "I just can't get enough of how cute they are."

But he started after her. Until Greg showed up, he guessed it was his job to act as a sort of surrogate husband here. Though before he made any commitments, maybe he ought to think over just exactly what that was going to entail.

His gaze fell on the letter she'd left lying on the table, and he stopped, hesitating. It wasn't nice to read other people's mail. But what the hell. He had a situation here. Reaching out, he took hold of the letter by the corner, as though he wasn't sure it wasn't contagious, and carried it over to where the light from the window was the brightest. Gingerly, he unfolded it and began to read.

It was the letter Greg had written to Chynna, but it didn't sound like his brother at all. The handwriting was Greg's. So was the signature at the bottom of the page.

But the thoughts he'd written down sounded like someone else's entirely. There were references to loneliness and love of the land, and those he could readily identify with his brother. But there was also talk of soul mates and walking hand in hand through life together, which made Joe want to laugh out loud.

What did he do, copy these romantic phrases from a book? he wondered to himself as he looked them over. The closest thing to a soul mate he could think of for Gregg might be a rabid wolverine.

He frowned, shaking his head. He and Greg had never been close. In some ways, they were the typical Cain and Abel siblings. Whenever Joe said black, Greg claimed white. When Joe wanted peace, Greg turned his radio on high screech. When Greg came home late, like as not, Joe would have locked the door. When Greg spoke, Joe tended to answer him sarcastically, and when Joe laughed, Greg found a way to turn the mood surly.

Now that Joe had been away all these years, he sometimes regretted the way they couldn't get along. He'd even decided, a few years back, that the rift between them was childish and should be over now that they were men, so he'd come home. But nothing had changed. If anything, Greg had grown moodier and more aloof. The planned-for reconciliation hadn't panned out.

And now this recluse, this mountain man was figuring to take himself a wife, was he? The situation made no sense at all. And yet it was obvious Chynna was right when she claimed to be here because Greg had…good Lord! Ordered her from a catalog?

His brother, Greg, was preparing to take himself this lovely woman as a wife.

"Over my dead body," Joe muttered aloud, thinking

of Chynna and her wide, hopeful gaze. "It can't hap-pen. I'd better get her out of here as soon as possible."

Unfortunately, that was going to be more difficult than it might seem. Unless there had been a radical and unexpected change, the only way out by air would be on the mail plane, and who knew what the schedule was these days. There was probably no other way out except by truck or car, and he couldn't leave. He had to find Greg.

He might as well resign himself to the fact that she was going to be staying overnight at least.

But then she would have to go. It would be much too dangerous to let her stay.

Two

This wasn't working out the way she'd planned it.

Chynna picked up the small table and vase, which luckily was made of some sort of sturdy ceramic that didn't break easily. After a nervous glance at the gold-fish bowl on the hutch at the window, which luckily hadn't been touched, she scolded her children for their behavior, her nervousness making her words a little sharper than they might usually have been. Kim looked up at her warily and popped a thumb in her mouth. Rusty's lower lip began to quiver. Chynna noted that fact, hesitated, then sighed regretfully and drew him to her.

Her kids were usually so good. She'd been so sure they would charm this man she'd come to marry, make him happy to have them as a family. Instead, things were slipping out of control.

"What is it, Rusty?" she asked, her instincts telling

her that something other than the overturned table was
bothering him. As she looked down into his earnest
face, it seemed to crumple beneath her gaze, and he
threw himself against her.

"I bit the man," Rusty told her, sobbing quietly into
her shoulder. "I bit him."

She frowned, holding him close and trying to under-
stand what it was he was saying. "What man? Greg
Camden?" He nodded, his face pressed into the hollow.
"You bit him? You mean with teeth?"

Rusty drew back so that she could see him, made a
face, then clamped his teeth together with a snap. "Like
that," he said, nodding tearfully. "I'm sorry, Mommy.
I d-d-didn't mean to."

Chynna recalled the sight of her son racing down the
hill and Greg coming behind him and she winced. "Did
he do anything to you?" she asked anxiously, studying
his dirt-streaked face.

"I was hiding," he said, gulping back a sob. Huge
drops of water stood in his eyes. "I thought he was
going to grab me. So I did this." He snapped his jaws
together again, his eyes brightening. Obviously, he was
beginning to enjoy the reenactments. "I did it hard,"
he said with just a hint of satisfaction. "He yelled."

"Oh, Rusty," she cried in horror, pulling him to her
chest and rocking him. "I wish you hadn't done that."

"I was protecting myself from a stranger," he reminded her, echoing lessons she'd taught him, his child-
like voice carefully enunciating the grown-up words.

Her son had bitten the man she was planning to
marry. She closed her eyes. Had she thought things
were slipping out of control? *Galloping* was more like
it. She caught her breath and straightened her shoulders.

There had to be a way to salvage the situation, but it had better be done quickly.

"Come on," she told Rusty, swinging him down to his feet. "Let's go into the other room. You have to apologize."

He hung back, dread filling his shining eyes. "Do I have ta?"

"Yes, you have ta. Come on. And make it sincere."

He slunk along beside her, trying to hide behind her skirt as they made their way into the living room, where the man he'd bitten was waiting.

Joe was still pondering the letter, his blue eyes frowning, but his expression changed as he looked up to see Chynna and Rusty coming toward him. His gaze narrowed appreciatively as he watched her neat form walking briskly through the room. No, it still didn't make sense. If you really could get something like this from a catalog, the mail would be swamped with orders. How did his brother get so lucky?

She stopped before him, tugging on her son's arm to pull him out from behind her. "Rusty tells me he bit you," she said, going right to the point. "He wants to apologize."

"Oh, yeah." He'd forgotten about that. He held out his hand and looked at it. The bite marks were still quite distinct, though the skin hadn't broken. Shrugging, he smiled at the freckle-faced boy. "This is nothing. Baby bites. You want to see where my brother bit me when he was about ten?" He pushed back his sleeve and revealed a long, jagged scar on his bicep. "Now, that's what I call a bite," he said rather proudly. "It tore flesh open. The traveling nurse had to be flown in to give me stitches."

Rusty stared at him with wide eyes, but if Joe had

been harboring any thoughts of bringing the boy closer with his old war stories, he realized he wasn't going to win over the kid this way. Instead of laughing or looking impressed, Rusty looked terrified.

Joe looked into those pained eyes and shrugged. What the hell, he was no good with kids. Never had been. And there was hardly any point in getting close to a boy he was never going to see again after...

Now, that was just the point, he thought as he rolled his sleeve back down. After what? How long was he staying and how close a relationship were they going to be forced into? He glanced into Chynna's lovely face. It didn't tell him a thing.

"We need to talk," he said evenly.

She nodded. "Of course," she said crisply. "But I need to feed my children. They haven't had anything since midmorning. I'll fix something for all of us and put them down for a nap, and then we can go over the ground rules."

His mouth relaxed into a lopsided grin. Her phrasing struck him as amusing. "The ground rules?" he repeated. "I only want a discussion, not a sparring session."

She tossed her head back and gave him a cocky smile that didn't quite warm her eyes. "You may just get both," she told him as she turned away. "Be prepared."

He gave her a Boy Scout salute, but she didn't see it. She was already halfway out of the room, Rusty clinging to her and glancing back as though afraid Joe might be following them.

Watching him, seeing the apprehension in his eyes, Joe winced, thinking of how the boy would deal with Greg. His brother wasn't known for compassion or tact. In fact, he'd always considered him a sort of goofy recluse, sort of a mountain man with no need for real human companionship. To think of him ordering up a woman came as something of a shock. And knowing his brother, to have the woman show up with two kids in tow would not go over awfully well. She would be lucky to get out of here before Greg got back.

But where was Greg, anyway? Why wasn't he here to greet his bride-to-be?

Joe turned and gave the room another quick examination. The place was surprisingly clean, though there was clutter here and there. He'd noticed dishes in the sink, but the food hadn't been on them long. Two long strides brought him to the storage-room closet, and opening it, he discovered that his brother had taken camping gear and cooking equipment. If he'd left that morning, it looked as if he wouldn't be back for a few days.

Joe swore softly and shook his head. "In the meantime, what am I supposed to do with your girlfriend, you idiot?" he murmured.

But there was no reply that made any sense at all.

He heard Chynna's steps and turned to meet her as she came through the doorway into the hall.

"We're almost ready," she told him, looking cool and efficient. "I'd like to put them down for naps right after they eat. Which bedroom may I use?"

"Bedroom?" She was obviously planning to stay, and he was going to have to decide what he was prepared to do to get her back on a plane to wherever it was she'd said she came from. "Uh...let me take a look."

There were three bedrooms in the house. The large one his parents had used still held a four-poster double bed. Next to it was what his mother had always called the green room, a place set up specifically for guests, with the best bed and nicest furniture. He assumed the bedroom at the end of the hall, which he'd shared with Greg, was still set up with twin beds.

He looked into the master bedroom and gestured toward the old-fashioned bed. "They could sleep here," he said.

She looked around him and nodded. "That would be fine," she said quietly. "Now, where do I sleep?"

He opened his mouth to say something, then closed it again. Looking down, he met her gaze, and something in the spark he saw in her eyes set him back on his heels. After all, she thought he was Greg. She thought they were more or less engaged. Funny. He'd never been this close to matrimony before. It felt spooky, and he wasn't real clear on just what she expected of him.

There was only one way to find out. He would have to be blunt. "You're not thinking about doing any sleeping together or anything like that, are you?" he asked, trying for a light, humorous tone, but ending up glancing at her suspiciously.

She grinned at him, and in that moment, he knew he'd fallen in a trap and he'd been sucker punched. "Of course not," she said primly. "Not until we're married." She turned and led the way down the hall. "How about this room?" she asked, nudging open the door to the middle bedroom. "Who sleeps in here?"

"I guess you will," he told her grudgingly. "At least for tonight. You might as well bring your things in."

"Great." She smiled at him. "I'll unpack as soon as we finish our meal."

He wanted to point out that unpacking would be premature, but she made her way back toward the kitchen before he got the chance, and he shook his head instead, angry with himself for not making it clear right away.

"You're not staying here," he said aloud, but there was no one there to hear him.

Kids were weird. That was the conclusion Joe came to after sitting down to a meal with two of them. The little girl, Kimmie, as they seemed to call her, had a hard time eating, seeing as how she refused to take her thumb out of her mouth. And Rusty ate quickly, glancing up at Joe as though he were afraid the large man would grab his food right off his plate if he didn't watch him carefully. Chynna tried hard to get a pleasant conversation going, but it was no use. For that, they needed a certain level of comfort and trust that just wasn't there.

"The countryside around here certainly is beautiful," Chynna remarked. "Flying in, you could almost see the curve of the earth. The forests look like they could go on forever."

Joe grunted, but his attention was diverted by the sight of Rusty's chipmunk cheeks bulging with food. Was he expecting a long, hard winter? Or just making up for lost time? Hard to tell.

"I imagine you're snowed in here most of the winter," she went on. "It doesn't look like snowplows would get out this way."

"Uh...no," he muttered, distracted as Kimmie, thumb firmly in place in her mouth, picked up a pea with her spare hand and calmly smashed it against her nose. He grimaced and looked up at Chynna, wondering where she stood on the playing-with-your-food issue and why she wasn't doing something to stop the child.

"Should she...?" he began.

He gestured toward the little girl, but Chynna was already cleaning the smashed vegetable off her daughter's nose with a napkin, making the move as though it were something she did every day, and going right on.

"This is going to be a very different experience for us," she said serenely. "The children have always lived in the city. And come to think of it," she added with a quick smile, "so have I."

"What city was that?" he asked, just making conversation.

"Chicago."

"Oh. Nice lake." Not a particularly compelling comment, but he had an excuse. His attention was being distracted by the eating habits of children, things he'd never dreamed he would see at the table.

At this moment, Rusty was returning a mouthful of egg to the plate, looking as though he'd been poisoned. Joe stifled a groan, his appetite completely gone. Chynna deftly whipped away the disgusting plate and handed her son a glass of milk, not mentioning what had happened and cleaning up the evidence as quickly as possible.

"I notice you don't have a television," she said, wiping a newly smashed pea from Kimmie's nose and stopping the hand that reached to get another one.

Joe was just glad one hand was occupied with the thumb in the mouth. If the kid had both hands free, who knew what she might rub into her face. He glanced at her, his eyebrows drawn together in a look of bewildered horror. So this was what it was like to be around children? How wise he'd been to avoid it in the past.

But the woman had been asking him something— whether they had television, wasn't that it? "Uh...no, no television. No signal makes it out this far very effectively.''

"That's just as well," she said. "Television is a major purveyor of exactly what I wanted to get them away from."

"No kidding." He threw down his napkin and glanced at the door, wondering if it would be rude to take a walk. A long, extended walk. Maybe go right past these kids' bedtime.

"We've brought along some music tapes the kids like to listen to. You do have a stereo, so they'll be able to use that."

"Children's songs," he muttered, hoping someone would warn him. He wanted to be out of the house before the chanting songs about beluga whales started up. He'd had a friend with a two-year-old once, and the sappy whale song he heard at their house still haunted his nightmares.

Chynna read the aversion in his face and she bit her lower lip, her dark eyes clouded in thought. This was turning out to be more difficult than she'd expected, but she wasn't going to let that get her down. She was used to coming up against brick walls and learning to dismantle them. Life had been like that for her so far. Not too many primrose paths in her background. Plenty of thistles and thorns and rivers to cross. When you came from times like that, you got tough or you crumbled. Chynna had no intention at all of crumbling. She was going to end up married to this man. That was a promise.

But for some reason, the kids were not cooperating. She glanced at them with a sigh, and then her gaze lingered and her heart filled with sweet love for them. Poor babies. What did she expect? They'd been wrenched away from the only home they'd ever known, flown across the country for hours, shuttled off in the small plane and plunked down in a gloomy old house in the middle of nowhere. And here was their harried mother, demanding they be on their best behavior. No wonder they seemed ragged and stressed out.

Sleep. That was what they needed.

"There's no telephone," Joe said, and she looked up, startled.

No telephone. That was going to bother her, and she knew it. But then, she reminded herself, that was what she'd come out here for. Maybe it was too many modern conveniences that had turned life upside down in the city. She'd wanted the opposite of that, and if giving up the telephone would help her get it, who was she to quibble?

"We'll get used to it," she said firmly. There would be no ordering out for pizza. But there would also be no crank calls, no banks calling to sell their credit cards, nobody selling tickets for the policemen's ball. Life would go on.

"Nap time," she murmured, untying Kimmie's bib though she hadn't really swallowed a thing.

Kimmie stared up, her dark eyes huge as she gazed around her fist at her mother, clinging to that thumb with all her might.

"I'm not sleepy," Rusty said fretfully, but he rubbed his eyes and yawned, and Chynna knew it was only a matter of time before his eyelids began to droop.

Softly, as she cleaned them up from their meal and began to shepherd them into the bedroom they would be using, she began to sing a lullaby.

"'Good night, say the teddy bears, it's time to close our eyes.'" She'd sung it to the two of them at bedtime since they were babies, and by now it worked like magic. They heard the gentle melody and they both relaxed, knowing it was time for a nap, knowing there was nothing that could keep sleep away. That was just the way it was.

Joe watched her with a frown. It was all very well that she was a wizard with her kids, but what did that mean in the long run? Greg and kids—no, the two concepts clashed like...like pickles and ice cream. It wouldn't work. He had to talk her into going back to Chicago, back to where she'd come from.

Rising, he began carrying dishes to the sink and tried to think of what he would use as his salient point. He was a lawyer, after all. All those years of training in logic and argument were finally going to come to something. No problem. Once he got going, she would be putty in his hands.

He rinsed off the dishes and stacked them, turning when he heard her coming back into the kitchen.

"They're down for their naps," she said simply, giving him a quick smile. "We can talk."

"Nice work," he said, complimenting her, his head tilted to the side as he looked her over. Nice work, he repeated silently to himself, but this time his comment was related to the state the woman was in herself. She still looked crisp and efficient in her blouse and skirt, but her hair had come undone just enough to leave wisps flying about her face in a very fetching way. She was one attractive woman.

"Shall we sit?" he offered, gesturing toward the chairs at the table.

She nodded and preceded him, glancing up in surprise when he helped her with her chair.

He took his place opposite her and narrowed his gaze, ready to lay down the law as he saw it.

"Let me see if I have this straight," he began. "You put yourself in a catalog for men who want mail-order brides. Greg answered, selected you and sent you money to come to Alaska. You brought along two kids you hadn't told him about, hoping he would take them as part of the bargain. But Greg wasn't here when you arrived. Is that about it?"

She stared at him for a moment, wondering how long he was going to try to keep up this pretense that he wasn't Greg. She was sure he was going to try to use it as an excuse to get out of their contract. He'd taken one look at the kids and panicked. That had to be it. Now he wanted to get rid of her so he could order himself up another woman, someone who would come unencumbered with little ones.

Well, she understood his angle. She'd been afraid something like this might happen. But she wasn't going to give up quite that easily. What she needed was time...time for him to get to know the children, time for him to get to know her and what kind of person she was. Once that happened, surely she would be able to talk him into taking them as a set. All she needed was time.

"That's about it," she said evenly. Leaning forward on her elbows, she decided to let him have his game without protest at this point. "The only part you left out was how committed I am to making this work out for all of us."

He gazed into her dark eyes and found only sincerity, but he couldn't hide his smile of skepticism.

"Hey," he said softly. "I didn't just fall off the turnip truck, you know. This doesn't make any sense, and you know it.''

She raised one delicately molded eyebrow. ''Do I?''

His short laugh said it all. ''Sure. Look, Chynna, you're a beautiful woman. I can't believe you've ever had any problem getting a man.'' He turned his hand palm up on the table. ''What would a woman like you need to resort to these measures for?''

For the first time, her gaze wavered. ''I never claimed I had problems getting men,'' she retorted stiffly.

He shrugged as though that proved his case. ''Then why did you do it? Why did you make this contract with my brother?''

She hesitated, her eyes cloudy. ''I have my reasons,'' she said at last. ''I'll explain it all to you at some point. But I'm not quite ready to open up on every private hope and dream I have. Not yet.''

His mouth twisted as he studied her. ''Why didn't you tell Greg about the kids?'' he asked.

She wet her upper lip with a quick slip of her tongue. ''I knew what your first reaction would be,'' she said simply. ''I wanted you to get to know them before you turned them down.''

''I'm not Greg,'' he said automatically, but he wasn't really thinking about that. He stared at her. Nothing she said added up. There had to be something else going on here. But what?

''Sorry. 'Joe,' isn't it?'' she amended, rolling her eyes only slightly but letting the tone of her voice emphasize the way she felt about this masquerade she thought he was playing.

'' 'Joe' it is,'' he stated flatly. ''Always has been and always will be. And Greg...'' He hesitated, then leaned forward, determined to get this cleared up and out in the open once and for all. "Listen, Greg is my brother. I know him well. And believe me, he's not husband material in any sense of the word."

She lifted her chin and met his gaze steadily. She had to admit, she liked what she saw. His face was tan, with grooves where dimples had probably once been, and tiny laugh lines around his eyes. From what she'd seen so far, she would say he was a very nice guy, and one who seemed to see the humor in most things. A man like that should be ready to love children. Why wasn't it happening?

"Not husband material?" she repeated. "I see. What's wrong with him?"

He shrugged, feeling uncomfortable to be spilling family secrets. But in this case, he didn't see any alternative. "It's not that there is anything wrong with him, per se. It's just that he's…" He narrowed his eyes, trying to think of the right words. "He's a real Alaska guy, you know what I mean? If this were ninety years ago, he'd be digging for gold in the mountains. If this were a hundred and fifty years ago, he'd be living off the land, tromping around in snowshoes and only coming down to civilization once a year for supplies. This is not a man who is set up, either psychologically or emotionally, to take care of a family."

"Oh?" She narrowed her eyes, too, staring right back at him. "Then why did he pick me? Why did he send me the money to come join him?" She picked up the envelope that was lying on the table between them and pulled out the photograph, dangling it from her fingers. "Why did he send me this picture of himself? And why did he say the things he did?" She shrugged delicately. "Maybe you don't know him as well as you think you do," she suggested.

He frowned, watching her wave the picture around and feeling like punching his brother in the nose once he found him again. This would have been a lot simpler if Greg had sent a picture of himself instead of using Joe as bait. "I can't really explain why he did those things," he said shortly. "Maybe he was playing around with a dream and then got cold feet when it looked as though it might actually come true."

She snapped the photo back into the envelope. "Yes, that's the thing, isn't it?" she said sweetly. "This has come true. Here we are. So let's make the best of it." She rose, starting toward the kitchen sink, but he stopped her with a hand on her arm.

"Listen, you don't seem to get it. I think you should pack up your kids and get while the getting's good. Leave. Take a plane and head out. Go back to where you came from."

Staring down at him, she slowly shook her head. "The pilot of the little plane that brought us from Anchorage said he wouldn't be back this way for four days," she noted. "We can't leave, even if we wanted to."

He swallowed hard. This was a reminder of what it was like to live out in the boonies. That just showed how quickly one could get used to modern life in a big city, where every convenience was at beck and call at any moment of the day or night.

"Oh," he said, letting his hand drop. "Well, I suppose I could drive you to Anchorage."

The lack of enthusiasm for that idea was evident in his voice, and she smiled suddenly, shaking her head again. "Don't bother," she said crisply, turning back toward the sink. "We'll stay. You need us."

"Like a hole in the head," he muttered to himself as

he made his way toward the front door. There was only one thing left to do. He had to find his brother, or at least find out where he was and when he was planning to drop in on this hardy little band of squatters who had taken over his house.

"Where are you going?" she called after him, leaning out of the kitchen door.

He looked back at her. "I'm going to see if I can find out where Greg went."

He expected to see a flash of annoyance in her eyes, but instead he saw a flare of fear. "You are coming back, aren't you?" she called.

"Of course I'm coming back."

He turned toward the car, not wanting to see her face, see the questions in her eyes. She still thought he was pretending not to be Greg. Well, it hardly mattered. She probably thought he was a little nuts, but then, if she were confronted with the real Greg, she would do more than think it.

And yet, that was hardly fair. He hadn't seen his brother for a number of years. It was possible he'd turned into a model citizen after all. Yes, it was possible. Just barely.

He swung behind the wheel of the long, low sports car he'd rented in Anchorage and started the engine, thinking how out of place a car like this was out here in the wilderness.

"And that's exactly why I love it," he murmured, avoiding a pothole and turning onto the two-lane dirt road that would take him to the combination post office and general store that served as the center of Dunmovin, the so-called town he'd been born in thirty-some years before.

Three

The place looked the same, only a decade and a half older and more run-down. Right next to it was a shiny new building. The sign in the window said Nails By Nancy, and Joe stopped for a moment and stared at the little yellow storefront, wondering who in the world there was for Nancy to do the nails of—whoever Nancy was. Shaking his head, he took the steps into the general store two at a time and burst in through the front door.

The theme inside was pure familiarity. Goods were still stocked to the ceiling, stacked precariously on long plank shelves. A lazy fan took a fainthearted pass at stirring the air. Two ancient residents sat on chairs tilted back until they leaned against the wall, and Annie Andrews stood behind the counter, working on her account books.

She looked up over her glasses when she heard him

come in and gave a snort of surprise as he walked into the dusty little building.

"As I live and breathe. Joey Camden." The gray-haired woman folded her arms across her chest and gazed at him instead of giving him a hug, but her snapping black eyes and crooked grin were filled with the warmth of her welcome, and he appreciated it, grinning right back. "What brings you to these parts, stranger?"

"The call of the wild, I guess," he said, hooking his thumbs in his belt loops and rocking back on his heels. "You always told me Alaska would call me back."

She nodded, looking pleased. "That I did. And I'm always right, aren't I?"

"Always," he agreed. He glanced at the two old-timers, but though they were eagerly hanging on to every word of this conversation, he could see that he didn't know either one of them. He gave them a nod and turned back to Annie.

"You going to be living with your brother in that old house?" she asked him, her eyes sparkling at the thought of it.

He hesitated. "No, not exactly. In fact, I'm just here for a short visit. I'm on my way to see Mom."

Annie nodded, taking a swipe at the counter with a rag. "How is your mother?" she asked. "She writes me every year at Christmas, but it isn't the same as having her a mile or so down the road. She was one of the few females I ever got on well with around here."

"She's okay. Not as young as she used to be, and she's worrying me a bit." He moved awkwardly, not used to unburdening his soul, but somehow the truth came pouring out. Maybe it was because he was talking to a woman who had known him since he was a baby.

"Actually, that's why I came. I've been trying to get

Greg to come into Anchorage and see her. But you know how he is. Cities give him hives. Or so he says.''

"Unlike you, who loves them.''

He shrugged and gave her a crooked grin. "You know me well, Miss Annie.''

Annie nodded her appreciation for his use of the old term he'd used for her when he was a boy, but her brow furled. "Joey Camden, you're Alaska born and bred,'' she accused. "How can you stay down in that forsaken place in California when you know you should be back here where you belong?''

"Here?'' He shook his head and laughed shortly. "Oh, no. I don't belong here anymore. I'm a city lawyer now, Annie. You remember. That's what I always wanted.''

She nodded, looking a bit sulky. "Oh, yes, I remember it well. Bright lights and big cities, that was what you always said. And I always told you it wouldn't satisfy you for long.''

"Well, that may just have been the one thing you were wrong about.''

She shook her head, stubborn as ever. "Nope. I'm never wrong about things that have to do with the heart. You're the one who just hasn't woken up and smelled the coffee yet.''

It certainly wasn't worth arguing about. "Maybe you're right,'' he allowed. "I see this town is going great guns. You've even got yourselves a nail parlor. How'd you get so lucky?''

Annie grinned. "Nancy came about a year ago. Calls herself an eco-feminist. Wanted to hunt and fish and live as one with nature. You know the type. Wouldn't know nature if it came up and bit her where the sun don't shine.'' She chuckled, enjoying her own little joke. "Turned out she was a total failure at the hunting-and-fishing stuff. Guns scared her, and she couldn't look a trout in the eye. Thought they were slimy. But I got to hand it to her—she wouldn't give up. I suppose partly it was that she didn't want to go back and face her eco-feminist friends with failure. Anyway, she decided she would stay, but go with avenues down which her talents really lie."

"Nails," Joe guessed.

"Yup. And manicures for the guys, things like that."

"Oh, come on, Annie. How many men around here want manicures?"

"Every dang one of them when the place first opened. You should have seen them. They were standing in line."

Joe looked shocked, then his face changed as the light dawned. "Oh. She's a looker, is she?"

Annie grinned. "She's about the prettiest girl we've had around these parts since the Babbitt twins left for summer jobs at Disney World and never came back."

Joe nodded. The twins had been about five years older than he, but he remembered well the sad day they left for the lower states. The men in Dunmovin had mourned for months.

"Anyway, that's neither here nor there. Let me fix you some dinner. How about it?"

He smiled. "Thanks, Annie. But right now, I've got other things on my mind." He glanced around the little room again. "Do you have any idea where I could find my brother?"

Annie pursed her lips thoughtfully. "I take it you've already been out to the house," she began, then her eyes brightened. "Say, wait a minute. Billy McGee was in here earlier and he said some woman had come in on the mail plane, come to see Greg. Had two little kids with her.''

Joe nodded. "That's right."

Her black eyes narrowed craftily. "Said she was coming here to marry Greg. Any truth in that?"

Joe hesitated, then shrugged. "I'm not sure about that."

Annie leaned forward and pinned him with her flashing gaze. "Said she was some sort of mail-order bride. Any truth in that?"

Joe sighed and gave her a long, lazy look. This was not a rumor he wanted spread. "I thought mail-order brides went out when the gold fields dried up," he said silkily. "I never did believe a woman would do something like that, anyway."

Annie snorted. "I know plenty of men who would jump at the chance to pick out a wife like they pick out their drill presses and their Sunday-go-to-meetin' clothes. Just choose a number and send in a check and she's yours, for better or for worse."

"Mostly worse, likely."

Annie raised an eyebrow. "Who knows? The divorce rate ain't so great on matches people choose for themselves when they supposedly fall in love first."

He grinned at her. "You've got a point there." His grin faded and he grimaced, leaning closer so that only Annie could hear him. "Tell you the truth, she does claim she's here because Greg…well, because he sent for her. You don't know anything about this?"

Annie's eyes glittered but she shook her head. "No, really. Greg has never been one to whisper his secrets in my ear."

Joe grinned. "I know that. I just thought you might have noticed the mail going back and forth."

One eyebrow rose. "Now that you mention it, there was a lot of correspondence there for a while. You know, Greg comes in with his bills once a month. That's usually the only time I ever see him. Oh, and when the *Field and Stream* magazines come in, he's always here the next day. But he was coming in almost every other day for a while." She gasped. "Wait a minute. I do seem to remember overhearing him talk about some girl he was going to get hitched with. I didn't pay it much mind—you know how your brother tends to..." She hesitated.

"Lie?" Joe supplied.

"Well, now, I wouldn't go so far as to say that. How about he just embroiders the truth a little? He likes to make life dramatic."

"Yeah, right." Joe nodded, his mouth twisting cynically. "Meanwhile...I've got a bride on my hands, and no groom in sight. If you see Greg, tell him to get his tail on home and clean up this mess."

"You can bet I'll do exactly that." She followed him to the door of the building and added gruffly, "And you come on back and see me again before you leave. You hear?"

"Will do." Surprising her, surprising even himself, he bent down and dropped a quick kiss on her cheek. "See you later, Miss Annie."

She pressed her hand to where he'd made his imprint and colored as he left, swinging down the steps and sliding behind the wheel of his fancy car. "You always were a little dickens," she muttered, but she couldn't hold back the pleased smile, and she shook her head as he waved, taking off in a dust cloud.

It was eerie walking into the house and hearing someone in the kitchen. Almost like the old days. But it was

even eerier hearing children playing in the living room.
That wasn't much like old days. Joe and his brother
never played happily like Rusty and Kim were doing.
They had mainly fought.

Joe stopped in the doorway, watching the kids.
They'd rigged up an old sheet between two armchairs
and were using it as a tent. Kim was under the canopy,
sitting cross-legged, swaying and singing a song to herself. Rusty was being an airplane, zooming around the
room, stopping to babble something unintelligible at the
two long-tailed goldfish who were swimming lazy laps
in their bowl on the hutch, then turning abruptly to
swoop toward Kim, making her shriek with delighted
fear. For a moment, Joe took in the play and wondered
at it. So this was what happy children did. He realized
he didn't know much about kids, when you came right
down to it. All he knew about was the way he and his
brother had been, and the word *happy* hadn't come up
much.

Suddenly, Rusty caught sight of him and stopped
dead. Kim whirled, saw him and her thumb went
straight into her mouth.

"Hi, kids," he said, feeling a little awkward.

They stayed still as statues, staring at him, as though
they had to be prepared to run if he took another step
toward them.

He searched his mind for a topic of conversation, but
came up with nothing. Then his gaze fell on the goldfish
bowl.

"Hey, how do you like these two guys?" he asked
heartily. "Aren't they cute?"

Rusty looked at the bowl and nodded. "What are
their names?" he asked.

"Uh…" How should he know? But pets had to have names. "Goldie and Piranha," he said off the top of his head. "Do you like goldfish?"

Neither of them said anything. Both just stared at him, and he found himself sweating under this kind of scrutiny. Swearing softly under his breath, he turned away. Obviously, he had no natural knack with children. That was hardly surprising. Still, it hurt a little to think kids hated him on sight.

On the other hand, women usually liked him just fine, and there happened to be one on the premises. Feeling better about it all, he made his way to the kitchen, where he'd heard those busy sounds when he'd first come back into the house.

Chynna was at the sink and he stopped, startled by the change. She'd cast off her business suit for jeans and a jersey top that hugged her curves like—well, it might be best not to go on with that simile. And it might be important not to let his gaze linger too long on the more spectacular elements. Shifting his attention to the dishwater, he came in and plunked himself down at the table.

"How did you know," he asked abruptly, "that you were going to like kids? Before you had them, I mean. What gave you the courage to take the plunge?"

She looked at him for a moment, turning her head so that her long, loose hair swung like a pendulum at her back, and laughed. "What did they do to you now?" she asked, one hand on her hip.

He managed an innocent look. "Nothing. Not a thing." Then his conscience got the better of him. "Well, if they were a little older, I'd say they snubbed me. But since they're just kids…"

"Kids can break your heart, too," she said softly.

"They're so open and innocent about it. They haven't learned to hide their feelings, so what they do comes straight from their soul. That can hurt a lot."

"Yeah." He shrugged it off. "I guess you're just a natural with children, aren't you?"

She threw back her head and laughed, surprising him. "Hardly," she said, her eyes dancing with amusement. "I made a lot of mistakes. I still make them."

He shook his head. "It's all too complex for me. I don't think I'll ever have kids. I have enough trouble keeping a dog happy."

The laughter evaporated from her face like spring rain on hot pavement. This was not the way she wanted things to go.

"Kids are great," she said quickly. "They grow on you."

"Like fungus?" He made a face. "No, thanks. I think I'll pass."

"You'll see," she said, gazing at him seriously. "You'll see."

He looked back into her deep, dark eyes, and something he saw there—or maybe something he didn't see—made him uneasy.

"Listen," he began, feeling as though he had to explain things to her, make her face the fact that he wasn't Greg, that he would never go for kids, that he doubted if Greg would, either, that she had made a big mistake coming here to Alaska.

But as though she read his mind and didn't want to hear it, she turned away, reaching for the pan she'd been scouring, and the words stopped in his throat. At the same time, he noticed she'd been cleaning.

"Wow," he said, examining the kitchen, first one side and then the other. The tile on the counters was shining, and the boxes of food that had been stacked there earlier had vanished. "You didn't need to do this."

She laughed again, more softly this time. "Let's put it this way—it needed to be done."

He shook his head in wonder. Even the old cookie jar was glistening. "I've never seen this place look so good."

"Really?" She turned back, pleased. "I've only just begun."

That caught him up short. He rose and came toward her, frowning. "No, listen. You shouldn't be doing this. This isn't your job. You're a visitor and…"

She put a hand up to stop his speech. "I'm no visitor," she told him calmly. "I told you. I'm applying for a job." She tried a fetching smile. "I'm going to make myself indispensable to you."

"Indispensable," he murmured, repeating her word in a bit of a daze. The concept was overwhelming, and he found himself backing out of the kitchen, not sure what to do or what to say.

He muttered something, and she turned back to the sink. After a last, lingering look, he left, but the effect she had stayed with him. He felt very strange. The thought of a woman like this fighting for a place in his heart—but wait. That was pure bull. This had nothing to do with him, per se. She wasn't trying to win him over. She thought she was working to win over Greg. And in the end, Greg's decision was the one that was going to count. What Joe thought wouldn't mean anything to anyone.

Feeling oddly resentful, restless and out of place, he sauntered into the hallway and then, slowly, made his way into the bedroom he'd shared with his brother for

all the years of his childhood. Once again, the past hit
him between the eyes.

"God, Greg," he muttered, gazing at the room.
"Don't you ever throw anything away?"

The same old madras spreads lay on the twin beds.
The same old rocking chair stood in the corner. His
dusty old L.A. Lakers poster still hung over his bed,
with Kareem Abdul Jabar stretching his long, long body
toward the basket. And there was his basketball, looking
like a partially deflated balloon, sitting on his old
dresser.

He glanced at Greg's side of the room. Greg had
mounted a collection of arrowheads in a case during his
last year of high school, and it still stood against the
wall. The only thing different was a stack of compact
discs and a small disc player on the nightstand. And
there, next to the disc player, was a catalog. A catalog
of women who wanted husbands.

Joe let his breath out in a long sigh as he grabbed
the book and brought it to his side of the room, sinking
down to sit on the edge of his old bed. This was it.
Shopping for wives. Very gingerly, he cracked open the
catalog and began to peruse it, feeling a strange sense
of reluctance, but unable to stop.

He gazed at the pictures as he flipped through the
book, studying the faces. Some looked half witted.
Many looked scared or desperate. The faces from war-
torn or poverty-stricken countries looked tight, determined, eager to escape their situations and try life in
the land of the free. He could see why they might be
ready to trade independence for a better life. That was
understandable. But why would a woman like Chynna,
a normal woman from Chicago—what reason could she
possibly have? It didn't make any sense.

And then he found her picture. She looked natural, but just a little reserved. There was a cool, self-possessed sense to her pose, to the look in her eyes, the tilt of her chin. And she looked damn beautiful.

Wow, he thought, frowning. It would take a brave and self-confident man to order up a woman like this. She looked like a handful, even in the picture she'd sent to sell herself with. It was hard for him to imagine Greg gathering that sort of courage.

But then again, maybe that was why he'd cleared out before she got here.

"He probably got drunk, wrote the letter and sent her a check, and then suffered buyer's remorse the very next day," he decided. "And was too chicken to call her and cancel."

The thought of it made him grin. Yes, that was what probably had happened. Which meant he was going to have to tell her, and watch those huge brown eyes cloud up.

His grin began to fade. "Thanks a lot, Greg," he muttered, closing the catalog and staring out the window at the pines. "Thanks a hell of a lot."

Chynna plunged her hands into the tepid dishwater and tried to make her mind go blank while she soaped down the parts of the ancient stove she'd just disconnected. There was something satisfying about scrubbing everything clean.

"It's another form of renewal," she told herself. Besides, it helped her keep her mind off things.

She frowned, trying hard to concentrate on making charred porcelain shine again, but the thoughts kept coming anyway. How could she help but think about it? It was here, it was now and it had to be dealt with.

She stopped and took a deep breath, letting her mind go, letting the thoughts flow in.

"Okay," she whispered to herself. "Here's the deal." She had to make the man fall in love with her.

That was the crux of the matter, and it chilled her blood. She'd never had a lack of male attention. Wherever she went, men tended to let her know by looks or actions that they liked what they saw when they looked at her. But those things had never ranked highly in her list of important reasons she'd been put on this earth. In fact, her good looks were often more a nuisance than a benefit to her. She'd always had a more serious bent, with goals and a good, strong work ethic. She had never had any interest in being a playgirl. And because she never played, she'd never been very good at flirting. She didn't think she could manage a coy look if her life depended on it.

"But it does," she whispered to herself, biting her lip. Her life and the lives of her two babies depended on it.

Shaking her head, she went back to scrubbing, but her mind was in turmoil. Greg was acting very strangely. And instead of meeting that fact head-on, she was washing things.

"That's because you didn't prepare properly," she scolded herself. "And now you don't know what to do next."

That was it. She needed time to regroup. This situation wasn't really turning out the way she'd pictured it would. She'd expected awkwardness at first, sure. After all, how did one act around a man one planned to marry when one had never had a real conversation with him before? They were tied together in the most serious way a man and woman could be tied, and yet they were virtual strangers. Intimacy was going to take time. That was only natural.

But did she have time? She wasn't sure. That was the problem. He wasn't acting as though he wanted her to stay.

And that was why she was going to have to make him fall in love. "Either with me or the kids," she told herself. But she knew it was going to have to be with her. She was going to have to make herself irresistible. She rolled her eyes and pulled the plug on the dishwater, watching it spiral down the drain.

At least she seemed to have made a pretty darn good choice. All you had to do was look at him. He was wonderful, really. When she thought of the sort of man she could have ended up with, this seemed almost a miracle. She'd taken a big gamble and she'd been prepared to put up with some borderline cases to get what she needed for her children. And in that way, at least, her gamble had paid off handsomely. He was a catch.

That didn't mean things looked rosy. Hardly that. He was still leery, still pretending not to be Greg. And he hadn't warmed to the children. That was going to take time. But it would come. It had to. Her kids were adorable. Everyone said so. They were just a little shy of him right now. Tomorrow would be different.

Tomorrow. She would clean like crazy, cook something unforgettable, show off her great kids and he wouldn't be able to resist. She would have him in wedding clothes by the end of the week.

"It's got to work," she muttered aloud as she dried her hands. "It's got to."

Evening was deepening into night, though the sky outside was light as ever, and there was no sign of Greg.

Joe was beginning to think his conjecture was right. Greg had no intention of coming back while Chynna was here.

He threw down the outdoorsman magazine he'd been reading and ran a hand through his thick black hair. He pretended to be looking out at the wind in the treetops, but all the while, he was looking at her, across the room with her children. She was pretty hard to ignore.

It seemed she was always moving. When a shaft of sunlight caught her hair, it glowed gold and silver, and her hands with their long, slender fingers seemed to flutter around her children. She reminded him of some mythical goddess, half animal, half human.

"A swan," he breathed to himself at one point as she hovered over Rusty, helping him find a place in his book. "A big, beautiful swan, protecting her children."

Like *Swan Lake*.

Ballet?

He blinked, startled. He was thinking about ballet? Good Lord, what was happening to his mind? He'd only been to the ballet once. Glee, a girl he'd been dating in L.A., had dragged him to the Greek Theater to see people leap around on creaky boards in tights and tutus. The men seemed to be impersonating forest elves, and the women looked as if they were wearing Frisbees around their middles and could easily have been launched into space at any moment. The music had been nice, but the dancing had not thrilled him.

"Don't take it all so literally," Glee had chided him when he grumbled. "Let go. Watch the movements. Feel the emotions."

Feeling emotions was not a well-loved hobby of his. He'd never thought much of feelings. As far as he was concerned, emotions were something to avoid, something to tamp down into a little corner of your soul and take out again only when you were alone and had time to deal with them. Emotions were not to be set prancing out on a stage on tiptoes for all to see. Emotions were things that couldn't always be avoided—but then, so were bad head colds. And he didn't like either one of them.

He was going to have to get her to leave in the morning. Did she realize that yet? Once she was gone, Greg would straggle back in from wherever he was hiding and Joe could get the job done he'd come to take care of. That was the only logical sequence of events. She was going to have to listen to reason. Maybe it would be best to get things settled tonight.

Looking up, she caught his gaze on her and she gave him a quick smile. "Is it ever going to get dark?" she wondered. "It's almost nine, and outside it looks like late afternoon."

"It's worse in late June," he told her. "There will be weeks when it never gets dark at all."

"Never gets dark," she repeated, shaking her head. "How do you convince children it's time to go to bed?"

He glanced at her kids and smiled. "My mother used to tell us if we closed our eyes, we could make it dark in our own heads and we wouldn't know the difference."

She laughed. "And that worked?"

"No. But we pretended it did so she wouldn't feel bad."

Rusty said something, and she turned her attention back to the children, but Joe couldn't stop watching her. Just being in this house was conjuring up memories he hadn't let surface in years. But having her here was

something else altogether. Her presence called up
thoughts and feelings he had no intention of setting
free—things he had no right to think about.

So he wouldn't. But he wasn't going to worry about
it. After all, she would be gone by this time tomorrow.
All he had to do was find her and her kids a ride with
someone driving into Anchorage. That was the ticket.

He watched as she got her children to put away their
things and start preparing for bed, gathering them together, coaxing them on. And on the way to the bedroom, she marched them past him.

"Say good-night to Mr. Camden, children," she told
them.

"'Night, Mr. Camden," Rusty said, staring down at
his chunky green tennis shoes.

"Good night, kids," he replied a little too heartily.

Kimmie said nothing. Her thumb was jammed tightly
into her mouth, and no sounds could squeeze out around
it.

Chynna sighed with resignation and dragged them on
into the bedroom, talking to them softly as she went.
Listening, Joe sank back into his chair. In a moment,
what he'd been hoping for happened and he smiled.
She'd begun to sing to them again. Her voice was light,
vaguely sensual, and it had magic in it. As he listened,
his muscles dissolved and he slowly melted into the
armchair, his head falling back, his eyes closed.

The next thing he knew, she was touching his shoulder.

"What?" He straightened quickly, blinking away
sleep. "What happened?"

Her eyes were huge, and she was leaning close.
"There's something outside," she whispered, obviously
alarmed. "Listen."

He listened, but he didn't hear a thing. Glancing at her, he frowned, embarrassed to have fallen asleep. A look at the clock told him he'd been out for half an hour. Probably his snoring was what she'd heard.

Her hand grabbed his upper arm at the same time he heard it—a low, mournful sound coming from behind the house.

"There it is," she said quickly, her fingers tightening on his biceps. "What was that?"

He liked the feel of her hand on him, and in his groggy state, he wasn't resisting her attractions as well as he should. An urge swept over him, something that involved grabbing and pulling her down on the chair in his lap, but luckily he was awake enough to resist it.

"It sounded like a wolf," he told her, though he was hardly paying any attention to the noise that had her galvanized. His gaze was on her face, her deep, dark eyes, the way wisps of hair flew about her face and framed it like a picture of pure beauty.

"Funny," he added vaguely, captivated by her closeness, but still trying to respond to her nervousness about the wolves. "They don't usually come out this way."

She nodded, though she could hardly have known that, and her nervous clutch on his arm didn't loosen. "A wolf? Right out there in the backyard?"

He looked at her more closely. "Sure. You knew there would be animals, didn't you? You knew there would be predators. Bears and cougars and wolves and foxes." That was it—scare her. Tell her she couldn't avoid animals that would tear her and her children from limb to limb. Then maybe she would be happy to leave in the morning.

But he didn't want to lay it on too thick, and he found himself sticking to the truth, the way he usually did.

"We're camped on the edge of the wilderness, you know. We share the land with animals of all kinds."

She swallowed hard and nodded again. Of course she knew. How could she not know? She was rational, educated, thinking—and completely shaken by this contact with the wild. It was one thing to think about animals in the woods; it was another to hear a wolf howl and realize there was something new she was going to have to protect her children from.

She turned from him, taking air deep into her lungs and steadying herself. She'd been so anxious to get away from the predators of the city, she'd forgotten there would be dangerous species out here, as well. Trying to raise two children on her own, she could afford only neighborhoods that were much too often filled with gangs and shootings and robberies. That was why she'd brought her children to this clean, pure wilderness. She should have remembered that there were dangers everywhere. They varied in type and style, but they had to be dealt with and vanquished, no matter where you went.

She would learn. Her children would learn. Greg would teach them. She looked at him, at his wide shoulders, his clear eyes, and she congratulated herself once again. Yes, he'd been the right pick. Of all the men who had contacted her when her ad came out in the catalog, he'd been the one she chose, and she'd done well. She had all the confidence in the world in him. And anyway, what choice did she have at this point?

"It's just going to take a little getting used to," she told him, managing a quick smile. "Do they...do they keep it up all night?"

"No. They'll be moving on, looking for something to kill."

Her face registered shock, and he swore softly, kicking himself for putting it like that. ''I didn't mean that the way...''

She shook her head quickly, stopping his apology in its tracks. ''No, I understand. That's the way it is out here, and we've got to adjust to it. I guess we're used to a life that's several layers away from nature and we forget how things really are.''

How things really are. Her words echoed in his head as he watched her walk away from him, on her way to the green room, where she would sleep for the night. The wolf howled again, a little farther away this time, and Joe's head rose, almost as though his instinct was to catch a scent in the wind, and a shiver ran through him. God, he'd missed that sound, the wild passion, the sense of the conqueror. The call of nature was strong in him for a moment. After all, he'd grown up here; he'd been bound to this land and its animals from birth. He couldn't very well erase that, even if he wanted to. And right now, with the sound of the wolf still hanging in the air, he didn't want to. For the first time in years, he was remembering how much he loved it.

Four

Joe couldn't sleep. He must have had an hour or so before he woke, but then he couldn't drift off again, no matter how hard he tried, no matter how many sheep he counted or muscles he forced to relax. Finally, he gave up, rolling out of bed and pulling on his jeans and a sweater and going out into the pale twilight night to find some space to breathe in.

The old, familiar sounds washed over him, the whirring of insects, the scuffling of small animals underfoot, the flutter of an owl's wings as it swept past him, the roar of the river in the distance. The atmosphere was very different from the quiet suburban street in Los Angeles where traffic was the main noise, along with your neighbor's stereo system. He turned to look at the mountains, the snowy peaks shining iridescent in the night, and even as the thrill of it caught at his heart, he laughed softly.

"Damn you," he whispered. "Alaska, you old tempt-
ress. You're not going to seduce me. I'm too old and
too strong to fall for this stuff."

But she was good. The very best. If he stayed too
long…

But he wasn't going to do that. He was going to find
his brother and force him to come visit his mother in
Anchorage. That was what he'd come for, and he
wouldn't leave until he'd done it. He owed his mother
that much—and so did Greg. Of course, he was also
going to have to take care of this new situation that was
complicating things.

Turning, he looked toward the forest and stared for
a moment, looking for movement.

"I know you're out there, Greg," he said aloud. "I'll
bet you're not even very far away. And you're going to
have to come in sometime. You're going to have to deal
with this situation that you've set up. Come on, chicken.
Come on in and face the music."

Greg didn't answer, though Joe waited a few minutes,
wondering. Finally, he turned back toward the house
and at the same time, saw a light go on in the master
bedroom.

He stopped, frozen, as he watched Chynna enter the
room and hover over her children, her white robe flowing around her like a cape. He could see her through
the bedroom window, bending over her son, soothing
him, a silhouette portrait of motherly love.

That was something he could admire from afar, but
he was as sure as death that he could never feel that
way about a kid. Never would happen. Not only did
kids not warm to him, but the fatherly spirit just
wouldn't gel in him. The question was, what made her
think Greg was capable of it?

Still, he was the one watching this all through the window. And instead of turning away, as he knew he should, he stood and watched, mesmerized. She still bent over Rusty, whispering something to him, then she leaned closer to kiss the top of his head. Rising, she let her fingers trail across him as she looked over at Kimmie with a faint smile. At the doorway, she threw a kiss back to her boy, then turned off the light and shut the door.

Something about the entire scene got to him, touched him deeply in a way he didn't understand at all. Still standing in the same spot, Joe felt an ache grow in his chest, a yearning. He shook his head, shaking it away. He didn't need any of that. But he did need to get some things clear and he might as well take this opportunity to do it. He went quickly to the back door, catching Chynna before she made it back to her bedroom.

"Chynna. Can you come on out here for a minute?" he called to her softly. "I've got to get something off my chest."

She turned, startled, but came willingly enough, stepping out on the back porch and looking apprehensively toward the trees. "Are the wolves still around?" she asked, trying to keep her fear out of her voice.

"The wolves?" He'd forgotten all about them. "Oh, no. They're long gone."

Looking relieved, she came down the steps and joined him on the grass. "It's still so light," she said, marveling at the blue gray midnight sky. "Like a full-moon night. But there's no moon at all."

"The sun's down—it's just not very far away," he said, strolling toward the old wishing well his father had built in the back many years ago. But he was looking at the sky, as well. All his years in L.A. had made him forget how eerie it was, and at the same time, how wonderful.

She followed him, not saying a word, seemingly caught up in some of the same feelings. The night was huge. It seemed to stretch to forever. There was definitely a certain magic in the air.

He dropped to sit on a little stone bench near the well, and when he made room for her, Chynna sat beside him, pulling her robe in tight around her, and he immediately regretted having let her come so close. Her hair tumbled about her shoulders, and he could smell her scent, something light and fresh that tickled his nose. The sensuality of her swept over him, and he clenched his jaw, willing himself to ignore it. She turned toward him, and he steeled himself to meet her gaze.

"Where are your dogs?" she asked, surprising him.

"My what?"

"Your dogs. There are dog dishes on the floor in the kitchen. There's dog food in the cupboard. That doesn't usually happen without dogs. So where are they?"

"Dogs." He laughed shortly. "You're right. There are always at least two dogs around. Greg must have taken them with him."

Sighing, she looked toward the snowy mountains. "Whatever you say," she murmured.

She still thought he was Greg and trying to hide it. He grimaced. This was getting old. It was time she faced the truth.

"Listen, Chynna," he said briskly, looking up at the deep sky, "you're a very nice woman. And your kids are, well, they're okay. But you're going to have to leave tomorrow. There's no alternative."

He didn't look at her, but he could feel her stiffen.

He didn't want to see her face so he kept staring into the blue.

"Don't take it personally. This isn't your fault in any way. It's Greg's. I don't know what game he thought he was playing when he sent for you. But it's pretty obvious he isn't willing to keep his side of the bargain. And to tell you the truth, you're better off this way."

"I don't agree," she said softly.

He glanced at her. Her voice was quiet, but there was a hint of steel in it. She wasn't going to give up easily. He was going to have to convince her to go.

"Listen, you really don't know what Greg is like," he began, wanting to explain the unexplainable.

"Don't I?" She broke in, sounding just a bit sarcastic. "Why don't you tell me all about him?"

He glanced at her set face, then looked away again. "I know this is hard to take, and I know you don't want to hear it, but I think you'd better know the truth. I have no idea why Greg put you to all this trouble, coming out here, and then taking off the way he did. But that's Greg. It's not really all that strange that he would act like that. In fact, it pretty much fits his character. He's always been moody, erratic, hard to handle. He'll go off for days at a time in the wilderness, just like he's doing now." He shrugged, wishing he was better with words to make this clear. "He's meant for this land and he'll never leave it."

"Who said I ever wanted to leave it?"

He finally turned and met her gaze full on. "You may not think so now, but you will. Women always do."

She frowned. "Are you saying women can't handle this wild sort of country the way men can?" she demanded.

"That's exactly what I'm saying. Chynna, I grew up

out here. I've seen it happen again and again. You don't know a thing about it." He shook his head. "But that's not really the point. We're not talking about women in general. We're talking about you." He gave her a baleful look, struck by the way she'd come out so defensively in support of women and their ability to handle the outdoor life. "What are you, some kind of feminist or something?"

She didn't rise to the bait. Instead, she stared at him for a long moment, then lifted her chin. "You just watch," she told him. "I know I can make it out here. I know I can."

There was plenty of determination in her voice, but he knew darn well she had no idea what she was talking about.

"Look, I know your heart's in the right place," he told her. "You mean well. But the wilderness will wear you down. You haven't lived here. You don't know. I've seen it happen so many times. Practically every man who brings a woman out here ends up alone in the long run. It's just the way things are."

The breeze blew a lock of her silvery hair across her eyes, and he had to hold back the urge to reach out and brush it back. She left it, let it fly, and his hand ached to touch her. Taking a deep breath, he forced himself to focus.

"Women like nice things. They like concerts and going out to dinner and dancing and shopping in nice stores. You can't do any of that out here. That sort of living might as well exist on another planet."

He didn't see it coming or he would have prevented it, headed her off at the pass. But she moved quickly and before he knew it, she had his hand in hers, her fingers laced through his, and she was looking up earnestly, as though her heart were in her eyes.

"Greg, please listen. I've spent all my life in the city. I've gone to fancy restaurants and seen plays and taken college classes. I know what that is like. I've purposely turned my back on all of it. I wanted to come out here where things are clean and free. This is what I need. This is what my children need. Let us stay. You won't be sorry. I promise."

Her hand burned on his, and her eyes were huge in the dim light. He wasn't a man to cave in, but this was some heavy artillery she was aiming his way. "Chynna..." he began, but he wasn't sure where he was going with it.

It didn't matter. She had her own plans.

"Hold still," she told him, her voice firm but softly husky, and suddenly her free hand was pressed against his cheek. "I think we need something like this about now," she murmured, and stretching up, she touched his cool lips with her own.

A kiss. He hadn't expected it, but once it began, he knew it was something he had longed for from the moment he first saw her. He fell like a ton of bricks. All his good intentions evaporated into thin air. She took over his senses, all sweet tastes, soft touch and intoxicating scent. She went to his head like a shot of brandy, and he didn't even try to stop it. He accepted the kiss, letting her lips press to his for a moment, then, catching a sharp breath in his throat, he reached out and pulled her to him, taking her mouth as though he'd found a continent to conquer and meant to make quick work of it.

She melted to his touch, her bones seeming to disappear as she molded herself to him. Her mouth was sleek and plush, and he sank into it as though it would heal something in him if he only could go deeply enough. The male in him came alive and wanted her, right now, right there, and for a moment, he thought he felt an answering hunger from her. But then he could feel her drawing back, pulling away, and he let her go, knowing this was so wrong; anything he did to extend it would only make things worse.

Chynna was turning from him, slightly stunned. Her heart was beating in her ears like a drum. This was not what she'd expected. This was no shy man who needed coaxing at all. A sudden shot of fear spilled through her, and she pulled farther away, breathing hard, her eyes very wide, her hands flattened against his chest as though she needed a brace to protect her from him.

"That's enough for now," she said breathlessly, gathering the robe in close again. "I...I'd better go in."

He didn't try to stop her. Just as shocked as she was by what had happened, by that tiny, quick release that had sent them both spinning off their tracks, he sat back and didn't say a word, though inside he was swearing at himself. He stared after her as her white gown fluttered around her ankles. She disappeared into the house and slowly, very slowly, he lifted his face to the stars.

"I didn't mean to do that," he told them earnestly. "I really shouldn't have done that."

But they didn't give him any satisfaction at all. Shining down coldly, they seemed to mock him and his futile regrets. He swore again, aloud this time. What the hell had he been thinking? He wanted to get rid of her and instead, he'd damn near made love to her right out here on the grass.

Turning toward the woods, he made a gesture. "Were you watching that, Greg?" he asked the emptiness.

"Did you see me kiss your bride-to-be?" Rising, he stared into the trees. "You'd better get home and take care of her, you jerk. If you don't, someone else will."

Someone else. Yeah, right. This was crazy, insane, and he had to get her out of here before something really happened. Groaning, he started off for the meadow. It would be too embarrassing to go in and take a cold shower at this point. A hard walk in the wild would have to do. And who knew? Maybe he'd find his brother out there.

Joe dreamed he was in Lilliput and a hundred little kids had him tied down on the beach, and when he woke up, he had the sense that someone was in the room with him. Blinking sleep out of his eyes, he looked around groggily. He'd left his door ajar, but now it was wide open.

"Who's there?" he called out accusingly.

There was a hush, and then a giggle, and then a flurry of moving bodies as Rusty sprang from behind the chair and headed for the door, and Kimmie leaped up from below the foot of the bed, running after him. And both children were shrieking at the top of their lungs, as though a demon were after them.

Joe groaned and pulled his pillow up over his head. This was not the way he usually greeted the morning, and he had no intention of encouraging it, especially after the night he'd had. He'd spent an hour searching the woods for Greg after Chynna had gone in to bed. He'd looked everywhere, even at Greg's favorite campfire pit, but there was no sign of him. Then he'd come back to the house, rummaged through the kitchen until he'd found a half-empty bottle of Scotch, and he'd slugged it down, glass after glass, hoping to find some sort of answer in inebriation. Instead, he'd learned the age-old lesson: alcohol gives no insights; it only makes you dumber than ever.

He wondered, fleetingly, if Greg might have showed up during the night. But he knew this bedroom was the first place his brother would have come, and since he hadn't seen him, it was doubtful Greg had arrived.

Good. He wanted more sleep. He closed his eyes and tried to find it, but a few things got in the way. First, he felt as if his head were being used for practice by a very rough basketball team. Then there were the problems to be dealt with. But with this head, he was in no condition to think things through. No, he couldn't let the day intrude just yet. It was too early for him. He was on vacation, after all. He needed sleep, and slowly sleep began to creep over him again.

Then something horrible happened. The strains of a children's song began to filter in through his doorway. The kids had found the stereo and popped in one of their own tapes. He pulled the pillow down more tightly, but it didn't help. The childish voices just seemed to grow louder and louder. And sure enough, it was a song about whales. He gritted his teeth until it was over, then sighed with relief.

But his sense of deliverance didn't last long. They'd found the Rewind switch. The song about the baby whales came on again, loud and strong. He really couldn't take this. Chynna's sexy voice crooning kids' songs was one thing. A chorus of chipmunk voices chirping about whales was something else. He had to get rid of the hideous noise or go mad.

Blearily, he surveyed the situation. If he could get the door closed, that might help. But he didn't want to get out of bed. He thought for a moment, much as it hurt his head to make the effort. If he threw his extra pillow hard at the door, it might go back and hit the wall and bounce out again, closing smartly. Yes, that was the plan. Half sitting, he grasped the pillow and heaved it, hard, at the door. As it sailed in the air, seemingly going in slow motion, Chynna appeared in the doorway, just in time to get smacked in the face with the thing.

It was strange how slowly it happened. He watched as the pillow seemed to hover in the air, watched as she looked in and started to say something to him, watched as the pillow hit and she staggered back.

And finally he sprang into action. Muttering a stream of curses, he leaped out of bed and ran to her, hitching up his baggy pajama bottoms as he went.

"Are you okay? God, I'm sorry, I really didn't mean to do that. I wasn't aiming at you."

She stood there, bemused and slightly disheveled, the pillow in her arms, and looked him up and down. He was next to naked, and she decided right away she liked what she saw. Hard, rounded muscles gave mute testimony to the fact that the man worked out or played a sport or something. A thatch of hair darkened his chest and formed a trail below his navel, tantalizingly revealed by the raggedy, low-hanging pajamas.

"Then whom were you aiming at?" she asked, more interested than annoyed. "My kids?"

"I...no, I mean..." he stammered, shaken by the fear that her kids were exactly whom he would have liked to have thrown the pillow at. But you couldn't do things like that to kids. Could you? Dimly, he was pretty sure that was a no-no. "My door. I was trying..."

"Your door?" she repeated, glancing at the thing, then gazing at him askance. "I see."

He ran a hand through his tousled hair. It was much

too early, and he was much too hungover to make sense of all this. "No, you don't see at all. I was aiming at the door so that it would hit the wall and then…"

She was shaking her head. "Greg, you don't have to explain. This is your house. You can throw pillows at people if you want to."

He started to say something defensive, then noted the sparkle in her eyes and realized she was teasing him.

He shook his head and gave her a quick grin, then held out his hand for his property. "Thanks for catching my pillow," he told her, pretending to be grumpy. "I'm going back to bed."

"Oh, no, you don't," she told him, hugging it to her chest. "It's late. You must be ready to get up by now. I feel like I've been waiting for you for hours."

Their eyes met, and the memory of the kiss from the night before flared up between them like a wall of fire. The kiss had told them both many things. It had told Joe he was attracted to his brother's bride, and it had told her he could be seduced by her. It had also told her she might find him a little harder to handle than she'd expected. But all in all, that wasn't bad. Still, it had been an experience neither of them would soon forget.

She looked away first, but he was the one who spoke.

"I didn't get much sleep last night," he explained, apologizing in his way. "I need to catch up. Another hour should do it."

Her head snapped up. "Another hour! It'll almost be time to go back to bed by then."

He gave her a flash of his crooked grin, even though it hurt his hair follicles to do it. "Great. Then I won't have to get up at all."

She rolled her eyes and glanced at the watch on her wrist. "Okay. We'll give you exactly one hour."

He held out his hand for his pillow again, but she ignored it. Coming on into his room, she made her way to the head of the bed, and put down the pillow herself, fluffing it up. But as she did so, her gaze fell on the empty Scotch bottle lying by the side of the bed, and her face changed. She glanced at his bloodshot eyes, looked back at the bottle and pressed her lips together.

"Just how much do you drink?" she asked, her voice tight, and he remembered that her ad in the catalog had specified no drinkers. Something told him that the man in her life—probably the father of these children—had been a drinker.

This was a lucky break, and he hadn't even planned for it. All he had to do was tell her he was a drunk, and she would be out of here like a shot. He could see it in her face. Just one little white lie and...

"I don't really drink at all." To his chagrin, he heard his own voice telling her the truth. "Last night was a special case. I had some things to think about and—" he shrugged "—I got carried away, and since I'm not used to drinking..."

She stared at him for a moment, searching his gaze, then seemed satisfied, though her eyes had a wary look she hadn't had before. She nodded slowly. "Okay."

He felt a sense of relief and could have kicked himself for it. What was the matter with him? He didn't want her to like him. That wasn't the point here. "Hey, don't forget," he told her quickly. "You're leaving today."

His announcement didn't seem to faze her. She glanced around the room and made a face. "You know, if you really don't want me for a wife, you might consider hiring me on as a surrogate mother," she said breezily, starting for the door. "From the condition this place is in, you need somebody."

Before he could answer, the tune struck up again and he winced, putting a hand to his throbbing head. Earplugs. That was what it was going to take. He rummaged through all the junk piled on Greg's dresser, but no earplugs appeared. Just as he was about to give up, he had a lucky break. There, on the floor, he spied a set of earmuffs left over from winter. Reaching down painfully, he pulled them out, and looked them over. They were very white and very fluffy, and he knew he was going to look like a fool if he put them on. But the baby whales were driving him crazy, and he tested them experimentally.

Chynna was still watching. "What are you doing?" she asked him curiously from the doorway.

He looked up and pulled one earmuff away from his ear. "What?"

"What are you doing?" she repeated.

"Defending myself from belugas," he admitted. The muffs were great for drowning out sound, but they were much too hot for this weather and would drive him nuts in their own way. He took them off and threw them back where he'd found them, then looked up at her again, annoyance plain on his face. "I'm thinking of joining a whaling expedition," he snapped. "Know where I can go to sign up?"

She stared at him for a moment, completely at sea, and then the words of the song sunk in and she smiled, realizing what the problem was.

"Don't think twice," she told him breezily. "I'll take care of it." She started toward the living room to stop the song in the stereo, but at the last second, she turned back. "How are you for songs about monkeys jumping on the bed?" she asked.

He made a face as he dropped to sit on the side of the bed. "Can't you find something soft and sultry? How about some Billie Holiday?" He rubbed his temples. "Now, there's a woman who understands these sorts of things."

"Hangovers?" She grinned as though she were doing so despite her better judgment. "I don't think the kids are ready for 'Lady Day,'" she told him as she disappeared from the doorway, closing his door as she went.

Probably not, he thought to himself as he lay back against the pillow and settled in. Children obsessed with baby belugas might not be ready to savor the intricacies of primal human tragedy.

"More's the pity," he muttered. "I'm feeling pretty damn tragic right now."

He put his head on the pillow and closed his eyes. The song had changed to monkeys, just as she'd promised, and she'd made them turn it down so that he could hardly hear it any longer. But still, he couldn't sleep. And it wasn't the music. Pictures of Chynna kept swirling through his mind, and as long as that was going on, he knew there was no part of his body that would let go.

It was nuts, this attraction he felt for her. Not only had she come to marry his brother, but she had two kids and a determined attitude that was the sort of thing that usually turned him off about a woman.

But when he came right down to it, he had to admit, over the years he'd developed a whole long list of things that turned him off about a woman. The older he got, it seemed the pickier he got. Deep down, he recognized the entire process was actually a way to guard himself against commitment. But that didn't bother him. Deep down, he didn't want to get married, so why not use every weapon he could against it?

Every now and then, he came up against a woman who shook his confidence in his bachelorhood. The last time it had been a painter he'd met on the beach at Malibu, an older woman who'd been as different as she was beautiful. She made pen-and-ink drawings of the passing scene, and he'd stopped by to comment. The next thing he'd known, they'd been involved in a deep philosophical discussion that had blown him away. She'd been a wiser, more original thinker than any professor he'd had in college. They'd gone for coffee, then for dinner, then for a weekend at Newport. She'd engaged his mind in the most-intellectual discussions he'd ever been a party to, and she'd shown him lovemaking like he'd never seen before. Only twenty-five, he'd fallen deeply in love, or he'd thought he had, anyway. He'd imagined their life together as a constant round of sex and contemplation, and he'd begun thinking marriage. Then her husband walked in to take her home, and Joe's plans, dreams and sense of being in love had fallen to ashes. That had taught him never to take anyone at face value. And he'd never let himself fall in love again.

"And never will," he told himself stoutly, and yet even he could tell there was a certain conviction missing at the moment. "That's a hangover for you," he murmured as he rose from the bed. Rationalization was the only way left to go, and sleep was going to continue to elude him, so he might as well get up and get this day over with.

Pulling on jeans and a polo shirt, and then his boots, he went out into the living room and headed for the kitchen, nodding at the children playing before the stereo as he passed them.

"Hi, kids," he grunted.

Kimmie's thumb went to her mouth as though it were magnetized, but Rusty managed an answer.

"Mornin', Mr. Camden," he said, watching wide-eyed.

Joe stopped and looked at him, appreciating the effort the kid had to make. "Call me Joe, okay?" he offered.

Rusty stared at him blankly, and he realized why as he made his way on into the kitchen and began to rifle through a cupboard. Rusty and Kim had followed him and were standing in the doorway. He glanced at them and saw they were still bewildered as he pulled down a box full of antacid tablets. They thought his name was Greg. Why would Greg ask to be called Joe? Poor kids. He glanced at them and hid a grin. Rusty definitely looked confused.

But this was no time for Joe to go into detailed explanations. His head was bouncing from one wall to the other, and he needed relief, fast. Grabbing a glass, he poured himself some water and dropped two tablets into it, watching as the liquid fizzed up, wincing as he thought of drinking the awful stuff.

"What's that?" Rusty asked, climbing up on a chair so that he could get a closer look.

Joe lifted the glass and looked at the bubbles. "This is a magic potion. It makes my head get smaller and my stomach stand still." Bracing himself, he gulped it down with his eyes closed, made a face and shuddered. He stood very still and waited for relief, and he got some pretty quickly. Looking down, he found both children staring at his head. For a moment, he was annoyed.

Then he remembered what he'd told them. They were waiting to see it get smaller.

He hesitated, wondering how he could explain things to them, but nothing came to mind and he shrugged. Leaving the glass on the table and the box of tablets right next to it, he turned and left, heading for the bathroom. He needed to splash some water on his face and give himself a shave. Then maybe he would begin to feel human again.

Meanwhile, back in the kitchen, Rusty was reaching for the empty glass. Carrying it carefully, he set it on the counter near the sink, then began to edge the chair into position to give him access to water.

Kim watched him solemnly, then pulled her thumb out of her mouth, making a pop, like a cork from a bottle. "You gonna make your head small?" she demanded of her brother.

Rusty shook his head, busy with his chore. "Naw. It didn't work. Didn't you see him? His head was the same size as ever."

Kim considered that for a long moment as Rusty turned on the faucet and filled the glass, then hopped down and got a handful of antacid tablets from the table, heading back toward the glass of water.

"But it's magic," she said at last.

Rusty nodded. "Yeah, I know. Look." He dropped two unwrapped tablets in the glass and they both watched it, openmouthed, as it did its fizzing routine.

"Wow," Rusty breathed.

Kim laughed and laughed, watching the bubbles with delight.

"Do more," she said when it began to calm down.

"Okay."

It was an easy reach from his position on the chair.

He pulled down glass after glass, filled each and plopped in tablets, making a torrent of bubbles that made Kimmie laugh until tears ran down her cheeks. He didn't stop until he ran out of glasses.

"More," Kimmie cried. "Do more."

He shook his head sadly, looking at the three remaining tablets in his hand. "The glasses are all used up," he told her, looking bereft. Then an idea struck him, and his eyes brightened.

"Hey. Maybe goldfish like bubbles."

Kimmie nodded vigorously. "Yes, they do," she announced with all confidence. "Let's go."

And the two of them ran for the door, barely fitting through it as each pushed to be first.

Five

Chynna paused to listen to the call of a hawk. Pushing aside a curtain to look out the window, she was in time to catch its gliding flight into the woods. Now, why did that cry set up a feeling of happiness inside her, when the cry of the wolf the night before had filled her with fear?

"Daylight," she murmured to herself. "Everything seems less threatening in the day."

Of course, here in Alaska, there was more daylight at this time of year than anywhere else. "Which is why I'm going to love it here," she told herself resolutely.

She'd been cleaning up the den, putting things in stacks, working with a vengeance, and she hadn't yet admitted to herself she was doing all this to keep from thinking, to keep from facing facts. And now the cry of the hawk touched something inside her, and she knew it was time she made an inventory of her situation and decided what she was going to do next.

Flopping down into a big easy chair, she sighed and closed her eyes, letting her head drop back for a moment. For weeks, her mind had been filled with plans and the necessary detail work to cut all ties to Chicago and prepare for a new life in Alaska. She'd sold all her furniture, got rid of most of her clothes, shed boxes of children's toys and packed only the essentials for the trip north. A new, clean life, she'd thought. A haven for her children, a place where they could grow up knowing nature as an intimate ally rather than something they saw occasionally on the cable channels. A safe place, a place to grow and spread their wings, with limitless opportunities for their futures.

This was what she'd dreamed about since before Kimmie was born, since Kevin had died, since they'd been set adrift, like a little Family Robinson, on a sea of uncertainty, where the jobs were never good enough to pay for rent and day care, where every bill paid was another mountain scaled, where she was afraid to let her children out to play.

So she'd hit upon a plan. Why not get married again? She knew she would never love another man like she'd loved Kevin. But she could make a decent home for a man, in exchange for a decent home for her children. It seemed like a fair exchange. Why not?

She'd never taken it to the next step in her mind. She'd never let herself wonder what would happen if she arrived, kids and baggage in hand, and the man decided he didn't want her. She'd been so sure she could win him over. And yet…and yet…

She opened her eyes and stared out the window and the low, scudding clouds. Greg wasn't exactly falling head over heels for her, was he? He was a nice guy, attractive and likable. She'd really been lucky to have been chosen by him. The only problem was, he was having second thoughts. She had to get him past that, somehow.

Seduction. That might be the only way. And when she thought about the kiss they'd shared the night before, she knew it had possibilities. All she had to do was toughen herself up a bit. All she had to do was throw herself at the man. She grimaced. A fiercely independent person, she'd never begged for love before, and the thought of doing it now curdled her blood. But sometimes a woman just had to do what a woman had to do.

"You can do it," she whispered to herself encouragingly. "Flirt, darn you. It's the only way."

And as if to test out her resolve, Joe appeared in the doorway, looking a bit bleary, but otherwise as darkly handsome as ever.

"There you are," he said, as though he'd been looking for her. He glanced around the room and noted the change in the place, saw that she'd been cleaning.

"You really don't have to do this," he protested once again, but before he could go on, he noticed a copy of the catalog on top of a pile of papers she was throwing away.

"Oh, come on, you're not throwing out the catalog," he protested, picking it up and riffling through it. "I haven't finished looking at it."

She hated that catalog. It was a symbol of her desperate decision. She was happy with the results of that decision so far, but hated the thought that she'd had to stoop so low to get to this point.

"What do you need it for?" she said pertly, covering

up the way she felt with a quick smile. "You've got me."

He looked up and into her eyes. "Greg has you. I'm not Greg."

Before she could react to that, his gaze fell on another pile of paper and magazines she'd made. "What is this?" he asked, frowning at what looked like a stack of old girlie magazines.

She looked down to see what he was referring to, then glanced up at his frown.

"Your reading material, I presume," she said, hiding a smile. "I'm trying to throw a lot of old things out and I'm making a pile of things I'm not sure about. You might want to look through it and let me know if you want to save any of them." She gestured toward the stack.

Joe looked from her down to the naked and very buxom woman on the cover. He stared at the picture for a moment too long, then quickly slapped another magazine on top of it, suddenly realizing, to his horror, that he was blushing beet red.

Chynna noticed and her eyes sparkled. "If these have been your girlfriends all these years," she said, teasing him with mock chagrin, "I don't know how you expect me to compete."

His mouth opened and then it closed again. He couldn't think of a thing to say. She'd thrown him off guard again, and he had to take a moment to get his coherence back. Funny how different she was from any woman he'd known before. There were times when he wasn't sure if she was laughing at him. Not that he minded. He was always ready for a good joke himself. Just as long as he was in on it. But these magazines were not his style, and he didn't want her to think they were.

Finally, he managed to defend himself. "These aren't mine. These are Greg's."

She winced and shook her head. "Greg, really, don't you think it's time to drop this charade?"

"No." He was getting annoyed himself, and when he slapped his hand down on the table to emphasize his point, the stack of magazines shifted, spilling out across the table and onto the floor, setting free a whole gallery of naked and half-naked ladies who laughed up at him. He hesitated, wanting to cover them, but short of throwing himself on top of them, there was no quick way to do it. Better to let it go, he realized. This was a case where he just couldn't win.

"No, because it's not a charade," he went on instead. "I don't know what I have to do to convince you I'm not Greg." He pulled out his wallet and flipped it open, wondering why he hadn't thought of this before. "Look at this. Joe Camden. I live in Los Angeles. See, here's my driver's license."

She stared at the document for a moment, nonplussed. What if he was telling the truth? She glanced at him. What if he really was not the man she'd come to marry?

Then who was Greg? And where was he?

No, she wanted this man to be Greg. She liked things just the way they were. There was only one adjustment needed. She had to make him want her.

"There's no picture," she noted, tapping her finger on the card.

He hesitated. "It's a renewal. I haven't had a ticket in years, so they just keep sending me these renewals. Here." He dug back into his wallet and pulled out the original, complete with murky picture. It had been in his back pocket so long, it had faded and was ragged around the edges. "There you go," he told her triumphantly. "That's me. See?"

She leaned close and scrutinized the picture. It looked to be a young man about fifteen years the junior of the man standing before her. The hair was lighter and worn long; the face was very different.

"That's not you," she said.

"What?" He looked at it, frowned and shook his head. He had to admit, it didn't look much like him now. "Sure, it's me. That was right after I graduated from college. Of course I looked different. But the basic guy is still the same."

He held it out, and she looked at it again, then smiled and patted his arm. "Nice try," she said dryly.

His tone mirrored his outrage at her obtuseness. "You don't believe a driver's license? An official document of the state government?"

She smiled at him. "Sure. I believe there is a Joe Camden. I just don't believe it's you."

"Listen." He swung to face her, his eyes shooting sparks as he tucked his wallet away again. "Let's look at this logically. If I'm Greg, I chose you out of a catalog, then sent you money to come join me. I would have been taking a gamble, sure, but you turned out pretty damn good. So why would I act like this? Why would I keep trying to send you away?" He shook his finger at her, obviously coming up with his trump card. "And why in God's name would I be keeping my hands off you?"

She shrugged, a bit taken aback by his vehemence. "I imagine you got cold feet about the whole thing, haven't you?"

He shook his head, exasperated with her. "What do you think I am, crazy? Or blind? A woman like you doesn't come along every day. If I were Greg, I'd have tested how things were between us by now. If I had a right to you…" He paused, aware that he was possibly saying things he shouldn't.

But she didn't want him to stop. A shiver of excitement sliced through her, and she moved closer, searching his eyes.

"What would you do?" she asked softly, touching his arm again. Her heart was beating hard in her throat, and she hoped he couldn't tell. Because this was it, the chance she'd been waiting for. If she didn't give things a little shove at this juncture, they might never get anywhere.

"What would I do?" he echoed numbly, his gaze riveted on her face. "That…that's not the point. The point is…" He hesitated. What the hell was the point? He couldn't remember. Her hand was moving on his arm, and his pulse was starting to throb.

"Chynna," he managed to murmur, reaching out to cover her hand with his and stop it from continuing to move on his flesh. "You'd better not…"

"What?" She still had another hand and she used it, placing it firmly against his chest and beginning a light massage. "Why don't we do it? Why don't we find out how things stand between us?"

A tempting thought, but one he had to ignore. He grabbed the hand on his chest, holding both still. "Because I'm not Greg," he told her gruffly.

She leaned toward him. "Then pretend you are," she whispered, lifting her face to make it simple for his lips to find hers.

He wasn't made of steel. Flesh and blood were all he

had, and neither was doing much to help him resist the temptation she placed before him. But he made one last attempt.

"No, Chynna," he muttered, shaking his head and trying not to notice how full and pink her lips were. "You don't belong to me. I can't pretend you do."

"I can," she said, slipping her arms from his and wrapping them around his neck, her body arching gently into him. "It's easy if you try."

The groan came from deep inside him. Her skin was smooth and cool, her mouth hot, her breasts soft and firm against his chest. He sank into her and felt as though he'd lost his balance, as though he were floating in a sea of sensation and only holding on to her would keep him from drowning.

She gasped softly as he took possession of her mouth. She'd had to coax him into doing this, but once started, the moves were all his, and she could feel his body respond, all hard muscle and hot desire. She hadn't been mistaken last night. He wanted her, wanted her badly, and this time his hands slid down her back and covered her bottom, drawing her hard up against him, as though he was determined to show her just what she was risking if she kept this up.

Sensation flooded her, scaring her with its intensity. She'd never responded to a man so rapidly, not even Kevin when they had both been so young and so deeply in love. What made her react to this man this way? She didn't know, and she wasn't sure she wanted to find out. Not yet, at any rate.

Gasping for breath, she pulled away from him, but this time it was much more difficult. He didn't let go easily, and as she slipped from him, he grabbed her hair and held her for a moment, looking into her face.

"Don't go starting things you're not prepared to finish, Chynna," he said huskily. "You can't turn me on and off like a switch."

"I...I'll finish this," she told him defensively, looking up into his smoky gaze and losing her breath again. "That's what I came for, after all. But not now, not with my kids in the next room. Tonight..."

He stared into her eyes, slowly shaking his head. "There won't be any tonight, Chynna." He let her go and turned away. "I told you you were going to have to go today," he reminded her. "And I meant it."

Her chin rose. She was shaky, but never a quitter. "And I told you, I'm not going."

Turning to look her over, he had to let a hint of a smile shade the light in his eyes. "What do you think you've got, squatters' rights on this old place or something?"

She caught the softening and gave it right back, smiling to take the sting out of her words. "I've got a contract, that's what I've got. Would you like to see it again?"

He groaned, shrugging his wide shoulders. "Don't you see that you can't stay here?" he demanded, then hesitated, knowing there had to be a better way to get to her, to get her to see this thing objectively.

"Listen," he said, striving for a reasonable tone, "you seem like such a modern, sort of feminist woman. If you lived here, you'd be quite isolated. How could you be happy staying home and raising kids? I mean, wouldn't you feel as though you'd been oppressed or something? It doesn't seem to be the thing to do any longer."

Chynna brightened. This was one of her favorite topics. She could be quite a crusader for traditional family values, and she was ready with her point of view. "Right," she said, letting a bit of sarcasm into her tone. "And while nobody's home raising the kids, you may have noticed that the world is pretty much going to pot in a lot of ways. Especially ways that have to do with turning good, healthy children into decent adults."

"I had heard some rumors to that effect." He gazed at her quizzically. He didn't know many women who would say a thing like that. But then, he didn't know many women like this one. "So tell me, what did you do before you began raising kids?"

"Career-wise?" She leaned back. "I worked for a large advertising agency. And believe me, while I was employed there, I lived for my job. And I did pretty well. But once I decided to have children, that became my job."

"And you've never regretted it?"

"Are you kidding? Landing a big account is nothing compared to watching your baby's eyes light up when he learns to read his first word or puts his puzzle together right for the first time. Those are the things that really count."

He had to admit, he still didn't get it. And he wasn't completely convinced. "So you're prepared to spend your whole life like this."

"What whole life? It's only a small chunk of my life. When they're fifteen or so, I'll probably start working again part-time, or start up my own business. And by the time they're off to college, I'll be ready to go back out into the world. And believe me, I'll still have a lot of life left in me." She smiled at him. "Life is a big cycle. A merry-go-round. You can jump on and off when you feel like it."

She certainly had herself convinced. He shook his

head. "Well, you see, that's another reason why you shouldn't stay. You'll never be able to get a job out here. Or even start your own business."

She didn't know when to admit defeat. Her chin rose, and she pinned him with a direct gaze. "Why not? I noticed someone had a nail parlor in town. I could do something like that."

"In town?" He snorted derisively. "You come from Chicago and you can call that bump in the road a town?"

He couldn't shake her enthusiasm for the place. "It's as much town as we'll need."

He shook his head, beginning to think there was no getting through to her. "But, Chynna, you've got to face it. You're not staying."

"Why not?" she asked, ready to fight for her future and that of her children if she had to.

He threw his arms out as though he could encompass the whole kit and caboodle. "You just can't. Can't you tell? Look how primitive it is here."

"I can take primitive," she said stubbornly. "I'll camp out if I have to. I signed a contract to marry Greg Camden."

He shook his head slowly, impressed despite how much she annoyed him. "And you're going to stick to that contract come hell or high water. Is that it?"

She met his gaze with head held high. "Damn right."

He stared at her for a long moment. That made it even worse. She was promised to Greg and she meant to stay that way. Joe had no right to touch her and he quickly vowed it would never happen again. Turning, he began to make his way out of the room.

"Where are you going?" she asked, as though she

was afraid he would head for the hills just as he claimed the real Greg had done.

"I'm going out to take a look at what condition the barn and stables are in," he told her without looking back.

"What should I do with these magazines?" she called after him.

He slowed, then turned back and looked her full in the face. "Burn them. Throw them away. What the hell? I don't need them. If I want to look at a sexy woman, all I have to do is look at you."

"Well, thank you, kind sir," she murmured, flushing just a bit, but he was long gone and she was talking to herself. Still, it was reassuring. Somehow she was going to turn him around.

She packed up her cleaning things and headed for the kitchen, humming a tune under her breath. She'd expected to see the children in the living room with the stereo, but she didn't worry when they weren't there. She was sure they were playing quietly someplace about. She was still humming when she stepped into the kitchen, but the hum stuck in her throat when she saw the mess that awaited her. Glasses stood everywhere, some still full of liquid, some on their sides with the liquid spilling out onto the floor. The empty antacid wrappers gave mute testimony to what had been going on, and when she heard Kimmie giggling in the front room, she spun and headed for the sound.

"Look at Goldie!" she heard Rusty saying. "He likes it. He really likes it."

And with dread in her heart, she ran into the room.

The barn was a mess. It hadn't been used in years. But the stables were okay. Greg seemed to have a horse, probably the animal he was on right now as he rode his way through the mountains, avoiding the bride he'd thought he wanted to marry.

Joe could remember when the stables had been full and the barn the best stocked in the valley. His father had been an unusual man, but he'd worked hard and run his piece of land like a ship at times. At others, he would disappear into the wilderness and not come home for weeks. The family had stayed on for a few years after he'd died, but things had gone downhill. His mother had done the best she could, but she'd never loved the place the way his father had. She'd spent most of her last few years there concentrating on preparing Joe for college, and then for law school. Meanwhile, Greg had headed for the hills every chance he got, playing at being mountain man. There was no one to take care of the land the way it needed, and Joe had settled in L.A., and their mother had moved to Anchorage, but Greg had stubbornly held on, not wanting any part of anything but the Alaskan wild.

"He's wasting his life out there," their mother had said time and time again. "If only he would get some education and make something of himself."

Joe had been impatient with him, too, but that hardly made a dent in Greg's enjoyment of life. In fact, the more angry he made Joe, it often seemed, the happier he was himself. If Greg had known his brother was coming to see him, Joe could almost see him setting up this situation with Chynna just to torture him. But he couldn't have known. Could he?

As he was pondering this mystery, he heard a new sound and it echoed in his memories before he placed it. Someone was arriving on horseback. Turning, he saw the man coming in through the gate. His hair was long, his beard full, his clothes old-fashioned and worn. His saddle was hand tooled, and an old Indian blanket lay under it.

For just a moment, he wondered if it might be Greg. But no, this man was older. He was the picture of a mountain man, though, the sort of man who'd haunted the mountains of the West for over two hundred years. From the evidence he saw before him, he would wager this man hadn't been anywhere within smelling distance of real civilization for decades. Or anywhere near a shower in quite some time, either.

The man reined in his horse and looked down at Joe.

"Howdy," he said. "Heard you got a woman needs taking care of."

Joe's head went back, and his eyes narrowed. "You heard what?"

The man shifted his weight and looked toward the mountains. "Heard you got a woman who came to marry your brother and he lit out."

Joe shook his head, amazed at the way news traveled. "Where did you hear about that?"

The man looked down at him and shrugged. "I was out drinking with some of the boys last night, and it came up."

"Wonderful," Joe said with all the sarcasm he could muster. "So we're the item of the week, are we?"

The man looked slightly puzzled. "I don't rightly know about that," he declared, quieting his restless horse with a touch of his hand on the neck.

Joe sighed, feeling beleaguered. "No, I suppose not," he muttered. He'd come on a simple errand. All he'd wanted to do was grab Greg and take him to Anchorage to see his mother. Instead, he was facing new complications at every turn. And people said living in

L.A. was stressful. He looked up at the man, who was speaking again.

"Anyway, thought I'd come on down and see if I could help you out," he said, his shifty gaze flitting from one side of the yard to another, then settling on the house, as though he was looking for evidence that the woman might be nearby.

Joe put a hand up to shade his eyes from the sun. "Oh, yeah?" he said, and he could hardly keep the belligerence he felt from his tone. After all, this man could couch it in these polite terms, but what he really wanted was to take Joe's woman away from him. At least, that was the way it looked to Joe. "And what had you planned to do to help me out?" he asked, amused that the man thought he had a chance.

The man leaned forward in the saddle, as though he was going to confide in Joe. "I just wanted to let you know, if she's pretty, I reckon I could marry her myself."

Joe held back his grin, but it wasn't an easy thing to do. "And if she's not so pretty?"

He shrugged and got honest. "She'd have to be ugly as a badger not to look pretty to me. I been alone so long, I pretty much forgot what a woman was until this thing came up about you having an extra one."

An extra one. It might be amusing to see what Chynna would think of that. But he really didn't want to get Chynna involved here. Much as the man might divert him, there was an underlying sense of menace he couldn't deny. Joe stared into the man's fiery eyes and noted his long, greasy beard and then his gaze dropped to the thirty-aught-six rifle he held in his callused hands.

"Well, she's pretty, all right," he told him. "But I'm afraid she's just not your type. She's real squeamish—

you know what I mean? She hates dirt and she hates the wind and she hates the wolves. She pretty much hates Alaska at this point, and she can hardly wait to get out of here. In fact, I'm trying to find a way to get her back to Anchorage.'' He shook his head sadly. ''Afraid you missed the boat on this one. She won't be here long enough to court and all.''

The mountain man shifted the chaw of tobacco he was chewing from one side to the other. ''Hey, a week might be long enough for me,'' he muttered. ''Let's have a look at her.''

Joe glanced at the rifle again. ''If you want a woman that badly, why not go on into Anchorage one of these days and find yourself some likely little gal who would come out here and do for you?''

The man gave him a look as though he'd suggested they try taking cooking classes together. ''I can't go near that place.''

Joe shrugged. ''Well, I'm sorry I can't help you.''

''No,'' the man said, leaning down and staring at Joe, ''I'm sorry *I* can't help *you*.''

''Oh. Right.'' He tried a pleasant smile. ''Well, so long.''

The man turned his horse, and then Joe remembered something.

''Do you know my brother, Greg?'' he called after him.

The man twisted in the saddle. ''Yup,'' he said.

''You seen him anywhere?''

''Nope.''

Joe grimaced. ''Well, if you see him, tell him I'm looking for him, would you?''

The man hesitated. ''I seen someone who's seen him,'' he offered.

Joe's hope perked up again. "Where?"

"Said he was up on yonder mountain. Said he was hunting."

"Oh. I guess he'll be back when he's back."

"More 'n likely. So long."

"So long."

Joe watched him go and debated telling Chynna about him. In the end, he decided to hold back the story at this time. But he knew even more firmly that he had to get her out of here and on her way back home. An unattached woman in a male bastion like this was bound to cause problems. He wasn't about to spend his days fighting off men who wanted to carry her off to live in their caves with them. He had enough problems fighting himself off her.

He made his way back to the house. Chynna met him at the door, and her pretty face was a mask of tragedy.

"Greg, I'm really, really sorry. I hope...well, I don't know for sure, but we may be able to save one of them."

"What?" A genuine sense of alarm flashed through him. What had happened? Was something wrong with the kids? "What are you saying?"

She hesitated, looking the very picture of regret. "Your goldfish. Goldie and Piranha."

He stared at her blankly, then realized what she was talking about. "Ah, yes, the goldfish. What about them?"

She bit her lip, her dark eyes troubled. She was well aware that he hadn't warmed to her children. This would be another black mark against them, no doubt. But she wouldn't hide it from him. The best way to deal with it was to be up front about it and take the lumps that came her way. Anything else would just poison things in the future.

"Well," she began, "the kids saw you using antacid this morning…"

"And?"

"And they dropped a couple of the tablets in the goldfish bowl," she added in a rush.

He frowned. "They what?"

"I'm sorry." She shook her head. "And so are they. Kimmie's crying now that she realizes it might kill the goldfish. I've got them in fresh water, and they're floating, but they still seem to be breathing, and…"

"Chynna…" He was laughing. She stared at him, appalled and outraged, but he couldn't stop. "I thought you were talking about your children at first," he told her between chuckles. "And then I realize it's only goldfish. Believe me, I'll survive the loss, should the worst come to pass."

"Well, I may not," she said in a harried tone, her hair looking a little wild, her eyes looking a little wilder. She was relieved that he hadn't reacted with annoyance, but she'd been through an emotional roller-coaster ride in the past hour and she was going to take time to recuperate. "Rusty's already planning a funeral service. He wants me to make a eulogy."

Joe grinned. "No problem. Goldfish eulogies are easy."

"Oh, yeah?" She let her shoulders sag. "Then why don't you do it?"

"Oh, no," he said, looking very wise. "It would be better coming from you. After all, you're the caring, compassionate sort of person. I'm the cold, heartless realist." He laughed softly, finding this entire situation vastly amusing. "And anyway, you spawned these little goldfish murderers. It's your responsibility."

Finally, she relaxed. It looked as though it wasn't going to be quite the crisis she was afraid of when she first found her two kids with the poor fish gasping for oxygen.

"They're good kids," she told him with a quick smile. "I hope you're considering leniency."

His smile faded, and he turned away. There was no point in beating around the bush. Things had to be faced.

"Actually, I'm considering banishment for all three of you," he said, trying to keep his tone light but not really succeeding. "Get your kids together. We're going into town. I'm going to get you transportation back to Anchorage if I have to hire sled dogs to take you."

Six

"It's going to be a long drive to Anchorage. I'll drop you off at the store so you can stock up with some snacks and things for the kids."

Chynna looked at her children in the back seat and then turned her attention to Joe. "Where are you going while we're in the store?" she asked him quietly.

He glanced at her. "I'm going to find someone to drive you back," he said shortly, then stared straight ahead as though he didn't trust himself to go into it any further.

Chynna stared ahead, as well, but she didn't see the landscape, or even the snow-covered mountain peaks in the distance. Her stubborn streak was rising in her chest. He could make all the arrangements he wanted to make, but what he did had no bearing on what she did. After all, if he wasn't willing to honor their contract, he had no claim on her. And there was no way she was leaving.

The little collection of shacks that masqueraded as a town came into view, and she leaned forward, eager to see it again. It reminded her of the set of a Western movie, with boardwalks and false fronts, and a severe lack of recent paint jobs. But there was something endearing about it, and she'd warmed to it, right from the beginning.

"Ask for Annie," he told her as he dropped her off in front of the general store. "She'll set you up with everything you need."

"What I need is a husband," she murmured to him with a significant look before turning to help her children get out of the car.

"Just ask Annie," he said, trying to maintain a light tone. "She's liable to have a supply of them, too."

Her look had daggers, and she tossed her head as she turned from him and started up the steps with her children. He drove off slowly, looking back in his rearview mirror, but she pretended not to notice.

She paused in the doorway, looking in. The place had an atmosphere that conjured up pictures of stores at the turn of the century, and in truth, had probably been established sometime around that age. A group of men sat around the stove, although the weather was too warm to need to have it lit, most of them on chairs tilted back, leaning against the wall. The room itself was well stocked with canned and packaged goods stacked on shelves that filled the walls, all the way to the ceiling.

The men were talking lazily, but as she entered, tilted-back chairs came back to rest on all fours with a thud, and a hush fell over the group. They each gaped at her and her children as though they'd never seen anything like them.

The reception was rather disconcerting, but she

smiled and asked, "Does anyone know where I can find Annie?"

There was a pause, and then they all tried to talk at once. At the same time, a gray-haired woman with lively dark eyes came out of a back room and stood behind the counter.

"May I help you?" she asked, looking Chynna over with an alert intelligence Chynna responded to immediately.

Chynna came forward and gave Annie her name and introduced the children. "We flew in yesterday on the mail plane," she began.

Annie didn't let her get any further. Her jaw dropped and her eyes snapped. "Don't tell me you're the one who came to be Greg's wife," she exclaimed.

Chynna hesitated. "Well, yes, I did."

"Oh, darling…" Annie grabbed her hand and pumped it up and down. "Well, what do you know. Greg hinted there was someone coming to join him, but I never dreamed you'd be so…you'd be…"

"So darn pretty," piped up one of the men who had been sitting around the stove. He'd risen and was coming over to join them at the counter. "Greg is a lucky man."

Chynna turned, flushing, and found that her children had gathered around another man who was pulling quarters out of the air much to the delight of the little ones. That was reassuring. She didn't want to talk about Greg in front of the kids, and now that they were occupied, she wouldn't have to be quite so circumspect. She turned back to Annie.

There was something in the woman's face that inspired confidence and brought up the urge to unburden herself. And she sure needed someone to confide in.

Annie looked ready to hear her out, and the man who'd come up to lean on the counter—Annie called him Roger—had a face full of sympathy. These were people she'd never seen before, but somehow that made it even easier to tell them the truth.

"Well, the problem is," she said softly, "it doesn't look like Greg wants me after all."

Annie's face registered shock. "Doesn't want you?" She slapped her hand down on the counter. "That sniveling little polecat. How dare he not want you?"

Chynna was a little startled by this description of the handsome man she'd been with for the past twenty-four hours. But Roger muttered his agreement with the sentiment.

"He's a fool—that's what he is. Always was a fool. Saw him keep a skunk for a pet once. Knew he was a fool ever since."

Chynna couldn't imagine the man she knew keeping skunks, but she supposed she didn't really know him very well. "At any rate, he wants us to go back to Chicago as soon as possible."

Annie shook her head. "Well, we heard there was some problem, but I was sure it would blow over as soon as Greg got his courage up."

"He should cut that wild long hair of his," Roger said, shaking his head. "Maybe then he'd be able to hear the advice everyone keeps giving him."

"Hair?" Chynna frowned. Greg didn't have long hair. He certainly must have had a haircut since the man had seen him last.

"Yeah, 'Grizzly Greg' we call him around here," Roger went on. He smiled at Chynna, looking a bit sheepish. "When he first told us fellas he was sending away for a bride, we all thought he was loco. But seeing you, I guess there are more men who will want to take a look at that book he found you in.''

Annie was impatient with this line of talk. She wanted to stick to the main point. ''You say Greg wants you to go back where you came from.'' She looked at Chynna sharply. ''He said this to your face?''

She nodded. ''He's made it very clear. He's out looking for a way to send us back to Anchorage to catch a plane for home right now.''

Annie pursed her lips. ''Listen. We don't have many women out here in Dunmovin. And the ones we got…well, we've got to stick together.'' Reaching out, she patted Chynna's hand. ''You come on into the back room with me. I'll fix you a nice cup of tea and we'll talk.''

''But my kids…''

''Don't you worry about them. We'll take care of them. Henry!'' She gestured toward the man who'd just found a dime in Rusty's ear, much to the boy's amazement. ''Take those kids out back and show them Cleo and her babies. They'll like that.'' She nodded at Chynna. ''Cleo's a fat old sow but she does have the cutest little piglets.''

Chynna began to shake her head, sure that her children, who'd been through a lot in the past two days, would want to stick close to her rather than go off with a stranger. But as she turned, she saw the old-timer reach out to Rusty and Kim with both hands, and to her amazement, she saw those same children reach right back, and in no time their pudgy little fingers were being held tightly and they were being led out back. And neither one of them so much as looked back over a shoulder to see what Mom was doing.

''Oh, Henry's a wonder with the kids,'' Annie told

her, reading the surprise in her face. "They'll be fine. You come on with me."

She did just that, following her through a doorway and settling down with a sigh as the older woman ran water for tea. The room was nicely furnished and looked nothing like the store area looked. She sat in a comfortably upholstered chair and examined the pictures on the wall.

"Your children?" she guessed, gesturing at the pictures of young soldiers and an airplane.

"Yup, those are my boys. Jack and James. They both went into the service and neither one of them ever came back."

"Oh, I'm so sorry," Chynna began, but Annie laughed.

"No, honey, I don't mean they died. They both ended up living in California. Both married. And I hardly ever get to see my grandchildren."

She poured out the hot water and stood back, smiling at the younger woman. "Oh, they invite me to come on down there and live with them often enough. But I tell them I've got Alaska in my blood. I can't leave her."

Chynna smiled. "It certainly is beautiful here," she said. "The scenery is so dramatic."

Annie nodded, pouring out the tea into two cups. "You should see it in the winter. It's like another world."

Chynna sighed. "I'm not sure I'll get to see that," she said. "Unless I find a way to avoid it, it looks like I might be leaving very soon."

Annie frowned, studying her face with a cool, perceptive look. "You don't want to go? You'd like to stay?"

Chynna hesitated, then nodded. "I don't want to go

back. I think this place would be perfect for raising my kids.''

"Your kids.'' Annie nodded slowly, as though she understood fully. ''They're why you came in the first place, aren't they?''

Chynna nodded. ''Not that I would have short-changed Greg in any way,'' she added hastily. ''I was prepared to be a good wife. But my main motivation was to find a place where I could raise my children.''

Annie made a sound of disgust. ''That darn Greg,'' she muttered, throwing down her napkin.

Chynna shook her head, anxious not to be misunderstood. ''Don't blame Greg,'' she told her quickly. ''It's really my own fault. You see, I tricked him. I...'' Funny how easy it had been to do this and how hard it was to explain it to people. ''I didn't tell him about Rusty and Kimmie.''

She stared. ''He didn't expect the children?''

Chynna nodded. ''I gambled that he'd learn to love them so quickly, it wouldn't make any difference. But I lost that gamble. And now I realize it was unfair of me to spring it on him this way. I'm only getting what I deserve. I just wish...''

''Well, I can see that the kids came as a shock to him. I'm sure he had fantasies of things children tend to inhibit.'' Annie looked at her fiercely. ''Are you in love with the guy?''

She hesitated. ''Well, I hardly know him. But...'' She looked at Annie's skeptical face. She would have been skeptical, too, only hours before. But now... ''Why? Does that seem so impossible to you?''

Annie shrugged and looked a little uncomfortable. ''To tell you the truth, I can't remember any other girl loving Greg. I wouldn't have thought it could happen that fast. I would have thought he would be more of an acquired taste.''

''I like him very much,'' Chynna said, realizing that what she'd just said was an understatement. ''He seems like a really quality person.''

Annie grimaced. ''Greg?'' she asked softly.

But Chynna didn't notice. She was thinking very hard, remembering his gentleness with the children, even though he obviously didn't understand them, how embarrassed he'd been about the girlie magazines, how he'd resisted her when she'd tried to coax him with sexual attraction—even though his resistance hadn't lasted very long. And then she thought of his kiss and how she had reacted, heart and soul, and a sadness filled her. She'd never thought another man could take Kevin's place. Even though he'd been dead for three years, she'd never been tempted to fall for anyone else. Until now. And she had to admit, she was tempted. Too bad he felt so very differently.

''Well, what does Joe say about all this?'' Annie was asking.

''Joe?'' Chynna's head rose in surprise, and after a heartbeat, a feeling of gathering doom began to settle in her heart. ''You mean Greg's brother?''

Annie nodded and grinned as she thought of him. ''He was in here yesterday. It was sure good to see him. He's been living down in Los Angeles for years. But I guess you know that.''

A strange buzzing had set up shop in Chynna's ears. She took a long sip of tea and said, her voice forced, ''They…they're not much alike, are they?''

''Oh, no,'' Annie said, laughing and motioning dismissively with her free hand. ''Tell you the truth, Greg has always been a bit of a pain in the neck. But Joe…''

She smiled. ''Joe's a sweetheart. I've always had a soft spot for that boy. He's almost like a third son to me.''

Annie went on, filling in anecdotes from years past, and though Chynna laughed and nodded, she wasn't listening. She was numb. He'd been telling the truth all along. Joe wasn't Greg. *Oh my.*

Finally, she had to laugh. Annie had just told about how Joe had sent away for a superhero uniform and worn it everywhere he went when he was eight, so the laughter seemed appropriate to her. But the more Chynna laughed, the more she realized that it had nothing to do with Annie's stories, but her own amusement and horror at the mistakes she'd made.

When she finally ran out of laughter, she turned very serious very quickly.

''Listen, Annie,'' she said leaning forward and fixing the woman with a direct gaze. ''We don't know each other well, but I need advice. Do you think you can help me?''

Annie blinked and nodded slowly. ''I took a liking to you from the moment I saw you,'' she told Chynna. ''And I'm seldom wrong about people. Go ahead and ask, honey. I'll do anything I can to help you.''

Chynna smiled and took the woman's hand in hers. ''Thank you,'' she said, her eyes full of sincere appreciation. ''Now, here's what I need.''

Chynna and the kids were watching for Joe and they came out as he drove up in front of the store. Annie came out with them, chatting with Chynna and herding the kids in to the back seat of the car while Chynna stowed the bags of groceries away. Finally, Annie bent down and spoke to Joe.

''You take good care of this girl. And tell Greg I'm

going to give him what for the next time I see him. Imagine, not wanting a girl like this, and after she's come all that way, too!''

Joe swung around in surprise and met Chynna's gaze. She smiled at him, looking just a bit sheepish, and murmured, ''Please don't say I told you so.''

He grinned, relieved and regretful all at the same time. ''Not even once?''

''No. You say it, and I'll find some way to make you pay.''

He chuckled. It was about time. There had been advantages to being thought of as Greg, he had to admit, but all in all, he preferred his own identity. And he was glad Chynna wasn't going to leave thinking this was all his fault.

They all waved at Annie as the car started down the road toward home. Glancing into the back seat, Joe's gaze met Rusty's, and he noted that the boy was fairly jumping up and down in his seat, his eyes alight, his face full of excitement.

''Hey, what's got you so stoked?'' he asked the child.

Rusty didn't need any more of an invitation to tell him. ''We had fun,'' he told him, his dark eyes huge. ''We saw baby pigs. They were little and they squealed, just like this.'' He gave a tiny sound that had both Joe and Chynna laughing, then went on. ''And the man— he pulled a dime out of my ear. Just like this.'' He demonstrated. ''Mom, could I learn to do tricks like that? Could I learn magic?''

''I don't know,'' Chynna said, tousling his hair. ''Magic takes a lot of work. You'd have to practice very hard.''

''Maybe the man could teach me,'' Rusty said.

"Maybe. We'll have to ask him next time we see him."

Joe looked up quickly, catching her glance. He'd noted the reference to a future in this area, and that didn't fit with the facts as he knew them. But she merely smiled at him, looking like the cat that ate the canary, and he felt he had to put in his two cents' worth.

"There are probably places you can take magic classes back in Chicago," he told Rusty, glancing over his shoulder at the boy. "Maybe your mother will look into them when you get back."

"But…but Mom says we're going to live here now," Rusty said, and then he seemed to remember that he wasn't supposed to be friends with Joe, that he'd made some secret and private pact against it, and he lapsed back into silence in his corner of the car. Kimmie spent the whole time with her thumb in her mouth, staring at the back of Joe's head, but not making a sound.

Chynna looked back at them both, smiled and winked and didn't say another word. Joe was silent the rest of the way back, as well, but he wasn't very cheerful. There seemed to be too much to think about for that.

First off, there was Chynna. She was acting far too happy. He knew she didn't want to leave, knew she had been upset to think he was making concrete plans to get transportation for her and her children. He'd felt guilty earlier, knowing how much it must have cost her to come, emotionally, mentally, and in giving up all that she'd left behind. He knew her well enough by now to know she would feel she had failed if she left. But she had to leave. He had to get her out of here before Greg showed up. The better he knew her, the more sure he was that she would be crazy to marry his brother.

At the house, the children tumbled out of the car as

soon as their seat belts were released and they ran across
the yard to swing on a loose gate, and Chynna leaned
on the porch railing, watching them with a bittersweet
smile. This was exactly what she wanted for them, a
place where they could run and play and explore life
without worrying about a kidnapper or a bus coming
down on top of them. She wanted them to watch ants
build a hill and find quail eggs in the bushes and see a
sunrise reflected on the nearby lake. This was what
she'd bargained for. And though she'd lost at her first
try, she had another trick up her sleeve. The only question was, did she have the guts to go through with it?

Joe came up behind her and watched the children
playing, as well. Turning, she smiled at him. "I'm
sorry," she said softly.

He gazed down into her velvet brown eyes and felt
something stir deep inside. "There's nothing for you to
be sorry about," he said gruffly, avoiding the emotion
that threatened to rise in him, pushing it back where it
belonged.

She nodded. "Yes, there is. I refused to believe you
when you were telling me the truth. I guess I just
wanted you to be Greg so badly...."

"Never mind," he said quickly. "That's all over
now."

"I came thinking I would be getting married. I guess
that's all over, too." She gave him a teasing, melan-
choly smile. "I don't suppose *you'd* like to get married?"

He shook his head. Though he knew if ever there
was a woman he might consider it with... But no, marriage was not for him. And children were something he
didn't understand and didn't want to know more about.
"I don't think I'm the marrying kind," he told her.

She nodded sadly. "I was afraid of that."

It was his turn to give her a slow grin. "But thanks for asking."

Her chin rose, and she turned back to watch the children. "Don't get too swellheaded over it," she advised him dryly. "I would have asked any good-lookin' man."

He grinned, recognizing a face-saving put-down when he heard one. "If it's just anyone you want, you won't have to wait long. I've had three men ask about you today. One of them rode right into the yard, ready to take you back to his cabin or whatever he lives in."

She turned as though delighted with the news. "Why didn't you tell me? I could have looked them over. Had my pick."

He gave her a look that said he still thought she was nuts and then he slumped down to sit on the top step. "Tell you what," he said, looking up at her with a grin. "If another guy shows up, I'll bring him right on in to meet you, and you can tell him to his face whether he makes the grade or not."

Dropping down to sit on the step below his, she gazed up at him with pretended skepticism. "Something tells me you wouldn't be laughing if this were really a good idea."

He chuckled. "Don't be so cynical. We've got some great men out here in Dunmovin. The fact that most of them haven't shaved in ten years and probably haven't had a bath since Christmas—that's all superficial stuff. You can turn a man like that around on a dime—I have no doubt." He shook his head, his eyes dancing. "It's almost a shame that you won't have your chance with Greg. It would have been interesting to see what you would have done with him."

Interesting, was it? That was a word that usually meant trouble in her experience. She drew her legs up and wrapped her arms around her knees. "So Greg really is up in the mountains hiding away someplace," she said softly, and she couldn't resist glancing toward the trees.

Joe picked up a pine needle and began to pull it apart. "Yup. He really is."

She didn't turn to look at him. "Why is he hiding?"

Joe was silent for so long, she almost turned to look at his face, to try to gauge what he was thinking. But he finally spoke. "I figure he ordered you in a drunken stupor and then liked the idea of you. But when you told him you were really coming, he couldn't quite face the reality of you. So he took off, figuring you'd leave when you couldn't find him."

She looked toward the woods again, almost imagining she could see movement in the shadows. "Are you saying he's out there right now, watching us?" she asked him softly.

He shrugged. "Could be. I wouldn't put it past him."

She was quiet for a few minutes, and then softly, very softly, she began to sing a song about a bird in a cage, and about its mate left alone in the forest, about how they both died of broken hearts.

Leaning back against the post, he half closed his eyes and let the sound wash over him. There was something about her voice that took the starch out of his muscles and made him feel about to melt all over, and that was unusual for him. He prided himself on toughness—in life and in the courtroom, but when he heard her sing...wasn't there some legend about a woman who could weave a spell with her voice, disarm an army? That was what Chynna's singing did to him.

Her song was over and she looked at him, smiling, and for just a moment, he thought she was going to lean over him and touch his face—maybe kiss him. The look was in her eyes. And his heart began to beat a little faster, anticipating.

But she merely patted his jeans-clad knee and drew back again. "If you won't marry me, maybe you ought to hire me," she said lightly. "It looks like I could put you to sleep anytime, anywhere." Rising, she laughed down at him, then turned and went into the house.

Joe sat back up and blinked, trying to analyze the way she could manipulate his blood pressure. He'd never felt so vulnerable to an outside influence before, and it sort of scared him. "Oh, well," he told himself. "She'll be out of my life soon. Then I won't have to worry about it."

She'd gone off before he'd had a chance to tell her about the arrangements he'd made for her trip. But that was okay. He didn't want to talk about them. He wasn't going to relish seeing her go. But he would be relieved to know she was on her way back to Chicago and out of Greg's sphere of influence.

She fixed the kids a late-afternoon snack, chattering with them, and including him when he came and sat at the table, drawn by the happy sounds. The children were subdued when he joined them, but Rusty soon loosened up and by the end of the meal, was almost natural. Kimmie, however, never took her thumb out of her mouth and never took her wary gaze off Joe.

"I'm starting to worry about her," Chynna admitted to him when Rusty had run off to play. Kimmie sat before her plate where not a thing had been touched. "I don't think she's eaten anything since we got here yesterday."

Joe frowned. Feeding kids was something he didn't know much about, but he didn't like to think of anyone going hungry on his account. "Has she had anything to drink?" he asked, just to make sure it wasn't time to call the doctor.

"Yes, she's had a little juice. And one glass of milk that I know of."

"Then she's probably okay," he said reassuringly, though they both knew he didn't have a clue as to what it all meant. He moved closer to the little girl and smiled at her. "Don't you want to have a bite of this sandwich?" he asked her, indicating the food on her plate. "It looks very yummy to me."

Kimmie leaned as far away from him as she could get without falling out of the chair. Her blue eyes were wide and vigilant. It was pretty obvious there was no way she was going to eat anything on Joe's say-so.

He stared at her, at the look in her eyes, at the lack of trust, and suddenly, he wanted more than anything in the world to make this little girl like him. It was something he had to do. He sat beside her and studied the situation. She wouldn't eat. She wouldn't speak. She wouldn't let him touch her. What could he do to get through to her?

Little girls liked dolls, but he didn't have any of those. They had tea parties, but he was afraid he didn't have tiny teacups in his old trunk in the bedroom. What else did they like? Animals?

Animals. Hmm.

"Hey, Mr. Camden, want to come watch me climb a tree?" Rusty was in the doorway, hesitating, looking hopeful, but ready to withdraw the invitation if he got the slightest indication it was unwelcome.

"Mr. Camden doesn't have time to..." Chynna began, but Joe rose and grinned at the boy.

"Sure, I'll come watch," he told him. "I used to climb that old elm outside my bedroom window when I came home late at night and my brother locked me out."

"Really?" Rusty was impressed. "Did you ever fall?"

"A hundred times."

"Yeah." Rusty looked relieved. "Sometimes you just gotta fall, huh?"

"Sometimes you do."

Joe threw Chynna a smile as he followed the boy out, and Chynna held her breath, holding back her heartbeat. The man was so...so... What could she say? Another man might have brushed Rusty off. Another man might have had to say he never fell, might have had to prove how manly and powerful he was, just to put the kid in awe. But not Joe. He saw immediately what the boy needed, and he gave it to him. For just a moment, her eyes filled with tears.

"Thank you, Mr. Camden," she said softly, and then she looked down to see Kimmie looking up at her, so silent, so watchful, and she bent down to kiss the top of her head. "And thank you, Miss Kimmie, for being my good girl. Now, how about eating just one bite? Look—this sandwich sure looks like a tiny airplane to me. Here it goes, taking off at the airport. And it's flying around and around." Swooping the sandwich through the air, she made the appropriate airplane sounds. "It's ready to land! Better open up the hangar! It's coming in." She slowly swooped the sandwich toward Kimmie's face, but the hand didn't move. The thumb still plugged the entryway. "Open up! Quickly!"

Kimmie's eyes looked very sad, but she resolutely shook her head. She was not going to eat. Not tonight.

"Oh, Kimmie." She dropped the sandwich down on the plate. "Look. The airplane had to crash. It couldn't get into the hangar."

She looked at Kimmie again, but the wall of determination hadn't softened one bit. Sighing, she rose from the table and began to clear it. Something was going to have to happen pretty soon. This couldn't go on much longer. Kimmie had to eat.

"We've got a plan." Joe and Rusty stood in the doorway of the family room, looking pleased with themselves.

"We're going out to the old water hole to see the animals," Rusty told her, his dark eyes sparkling with excitement. "It's a place where Joe used to go when he was a kid."

"Joe?" she asked, raising an eyebrow, but Rusty had already run off to tell Kimmie about the planned expedition.

"I told him to call me that," Joe explained, leaning against the doorjamb and watching her. "I wanted to be something closer than a 'Mr.'"

"Oh, really?" Turning, she gave him an appraising look. "And why is that?"

"Why do I want to get closer to him?"

She nodded slowly, her arms folded across her chest. "What exactly is the point?"

He hesitated, not really sure himself. "Because I like him," he said at last, a bit defensively. "He's a great kid."

"I know that." Frustration laced with a touch of anger made her voice tremble just a bit. "But he doesn't need you to break his heart."

"Break his heart?" Joe looked bewildered. "Damn it, Chynna, I just wanted to be friendly. I'm not trying to...to..."

She stared at him, then relented a bit and gave him a half smile. "I know that. You mean well. You're a nice person." She turned away, shaking her head. She'd been alone with her children for so long, and she'd watched their needs go unmet much too often. How could she make Joe understand?

She turned back and gazed into his eyes. "But don't you see what this could do to Rusty? He doesn't have a father and he so desperately wants one."

He wasn't going to give in to this psychological analysis. Stubbornly, he said, "Look, all I did was tell him to call me Joe."

"Okay." She held her hand up to stop the subject in its tracks. "Okay."

He shifted his weight restlessly. "Can we still go out to the water hole?"

"Sure."

"Good."

He sounded relieved, and she couldn't help but smile at him. She turned, pointing out the stack of old magazines. "I brought these back in. Since they aren't really yours, I guess they're not yours to throw away. Shall I put them in the bedroom?"

He hesitated, stealing a glance at the cover of the top item. "Uh...no, why not just leave them here?"

She made a face. "Because I don't want the kids to see them."

"Here." He looked around, then picked up the lot of

them and shoved them into a cabinet. "Now they're gone. Out of sight, out of mind."

Unfortunately, the cabinet was not secure. His words had barely completed their echo in the hallway before the cabinet door flew open again, and the magazines came spilling out all over the floor, some of the most blatant pictures making a return engagement to the space between the two of them. They both stared down for a moment, then looked up and met each other's gaze.

"Back in sight, back in mind," she murmured, biting back a laugh as she sank down to sit on the couch.

He was still embarrassed by them, and that made her want to grin all the more. She watched while he bent down and began to scoop them up. Reaching out, she picked up one with a picture of a woman with the largest breasts she'd ever seen—both quite naked and being projected toward the cameraman as though they were turrets on a big gun and the enemy was at hand. Studying it for a moment, she shook her head.

"Why do men like that sort of thing?" she asked, just making conversation. "You know, I really don't get it."

He had most of the magazines back up in a pile and he glanced over to see what she was looking at, then looked away again very quickly. "That's as it should be," he said evenly. "You're a woman. You're not supposed to get it."

She leaned forward, her chin in her hand, and frowned at him. "But what do you get out of it? I mean, a nice-looking man is fun to look at for a minute or two, but I can't imagine buying a whole magazine full of them and looking for hours. What a waste of time."

He snatched the offending magazine away from her and put it on the bottom of the stack.

"You see," he said wisely, "that's because in the grand scheme of things, when it comes to stimulation, men are visual."

She watched him trying to jam the magazines back in the cabinet with amusement. "And what are women?"

He didn't look at her. He was concentrating on his job. "I don't know."

"I do. Women are sensible."

He got the last of the magazines in and slammed the door shut, turning the key in the lock, then stood back and waited to see what would happen. Nothing, it seemed. Finally, he turned to look at her.

"Women are a complete mystery to me," he told her breezily. "But I must admit I feel a strange, mystical attraction to them."

She grinned at him. "No kidding. How unique."

"You think so?" He pretended to preen in the long mirror that decorated the far wall.

She threw a throw pillow at him, and he laughed, ducking it, but tackling her as she tried to get away, pulling her back down onto the couch in his arms. The moment was ripe with provocation, but he hesitated, and so did she. Their gazes clung together for a long ten seconds, and then the moment had passed, and they slowly, reluctantly, drew apart.

"Get ready," he told her as he rose and started for the doorway. "We're going to the watering hole."

"What should I bring?" she called after him.

"A canteen. Maybe some snacks. And a jacket. It'll be cold before we get back."

She nodded to herself very slowly. "Cold," she whispered to the air. "And very lonely."

Seven

"Why do you call this a water hole?" Chynna asked him a little over an hour later as they trudged down the hill into the valley that held their destination. "It looks like a small lake."

"It is. But when we were kids, Greg and I saw some documentary on water holes out on the Serengeti Plain, and it worked just like this place does. At nightfall, all the animals for miles came to the water hole to drink. And the same thing happens here."

"Except you don't have any nightfall," she said, looking at the brilliant sky.

"Sure, we do. It's just longer and more drawn out." He kept moving, surveying for a good picnic area. "We'll go down to the edge in a bit. You'll be surprised at what we'll see."

They'd come out of the trees into the valley. A small river ran down the center of it, emptying into the lake, and a series of waterfalls let water back into the river at the far end of the body of water. Chynna fell in love with the area at first sight.

"Paradise," she whispered to herself as she put down the picnic basket on a flat rock and began to help Joe spread out the blanket. A hawk flew by, and birds sang in the trees. The rushing of the water seemed to mirror the flow of clouds across the sky. The children began to run and play in the meadow, running over tufts of jade green grass, falling among cascades of tiny yellow-and-blue flowers, poking at stashes of snow that still lingered in the shady nooks and crannies.

"Look," Rusty said, pointing at a puddle. "Something's moving." He bent over and stared into the water with Kimmie right behind him.

"Pollywogs," Joe told him. "Tadpoles. They'll be frogs pretty soon."

And sure enough, a battalion of tiny frogs began to hop out of the puddle, making the children scream, first with surprise, then with delight. Chynna watched while Joe helped them catch a few and gave them safety tips, showing them how to hold the tiny animals without hurting them, and then release them again into their natural environment.

She smiled as he came up to join her on the blanket. "It must have been wonderful growing up here," she noted.

He slumped beside her and frowned, considering. "Looking back, I guess it was pretty good. Better than concrete and drive-by shootings. But it wasn't perfect."

"No?" She glanced at him sideways. "Why not?"

He started to say something, then caught himself and growled at her. "Oh, no, you don't, Mrs. Freud. You're not going to get me to unburden the painful experiences of my childhood so that you can pick my psyche apart.''

"Aw, come on," she teased. "Be a good sport. It'll be fun."

"For you, maybe." He gave her a half grin, looking up into the low sun and noting the way the sunbeams shot out around her head like a halo. "Anyway, I'm not the one who put my picture in a catalog so that I could marry some stranger. You're the one we ought to be analyzing. Why the hell did you do that, anyway?"

She folded her hands in her lap and went very still. "I don't know if I can make you understand."

But he had to understand. He needed to. "Give it a try," he said softly.

She hesitated, looking at him speculatively, at the way his hair fell over his forehead, at his broad, competent hands, his strong arms.

"Have you ever had anyone in your life that you loved better than yourself?" she asked him. "Have you ever cared more for the welfare of someone close to you than you did for your own comfort?"

He frowned. "Sure," he began, but then he thought for a moment and couldn't come up with anyone. He'd been about to say his mother, but that wasn't really true. Not the way she seemed to mean it. He did go out of his way to do things for his mother, but he'd never been forced to make a choice that would put him at a disadvantage. He couldn't honestly say that he'd experienced what Chynna was asking him to consider.

"I guess not really," he admitted. "Not yet."

She nodded. "You don't have children," she told him. "Once you have your own children, you'll know what I mean and why I did what I did." She looked at him for a moment and decided to tell him a bit more.

"I'll tell you what finally made up my mind to take the chance. Rusty has a slight learning disability, and I knew they would never help him in the schools where we lived, not the way he needed to be helped. I knew I could do a better job teaching him at home. I'm the one who cares if he learns or not. And at the same time, Kimmie was having problems at the day-care center where I was leaving her while I went to work. She's so shy, the other kids were teasing her and she...well, she just wasn't doing well."

He looked out at where Kimmie was playing and felt the urge to protect her. If he, hardly knowing her, had that urge, what must Chynna feel like?

"The problems seemed to build up day after day. And I couldn't see any solutions. I spent so much time at work, worrying all the time about what was going on with my kids...I had to find a way to make a change. You only get one chance to raise each child. You have to try to do the best for them that you can."

"Okay," he said, frowning. "I get that part. Now, here's the part I don't get. How did you get to the point where you could treat marriage like a blind date?"

She met his gaze and didn't waver. "I don't look at it quite that way," she told him levelly. "I wasn't in need of a man so much as I needed a job, and a life-style. That was what I was in the market for. And when I made an honest appraisal of my resources, I thought the only way I would have a chance of doing it well— of giving my children a better situation—was to marry someone who lived where I wanted my kids to grow up."

He stared at her, but before he could respond, the children were back, ravenously hungry and, in Rusty's case, full of stories of what they'd encountered in their trip through the meadow. He sat back and watched her with her children and wondered at a love that could be so selfless.

Oh, no, he could almost hear her whispering to him. *It's the ultimate in selfishness. Don't you see? They're part of me.*

Looking down, he met Kimmie's dispassionate gaze. He tried a smile, but she looked stern, so he gave it up pretty quickly.

"When are you going to trust me?" he asked her softly.

But she didn't have an answer yet, so he shrugged and ate his sandwich.

Chynna saw the look pass between them and she bit her lip. She knew, deep in her heart, that they could become close with the right circumstances. What she didn't know was when that might happen—how long it would take. And there wasn't much time. Very soon, Joe was going to walk out of their lives.

Could she let that happen? She didn't have a whole lot of choice. If only she could think of some way to hold him, to make him want to stay. She'd never known a man who seemed so right for her and her family. If she could have picked a man out of a catalog, and had waited for the perfect one to come along, it would have been Joe. They said women often fell in love with the wrong men. Here she was feeling very much on the verge of falling for the perfect man—and it didn't really matter. She wasn't going to be allowed to have a real chance at him, was she?

She didn't have much time. If she was going to devise a battle plan, she'd better do so quickly. Sitting back, she watched him and wondered.

When the food was devoured and the basket packed

away, Joe gathered them all together for the trek down to the water.

"You've got to be very quiet," he told the children as they walked along. "If the animals hear you, they won't come near."

Their side of the river was lined with thick brush, and the other side had trees coming down almost to the water, but no brush to speak of. Joe led them into a thicket where they settled and sat quietly, parting the branches with their hands and waiting to see animals come to drink on the other side.

"I don't see any," Rusty said in a loud stage whisper, after watching for about thirty seconds.

"Be patient," Joe whispered back. "We just arrived like a conquering army driving elephants across the land. They'll have heard us. They'll be wary for a while. We'll have to wait until they think we're gone for sure."

They waited another five minutes, and just when the kids were beginning to fidget again, there was a sound on the other side. They sat very still, holding their breaths. A rustling was heard in the trees, and then a beautiful blacktail deer came from the woods, stepping carefully, nose up for danger. She stopped for a moment and sniffed the air, then stepped toward the water, and from behind her came a fawn, a quarter her size and dappled where she was tan. It scampered past her and made its way to the bank while she moved with a more stately pace. They both began to drink, the mother raising her head every few seconds, checking for threats from up the valley, then down.

Joe glanced down at Chynna and the kids. Each seemed to be holding a breath, watching with wide eyes. Kimmie's thumb had dropped out of her mouth. She was staring at the deer with all her might, her mouth slightly open, her eyes big as saucers. Warmed, he looked back at the animals, and he had to admit, he felt almost as thrilled with the sight as the others did. All his years in suburban southern California had dulled him to this sort of experience, and now he felt as though he were awakening to it again. This was real. This was Alaska.

It wasn't until the deer had retreated into the woods again that anyone spoke. Rusty and Chynna were brimming with reaction, but Kimmie didn't say a thing, and Joe leaned down to catch her attention.

"Did you like that, Kimmie?" he asked her, and she looked up at him solemnly, took her thumb and very carefully, deliberately, popped it back into her mouth. He had to laugh. She'd decided he wasn't to be tolerated, and she meant it.

But he was growing more and more determined to break open that little ice-cube heart, and he meant it, too.

Another sound came from the opposite bank, this one louder than the first, and they lapsed into silence again, staring out and waiting. Joe was hoping for a fox, or maybe a small brown bear, but when a horse with rider came into view, everyone in the thicket heaved a sigh of disappointment.

The rider seemed to hear them as he loosened the reins and let his horse drink. At any rate, he spotted them in the brush and tipped his hat. "Howdy," he called out.

Joe rose and nodded to the man, and the others followed him, stepping out so that they could be seen. The rider was a clean-shaved, handsome man in his thirties, dressed in buckskin with fringe that blew in the breeze

and a wide-brimmed hat that shaded his face. He looked
sharply at the party across the body of water and seemed
to know who they were.

"Say," he called out to Joe. "You the fella's got an
extra woman on his hands?"

Joe's head came up, and Chynna gasped softly.

"No," Joe said, his voice gruff. "You must have me
mixed up with someone else."

The man frowned. "You're Joe Camden, ain't you?"

Joe nodded slowly.

"Well, then you're the one," he noted, sliding down
off his horse and coming to the edge of the water. "And
if that's the woman you're trying to get a place for, I
would take kindly to being introduced."

Joe turned and looked at Chynna. She looked back
with panic in her eyes. It had been kind of funny and
flattering to hear that men were around offering to take
her if one of the Camden men didn't want her, but to
come face-to-face with it was something else again. The
man was clean and handsome, and still, going off with
him like this would be madness, and she knew it. She
stared at Joe, shaking her head imperceptibly, and wondered what he was going to do.

Joe searched her eyes, then turned back to the man.
"You're too late, buddy," he told him. "I've decided
I do want her after all."

The man nodded. "I can see why," he noted. "But
say, if she's got any sisters, send one of them my way.
I need a wife bad. I've been lonely too long."

Joe met Chynna's relieved glance and grinned at her,
feeling suddenly lighthearted and particularly friendly
to the man.

"There are other women," he noted.

"Not around here there aren't."

Joe frowned, knowing he was pretty near right. "If you want a woman that badly, why don't you go ask that woman named Nancy?" he suggested. "I hear she's a looker."

"Nancy?" The man grunted as he began gathering up his horse's reins in his hand. "That little gal who does nails?" He shook his head and swung back up into the saddle. "No, thanks. I went in and got myself a pedicure, and she darn near talked my ear off. She's got a sharp tongue, does Nancy. A man should think twice before saddling himself with a wife's got a sharp tongue. That's like signing up for a season in hell."

"You got that right," Joe called back.

They stood on the bank and watched as the man began to ride away, Chynna watching the scene in amazement—mostly wondering why the explicit sexism of the situation, why the exaggerated maleness of the environment—didn't bother her more. Back in Chicago, she would have protested their assumptions. But somehow, it seemed right and fitting out here in this wilderness. Fitting, and comfortable.

Once the man was out of sight, Joe turned back to Chynna, shaking his head and looking her up and down.

"The man just wanted to look you over," he told her, leashing his amusement as best he could. "He was in the market for a wife and he thought you might do." He grinned, then bit it back, while she gagged. "Now, tell me why that bothered you so much?" he asked her. "How was that much different from signing up with an agency and taking a stranger who writes to you to be your husband?"

She thought for a moment. "Because I got to participate in the choosing," she said at last. "That was very different."

Before he could respond, a shout turned them around. Suddenly, they realized that the children were no longer with them. Rusty was running toward the far end of the little lake, and as they looked, they saw something else in the water.

Chynna gasped, her hand to her throat. "Kimmie!" she cried. "She fell in!" Then she was running, stumbling over twigs and fallen branches, trying to get to her baby.

Joe had seen her, too. Her little head was bobbing, and she'd been caught up by the current. She was headed for the falls.

He didn't have to think; he just reacted. Running alongside the water, he began stripping off clothing, and by the time he'd almost caught up to where she was, he was down to jeans and socks. Without a moment's hesitation, he dived into the icy water and swam strongly toward her. In seconds, she was in his arms.

"Hold on, Kimmie," he called out, grabbing her away from the rocks. "Hold me tightly. I've got you, but you've got to hold on."

She did, clinging to him like a burr, and he worked against the current, fighting the strong pull toward the falls. The water was horribly cold, numbing, and he began to lose feeling in his feet. But he went on. There was no choice. He had to go on, or Kimmie would be badly hurt.

They struggled, fighting for land. The cold and the sweep of the river worked against them, and Joe cursed the fact that he wasn't in as good shape as he could have been. He had to hold Kimmie with one arm and swim with the other. There were flashes of fear when he wondered if he would get her back in good shape. But finally, the bank was in reach, and he pulled up on the sandy shore, panting, exhausted, lying on the ground with his eyes closed.

Chynna and Rusty were there, saying things, touching him, trying to check Kimmie out to see if she was hurt. But she wouldn't let go. Her little arms were around his neck, and she wouldn't release them. The more they pulled, the more tightly she clung, until finally he'd caught his breath and revived enough to sit up and gently pry her away.

They went back to the house as quickly as they could, and Chynna gave Kimmie a warm bath and wrapped her tightly in warm clothes. She had a few cuts, a few bruises, but otherwise she seemed to be all right. Joe had a gash over one eye and a couple of pulled muscles, but he was fine. When he went in to say good-night to Kimmie, her thumb was back in her mouth and she followed his every movement with her dark-eyed gaze, but she still wouldn't talk to him. He left disappointed and beginning to think there was no way to reach her.

"Thank you," Chynna told him when both children were in bed and they were alone. "I can't tell you how much..." Her voice choked, and he drew her close, patting her awkwardly before he drew away again.

"It's no big deal," he said. *I would do just about anything for that little girl,* he could have added, but he didn't. Still, he realized it was true. He couldn't stand her silence, and her huge eyes haunted him. If he could have thought of some way to win her over, make her smile just once, he would do it, regardless of what it took.

Still, he was glad she seemed to be basically unhurt. He wandered the house restlessly while Chynna cleaned up the kids' toys, telling himself he was anxious to get going. Once he had Chynna and the children out of the house and on their way, Greg would probably appear in the yard, and he could get on with the errand that had brought him here. His mother's birthday was days away, and he wanted to make sure Greg came to see her for it. Nobody had been able to persuade him to come to Anchorage yet. This time, Joe was determined.

But first, they had to get through the night. He ran a hand through his hair and swore softly at himself. He was making this whole thing more difficult than it needed to be and he knew it. It would be so much easier if Chynna wasn't...if she weren't so...if he could only stop thinking about what it would be like to take her to bed.

There. He'd admitted it to himself. She was driving him crazier than a june bug on Memorial Day. The curve of her cheek, the way her hair flew out around her face, the scent she left behind in the room when she left it, everything was eating at him. He could hardly stand it.

"What's the name of that perfume you're wearing?" he asked grumpily as she walked past, picking up the children's toys.

"Perfume?" She straightened and smiled. "I call it good old soap and water."

"You're kidding." He frowned, annoyed and not sure if it was at her or at himself. "Then how does your scent last in the air like that?" he asked begrudgingly.

"Magic," she told him with an impish grin.

"Magic," he repeated under his breath as he watched her sway from the room. That had to be it. Otherwise, why would he be feeling so nuts?

He had to get back to L.A., back to the life he knew, back to things he was used to. He had friends there, his job. No girlfriend lately, but that was just because he'd

grown tired of dating empty-headed starlets and suc-
cess-hungry lawyers. It seemed all he met were from
one group or the other. What he needed was a nice
woman who had brains and a metabolism about half
that of your average hummingbird. A little class would
be nice. Maybe a caring personality. A pretty face.
Someone very much like...

No. He wasn't going to say it, not even to himself.
Chynna was great, but she wasn't his dream girl. How
could she be? Dream girls didn't come with two little
kids clinging to their legs. And anyway, she was supposed to marry his brother.

Not that he had any intention of letting that happen.
But still, ethics were ethics.

A glance out the window told him she was outside,
leaning on the fence and staring at the mountains. He
went out the front door and swung across the porch,
coming up behind her and looking at what she must be
seeing.

"It is beautiful," he acknowledged, as though he
knew she was going to tell him so any second and
wanted to beat her to it. "And deadly. You know how
many men die up there every year?"

She nodded slowly. "So you aren't one of those who
think beauty is worth dying for," she said.

He gave a short laugh. "Listen, you want to see
beauty, you ought to get a look at the beach at Malibu
on a sunny spring afternoon."

Chynna looked at him over her shoulder. "Lots of
itsy-bitsy teeny-weeny bikinis?" she guessed.

He pretended outrage at her suggestion. "I was talking about the sunlight on the water," he told her. "And
the view of Catalina on the horizon."

She grinned. "Oops. I stand corrected."

He moved next to her and leaned beside her. Their shoulders were almost touching. The mountains stood out against the liquid blue sky, a silhouette of power and majesty that tended to take your breath away. Neither one of them spoke for a long moment.

"Makes you feel sort of small, doesn't it?" she said at last.

He blinked, realizing suddenly that she'd hit the nail on the head. That was exactly why he'd been so hot to get out of Alaska when he was young. He had to find a place where the landscape didn't dwarf you, where expectations were kept to human size. So he'd picked southern California, which had its own laundry list of intimidating circumstances—but they were all new to him, and he'd prevailed over them in time. He'd done well. He had a good job making good money, living in a beautiful area, with all the perks that came with the good life. Everything was perfect, damn it! So why did he feel like snarling?

"So tell me, Mr. Joe Camden," Chynna said, when he'd been silent too long and she had to say something, "how have you managed to reach this point in your life without getting shanghaied into marriage somewhere along the way?"

"I live in L.A., remember? It's not exactly a marrying town, at least not the part I live in."

She looked toward the white clouds scudding across the sky. "You could always move," she noted quietly.

He turned to look at her and tried to grin, though it felt as forced as it probably looked. "Not if it made me more vulnerable to marriage. What would be the point?"

She faced him and almost smiled. "How silly of me.

Well, then, it seems you've chosen the perfect place to live. You must be very happy."

"I am happy." He sounded defensive and he knew it, but once the words were out, he couldn't take them back, nor could he modulate the tone.

But she was smiling, as though she knew she'd touched a nerve and was glad to have done so. "Well, you don't have to bite my head off," she said mildly.

"I wasn't."

"My mistake." She grinned like a woman who'd won the last point in a tennis match. "It must be that all that happiness beaming out from you that blinded me to the truth."

He glared at her helplessly. Why was it so hard to get through to her? And why was it bothering him so much that she continued to laugh at him this way?

"Listen, I'm living the way I want to live."

She nodded, acknowledging his point, but that didn't stop her. "You really don't think you'll ever want a real home, with children and all that goes with it?" Catching the look on his face, she laughed, patting him on the arm. "Don't look so scared. I'm not trying to trap you into anything. I'm just concerned about you."

"About me? Hey, we're just two proverbial ships passing in the night. What do you care about what happens to me?"

She stared at him for a long moment, wondering if she were wrong about him, wondering where the real soul of Joe Camden was hidden. It was obvious he didn't feel the same bond growing between them that she did, and she looked away, hiding the slight tremor in her smile. She'd had hopes. But prospects looked fairly dim at the moment. He was bound and determined not to fall in love, wasn't he? And she wasn't going to have time to work on changing his mind.

"I just have a natural urge to nurture, I guess," she said lightly.

But he wasn't listening any longer. Her hair had brushed his face as she turned, her scent, perfumed or not, was drowning him and he could hardly breathe.

"What happened to the kids' father?" he asked abruptly. "Were you married to him?"

She glanced down at her hand and saw, with a start, that her ring finger was empty. Of course, she knew that. She'd taken off the ring before she'd left Chicago. After all, if she was going to marry someone new, it wouldn't do to arrive with the first husband's brand still on her, so to speak. But she wasn't used to the nakedness yet, and it still gave her a shock when she noticed it.

"I was married to him," she answered calmly. "We went together from our junior year in high school on and were married right out of college."

"Young love," he muttered, hoping he didn't sound as jealous as he felt, and at the same time, shocked at himself for feeling that way.

"It was," she said simply. "We had Rusty and Kimmie and were very happy for as long as it lasted."

"And what broke up that old gang of yours?"

"Kevin died."

"Oh. Sorry." He winced, wishing he could take back this feeling of frustrated anger. He wasn't even sure what it was or whom he was angry with, but he knew he was acting like a jerk, and he couldn't seem to shake it. "How did it happen?"

"He died in a car accident." She paused, steeled herself, and added, "He'd been drinking."

Joe thought immediately of the look on her face when she'd found the bottle beside his bed, and suddenly his anger turned toward this much loved Kevin, a man who would risk losing his life and leave a family like this, a woman like Chynna, kids like Rusty and Kimmie, alone in the world, all for the sake of a drink.

He wanted to comfort her, but the set of her shoulders told him she wasn't asking for solace and wouldn't necessarily welcome it should it come. Everything about her was sending signals, beating a rhythm in his blood, making his brain go fuzzy.

It had been a long time since a woman had sent him into this sort of tailspin. Eighth grade might have been the last time, when he'd walked Elinor Bingley home from the junior-high dance, his palms sweaty as he planned how he was going to kiss her. First, he was going to casually lean over her as they stopped to try out the echo at the empty old brick brewery, but she started to teach him how to whistle between two fingers and he got sidetracked and forgot. Then he planned to pull her back just before the pothole on the corner, saving her from the mud and grabbing a quick kiss at the same time. But she dashed ahead of him and sailed over the pothole, leaving him, off balance, to catch the edge and splash mud all over his best slacks. Under the single town streetlight, behind the bleachers at the baseball diamond, even on her front steps, every plan fell through for one reason or another, and he'd just about given up when he heard her father's gruff voice and heavy tread as he made his way to the front door to let his daughter in. But Elinor gave him a cocky grin, reached up and planted her lips full on his, and even held it for a count or two, before darting away and disappearing inside her house, leaving him alone on the front porch.

He could still remember the flush of absolute joy. "I did it," he'd muttered to himself, flush with triumph.

"Fooling myself even then," he muttered now, realizing it was Elinor who had done it, not he.

"What?" Chynna asked, catching the tail end of his statement.

He turned and stared at her, studying every curve of her face, the light glow of her cheek, the way her eyelashes shaded eyes that sparkled like spring snow on the lake.

"I'm going to have to kiss you one more time," he told her distractedly, taking her by the shoulders and frowning down into her face.

"Why?" she asked solemnly, her eyes huge, her heart beating and hope rising in her chest.

He grimaced. Her mouth looked soft and warm and full and damn near irresistible. "Mostly so I won't want to so much anymore," he told her honestly. "So I'll stop thinking about it."

She met his gaze and searched it. "You really think that's going to work?" she asked him softly.

"No," he admitted, his fingers tightening on her shoulders. "But I can't think of anything else to do."

"Okay," she whispered, raising her arms and slipping them around his neck so that her body molded itself to his. "Let's give it a try."

So he did. He meant for it to be quick and clean, a good, solid kiss that would tell him she was like any other woman, that the lingering effects of the other kisses they'd shared lived mostly in his mind and imagination, that he'd been dreaming. But he knew right away that he'd been trying to fool himself again.

Only this time, it wouldn't work. He was under the spell of her magic, like a bug in a spider's web, and the more he twisted and turned and tried to free himself, the more he was wrapping himself in the silken threads that would bind him forever if he didn't watch out.

A cool breeze sprang up, blowing across their faces, but her mouth was so warm, he hardly noticed anything else. He was sinking into her, letting her pull him in and take him with her, sailing on that breeze, holding her so that he wouldn't fall, so that she would stay afloat, so that they both could share in the glide that might never end.

He wanted her, and yet he'd wanted women before and it had never been like this. He wanted to plunge inside her and take the sweet pleasure her body could give him, but at the same time, he had a strange urge to hold her high, like an offering to a sun god, like something to be guarded and cherished. He wanted to own her. There was no other way to put it. He wanted to take possession, body and soul, and make her his own.

And that was plain insanity, because she wasn't his and could never be. She'd come to marry his brother. He had no right to her, and couldn't have had her in any case. She was off-limits, and here he was kissing her again.

He drew back slowly, because she was so good and it was so damn hard to resist her. She looked at him coolly, as though she had hardly been affected by what had happened between them, and she said in a calm, clear voice, "What's the verdict?"

He gazed at her groggily, his sense still whirling. "Wh-what?"

"On the kissing cure." Reaching up, she touched his

face with the flat of her hand for a split second, then drew away, confusing him again. "Did it render you immune to my charms?" she asked, teasing him.

He stared at her for a moment, clearing his mind, then swore softly and obscenely and turned away.

"We can't do this anymore," he said gruffly, as though set to take action. "We've got to forget this ever happened."

She laughed softly, but managed an innocent look. "Forget that what ever happened?" she asked, her eyes wide.

He frowned and waved a hand. "The kiss..." he began, then saw the look on her face. "Oh, I get it." He half smiled. "I'm slow, but I do get there eventually."

She wanted to answer that, to tease him again, bait him, cajole him, even flirt a little, but she held off, knowing it wouldn't be fair. He was trying so hard to be honorable, and she had to respect that. Much as she regretted it, they weren't a match made in heaven. That was just not to be. He'd tried to tell her again and again, and she might as well let the lesson sink in. He wasn't going to marry anyone, and much as she was attracted to him, much as she respected him and thought he might just be the one—without marriage, a relationship of any kind would be impossible. She had children to think of. If it just wasn't going to be, it was best they hold back and try to forget it, just as he'd demanded.

She left the fence and started back toward the house, moving toward security, but he stopped her with a hand on her arm.

"You know, I haven't given you the details yet. I should have told you before. I've got you a ride back to Anchorage tomorrow."

There. He'd said it. Bracing himself, he looked down

into her eyes, but to his surprise, her face was serene and she was almost smiling.

"Cancel it," she said calmly. "I'm not leaving."

"What?"

"Don't worry," she told him, just in case he thought she meant to latch on to him for the duration. "We'll have to stay here tonight, but after that, we won't be imposing upon your hospitality any longer."

He was gazing at her as though she'd proposed contacting space aliens and planning a get-acquainted dinner party. "Where will you go? What are you going to do?"

She turned and looked him square in the eye, like the professional woman she meant to become. "Don't worry. I've laid the groundwork. I've got some money saved, and Annie is going to help me. She knows of a place I can rent with a storefront and living space in the back."

He was gazing at her in complete bewilderment. He still didn't have a clue as to what she was talking about. She took a deep breath and came out with the coup de grâce.

"I'm going to look into starting a business."

"A business? In Dunmovin?" He blinked, stunned. "You're kidding. What sort of business?"

She licked her lips and told him. "A coffee bar." Holding her breath, she waited for his response.

It took a minute. At first, he didn't seem to understand. But then realization dawned in his eyes. "A coffee bar?" He stared at her, appalled. "Oh, now I've heard everything."

Her chin rose and her jaw tightened. "Why not?"

"A coffee bar?" His chuckle held more disdain than humor. "These people won't drink cappuccinos and lattes. They want beer and they want it thick and dark as molasses.''

She tossed her head, turning from him and beginning to walk toward the house. "This is almost the twenty-first century, you know," she reminded him over her shoulder. "I think you'll find that times, they are a-changin'." Turning back, she found he'd followed her, and she set her hands on her hips. "Besides, I won't just make coffees. I'll make sandwiches, too. I'll fix pack lunches for the men going out to hunt and fish, and the men going out to work on the pipeline, and..."

He was shaking his head in astonishment and finally he couldn't contain his comments. "Maybe I'm the one who's nuts, but I can't see those big burly men coming into your shop for a quick mocha with whipped cream and picking up an avocado-and-alfalfa-sprout sandwich to take up into the mountains with them."

He shook his head. "Chynna, I know these men. I grew up here. They don't act like men in the city, because they don't like the city. They like the wilderness and they want to act like wild men. You're not going to tame them."

A stubborn light shone in her dark eyes. "We'll see."

He hesitated, wanting to stop her, as though she were walking too near the edge of a cliff and he was the one who could grab her back away from danger, wanting to shield her from pain. "You're going to end up with a broken heart," he warned.

"Maybe." She stopped, thought for a moment, then turned back and told him what she thought in no uncertain terms. "And maybe I'll end up with a business that makes enough of a living to make it possible to keep my children out here in this beautiful, clean and healthy place. And maybe I'll be able to do all that without having to sell myself in marriage to some man I don't love.''

That shut him up, and as she flounced away, he watched her go and found himself chuckling softly. Well, maybe so. If all it took was pure guts and determination, she would have it made. Maybe so.

Eight

Chynna woke and found herself in darkness. For just a moment, she thought she was back in the apartment in Chicago, and every muscle tensed. Then she remembered. Alaska. Suddenly, the bed felt softer, the air lighter, the sounds of crickets reassuring. Yes, she loved it here. She had to stay.

But something had woken her. What was it? Had one of the children called to her?

She lay very quietly for a moment, but there was no sound. Still, something wasn't quite right. She could sense it.

Slipping out of bed, she padded into the hallway and pushed open the door to the room where the children were sleeping. Rusty's head lay on his pillow, and his eyes were closed, a picture of peace and tranquillity. But Kimmie's side of the bed was empty.

"Kimmie?" she whispered, glancing around the room. "Where are you, honey?"

She looked up and down the hall, then made her way through the darkened living room to the kitchen, where she switched on the light. No Kimmie. Her heart began to beat just a little faster, and her steps were more hurried as she moved through the house, turning on lights as she went.

"Kimmie?" she called in a normal voice.

Memories of the wolf howl from the night before came creeping into her mind, and she shook them away. Kimmie wouldn't go outside. Would she? She hurried on through the house, searching, dreading....

What if she had gone outside? What if she'd been looking for her mother and lost her way and ended up outside, alone and frightened. What if...?

Finally, there was only one room left to look in. Walking quickly to the end of the hallway, she found that Joe's door was ajar and she pushed it open. The light from the hallway fell into the room, and there on the floor, at the foot of the bed, on a little round rug, lay Kimmie, her eyes closed, her thumb in her mouth.

Chynna drew in her breath, and her eyes filled with tears of relief. For just a moment, she stood there, giving thanks that she'd found her baby unharmed, but also taking in the atmosphere. Joe was sound asleep, lying on his side with his arm around his pillow. And there was Kimmie, at the foot of his bed, as close as she dared get to him, with her blanket clutched to her chest and her stuffed koala bear in one arm. Chynna laughed softly, and all her love was in her eyes as she watched her baby sleep.

But she couldn't stay there forever, watching. She was going to have to pick Kim up and carry her back to her own bed. Still, she hated to have Joe miss this. She hesitated. Would he care? But this was too good, too cute. She had to share it. It had been so long since she'd had someone to share things like this with, it would be wonderful to have the closeness, even if just for tonight.

"Joe." She put a hand on his bare shoulder, and he rolled onto his back, his eyes wide open.

"Chynna?" For a moment, he thought he was dreaming. She was leaning over him, her hair sweeping down and tickling his bare chest. Could this be real? But then her scent filled his head, and he knew she was really there. He reached out to pull her down into his arms, but she was laughing softly and avoiding his embrace.

"I didn't come in here to seduce you," she whispered, batting his hand away. "Come here. I want you to see something."

He rose sleepily, hitching up the drooping pajama bottoms he wore, but when he saw what she'd called him to see, he was suddenly wide-awake.

"Kimmie," he said in a stage whisper. "How did she get here?"

Chynna smiled at him. "She came on her own. She snuck in during the night. I was looking all over the house for her, and finally I came into your room...."

He frowned, bewildered. "But why would she come in here? She hates me."

Chynna shook her head, her gaze softening as she looked at him. "She adores you, you idiot. She's just afraid to show it."

Her eyes were telling him more than he wanted to know, and he looked down at the child. Females were hard to read, no matter what the age. But if Chynna said Kimmie liked him, that was enough for him. Reaching down, he scooped her up into his arms, koala bear and all. "I guess we'd better put you back in your bed," he told her softly.

She surfaced for a second or two, pushing her way through the cloud of sleep, her dark eyes blinking in the pale light. Then she put her arms around his neck, holding on tightly, and when her head fell against his chest, she was out again, secure in his arms, happy, it seemed. Joe swallowed hard and felt a lump grow in his throat.

"Come on," Chynna said, leading the way. "Let's put her down."

She watched him, saw how tenderly he held her child, and something broke open inside her and suddenly she knew, as though someone had spoken the words, that this was the man she wanted. This was the man who was slipping through her fingers.

But there was something else. As she watched him, she knew there was more. She was in love with Joe Camden. Far beyond how good he would be for her children, how perfect a match they could make, she was in love with him. Head over heels like she'd only been once before. What was she prepared to do about it? Nothing? Standing back, she bit her lip and felt the stirrings of a pain that was to come.

Joe removed Kimmie from his arms reluctantly. She felt so good there. An angel. That was what she looked like when he put her back in her bed and pulled the covers up around her. He looked down at her, and something hurt in his chest, and suddenly he was backing away. He had to get out of here, get away from these kids. If he didn't watch out...if he didn't watch it...

He didn't put into words what he was afraid would

happen, but he knew what it was and he knew how to avoid it. Get away from these kids, get Chynna out of town and go back to L.A. and the life he'd been living for all these years. Get back to normal. That was all there was to it. Should be easy.

All he had to do was get past Chynna in the hallway, get into his own bed, go to sleep and in the morning things would be calm again. He could handle that, couldn't he?

Closing the door to the children's room, he turned and saw exactly why that scenario wasn't going to work out quite as efficiently as he'd projected. Chynna stood between him and his room, her hair down around her shoulders in a golden haze, the light from behind her shining through her sheer nightgown, outlining her slender curves. He took a ragged breath and steeled himself to resist.

"We'd better get some sleep," he said, starting to edge past her. "We still have to discuss what you're going to do."

She stood very still, not giving him any ground. "There's no discussion needed," she said simply. "The children and I are moving into the place Annie has to rent. You don't have to worry about us any longer."

He hesitated, knowing he should move on, knowing to stay and argue was pointless, and more likely dangerous. But he had to say it.

"You can't stay here in Dunmovin," he told her earnestly. "It's crazy. It won't work."

She sighed, shaking her head. "Why not let us sink or swim? What do you care?" she asked him softly. "You won't be here. You'll be going back to Los Angeles."

There was a buzzing in his head. She was too close,

and her scent was too strong. He couldn't avoid seeing the way the fabric of her nightgown clung to her breasts, and it was making him light-headed.

"Do you want to come with me to L.A.?" he heard himself asking, to his own dismay. "There are more jobs there lately and…"

What was he saying? Was he out of his mind? And yet, he couldn't stop. Something inside was coming out, as though he had no will of his own.

"…and I could help you find a place to live and a job with a good day-care center."

But she wouldn't take the bait. That wasn't what she wanted at all, and she wasn't ready to settle yet.

"No," she told him firmly. "In Los Angeles, I would run into the same problems I had in Chicago. This is the best place for us. Right here in Alaska."

He was conscious of her nearness and of his own nakedness, except for the baggy pajama bottoms that hung low on his hips. He thought he could feel her warm breath on his skin, and it sent his senses spinning.

"Why do you want to stay?" he asked her, no longer thinking about what he was saying, just making sound to try to cover up the way he was reacting to her. "Are you still hoping Greg will want to marry you when he shows up?"

Her head came up, and she stared into his eyes, her own eyes dark pools in the dim light of the hallway. "Greg has made it very clear that he's not really interested in marriage," she told him softly. "I think we've moved beyond that, don't you?"

He didn't know what she meant, but it hardly mattered. He stood very still, frozen by the electricity in her dark, velvet gaze. She was so beautiful. What had she said earlier? That he wasn't prepared to die for beauty? Right now, he felt as though he could. Everything in him wanted her, wanted to take her the way a man conquered land. And yet, who was conquering whom? As he stood paralyzed, she lifted her hand and flattened it just above his heart, as though she were searching for his heartbeat. He felt the muscles of his stomach contract and he gasped, reaching up to cover her hand with his own.

"Chynna," he murmured, fighting for strength, choking out the words, "you'd better go. You'd better..."

But his words evaporated as her hand moved on his flesh, and he lost the power of speech for a moment.

"If you can give me a good reason," she told him softly, her gaze holding his, "I'll go off to bed and leave you alone. But if there's no reason..."

He grabbed her wrist and held it tightly. "You came to be my brother's wife," he said, his voice gritty. "Isn't that reason enough?"

She shook her head slowly, her gaze locked on his. "I don't know your brother," she whispered. "But I know you."

What she said didn't make a lot of sense, but it didn't have to. They both knew where this was going and they both had to agree for it to get there. He stared into her eyes and silently made a bargain. Reaching up, she pressed her palm to his cheek and kissed his lips, and his arms slowly slid around her, holding her tightly while he soaked in her warmth and held it to him. He closed his eyes and let himself feel. Words were no longer enough to say what they needed to say to each other. Something else would have to take their place.

He took her to his bed, the same bed he'd slept in all his young, growing-up life, the same bed where he'd dreamed of girls and escape from Alaska, and bringing

her there somehow seemed to bring a closing to his
circle. Security conscious, she locked the door to his
room and made sure he had protection. Then she slipped
off her nightgown and let him glory in her body.

Her body. He'd never seen anything so beautiful, so
lush, so smooth, so infinitely desirable. He let his gaze
follow the long line of her leg, the rounded elegance of
her breast with its tight, dark tip, the smooth dip of her
navel, the curve of her shoulder, the pulse that beat at
the base of her throat as her excitement grew, and then
he made the same trip with his hand, until his breath
was ragged and he had to fight to keep from spoiling
the moment.

It had been a long time since he'd wanted a woman
this badly, a long time since sex had been special. He
buried his lips in her soft skin and melted with her, his
hands molding her, his body coming down on top of
her, taking her with him on the slide into delirium. As
his instincts took over, as his maleness rose and surged
inside him, he felt a sense of power he'd never had
before. She was his. For this moment, anyway.

Lovemaking had always been pleasant but not particularly urgent to Chynna, and she expected the same
slow response this time. But as she watched him,
watched the way his desire grew as he explored her,
watched the way the light in his eyes went from admiration to lust to stark, hungering need, very soon his
touch was conjuring up answering sensations that surprised her. Her flesh seemed to burn, her hips began to
move of their own accord and suddenly she wanted him
the way a drowning man wanted air. She had to have
him, have him deep and sure and strong within her, and
she made soft sounds that told him exactly that, while

her hands urged him to join her, come together in a dance as old as life itself.

He took her as though he were claiming her. That was the way she felt it. She accepted his mastery, needed it at that moment, knowing in her bones the ancient irony that made his power her triumph. Deep, deep inside, she ached to make him hers and for a moment, just a moment, it seemed to come true, as they spiraled higher and higher toward the sun.

I love you, she thought as their bodies clung in the last ebb of the intensity. And it was true. She loved him in ways she had never loved Kevin, though she had loved Kevin with all her heart.

But this…this was something more. He'd taken her further, higher, harder, and that was part of it. But there was much more. She loved him with a fierce sense of bonding, something she'd never experienced quite this way before. She felt a part of him.

Rolling over, she looked into his eyes to see what he was feeling, to see if he'd known what she'd experienced, if he in any way felt the same.

But his eyes were troubled, and her heart sank. He reached out and combed his fingers through her hair, caressing her, but his eyes didn't give back the love she needed to feel there. Leaning down, she kissed his shoulder, his chest, his stomach, as though kisses could somehow make him feel it, too. But he pulled her up to face him, and his smile was bittersweet.

"This was crazy," he told her. "You know that. Chynna, I can't promise you anything. You understand that, don't you?"

"Shh," she told him, putting a finger to her lips. "Don't talk. If all we have is tonight, I want to make the most of it." She dropped a kiss on his mouth, her hair falling down around their faces like a protective curtain. "We can talk tomorrow," she whispered. "There's a long night ahead."

He groaned and laughed softly. "How did you get to be such a vixen?" he asked her. "Somehow, that wasn't the impression I got when you first arrived. You didn't seem so bold."

She gazed down at him. "I'm not," she said, giving him a slow half grin. "I've never made love with any man other than Kevin, my husband. I was scared to death. Couldn't you tell?"

He shook his head, frowning at her in a sort of wonder. "I don't believe you're scared of anything," he told her. "You take my breath away."

She grinned. "Here." She kissed him playfully on the lips. "Have it back. You're going to need it."

He laughed and reached for her, and in a moment they were wrestling, teasing each other and reminding each other to keep the noise down, but driving each other closer and closer to desire, until it overtook them once again and they came together with a gasp on his part and small cries of delight on hers, rising once again and finding an even sweeter joy.

She woke up in the morning in her own bed and stretched, feeling luxuriously wonderful and not remembering why at first. Then she did, and the smile broke on her face, filling her body with happiness. Joe was a wonderful man, and the night they had shared was something no one could ever take away from her. She had it for keeps.

And then someone cleared his throat, and all her good feelings fled, not to return again for a long, long time.

"Good morning," a male voice said before she'd had

a chance to finish reacting to the throat clearing. "You must be Chynna Sinclair."

She whirled in the bed, pulling the covers up to her chin, and gazed out at a wild-looking, very hairy man who sat in the armchair across the room. His blue eyes were lively, his face rather handsome even though she couldn't see much of it because of the beard, and his form long and lanky. He looked like a younger, wilder version of Joe. But something was missing, and she knew right away it was the look in the eyes. Greg's look was slightly blank where Joe looked warm and quick to understand.

"You must be Greg," she said, her voice cracking with sudden stress.

"I must be," he agreed, nodding. He looked friendly but wary, like a huge puppy dog who had suddenly grown into his big paws and didn't quite know how to handle that yet. "Sorry I wasn't here to greet you when you arrived. But hey, I left the door unlocked for you."

"I noticed."

He nodded again and looked a bit embarrassed, glancing around the room as though looking for a new topic of conversation. "Say, who are these kids you've got with you?" he asked her as he thought of it.

Funny how easy it was to tell the man she was contracted to marry about Rusty and Kim this time. "They're my kids. I didn't tell you about them before. But they're mine."

He shrugged, obviously ready to adapt to anything. "That's cool. I always wanted kids. Now I can have them without all the work." He grinned. "Kind of like getting a dog that's already house-trained."

"Kind of like," she echoed, blinking at him groggily, still too stunned to know what to say to him.

"Hey, having kids will be fun," he went on, looking very happy about it now that he'd thought it over. "I can teach them how to ride and fish and hunt. We'll have a great time together. And you can stay home and cook the food."

Chynna blinked at him, trying to clear her mind, wondering just how old he actually was. He'd said thirty in his letter, but this young man seemed about eighteen and not too sure of how to deal with the world as yet.

"Are you sure what you want is a wife?" she asked him, letting a tiny dose of acid edge her tone. "It sounds more like you might want a mother and a couple of new siblings."

"Oh, no." He was very sure of this. "I've got a mother. She's in Anchorage. I wanted a wife be-cause…well…" He turned beet red for a moment. "There aren't any girls around here except for Nancy, and she turned me down."

"I see." Sounded like Nancy might be one smart cookie after all. Chynna shook her head, mostly to clear it, but also in amazement. This was the man she'd come to marry. What was she, nuts?

But looking at him, she relented. He looked nice enough, even sort of endearing in a bearlike way. She shouldn't be too harsh too quickly. Maybe it was just too early to make snap judgments. Maybe she ought to give him a chance.

She glanced at her clothes on the nearby dresser and looked at the door, about to ask him to leave while she got ready to face the day, but before she had a chance to speak, Joe appeared in her doorway.

He'd pulled on jeans, but his chest was still bare, and he wore a very sexy smile when he first looked in on

her, was just about to say something and caught sight
of Greg, stopping his words just before they'd formed.

"Hey," Greg said, still friendly as a young mala-
mute. "Look at me. I finally showed up."

Joe looked from his brother to Chynna and back
again, not saying a word. Chynna thought she could
guess what he was feeling by the look in his eyes, but
he didn't say anything. Turning abruptly, he left the
room.

"My big brother," Greg explained, nodding toward
the doorway. "He's a great guy when he's in a good
mood." He grinned. "I just haven't seen him in a good
mood for a long, long time. Like, since the day I was
born."

Chynna had to laugh, despite everything. Greg and
Joe, what a contrast. But they were definitely brothers.
She could see the similarities everywhere.

"I guess he's one of those people who needs a cup
of coffee before he says anything in the morning," she
said, sighing. "Maybe you ought to let me get up so
we can go out and all three have a talk."

Greg shrugged. "Sure. Why not? I'll just go stash
some of my things in my room. Be back in a second."

She nodded, watching him go. "Oh, my," she whispered to herself. "What now?"

Joe was tight-lipped, all right. And it wasn't that there
wasn't plenty to say. As he walked stiffly to the kitchen,
he could hardly contain the things welling up in him.
But experience had taught him that saying them would
only make things worse. He had said them so often
before.

What the hell were you thinking? he would have liked
to have said to his brother. *You've got a mother sitting*

all alone waiting for you to visit her just once, and you can't be bothered. She's got a birthday next week. And I know damn well you're not planning to do a thing about it. I came to make you go to see her, but what do I find when I get here? There's a woman here you promised to marry. But you're not here. You left her dangling, just like you leave everyone. What kind of a numskull are you? Can't you keep a commitment to anyone or anything? Can't you honor or respect any relationship? What's the matter with you?

He'd been making speeches very like that one to Greg for years, and it never changed anything. Because deep down, he knew what was the matter with his brother, knew he'd never change and knew why. Greg was just like their father.

He filled a glass with water and drank it down slowly, counting as high as he could, trying to settle his temper. There was no point in yelling all these things at Greg. He'd finally learned to hold it back. But he still hadn't figured out how he could get to his brother, how he could begin to make him see, begin to make him change.

He heard Greg's tread in the hallway. He was coming into the kitchen, and Joe steeled himself, but he still wasn't ready for what his brother had to say next.

"Hey, do you think Annie can perform a wedding ceremony?" Greg asked him lightly, slumping into a chair and looking like a happy man. "I mean, she's kind of like unofficial head of the town. If we had a mayor, she'd be it, you know. So why couldn't she marry people? Captains of ships do, don't they?"

"A marriage ceremony?" Joe said, turning to glare at his brother. "What the hell for?"

"For me and Chynna, of course."

For a moment, Joe couldn't speak. Anger choked him. Finally, he croaked out, "You want to marry her?"

"Sure. I wouldn't have sent her the money to come if I didn't want her."

"Then why weren't you here when she arrived?"

Greg grimaced and looked like a kid who'd forgotten to take out the trash. "I would have been, but Jim Barley came by, said there was a brown bear as big as a barn up near Cross Creek Meadow, so I had to go up and take a look. We don't get bear up there anymore, and I had to see what was going on." When he saw the look on Joe's face and realized this explanation wasn't cutting it, his tone became more defensive.

"I was only gone a couple of days. That was hardly anything. You know the trips I usually take. I came back way early..." He thought for a second, trying to find the right word, preferably a word Joe had used to him before on this subject, and then finished his sentence with a pleased smile when he thought of it. "I came back way early to take care of my obligations." He looked up expectantly, obviously hoping for some brotherly praise.

But Joe wasn't ready to reach for compliments just yet. "You've been gone three days," he began.

"Uh-uh. One and a half. I was back last night. I saw you guys at the water hole."

Joe frowned. "Why didn't you make yourself known?"

Greg leaned closer, his face earnest. "Tell you the truth, Joe, when I saw her, I got sort of scared. I mean, she's so beautiful. I was pretty sure her picture in the catalog was rigged. But when I saw she was even prettier than that..." He shook his head. "I gotta admit, for a while there, I lost my nerve."

Joe stared at him, touched by a twinge of compassion for this man of his blood for the first time that day. "What about the kids?" he asked. "Did you see them, too? What do you think?"

Greg shrugged. "They're great. I like kids. This way, I won't have to make my own family. I'll already have one."

Anger swept through Joe again. "What's this all about, Greg? What do you want to do, play house? This is real life you're playing around with."

"I know." His face registered outrage that his motives might be questioned. "I want a wife. I want a family, just like every other guy. I want what every other guy wants."

"Yeah, but you don't want to do what every other guy does to get that."

Greg was beginning to get impatient with Joe's carping. "What else was I supposed to do?" he asked, scratching his head. "I ordered up a wife, and I'm getting kids thrown in free. It seems like a good deal to me."

Joe was slowly shaking his head, his eyes hard as tinted glass. "She won't marry you," he said softly.

Greg looked surprised, then amused. "Sure, she will. We've got a contract." He gave a short laugh. "Hey, man, you're the lawyer. You know about contracts. They're binding."

Chynna entered the kitchen just in time to hear his last statement. She looked from one brother to the other, her eyes huge and dark. "Well," she said, sinking into a chair at the table, "this changes things."

"No, it doesn't," Joe argued. "It doesn't have to."

She looked up at him, her chin at a challenging angle.

"As Greg says, a contract is binding. And we have a contract."

Greg frowned. He could sense something going on underneath their words, something conveyed by the way they were looking at each other, but he wasn't sure what it was.

"Contracts are often broken," Joe said firmly.

"But only for good reason," she countered. "Do you know of a good reason why this one should be?"

He met her gaze and held it. He saw the question in her eyes and he knew what she wanted, but the one thing she wanted was the one thing he couldn't give her. Dragging his attention away, he turned back to Greg.

"Are you coming to see Mother or not?" he asked tersely.

Greg shrugged. "I told you before, I won't go to cities. I'll never set foot in that place. I didn't tell her to move to Anchorage. She should have stayed out here where she belongs."

Joe hesitated. He'd come with plans to hog-tie his brother and drag him back to see his mother if he had to. But circumstances had changed. Everything had changed. Now all he wanted to do was to get out of here.

"Just come for her birthday," he said. "It won't take long. She needs to see you."

Greg smiled, guileless as a child. "How can I go now? I've got a wedding coming up."

That did it. If Joe stayed in the kitchen any longer, he would end up hitting something—very likely his brother's chin. Turning, he grabbed a shirt off a chair and shrugged into it, heading for the front door. Walking out onto the porch, he found himself in the midst of a glorious Alaska morning. The sun was just up, and the birds were coming alive. The air was cool and crystal clear. The snowcapped mountains looked so close, he could almost touch them. Slumping down onto the top step, he sat and drank it all in. He had to admit, this was something magnificent you couldn't get every day in L.A.

He heard someone coming out the front door behind him, but he didn't turn. Still, he was surprised when it was Rusty who sat down beside him, resting his chin in his hands in a direct reflection of Joe's posture.

"Good morning, kid," he said gruffly.

"Good morning," Rusty said back. "Can we go out to look at the animals again?"

Joe smiled at his hopeful face. "Not this morning. Maybe later today." But he knew he wasn't going to be around to take the boy, so why was he setting him up for a letdown? Maybe Greg would take him. For all he knew, Greg was going to be this boy's father soon. He couldn't believe it, but so far no one had told him it wasn't going to happen.

Rusty was looking at his hand, and suddenly he asked, "Remember when I bit you?"

Joe nodded. "I'll never forget it," he promised.

Rusty's gaze shot up to meet his, wary at first, then smiling when he realized Joe was teasing him. "I wish I didn't do that," he told him earnestly, but before Joe could say anything in return, he'd jumped down from the porch and was running toward the swinging gate.

Suddenly, there was a commotion from around the corner of the house, and before Joe could prepare Rusty, the yard seemed to fill with dogs. In the end, he realized there were only three of them, but they ran so fast and barked so loud and jumped so high, at first it seemed like a lot more. Joe rose, about to go to Rusty and help him, knowing he wasn't used to dogs like this and might be terrified. But Rusty was doing fine. Though he stayed up on the gate, he called to the dogs, and when they came jumping around him, he clung more tightly, but he laughed, and a big black Lab licked his face, delighting him.

These had to be Greg's dogs, and they'd been with him in the mountains, no doubt. Joe had forgotten how friendly dogs could be, how goofy and yet comforting. As he watched them with the boy, he remembered. A boy and a dog. There was sometimes something magic there.

While he was mulling this over, someone else slipped in to sit beside him. Startled, he looked down into Kimmie's tousled hair. She sat very still, just inches away from him, dressed in a pink shirt and tiny jeans, her legs sticking straight out, her feet in little red tennis shoes—and her thumb firmly planted in her mouth. He smiled down at her, and she looked up, but her face was as solemn as ever.

"Won't you smile for me?" he asked her softly.

Slowly and very deliberately, she shook her head.

So he sat beside her, and they both looked out on the morning and watched Rusty with the dogs, watched him get down off the fence and begin to run with them. Nothing more was said, but he felt a strange companionship with the little girl and he had to admit, it was rather nice having this sort of company—even if she wouldn't smile.

Nine

"**A**re you really going through with this?" Joe asked as he turned the car down the only main street in town.

"It's starting to look that way, isn't it?" Chynna's eyes danced with excitement. In her hand, she held the key to the building Annie was going to rent to her, if she decided it would suit her needs.

"Well, which is it?" he asked, frowning. "Are you going to start a business or marry Greg?"

She cocked her head to the side as though considering. "I don't know. Can't I do both?" she asked lightly.

After a shocked look in her direction, he lapsed into silence, and she stole a look at his strong profile. Just over two days ago, she hadn't known him. Just over a few hours ago, she hadn't known she loved him. And now...now she was about to lose him. But she wasn't going to let it crush her. She was starting a new life for herself and her babies, and nothing was going to stop her from making that work.

"There it is," he said, pulling the car up in front of a small green building with a front porch and false front. "Do you love it already?"

The funny thing was that she did. It was darling—a little run-down around the edges, but it had a Victorian charm, created mostly by the gingerbread someone had thought important at the time it was built, and the way wildflowers twined around the corners.

"How long has it been empty?" he asked as they got out of the car and walked slowly to the front door.

"A little over a year, Annie said. The couple who had it before ran a sort of trading post, selling Native arts and crafts."

He looked around and shook his head. "This isn't exactly a tourist haven. I don't imagine they got rich."

"No." She laughed. "In fact, they gave up and moved to Florida. Annie says they run a scuba-diving center somewhere on the Keys."

She put the key into the lock, but her hand was shaking and she laughed again as he reached down to help her. The door swung open, and a musty smell came toward them, but the place inside was clean and neat, the front room completely empty, the back rooms completely furnished.

"Oh, look! This will be perfect." She turned, surveying as much as she could from one spot in the middle of the floor. "I wish we'd brought Rusty and Kimmie. They're going to love this."

"Rusty and Kimmie are more interested in baby pigs than they are in real estate," he muttered, frowning as he turned with her. "And Annie's enjoying having them at her place for the moment."

Chynna nodded and began to pace the floor, as though measuring for renovations.

"Look. We can put the counter right here. And the burners back here. And there's already a sink...oh, this is so perfect!"

He watched her and couldn't help but show the trace of a smile. It was pretty clear she had her sights set on starting a business. Where that left his brother he wasn't sure. She'd been very cagey about that ever since Greg had shown up. He couldn't believe she would still consider the marriage, but still, she hadn't definitely ruled it out. Who knew?

"Are you going to have enough money to get this started?" he asked at last, turning to watch her as she examined the room.

She turned and looked at him in surprise. "Don't worry about me. I told you I have some money saved," she said.

He shrugged. "Do you need a loan or anything? Just to get you started."

She did a double take, then stepped closer and searched his face. "Why would you loan me money for this? You hate the whole idea."

He hesitated, then gave her a lopsided grin. "I hate the idea of you failing at it more. So let me know."

She stared at him as he turned away and wandered through the building, looking slightly embarrassed. How could she not love this man? Full of contradictions, yet always basically compassionate, he was also the sexiest man she'd ever seen. Was she crazy to let him slip through her fingers this way?

Sighing, she followed him into the back rooms, which would be the living quarters. The furniture was simple but clean and tasteful. A couch sat against the wall, along with a coffee table and two chairs. There was a dining-room table with six chairs around it, and an empty china cabinet.

"It's going to be perfect," she said again, dreaming of the future. "I'll open the café in the mornings and in the late afternoons. The rest of the time, I'll be preparing food, then I can be with the children, home-schooling them until they're ready for the local school."

He looked up from a book he'd been cradling in his hand. "It's a one-room schoolhouse, you know."

She nodded happily. "Can you imagine? What could be more wonderful?"

He frowned, putting down the book. "I don't know. Most communities seem to think graduated classes with separate teachers for each grade do a better job."

"I don't." She waved an arm in the air. "Just look at what sort of people came out of those little school-houses in the old days. And look at what's coming out of our modern schools these days. I'll take that old-time schoolmarm any day. She knew how to make kids crack the books."

He chuckled. "You may be right," he admitted, enjoying her.

"The thing is," she said, head tilted to the side while she thought it out, "I'll be working out of our home, so I'll always be here when the children are out of school. They will have to help with the work, and good honest work never hurt anyone." She shook her head, her eyes shining. "No, this is going to be everything I've dreamed of."

Her enthusiasm was contagious. He smiled, watching her. "If you feel you've got to do this, I hope you make it."

She turned to him, looking into the depths of his crystal blue eyes. "You do, don't you?" she asked softly.

He nodded. "There's just one thing," he added, his gaze hardening. "Don't marry Greg."

Turning away, she leaned on the windowsill and looked out at the brambles in the backyard. It was going to take a lot of work to clean that up, but she was looking forward to it.

"I'll file your comment away under Biased Advice," she said lightly.

He came up behind her. "You can file it wherever the hell you want to file it, just don't do it."

She licked her lips and pressed them together. "Why shouldn't I marry Greg? It's what I came here to do."

"Because it's wrong for you, it's wrong for the kids and it's darn well wrong for Greg."

She glanced over her shoulder at him. What did he think she was, a fool? Marrying Greg was the last thing on her mind. But she didn't want to tell him. She didn't want it to be too easy.

"Just because marriage isn't your cup of tea..." she began.

Not waiting to hear the rest of it, he seized her shoulders and held her to him.

"Come with me to L.A.," he said impulsively. "You could live with me, you and the kids. You wouldn't have to get an outside job. We could work something out. You could stay home with them and..."

"No," she said firmly, though it cost her a lot to say it. She turned back to look out the window again, and to avoid his eyes. "Don't you understand? That just wouldn't do."

Impatient frustration swept through him. "Why not? Why would marrying Greg be better than that?"

"Because in a marriage, I would be an equal partner. Living with you, the children and I would be supplicants."

He frowned, knowing there was a grain of truth in what she was saying, but refusing to accept it. "That's hogwash."

"No, it's the truth." She shook her head, letting her heavy hair sweep across her back, tiny strands brushing against his face. "I wouldn't live with you without marriage."

He tried to get back to a light note. "Why not? It's all the rage. Everybody's doing it."

She nodded. "And we have a nation filled with lost children who don't know who their parents are. I won't do that to mine."

His hands slid down to curl around her upper arms, caressing them. She felt so good, so clean and healthy and strong. "But you would like to go with me, wouldn't you?" he asked softly. "If there was a way."

She turned her face away, but he forced her to look up at him, holding her chin and turning her.

"You want me, don't you?" he asked her softly, his eyes as deep and darkly blue as a midnight sky. "Tell me the truth."

She touched his face, taking him in with her gaze. "Do I really have to put it into words?" she asked him, her eyes shining. "Can't you feel it?"

He winced, grabbing her hand and putting it over his heart, holding it there. "You can't marry Greg," he insisted.

She smiled up at him. "Why not?"

He hesitated, but her beautiful face was too close.

"This is why not," he said huskily, drawing her closer.

He told himself he was just going to prove something to her, just wake her up, and then he would release her. He pulled her into his arms, and his mouth closed on hers and all his plans and rationalizations fled. All he knew was her. She melted against him, clung to him, accepting him and giving an answer to his question, and he knew she was right. She didn't have to say it. She knew how to show him with her eyes, her mouth, her body, in ways words could never explain.

It was nice the couch was handy, but it hardly mattered. The hard floor, a sandy beach, rocks in the mountains—it would all have been the same to them. The urgent hunger that filled them both seemed to grow like a wildfire between them, consuming everything in its path. He pulled at her clothes, and she yanked at his, needing to feel her hands against his naked flesh, desperate to feel his lips on her breast, his hand sliding between her legs. It had never been so fierce for her before, and she couldn't stand to be without him. Desire was like a wild thing beating inside her, and only he could tame it.

And he did, rising above her, plunging in and taking control, so that she cried out, her fingers digging into him, her hips churning high in the air to meet him, her eyes wide open as she stared into the fire.

He took her, and it was like nothing he'd ever done before. No woman had made him feel like this. As they lay together, panting, body parts tangled, he knew he would never know another woman like her. She was his, body and soul, and there was no way he could deny it.

But that didn't make anything different. He was the same person he'd been before he met her. She was just as determined to live in Alaska as ever. He looked down at her, at her beautiful hair spread out across the pillow, and he wanted to shake her, make her promise she wouldn't marry his brother, that she wouldn't marry any man. But he had no right to do that. He knew very well, if he wasn't willing to offer her anything himself, he couldn't ask her to resist all others. There was nothing he could do about it.

Still, he could dream.

"You are mine," he whispered fiercely into her hair.

"What?" She thought he'd said something, but she'd only heard part of a word. She raised her head and looked at him. "What did you say?"

"Nothing." He brushed back her hair and looked at her, and she couldn't tell if the emotion she saw in his eyes was laughter or something very different. "Nothing at all."

She nodded slowly. She knew it made no difference. They could make love all day. They could make love every time they saw each other. It made no difference. He was leaving. She was staying behind.

Still, she would always have this. As she traced the outline of his muscular chest with her fingertip, she knew that. She would always have a part of him. But would that ever be enough?

Joe left that evening, driving off in a cloud of dust that lingered for what seemed like hours. Every time she looked out the window, she thought she could still see it, particles still floating helplessly in the air with no place to land. But he was gone, and she'd made no promises.

The children didn't ask where he was going, and she didn't know what to tell them, so she ignored the issue and they spent the afternoon playing in the backyard.

They were getting to be country kids so quickly, getting used to running free and finding small animals everywhere. It made her heart glad to see them this way.

She'd spent the afternoon cleaning the little building that would be their new home, and now she and the children were spending the evening moving in.

"Why don't you wait until tomorrow?" Greg asked, puzzled at why she would want to leave so quickly. "What's the hurry?"

"I want to be on my own," she told him firmly. "And the children need to have their own rooms."

He frowned, not sure how to take all that. "Now that Joe's gone, we could have really gotten to know each other," he grumped.

She smiled at him. "Come to lunch tomorrow. We'll try out our recipes on you."

That brightened his outlook. "Cool. Could you make me a peanut-butter-and-bacon sandwich? That's my favorite."

"Then that is what you shall have."

She was thrilled to be getting started so quickly. Annie had supplies for the short run, and she would order from distributors Annie recommended in the future. The older woman was also expediting the process of getting a business license and health inspection.

"If only Joe could see me now," she said that night as she surveyed her handiwork—and it was only four hours since he'd left.

But he was constantly in her thoughts. Funny how a man she hardly knew could change her life this way. Funny, but true. Would she ever see him again? She had to believe she would. Somehow—somewhere. She would have to think about it. What she needed was a plan.

Ten

"**Y**ou're just a big baby, you know." The handsome gray-haired woman looked at her son lovingly across the table in the chic restaurant where they were celebrating her birthday with a trendy nouveau meal. "You have that look on your face you've always had when you didn't get your way."

A rebellious spark flashed in Joe's eyes, but he took a sip of his amber-colored wine and said smoothly, "What could I possibly not be getting my own way about?"

His mother frowned thoughtfully.

"I don't know, but you have that look." She picked up a roll, broke off a piece and buttered it. "Just exactly what happened while you were at Greg's?" she asked with studied indifference.

He grimaced involuntarily. "Nothing. I told you.

Greg and I had an argument and he refused to come to Anchorage once again and I left.''

She shook her head, pushing back her sleeves and letting her silver bracelets jangle. "I wish you and he would get along better."

He looked up in exasperation. "He's such a flake. What can we do to make him change?"

She smiled. "Nothing. Oh, I know exactly how you feel. Lord knows I've spent enough time trying to make him change myself. But you finally have to face it. Greg is what he is. Accept him that way. Your life will be simpler."

He barely controlled a snarl. "My life is fine. It's his life that's screwed up."

"So let it be. That's Greg." She waited a moment, then went on. "You were there longer than you expected to be."

He nodded, avoiding her eyes. "Yes. When I first arrived, Greg was out hunting. I had to wait for him to reappear."

She smiled, watching him. "And what happened while you were waiting?" she asked quietly.

He met her gaze and hesitated. They'd always been close, and he'd told her a lot about his life. But somehow, he couldn't tell her about this. Not yet.

"Nothing," he lied, looking back down into his drink. "Nothing at all."

But his mother saw the clouds in his gaze and she ached for her son. She had no idea what was troubling him, but she knew it was deep and painful and that it was going to hurt for a long time.

Chynna rested her arm on the ladder for a moment and surveyed the paint job she was doing to her new walls. It looked pretty darn good if she did say so herself. It had been three days since Joe had left, and things were falling into place here at Chynna's Café, as she was thinking of calling it.

Greg was here helping at the moment. He would work for hours if she promised peanut-butter-and-bacon sandwiches at the end of his stint. She watched him work for a moment. He was sanding down shelves they were building to go along the back of the shop. She appreciated the help and enjoyed the company, but he reminded her of Joe, and those reminders were beginning to hurt more. She'd thought they would begin to fade. After all, it wasn't as though he'd become a major part of her life in two days. But he had become a major part of her soul. And in her heart, he seemed to be growing rather than fading away.

As far as she knew, Joe was still in Anchorage visiting with his mother. So near and yet so far.

She glanced down at Greg again as she began to descend the ladder to put away her paintbrush.

"Why won't you go see your mother?" she asked as she went.

He looked up in surprise and then he frowned. "She doesn't really want to see me. She only cares about Joe. He's her favorite."

She didn't know the woman, but she knew women, and she couldn't believe that for a moment. "She cares about you, too. You're her son, her baby."

He shook his shaggy head. "Naw, I was my dad's son. He taught me everything I know about the wilderness."

She began to rinse out her brush. "What about Joe?" she asked above the sound of the water.

Greg shrugged. "What about him?"

"Did he go out into the mountains with you and your dad?"

"Sometimes. But he didn't like hunting. We mostly left him home."

"With your mother." She finished with the rinsing and came over to stand beside where he was working.

"Yeah, they are a lot alike." He made a face and put down the sanding block he'd been using. "Their favorite sport is to sit around and tell me what a loser I am. I don't need to go all the way to a crummy city to have that thrown at me again."

Chynna nodded. So that was it. Well, she could hardly blame him. And yet, everyone pretty much went through that with family. There ought to be some way to get these people together. She frowned, thinking.

"Has she ever visited you since she left? Has she ever come here?"

He shook his head with his lower lip out. "Nope. She left, and that was that." He looked around at where his empty glass was sitting. "You got any more of that chocolate stuff?" he asked.

She went to the thermos and poured out a café mocha for him, thinking all the while. "Maybe you should invite her," she said as she handed him the drink.

Greg nearly dropped it. "Who? Me?"

She gazed at him speculatively. "How about if I do it?" She began to get excited by her own idea. "Why don't we have a birthday party for her right here? We could invite Annie and all her old friends."

He stared at her, then shrugged. "Well, if you think so. I guess it would be okay."

She smiled, charged up now. They already had phone service hooked up to the café. It was about time she used it. "This will be great. Give me her phone number. I'll call her right away."

She glanced at Greg as he obligingly began to look through his wallet for the number. Would he think this through? Would he consider the fact that Joe was probably still there? Would she blow her cover?

It wasn't as if she'd plotted here. The idea had just fallen into her lap. But she would run with it now. And maybe, just maybe, something would come of it. Unless Greg realized...

But no. He found the number and handed it to her. "Tell her hi for me," he said casually as she walked toward the other room, where the telephone was kept. "She's pretty nice, actually."

Chynna's heart was beating like a drum as she listened to the telephone ring. What if Joe answered?

But it was a woman's voice she heard on the other end of the line.

"Mrs. Camden? You don't know me, but I know your sons."

"Oh?"

"Yes. You see..." Suddenly, she realized that this was going to be very awkward to explain. "I came to Alaska to marry Greg, but..."

"What? Where did you meet my son?"

"I didn't. I mean..." She sighed. The truth was the only way. "I came as a mail-order bride. But Greg wasn't here and Joe arrived and waited with me for Greg to come back, and by the time Greg came back... well..."

"You are no longer planning to marry Greg." The woman made it a statement of fact, and Chynna couldn't dispute it. She glanced toward the front room, but Greg was out of hearing distance.

"No. I'm not going to marry him. But I've gotten to know both your sons very well, Mrs. Camden, and I know how much they care for you. The thing is...I would like to have a birthday party for you here in Dunmovin."

There was a moment of silence while she absorbed this. "Why would you do that?"

"Because I think you should see Greg."

She paused, then asked, "Why can't he come see me here?"

Her fingers tightened on the receiver. "I think he would like to, Mrs. Camden. But I think he's just too close to the wild to make the trip. It breaks my heart to see a rift between a mother and child. I have two children of my own. So I'd like to try to do something for the two of you. Will you come?"

Mrs. Camden was silent for a long moment. Finally, she spoke. "Yes, my dear," she said firmly. "I will come."

Chynna's heart leaped. They went over the particulars of the time and place, and when she hung up, she was glowing. Joe's mother was coming. She hadn't had the nerve to ask if Joe would be coming with her. But at one point, she'd heard his voice in the background. Surely he would come. Surely.

Joe looked out the small airplane window at the city below. L.A. He was coming home. Alaska was like a dream to him now. He'd been thinking over what his mother had told him about Greg, that he had to accept his brother the way he was, and he was beginning to come to terms with it. Finding out that Chynna wasn't going to marry him had helped enormously. Somehow, he could feel much friendlier toward him now. Would he ever be able to be around him and not be annoyed? Probably not. But he thought he was getting over the need to try to reform him. He had to admit, chances were it was no use.

But now he was back in California and he could forget all that. He only wished he were looking forward to getting back to work more. He'd enjoyed legal work for a long time, but lately things had gone very stale. He needed something new to pep him up. Something to start his blood flowing again.

"Please fasten your seat belt, Mr. Camden," the pretty redheaded flight attendant asked. "We'll be landing in a few minutes."

She'd been flirting with him all the way from Seattle. As he leaned back in his seat he watched her tight little bottom wiggle down the aisle. *Ask her out,* a voice said. *Come on. She's given you every signal. Ask her out and go have some fun.*

Okay. He was ready. The next time she came this way, he would do it. *Would you join me for dinner?* he would say, very suave and confident. She was coming back down the aisle. He got his smile ready. He was going to do it.

The plane hit a pocket and gave a jolt, and she turned back, bracing herself with the back of a seat some distance away. And at the same time, a little girl jumped up, out of her seat, and tried to run down the aisle herself. Her mother called her back sharply, leaning out to do so, and Joe got a good look at them both. They could have been Chynna and Kimmie, both so blond, both so sweet looking. The flight attendant came his way again, throwing him a dazzling smile. But he barely noticed and barely returned it. His mind was back in Alaska. Back in the dream.

There would be no dinner with the flight attendant. He only hoped he'd be able to eat at all.

Chynna and Greg were making preparations for the party, blowing up balloons and tacking down streamers. The whole town had gotten involved. Everyone was coming. Chynna was having a hard time holding back her excitement. Her new life was starting off with a bang. The party and her grand opening were coinciding. The icing on the cake would be if Joe came. But that was almost too much to hope for, wasn't it? In the meantime, she babbled on and on about her plans to Greg, until he grew a bit testy.

"Now, wait a minute," he demanded at one point. "What about us?"

"What *about* us?" she returned, blinking at him.

He frowned at her. "Are we getting married or what?"

She drew in a deep breath. She'd been expecting this conversation for days, and now it was finally here. She had to be honest with him. "Greg, I'm very sorry, but I don't think we should do that."

His blue eyes widened. "But you promised."

She took his hand in hers. "I know I promised. And I'm very sorry. But you know, if you look at the contract, you'll see that there is a back-door clause in case either one of us gets cold feet."

"You've got cold feet?"

She nodded. "Freezing," she murmured.

He looked more confused than angry. "So, there's a clause in there for me, too?" he asked her.

She looked at him for a moment, then laughed. "You didn't really want to marry me, either, did you?" she accused.

But he denied it. Well, he halfway denied it. "Sure, I did. Only…" He flushed and avoided her gaze. "Only I saw Nancy last night, and she heard all about you and she was real impressed." He looked very pleased with himself. "The way she was making eyes at me, I figure I might have a chance with her after all."

She stared at him with her mouth open. "Why, you little devil. If I find out you dragged me all the way to Alaska just to make Nancy jealous—"

"Oh, no. Oh, I swear that wasn't why."

"—I'll be grateful to you until the day I die. Coming up here was the best thing I ever did."

He blinked. "Oh." He blinked again. "Okay, then I guess it *was* my fault."

With a shriek, she attacked him and they wrestled for a moment, both laughing, both feeling more like brother and sister than anything else. But it brought back memories of wrestling with Joe. And the contrast was startling. So much so that later that night, she watched the faint stars and wished on one.

"Please make Joe come back," she whispered.

Did wishes get granted in Alaska? She would soon find out.

It seemed that in Alaska, wishing on stars didn't work. Maybe it was because of the short nights. At any rate, Mrs. Camden arrived for her party without her oldest son in tow, and Chynna's heart sank when she realized it.

Still, it was touching to see Mrs. Camden's reunion with Greg, who actually shaved for the occasion. It was especially heartwarming when his eyes filled with tears as his mother hugged him. His crusty defenses shattered in that moment, and as the evening wore on, he was the life of the party, and especially dazzling when the lovely Nancy was nearby.

Mrs. Camden herself had a wonderful time. People came from miles around to see her, and she was astounded at how much she'd been missed.

"I'll be back again soon," she promised everyone. "I won't stay away so long next time."

There was dancing and singing and lots and lots of food. Chynna was already feeling like an old-time member of the community. Annie had taken her under her wing, and that was enough for most residents. One after another, mountain men came by to tell her they would be trying her sandwiches on their next trips. And everyone was looking forward to her cappuccino concoctions.

As the evening wended its way toward midnight, she had a chance for a talk with Joe's mother. They felt a bond immediately, and Mrs. Camden didn't waste any time.

"Are you in love with my son?" she asked.

Chynna stammered. "I…I thought I explained…."

"I don't mean Greg," she said. "What have you done to Joe?"

"Done to him?" She realized she was blushing. It was too late to deny anything.

"Yes, done to him. He was mooning around like a love-sick puppy. Well, out with it. What happened?"

Chynna gave her a brief outline, leaving out a lot of details, but including the fact that she'd never known a man like him.

"He's so strong, and yet so good and kind," she told his mother, as if she didn't know the fellow herself. "I don't understand why he won't consider staying here where he grew up. I would think he would love it."

Mrs. Camden nodded. "Joe felt, all his life, that Greg

was like his father, made for Alaska, and that he was
like me. He felt out of place here. When he was young,
he was sure there were things out there in the rest of
the world that would suit him better. He could hardly
wait to leave.'' She sighed, thinking of the old days.
''But he's been gone a long time now. I think his sense
of alienation went too far, and it's time for him to realize that. Alaska is in his blood, just as much as it's in
Greg's.''

Chynna hesitated. ''Well, if that's true, he won't admit it.''

Mrs. Camden smiled. ''We might have to trick him
into it,'' she said softly. ''Do you have a telephone?
I'm feeling a little light-headed. I think I'd better make
a call to my son in California.''

Chynna watched, holding her breath, as the woman
left the room and headed for the telephone. She wasn't
sure this was going to work. But what the heck. It was
worth a try. Anything to get the man back in town.

Joe hit the road to Dunmovin at eighty miles per
hour, swearing all the way. He didn't want to do this.
He'd just left Alaska. He hadn't wanted to come back.

But as he drove along the highway, he couldn't help
but see the landscape, and he couldn't keep from being
enchanted by it again. Was there any place on earth as
beautiful?

Alaska was a big country. A man ought to be able to
do big things here.

He pulled into town, driving right past Annie's. His
mother had said she was staying with Chynna at the
café, and that made him swear again. How the hell had
those two got together and got so cozy so fast?

Pulling up in the driveway, he got out of the car and

stretched, stiff from the long drive. He heard the sound of running feet and turned to find Rusty coming out on the porch.

"Wow," the boy called out, eyes wide. "It's Joe. You came back."

Joe moved awkwardly, wishing kids weren't so darn vulnerable. "Just for a visit," he said quickly, but Rusty didn't seem to hear him.

"Did you come back to be our daddy?" he asked, as though it were the most natural question in the world.

Words stuck in Joe's throat. He couldn't have been more shocked if Rusty had shot him. He had to reach out and put a hand on the gate to steady himself, and then he heard his own voice saying, "Do you want me to be your daddy?"

The world seemed to stand still. The air didn't move; the sun held its breath. And Rusty's eyes clouded for a moment, as though he wasn't sure he should answer that. He thought for a moment, staring at Joe, mulling over the question.

Finally, he bobbed his head shyly. "Kimmie does," he said brightly. "She told me."

Joe turned, feeling like a man in a dream, moving in slow motion, because Kimmie was coming through the doorway, and when she saw him, her thumb popped out of her mouth and she cried out, "Joe!" and dashed toward him.

He wasn't sure how it happened, if she leaped into the air or if he reached down and swung her up, but she was in his bear hug of an embrace and her little arms were around his neck and she was saying, "Joe, Joe," over and over, and when he drew back and looked at her, she was smiling.

His eyes were stinging, and at first he didn't know

why. But he couldn't let that little girl go, not until her
mother was there, walking toward him, and then his
sense of the surreal went into overdrive.

It was like one of those movies, he thought later,
where the man and the woman come together across a
field full of daisies, where they see one another in the
distance and just start moving together, like two halves
of a whole that must unite. All he had to see was the
deep darkness of her eyes and he was drowning in them,
reaching for her, taking her up in his arms.

She was crying. Her face was wet and—funny thing,
so was his. But he was kissing away the tears, kissing
her again and again, kissing her eyes and her nose and
her lips and her ears, until his lips were sore from the
kissing and she was laughing and pulling away. The
kids were hanging on to his legs, one on each, and they
were laughing and he was laughing and it all happened
without warning. He found his family and bonded with
them, and no one had told him it would be like this.
But by the time he'd realized what had happened, it
was too late to stop. He heard his own voice telling
Chynna he loved her, so where could he go from there?

"Why not have the wedding right here in Clarks'
meadow?" his mother was saying, referring to the yard
behind the café. He didn't care where it was because
the wedding was a thing for women to plan, and all he
cared about was that he would have Chynna with him
for the rest of his life and that her kids would be his.

"You can live in Alaska?" Chynna was asking him,
and he could tell he was nodding yes, though he wasn't
sure why.

"Computers make everything easier," he heard his
voice saying. "I can work here. I love Alaska."

"Good," his mother said, and he vaguely remembered that she was supposed to be having fainting spells or something, wasn't that what had brought him here? But she looked okay now, walking off across the meadow with the kids to give the two of them some time alone. And as Chynna drew him to her and wrapped him in her arms, he sighed and shook his head.

"I'm not really sure how all this happened," he told her, looking a little bewildered.

She laughed deep in her throat. "Just consider yourself a mail-order husband," she teased him. "I ordered you up, and here you are."

He dropped a kiss on her lips, and somehow it grew and wouldn't quit. This was what he'd been missing all his life. Funny how long it had taken him to admit it.

"I love you," he told her huskily, her face between his hands.

"I love you, too," she told him, her eyes filling with happy tears. "We all do."

"Even Kimmie?"

"Especially Kimmie." She gave him a ragged smile and pulled him closer. "No, I take that back," she whispered as her body melted into his. "Especially me."

And he wouldn't have had it any other way.

* * * * *